The Outcasts

Book I:
The Lies of Autumn

by

Chuck Abdella

ISBN-13: 978-1-51-430314-6

Printed by Createspace

Visit www.chuckabdella.com

About the Author:

Chuck Abdella is a History teacher at St. John's High School in Shrewsbury, MA. With degrees in History from Boston College and Columbia University, Chuck has spent many long hours in the embrace of ancient and medieval civilizations. During July, he also directs an academic enrichment camp called College Academy, where he usually saves the world at least once per summer by spearheading an adventure during the camp's popular Time Machine Day. Studying all that history, telling stories as a teacher, and seasonal world-saving have all helped inspire his writing.

Chuck has written poetry and prose for at least 25 years and has been published by the St. John's *Icon,* the Boston College *Stylus, Worcester Magazine,* and the *Boston Globe.* He estimates he's written at least eight novel-length manuscripts of varying levels of horribleness since he was in high school, but feels as if this novel might help to prove that the ninth time really is the charm.

When he's not spending his time reminding adolescents that the Romans were much cooler than they thought, Chuck enjoys reading, cooking, traveling, coaching youth softball, playing basketball, and watching Boston sports. He is grateful for the support of his loving wife, Kerry, and his two daughters, Zoe and Molly, whose writing and story-telling he tries to encourage daily.

You can follow the author on www.chuckabdella.com where there are links to his Facebook and Twitter pages.

Dedication:

This book is dedicated to my wife Kerry, who transforms the prose of my life into poetry with her love and support. Her encouragement for me to take this dream and make it a reality meant everything, and I dedicate this book to her. You can well imagine the chores that were left unfinished while I spent time writing. My wife's understanding in such matters has been truly remarkable and filled with love. I am most grateful.

A list of gratitude:

The Roman Emperor Marcus Aurelius notes that the best advice he ever received was from the oracle of Caieta which simply said, "It's up to you." While there is wisdom in that, the success in writing and publishing this book was certainly not up to me.

Thank you to my daughters, Zoe, the "darling of my eyes" and Molly "my sweet little bunny" for making my life complete and showing the enthusiasm for my writing that only children can. You both inspire me to keep trying to tell better stories.

To my dear friends who agreed to serve as my primary test readers: Greg Smith, Rich Byon, and Rick Subrizio, who read early drafts, and fellow author Diane Mulligan, who read the final draft. All four test readers gave me phenomenal feedback to improve the story—without their assistance, this would be a vastly inferior piece of writing. Thank you so much.

I am also grateful to those friends and relatives who kept showing excitement about my writing. Maybe you kept encouraging me about the project, read a draft, kindly asked for updates, or said supportive things like "I'd read any book you wrote." If so, I want you to know it made a real difference and I want to thank you: Andy and Meaghan Troiano, John and Andrea Berger, Sara Hendricks, Jim and Joan Monahan, Kelly Benestad, Katie Mylroie, Mike Nicholson, Andy and Rebecca

Abdella, Mike Smith, and Mike Foley. I also want to thank my nine year old niece, Lila, for believing that I'll be as successful as J.K. Rowling someday. ☺

My parents (Charlie and Monica) have encouraged my writing from an early age and I am grateful for that support. Thanks, as well to my mentor, Professor John Rosser of Boston College, who has built up my confidence for any project I undertook. Thanks, as well, to all of my colleagues and my students at St. John's, who have taught me as I taught them—special thanks to my former student, Max Richman for his publishing advice.

This novel began with some writing I did for Medieval Day at College Academy. I am grateful to all of my office staff who helped inspire the first stirrings of my story, including Louise McGee, Michelle Wasiuk, Helen Silkonis, Pete Jackson, Kira Rasmussen, and Scott Brahman, as well as the Harrington family for inventing College Academy and helping it thrive.

Thank you to Ric Wasley for his class on publishing which helped me with the technical terms of the industry and gave me confidence that this hobby of mine could entertain others.

I wrote the first draft of this novel while recovering from vocal cord surgery. I could not speak for three weeks and writing this book was the only way words could escape. Thanks to Dr. Philip Song, Dr. Dan Massarelli, the nurses, and voice therapists for their healing.

Thank you to you. Whether you are politely reading this book because you know me or whether you just picked it up because you liked the cover, I am grateful. Writers need readers, so thanks for giving me a chance. I hope that I might repay the debt by entertaining you in the following pages.

Chapter 1: The Motherless Boy

Marcus opened his eyes slowly as his surroundings resolved into sharper contrast. Inhaling deeply, he tried to discern individual sounds from the cacophony of bird shrieks, Human grumblings, and wind gusts. "It's cold," he noted, as reality penetrated his sleep-haze. That was his first thought of the day, a starkly logical observation characteristic of the Wizard side of his lineage. Marcus sat up and tugged his dark cloak around his broad shoulders. All around him, the camp was buzzing with men and women packing up their meager belongings for the decision had been made to hike further into the mountains. A hostile army had been spotted in the distance and Rangers were to be killed without trial by Human armies. He peered at the Rangers with his violet eyes. Human men and women, he mused. Like me, but not. He was only half Human and often felt the tug between their passionate take on life and the Wizards' complete indifference to "emotional slavery."

"Glad to see you've awoken, Marcus," Quintus said with a half-smile, "The snow is coming down so quickly that we can't get a fire started to boil water for tea. You could be of some help." Quintus was his best friend, essentially his only friend, as much an outcast as Marcus in this small band of Rangers—themselves all outcasts in varying degrees. Quintus's exile had nothing to do with Human mothers and Wizard fathers. But it had everything to do with the war and the strife amongst the races. Perhaps that's why Marcus and Quintus got on so well. Some say love is the unifying principle of the world, but too often hatred seemed ascendant—at least everywhere that Marcus looked.

"Wizard, will you please help us with the fire?" a Ranger woman named Terentia asked. Few of the Rangers ever called him "Marcus," as it was odd for a Wizard to have a Human name. They seemed to fear speaking the two syllables, as if their very pronunciation might invoke some of the forces which had sparked the bitter war between Humans and Wizards, now in its third decade. Quintus was the exception in all things. He never referred to Marcus as simply "Wizard." Nor had the slur "Sorcerer" ever escaped his lips. It was a word much-used

1

by the Rangers when Marcus was out of earshot, or at least when they presumed he was. Terentia looked impatient while she crouched over the sodden wood of a hopeless fire. Hopeless for Humans, anyway. Marcus nodded, stood up in his boots, and spoke the ancient words. With a simple hand gesture, flames arose on the cold, soaked wood and quickly consumed it. The gesture seemed as simple as making a fist or hopping on one foot. Through Human eyes, it was *magic*, a small miracle every time the spell was cast. There was awe in the woman's gaze, but also some measure of contempt. "It's so easy for you," she spat out sourly.

She had no idea, Marcus thought as he walked away. Simple did not equal easy. She had no idea the years of study, the hours of practice, the agony of mastering the powers within his flesh. To her, it did seem easy to start a fire with some archaic words and a casual sweep of the hand, but nothing was easy. These Rangers could track animals or fire arrows or put up camps in much the same way. It looked easy to the uninitiated, but a closer look revealed the toil which produced these skills. Why would they never understand that it was same for Wizards? In fact, if anything, it was ten times as hard for one who was only Wizard on his father's side.

As if reading his mind, Quintus clapped a hand on his shoulder. "Banish those thoughts," he advised, "I know nothing comes easy for you. I know you only succeed because you work harder than other Wizards. I know, brother." Marcus nodded soberly. Quintus understood. Quintus always understood. It was a gift. You could call it magic of a different sort, perhaps.

"Nor have things come easily for you, Quintus," Marcus offered, as he felt the anger drain from his veins.

"At least both of my parents were Human," Quintus said with a shrug, a faint smile appearing beneath his trimmed beard, sandy brown, but occasionally flecked with gray.

"That doesn't seem like it helped, as you're still living here amidst the Teeth," Marcus said, gesturing at the bleached landscape which surrounded them in the frigid white mountains of the east, known to most as the Dragon's Teeth. The name

2

was derived from a story about the last dragon in history being slain and its teeth landing to form the mountains of the east, while its falling claws became the gray mountains of the west. Marcus, like most Wizards, simply called them the White Mountains and Gray Mountains in his head, but tried to use the silly mythic names to appease his Human friend.

"True. I am a long way from the castle of my youth," Quintus observed, "But I feel more at home with these Rangers than I ever did with my own family."

"The Rangers love Elves like you do..." A faint wisp of sadness seemed to crease the Wizard's features, "in ways your parents could not understand."

"True," Quintus replied, his voice trailing off into a slight quiver. He was thinking about her. The Elf-girl. Marcus winced. It is true that Wizards are known to be stoic about love and suffering. Of course, if you know any Wizards, you recognize that it is more complicated than that, but it is fair to say that they feel things less strongly than Humans do. Nevertheless, Marcus was both Wizard and Human and he grieved with his friend for that loss. Marcus was learning more about his mother's people each day he spent with these Rangers—who were, of course, not seen as properly Human by the Human world. Marcus's first 20 years had been spent in the exclusive company of Wizards, a motherless boy, whose half Human roots were gently mocked when he was young. 'Twas a gentle mocking, but no more. As the situation beyond the Gray Mountains deteriorated, the childhood taunts morphed into something more hateful—embraced or at least, tolerated by those around him. When the war between Wizards and Humans finally caught flame and tragedy consumed his little world, Marcus's father had spirited him out of the Wizard's Realm. By that time, he was no longer a curious hybrid, but rather a monstrous abomination. Funny, Marcus thought, he hadn't changed at all. He was the same as he'd always been, but his world had changed so utterly that he could no longer exist in it. Quintus understood. It was, Marcus noted again, a gift of sorts.

The darkness which followed the war's outbreak could no longer be felt directly by the Wizard, but only in echoes.

And even those echoes were still painful enough to cause him to physically wince in response. Yes, Marcus's father had sent him to the three exiled Wizards who dwelt on a remote island in the Burning Sea. Yes, this had saved his life. If saving the life he had left was a blessing or a curse, Marcus had never been entirely sure. What life could he hope to live after the tragedy which he had suffered? The curse of the island had insulated him from the war, but it was lonely. After several years of fruitful study, he had felt compelled to leave the lonely island, only to find the rest of the world just as lonely. Marcus had bounced from place to place in the other three Realms, solving local problems with his powers, bedding random girls to numb the pain, drinking his share of ale on the house for the same reason. He had become a stock character in epic tales—the wandering Wizard. It was not epic. It was an empty life. A small part of Marcus's Humanity still soldiered on, despite the evils which had befallen him. As if to encourage that Humanity, he had met Quintus nine years ago. They had saved one another's lives in a most unexpected way. Marcus smiled as he thought of it.

The two men had been with these Rangers for about a year or so, which made it easier on Quintus, who yearned to be with his own kind. Marcus had told Quintus he would agree to join these Rangers because it would make food gathering easier and protection stronger. Quintus acknowledged the cold logic of Wizards, even if he suspected that Marcus's Human side had made the choice to improve the life of his one friend. The Rangers were all wary of the Wizard, but they had been good people and a reasonable community. Quintus had befriended them, but he was good at such things. Marcus was more guarded. But if you knew his entire story, as Quintus did, you would understand completely. Marcus's thoughts had consumed him and Quintus noticed, as he always did. He shook his friend by the shoulders to snap him out of his dark reverie.

"Let us talk no more of sad things with the Golden One still so low in the sky," Quintus shouted, composing himself as he pointed to the sun that represented divinity for the Humans.

"The day stretches out in front of us, Marcus. Let's see if we can't find some delicious beast to roast on that fire."

"Well said, my friend," Marcus agreed, "We'll see if your bow is quicker than my Wizardry." Both men smiled—each as sincerely as his fashion allowed—and they went on the hunt. The other Rangers wished them well, but no one joined them. Having a Wizard in your group can prove immensely useful, but also quite awkward. Few Rangers were sad to consider Marcus would be away for an hour or two, as it would permit them to speak more freely and breathe more easily. Had they known what this day would hold, they'd have regretted their petty feelings, but alas the future is hidden from all—Wizards included.

Quintus knew there was plenty of food in their stocks, but he had thought that Marcus was more glum than usual this morning and a hunt would perhaps cheer him up. He knew he could not lift the weight from his friend's shoulders, but he could help him bear that weight from time to time. A motherless boy who had lived through unimaginable horrors... It was a miracle that Marcus did not wake up so grim every day, Quintus mused. Marcus peered at him as if reading his thoughts—although Quintus knew that Wizards did not have any such powers. As the snow cascaded down his face, Quintus pulled his hood over his thinning tan hair and smiled broadly at Marcus. Marcus did not return the smile—three Wizard smiles would be too much to ask so early in the morning—but his violet eyes seemed to brighten a little.

"I presume we have no Elvin Morning Elixir," Marcus said flatly, drawing his own dark hood over his black, but graying hair, while the cold snow pelted him in an almost taunting fashion.

"No, we will try to meet up with some Elves soon enough and engineer a trade," Quintus said, "I can ask Terentia to brew you some tea." He grinned boyishly.

"Tea? I detest the bitter water of Humans. It is not the same," Marcus spat, "Remind me again why we are so far North in this detestable mountain range?"

5

"Must you ask questions to which you know the answers?" Quintus said, cocking his head with amusement, "We were asked by the Elves to search for a missing group of clerics who were on a mission to Monk's point."

"Religious Elves seeking religious Humans…" Marcus muttered and if you'd heard his voice, it would have been as if cynicism were drowning his words.

"They wished to end the war," Quintus insisted, "As it happens, so do we. Wouldn't that make their disappearance our concern?"

"I spare little concern for clerics or monks," Marcus grumbled, "And I do not fully comprehend why Elves cannot conduct a search for their own kind."

"We are too far north for Elves," Quintus explained, "You know that Rangers are better suited to such matters."

"How you Rangers love the Elves," Marcus marveled, "You are willing to endure winter's cold despite it being out of season just to find some Elvin clerics. Curious."

"You think they've been killed and we are wasting our time?"

"Just as likely they froze to death," Marcus shrugged, "I do not think Elves are suited to the cold."

"All creatures who walk the black earth are adaptable," Quintus chided him teasingly, "This, you know."

"This, I know," the Wizard agreed, allowing his friend the small victory, "Let us begin the hunt, Quintus."

"Who knows what adventures await us!" Quintus declared with a false exuberance he'd hoped he'd pulled off.

"Your brushstrokes are too thick for the portrait you seek to paint, old friend," Marcus said with a dark chuckle, "I see through you. I know why we are going hunting. You need not over-sell it." Quintus's eyes turned downcast for a moment at the Wizard's penetration of his ruse. Marcus swallowed audibly and looked directly into Quintus's eyes. "I do appreciate it, brother," Marcus added softly and the quality of his voice seemed different, more Human.

Chapter 2: Non-Combatants

"He is just a child," she declared, brandishing her battle axe menacingly.

"He is not one of us. His age is irrelevant."

The child seemed blissfully unaware of the disturbance he was causing. He might have been three years old, maybe four at most. He was definitely a Wizard—there was no hiding that. Everyone knew you could always tell Elves by the ears. Many Humans said you could tell Morphs by their smell, although Octavia had always kept her distance from the Morphs, even if they were technically her people's allies. And Wizards? Well, their eyes were violet and they couldn't hide that, although some stories said they could. She knew Humans and Wizards were at war; she'd been fighting in that war— fighting quite well, if she did say so herself. She hated Wizards and their weird magic; she hated Elves and their uncivilized ways; she hated the traitorous Rangers who refused to stand with Humanity. If pressed, the warrior-woman didn't really *hate*, but she did kill, all the same. It was the job. Octavia Flavius was proud to be a Human. Humans were the most numerous race in the world by far. They excelled at building, forging weapons and armor, and letting their hearts guide them to what was right. Wizards were cold and detached, Elves rigid and pious, and Morphs were just plain bizarre. Still, being Human meant that Octavia was filled with emotions and one of those emotions was a belief that three year olds were always non-combatants—no matter the war being fought.

"Step aside," ordered her gray-haired commander, General Gnaeus Cornelius, who had been fighting the war since its inception. "If you don't want to kill the child, Lucius will do it. If you don't want to watch, then go join the rest of the army, Octavia."

"We don't kill children," she announced, her muscles tensing.

The general exhaled loudly. He knew that one of the things which distinguished his race was a belief that women were equal to men. He was brought up to believe that the Elves were wrong to mark out separate roles for men and women. And yet as he looked to his left and his right, he saw four men who would simply kill the Wizard boy and be off without a hesitant breath. Lucius, in particular, would dispatch the child in one stroke and they could ride back to the camp, having fulfilled this scouting mission. General Cornelius respected Octavia—she was as good a warrior as any man. Actually, better than most men in the two years she'd been assigned to his unit. But he felt that there was a softness to her, deep down. Her limbs were hard, her abdomen was hard, her look was hard, but a soft womanly heart beat beneath her chest. He could forgive this when Octavia was cleaving Wizards and Elves in two with her axe. But right now, it was putting him off schedule and he could not abide by that.

"What are you going to do?" asked Lucius, "Raise the boy as your own, Octavia? Is that why you left your breastplate behind, so you could nurse this boy with those lovely breasts?" All five men chortled at the absurdity of Octavia Flavius nursing any child, let alone a Wizard. Her large breasts seemed wasted on such a fierce soldier.

On most days, Octavia endured the earthy camp-talk about anatomy with little notice. This was one of the other days, when she had no patience for their crassness. By now, they should have been able to discern which day was which. That was their fault. "Come any closer and I'll split *your* breastplate in two," she threatened in her too-deep-for-a-woman voice, "We could take the boy captive and offer him in exchange for a Human prisoner. We are not savages. We kill Wizards, but we don't kill children."

The Wizard boy was delighting himself by making a handful of acorns levitate and then drop, only to levitate them again. "He already has magical powers," the general declared, "He will grow up to kill you and those you love, Octavia. If his parents cared, they would not have abandoned him. But Wizards don't care about anything."

There was a point in that. Octavia wavered for a moment, but only a moment. "Wizards are unemotional, but they would not abandon a child. We're missing something, sir.

What happened to his parents?" She looked around for the menace she believed might had caused this boy to be alone. They had seen some animals running and had heard vague combat sounds a few minutes ago. General Cornelius had chosen Octavia and four of her comrades to check it out. It could not have been some little Wizard boy, playing with magic, so what else was out there? Cornelius had pointed to her and the others so quickly that she had just grabbed her axe and mounted a horse. Given the current tense stand-off, Octavia wished she'd taken the time to dress in her armor, in case words failed to sway her comrades. She shook her head. There was a way out of this. Lucius could be an animal at times and General Cornelius had his faults, but they would surely listen to her logic. Wizards did not have exclusive hold on logic. Humans could think with their head as well as their heart. This wouldn't go bad. Not as bad as her vivid imagination was conjuring, as she stood between them and the boy with only her treasured helmet as armor.

"Come on, Octavia," moaned one of the other soldiers, Junius. "We haven't even breakfasted yet and you must be cold. You're half dressed."

She was cold, but she refused to shiver. Coldness had dominated her life in so many ways, but she would not let them see her shiver. "All I am saying, sir," she turned to face her commander, "is that this could be a trap. There may be Wizards in these woods and Elves, as well. We've had reports of Elves this far north, have we not? I have never heard of a child so young being left alone. Let's bind him with the Wizardsbane and take him back to the camp." Bound with that plant, he would not be able to cast and would be as harmless as any three year old boy.

General Cornelius peered into her eyes and then walked his gaze down Octavia's body, lingering on her exposed flesh which was reddening in the coldness. "I am losing my patience," the commander snapped, "Enough of this nonsense. Lucius, dismount and kill the child. Octavia, get back on your horse and fall back to camp. Those are orders." Lucius lunged at the child with his sword and found his death-stroke blocked by Octavia's battleaxe. Her green eyes seemed aflame.

"Order him to withdraw," Octavia growled. "We are soldiers, not butchers. We will not slay a helpless child. We are Humans. We are better than that." The Wizard boy looked curiously up at her and smiled as if it were all a game.

"You are disobeying a direct order, Octavia Flavius," General Cornelius snarled, "Drop your axe and let Lucius fulfill my command or that broad back of yours will be licked by 20 lashes when we return to camp."

"I will not follow an unjust command, sir," she said. Lucius was strong, but she was stronger. Lucius was fast, but she was faster. She knew it. Lucius knew it. The general knew it. He could not go down this path with her. He had to give in.

Cornelius seemed to be pondering the endgame. Then, his face hardened. "Take Octavia prisoner for insubordination and kill the Wizard," he said in clipped tones. "I will enjoy watching your body squirm as the sergeant administers the lashes in full view of the company, Octavia. Soldiers obey commands. I was given to understand that you had already learned that lesson." His lip curled into a sneer and Octavia knew at that moment that she would not give in on this issue. Nor would she take commands from this man ever again. He knew her secret. He mocked it. He was a general, but he was wicked. Her father had taught her never to follow the commands of wicked men or women. She would die, but she would not die alone. The only question which remained was how many of them she would take with her. One would have to presume two or three would be a fair assessment if one knew anything of Octavia Flavius's prowess in combat.

Nodding to Cornelius, Lucius turned his fury to Octavia and swung clumsily, in her estimation. She did not think, but acted in reflex. True to her word, she split his breastplate in two, the blade of her axe biting his flesh. It only took another blow and his eyes closed forever. The general and the other three soldiers appeared stunned for a moment, but then leveled their spears and spurred their horses. Octavia knew she was doomed. She had killed a fellow Human soldier in defense of a Wizard.

The penalty for such treachery was death. Her only consolation was that it would be a quick death with her helmet on. She could not defeat four men on horseback, but if she was lucky, she could kill at least one more—hopefully, Cornelius. She'd never liked the lecherous looks he gave her. Those looks brought her back to four years ago in another place... For this, he would be the one to die. Octavia shook her head to clear those thoughts. She was glad she had her axe and the helmet her father had once fashioned for her, but Octavia wished she'd had time to put on a breastplate or greaves. She felt exposed wearing just deerskin pants and a band of leather which only existed to support her breasts. This wasn't supposed to be a combat excursion, just a quick scouting job. At least she had her helmet on. Her only hope about her death was that she'd die wearing her father's helmet, so well-crafted and filled with his love. Death wearing the helmet would be sweet. "How nice to have a dream come true," she thought bitterly, as she braced for the inevitable.

Thwump! An arrow appeared from out of nowhere and pierced the throat of the lead rider, Junius. He crumpled to the ground as his horse peeled off. An unnatural wind then blew from Octavia's left and toppled the other three riders. She did not look to see what was happening, she simply finished off one of the unhorsed warriors. A clean-shaven man, hooded in a dark cloak appeared. He was wielding a sword which glowed orange, as if it were just being forged. This man cut down one of the soldiers who she hadn't even seen approach. A bearded man clad in greens and browns pulled out a shorter, more conventional sword and headed towards the general. But General Gnaeus Cornelius had sensed the doom, remounted, and began to ride off. The man in green and brown sheathed his sword and drew back his bow—it must have been he who had sent Junius to his death—but the general evaded the shot. The cloaked man with the glowing sword muttered something and pointed his hand at Cornelius. Octavia saw a lightning bolt emerge from his finger and move impossibly fast towards its quarry. But at the last moment, General Cornelius had banked right and the bolt hit a tree instead, exploding it into flames.

The horses scattered everywhere, their neighing echoing against the cold, white mountains.

Octavia swallowed and caught her breath. She felt the bare skin of her arms, ran a finger down her stomach, searching for blood. She found none. She removed her treasured helmet and shook the ponytail of her red hair free. It tickled her bare shoulders. The Wizard child was nowhere to be found.

"Who in the name of the Golden One are you two?" she asked when she finally caught her breath.

Chapter 3: The Girl with the Winged Helmet

"I am Quintus Agrippa Aureus, formerly the noble heir to the Dukedom my family still holds, now a simple Ranger with a small band in these Dragon's Teeth," said the man in green and brown, bowing courteously. There was irony in his bowing, she could detect that—as if he did not believe the tone he had adopted. There seemed to be a joke between him and the other man to which she was not privy. He added as an afterthought, "This is my friend, Marcus."

"You must be awfully cold, dressed like that," Marcus observed, pointing to Octavia's exposed flesh.

"Cold does not affect me," she announced, confidently, "I am a woman of the North. And I am not ashamed of how my body looks. It takes a lot of training for a body to look like this."

"Seems foolish to go into battle with so much of one's body unarmored, even if one is proud of how it looks," Marcus said with a shrug.

"Don't mind him," Quintus said in an apologetic tone, "It's his Wizard blood."

"I knew he was a Wizard," she retorted.

"The purple eyes? Good investigation, Red," the Wizard said with a smirk, "But I am only half Wizard."

"Marcus? Odd name for a Wizard, even if you are only half of one. Is the child yours?" she asked.

"No, I have not lived amongst the Wizards for many dark moons," Marcus replied, his voice sounding distant, "But it was very brave for you to stand up for him to your own kind. Of course, you are clearly brave if you wear so little clothing while snow buries us all."

"I was not expecting to fight or I would have been wearing armor," she snapped. She *was* cold as she was nearly shirtless and the snow was coming down, peppering her pale flesh with its frosty darts. Yet she would not let *them* see her shiver, either. She changed the subject, "Where did the little Wizard go?" The Wizard with the peculiar name looked around intently, shook his head, and muttered something to the Ranger.

Octavia did not catch the words, but the tone was sad and resigned.

"The child must have taken advantage of the chaos to slip away. We must hope his parents found him and he is safe," Quintus said, "If you'll pardon me, I think we should continue this conversation elsewhere or your white haired friend will soon be back with more men than Marcus and I can handle." The Wizard's face changed from sad to smug.

"More men than we can handle *easily,* anyway," Marcus chuckled darkly.

"So you think I should go with you two?" Octavia asked skeptically, "A Ranger who claims to be a disgraced noble and a Wizard? Pardon me, half-Wizard?"

"Do you have any better options?" Quintus asked. Octavia inhaled deeply and tried to ponder her dwindling options.

"You're an outcast like us," Marcus said mock-cheerfully, "Join us and our Rangers. The food is terrible, the company dreadful, but sometimes they play music and it's not the worst I've heard…"

"Rangers aren't Humans. They forsook our ways to support the Elves."

"That is the one thing I like about them," Marcus offered, "Except the music, of course."

"There are 20 of us," Quintus explained.

"Are there any women?" Octavia asked in a suspicious tone. What were these men's intentions?

"Eight," said Marcus, "And you'll certainly be the best looking one there, but as you will see, that compliment doesn't count for much. What's your name? Or should we just call you 'The Girl with the Winged Helmet'?"

"I am Octavia Flavius," she said, "Don't mock the helmet. My father made it for me when I left to train as a warrior. He said I was his sweet little dove."

The Wizard failed to stifle a snicker. "You don't fight like a sweet little dove."

"No," she said, narrowing her green eyes, "I do not." She glanced around and assessed her situation. It was dire; still she knew only one person on whom she could rely when situations got dire. She tucked her hair into her helmet as she placed it onto her head. "I thank you for your kindness and consider myself in your debt, should we ever meet again."

"You will not come with us?" Quintus asked, incredulous. She nodded with a trace of resignation.

"You would be wise to reconsider," Marcus said flatly, his eyes darting to and fro, as he searched for more Humans or the Wizard boy.

"As I have said, you have saved my life and I am grateful," Octavia said, standing as tall as she could, "But I will make my own way."

Marcus and Quintus looked at one another and exhaled in unison. Quintus bid her farewell. Marcus nodded in a non-committal fashion and they continued their hunt. Surely, insults would have been hurled their way if they had returned with a woman rather than a beast for roasting, Quintus consoled himself. Her powerful legs carried her west until she was a speck against the horizon and then, nothing at all.

"It's a pity she decided against coming with us," Marcus said after she had left.

"Do you like red-haired maidens, now?" Quintus asked playfully.

"Just seems a shame that the only broad-minded Human in the world other than you is going to perish before your Golden One dips below the horizon," he said with a shrug. "Her choice makes no sense. This vexes me."

***

Octavia wasn't sure she'd made the right decision, either. The Wizard and the Ranger had helped her and seemed genuinely sympathetic to her plight. Still, she'd not been brought up to trust strangers, especially the traitorous Rangers or the wicked Wizards. Of course, she hadn't been brought up to save Wizard children, either. No, she thought, that's not entirely right. Her father always taught her that the mark of a great warrior was if he or she protected the weakest. "Anyone can protect the mighty, Little Dove," he had said, "But to be a true heroine, you must pledge your strength to shield the vulnerable and the helpless." He had never specified that it had to be a Human, although she presumed that was his meaning. Perhaps she'd presumed too much. All Octavia knew now was that the entire army had been informed that she was a murderer and a traitor. The snow was falling so quickly that she could barely see an arm's length ahead. She was not wearing nearly enough clothing. She had no food. However, she did have her axe and her strong arms, which had solved most of her problems. But this was a problem like no other.

Where could she go? Octavia cursed herself for making her decisions so swiftly—to save the Wizard boy, to defy the general, to kill Lucius, to reject the offer of the Ranger and the Wizard with a Human name. None of those decisions had cost her more than a moment's thought. But the consequences were severe. All she knew was that she had to put as much frozen ground between her and Gnaeus Cornelius before she could take a moment to figure out her next move. Octavia inhaled the frigid air and almost choked—whether from the cold or the situation, she did not know. She knew one of her brothers lived a week's hard walk from here. Perhaps he would take her in, even if she were a fugitive. Then again, perhaps her sister-in-law would say no, that it was too much of a risk for Octavia's nieces and nephew. Her sister-in-law would be protecting the vulnerable. A great warrior's duty, for sure. Although Octavia mused, her sister-in-law had never picked up a blade in anger and her protection of her children would be laced with judgment and lack of pity for Octavia. Not terribly heroic. But not terribly unfair to turn away a fugitive to protect one's children. Why hadn't the Wizard boy's parents protected their child? Why did it fall to Octavia? She cursed under her breath, as she quickened her pace.

The next thing she knew, she was face-down in the snow, the cold burning her bare belly. She lay there for only an instant. Octavia's training quickly kicked in and she rolled immediately to her left, clutched her axe, and brushed the snow out of her eyes with her free hand. She spun around, looking for her assailant, but saw none. Within a few seconds, Octavia realized she had no assailant and that she had clumsily tripped over something. She looked closer. Not just something. A body. A Wizard's body. "The boy's father?" she softly asked no one in particular. The purple eyes were frozen in death. The corpse had been mistreated. Mutilated unspeakably. No Human would do such a thing to an enemy. Even a warrior with experience in combat had the right to be horrified by the sight. Who did this? Fear settled in her breast. Her breathing quickened. Suddenly, her choice to leave Quintus Agrippa whatever-his-name-was and the sharp-tongued Wizard with the Human name seemed very foolish. She closed her eyes and shook her head and then determined to rectify the situation while it was still her power to do so. Sprinting through the snow on those powerful legs, Octavia retraced her steps and discovered the Ranger and the Wizard within the hour.

***

"Does your offer still stand?" she asked, breathlessly, removing her helmet.

Quintus looked at Marcus and they seemed to have a wordless conversation. Octavia could not detect anything from the Wizard—not a word, not a gesture, no sign of his opinion on the matter. The Ranger read his comrade better and said, "Yes, our offer still stands, although we cannot offer you a beast for roasting."

She looked at them quizzically, "What?"

"Some broad shouldered, red-haired creature scared away our quarry," Marcus said. "We ought to return to the camp and warn the others that the Human army is likely moving quicker than we anticipated, although I expect the Rangers already know. Armies are rarely stealthy."

"Non-Rangers move very loudly," Quintus agreed.

Octavia thought about telling them what she'd seen, the mutilated Wizard. But she bit her lip and demurred. She excelled at suppressing horrible images. She felt that skill alone had preserved her sanity.

Halfway back to the camp, Octavia grabbed Marcus's arm. He seemed unsurprised and unconcerned at this. She blurted out, "Why did you save me?"

She expected another sharply-worded Wizard answer. Instead, he threw back the hood of his cloak to reveal his black hair with a healthy sprinkling of gray. He stared at her with those violet eyes. "We saw the whole situation unfold. You have been raised to hate Wizards and Elves, to tolerate Morphs only because they are allies, and to look down on Rangers as those who denounce their own Humanity. Yet when faced with an immoral order, you did not let these feelings win. You are rare. Quintus and I thought that you might believe all living creatures are the same. If so, you are like the two of us. I can sense that you struggle with this, even as I say it. But it is true, or else you'd have killed that child. You were lucky we were there, that is indisputable. But if I am right, then we are lucky to have found you, too, Octavia Flavius." He looked deadly serious.

She looked at Marcus and studied his face. He was right that she didn't believe all that she'd been taught. Of course, she wasn't sure he had so easily analyzed her correctly even if he did wield magic powers. Still, she had been a dead woman. A few more seconds and they'd have pierced her soft throat, dragged her naked body back to camp, and used her meaningless short life as a cautionary tale about why Humans defend Humans. Quintus and Marcus were strangers, but they'd saved her life. "I have lived my life owing nothing to anyone," Octavia said proudly in her deep voice, "But I owe you two my entire life. I will walk with you as long as you'll have me and my axe will defend you so long as there is breath in my chest."

Quintus and Marcus nodded somberly for they knew the oaths Humans swore when their lives were saved. Too many of those oaths could be written on a rushing river as the old poetic fragment from Classical Civilization once said, but this warrior girl seemed different and that was why they'd saved her in the first place. It would have been easy enough to save the boy and let the Humans kill each other. Marcus wondered where the boy went and what had happened to his parents. It nagged at him, but he tried to brush it off like the snow. They had chosen correctly. The girl's return had proven it.

They arrived at the camp to find Marcus's fire still smoldering but everything else in a state of chaos.

"Where is everyone?" Quintus asked. He could have been speaking to Marcus and Octavia, but it was just as likely he was asking a mountain.

"Could your Rangers have left you?" Octavia asked.

"They might have left without *me*," Marcus said, "But never without Quintus. He's more charming than…" His voice disappeared as he focused on something. "All the tents are still up and the supplies are still here. Rangers don't leave without their supplies." Another illogical fact. They were starting to pile up for the Wizard.

"My army was looking for Rangers and a report of Elves," Octavia said with a wince, "Could they have killed your friends?"

"Where are the bodies?" asked Marcus. "If your army killed the Rangers as a message, they'd have nailed up the bodies. It's their way." As you can tell, Wizards get easily flummoxed when logic is abandoned and Marcus was Wizard enough to be furious as such an odd state of affairs.

"There's no way that army could have come up here so quickly," Quintus said, as he studied the wind. "This was not the work of Octavia's army."

"Then what? A pack of animals?" Octavia asked.

"There were 18 well-armed Rangers here," Marcus said, "It would have needed to be a pack of dragons to kill them all so swiftly."

"There's no such thing as dragons," Quintus said flatly.

"Good, we can eliminate that angle," Marcus replied sharply, "Let me feel the earth. Sometimes, it can speak to me, although it is not a magic with which I am strong." Quintus met his eyes and nodded knowingly. Marcus knelt down and placed his hand on the exposed soil. He closed his eyes and muttered strange words.

"Anything?" Octavia asked.

Marcus shook his head. "Earth magic. Not a spell I was ever particular good at. Quintus, you can track anything that moves. What do you see?"

"The snow is coming down so fast, it obscures everything," Quintus remarked bitterly. He called out to his brethren and sistren with their special coded calls and when those failed, he fired a whistling arrow and waited for an answer. None came.

"What is this?" Octavia asked, as she dug into the snow with her axe. "It looks like blood, but it's black." A pool of black liquid was just beneath the snow.

"Blood?" Quintus asked no one in particular. "Nothing bleeds black blood. No Human, no Elf, no Morph, no Wizard, no beast..."

Marcus felt the ground near the black liquid. "I feel a darkness," Marcus announced solemnly, "I cannot explain it, but it is very cold here. Not snow cold; not ice cold; it is a different kind of cold. A hollow cold. A dark cold. A foreboding cold."

"I am going to track for a little while," Quintus announced, "Why don't you two keep an eye out for the Human army in case they do find their way up here." Octavia and Marcus nodded. Quintus slipped into the forest, his eyes as wide as they could be, an arrow already notched in his bow.

"How long has he lived with them?" Octavia asked, "Longer than you, right?"

"Indeed, he has been with many Ranger groups. This one, Quintus has run with sporadically for years. I came to them relatively recently, about a year ago. Because of Quintus," Marcus explained. He found a cloak, possibly Terentia's, and thrust it to her. Octavia was reluctant, but she wrapped it around her bare torso for warmth.

"Was he really a Duke? I know the Aureus family, but I've never heard of Quintus. I know all Rangers are exiles, but did he really leave a noble's life to live in the woods, wearing greens and browns?"

"Strictly speaking, he did not exile himself—although I suppose in a way he did," Marcus said with a world-weary smile, "His family was rich and powerful—they still are, although they are no longer his family. Our Ranger was the oldest son of the Duke of Aureus and was brought up with all the luxury that entails."

"I was the daughter of a blacksmith with all the soot that entails," Octavia smiled. Her joke had found fertile ground, this time, for the Wizard half-smiled.

"I was never Wizard enough for my father's people nor Human enough for my mother's, so I have more in common with a blacksmith's daughter than a Duke's son," Marcus observed, "But being well-born is no guarantee of happiness. Quintus was a model son. He grew into a great warrior, learned his history—at least as well as a Human can, wrote poems, danced at balls, excelled at athletic pursuits. He had one fatal flaw: he fell in love with the wrong girl." The Wizard stopped and silence hung over them.

"Tell me more," she demanded. He looked at her, appeared to be judging her worthiness, and then nodded.

"It was nearly two *decem* to use the Wizard word, about 19 of your years ago that Quintus was sent to the Elf Kingdom to represent the Humans, a great honor. This was not terribly long after the Human/Wizard War had begun and there were some Humans who felt the Elves would be good allies. On behalf of your ruling Council, Quintus was dispatched to secure a treaty from the Elf King Ealdric in complete secrecy."

"19 years ago?" Octavia marveled, "I was only three." Marcus appeared unimpressed with her youth. "Quintus's secret mission must have failed. The Humans decided to ally with the Morphs," Octavia said with a rueful nod. Marcus exhaled through his nose.

"While he was there, Quintus fell in love with a beautiful Elvin girl. Her name was Valeria, a high-born Sunrise Elf. He tells me her hair was like gold and her eyes were like the sea. Humans are poetic about their loves, and Quintus is more poetic than most with such matters." He permitted himself a warm smile, then it soured. "He came back with both Valeria and the sought-after treaty with the Elves."

"It was too late," Octavia observed, wincing.

21

"The Human Council had allied with the Morphs and declared the Elves to be as hateful as Wizards while he was away. It appears that his mission was a ruse, so the Human-Morph Allies could sneak attack an Elvin target in the Far South. Quintus showed up unaware of what had happened in his absence. He returned home, expecting a warm welcome due to the treaty in his hand and the girl he expected to marry."

"Marry? They couldn't have known one another long," Octavia observed.

"Falling madly in love in a few weeks? That is the way of Quintus, I am afraid," Marcus said, shaking his hooded head with a small laugh you could describe as warm, but with bitter dregs at the bottom of it. "Anyway, they put him in chains and tortured the Elf girl mercilessly. His parents told Quintus that the only way he could regain his honor was by killing her. He steadfastly refused. That is the way of Quintus, as well. Had he consented to pull back his bow and pierce her throat with an arrow, he'd still be a noble, although he would no longer be Quintus. He knew she'd die, but he refused to be a party to it— even if it would have saved the life he'd always known. On orders from the Council, Valeria was killed right in front of him. Slowly. With sharp knives, they tore strips of her white flesh, little by little, hour after hour. It is said she was driven mad before she finally died. I cannot imagine how Quintus avoided being driven mad by the sight of it, although I expect that he was never the same."

Octavia's hard eyes softened slightly for a moment before returning to their steely natural state. Marcus decided that few execution stories would have an effect on a soldier like Octavia Flavius. This was clearly one of them. She said nothing, but he had noticed the impact of the story on her.

"He'd have been killed too if his father wasn't a Duke," Marcus went on, "His father disinherited Quintus and they sent him into exile. No one spoke up for him. Not one friend. Not one of his siblings. No one." His words were laced with bitterness. "On that day, he became less than a man in the eyes of your people, but more of a man in my eyes, if you are curious. He was an exile, with nowhere to go."

"Couldn't he have fled to the Elves?" Octavia asked.

"By then, the Elvin King Ealdric was being called as 'Ealdric the Unready' for trusting the Humans—a name which has followed him into the recent histories. Valeria was his niece and now she was dead. The Elves thought it was all a trick and that Quintus was in on it from the start. It was a trick, but Quintus was not a party to it—I have never figured out who set him up, although I have my theories. Anyway, King Ealdric was deposed and killed by his brother, who still rules the Elves today, and not a whit of his hatred for Humans has diminished in the years of the war," Marcus explained, "As far as his own people, the de-nobled Quintus was forever branded an Elf-lover, quite the slur in the Human world."

"Nineteen years ago? That's when the Rangers started forming," Octavia noted, connecting the dots, "Some Humans felt that Elves and Humans should be allied and broke away to live like Elves in the wilderness. We call them barbarians."

"Of course, I might offer that few things are more barbaric than torturing and killing an innocent girl because her ears look different and she knows more about plants."

"You don't have to preach to me, Wizard," she said, holding up her hand, "I am with you."

"I know, I'm sorry, too few beings have been 'with me' during my life," Marcus explained, "Sometimes, I don't know how to handle that. All three of us could be killed on sight by Humans or Wizards. I don't know how much sympathy the Elves would have for us, either. And the Morphs? Who knows what they think?"

"I've never spent much time in the company of Morphs," Octavia stated.

"You probably have and just did not know it," Marcus offered, "If you've ever seen a bear or a wolf or an eagle; it might have been a Morph. Or perhaps you just met a person with a very good sense of smell."

"I once slept with a guy who had very good eye sight." It was a lie, but Octavia wanted to establish a rapport with her new comrade and ease in speaking about sex was the surest way for a woman to fit in with men in the Human world.

"A lover with good eyesight? Probably an Eagle Morph," Marcus said grinning, "Did you wake up with feathers in your bed?"

"I thought it was just the pillow exploding," she joked, "Who am I kidding? There was no pillow." Their moment of mirth ended abruptly.

Quintus returned, pale as the snow. "There's more of the black liquid if you track well enough," he said flatly, "And the trees have claw marks that I can't recognize. I can't feel the coldness that you feel, Marcus, but I am getting the sense that something happened here which I cannot explain."

"Why do you say that?" asked Octavia. Quintus looked at her blankly, steadied himself against a tree, and vomited. Marcus had known Quintus well enough to know that his stomach was made of iron. He had eaten three meals a day cooked by these Rangers and had never retched like that.

"There is something else," he said when he had finished. He took a breath, turned, and walked away. "Come." Marcus and Octavia followed. After a brief walk, they came to it: four bodies in a pile.

"Humans did not do this," Octavia said shakily as she surveyed the dead Rangers. Her legs wobbled a bit, but she kept her balance. She felt a burning at the back of her throat, but swallowed it down.

"Humans did not do this," Quintus repeated softly. He gestured at one of the corpses, a corpse which hours ago had been his brother-in-arms. "Not only did they murder our comrades, they cut out their hearts."

Octavia's throat closed up completely for a moment and she only swallowed with great effort. It was exactly like the Wizard corpse she'd tripped over. "Who?" Octavia demanded, incredulous, "Who in the Four Realms does that?"

"I have never heard of a being which steals the hearts of its enemies," Quintus said, exhaling through his nostrils. "Marcus?"

Marcus just looked at him, his brow furrowed. For a moment, he seemed ready to speak, then stopped himself. After a short eternity, Marcus nodded somberly to himself, "What do you want to do?" the Wizard asked, disregarding Quintus's question.

"I want revenge!" Quintus bellowed, "I want to empty my quiver in whatever man or beast did this. I don't care what color they bleed." Octavia cleared her throat and made a decision.

"I must tell you, I saw a Wizard back there—the child's father I suppose—and his heart was cut out, too," Octavia admitted, "So whoever does this hates Humans and Wizards. Who could that be?" Marcus looked at her gravely, or more gravely than usual. He said nothing but looked as if he were doing mathematics in his head. Octavia strode over to the Ranger, "I am shoulder to shoulder with you, Quintus," Octavia said, "Let's find whoever did this and carve them up."

"Humans," Marcus muttered under his breath, shaking his head. "I think a better plan is to gather our belongings and get away from here before that army catches our trail. If you listen carefully, you can hear them getting closer." The faint sound of hooves crunching snow was audible, even over the blood drumming in Quintus's ears.

"The rest of the Rangers must be out here," Quintus insisted.

"For them to abandon you, something must have occurred which rivals the worst nightmare imaginable," Marcus explained calmly, "That nightmare lurks in these mountains and the Human army approaches. We must flee, lest we be caught in that vise."

"So we just let this go?" Quintus asked, incredulous.

"Never," Marcus boomed, grabbing his friend by the shoulders, "But we cannot undo whatever was done here. We can find out what occurred. But that will require significant assistance." Quintus pondered, struggled with himself, and nodded with wordless resignation.

"Whose assistance?" asked Octavia.

"Three wise Wizards," Marcus explained. "Trust me. If am reading the signs correctly, then this is bigger than us. Much bigger."

***

In that moment, he saw them. The edges were blurred, but he saw the three figures as clear as the magic would allow. This was the moment, then. The moment they had long anticipated. He knew of the Wizard, but not of the Humans. No matter. They could be the instruments. He pondered whether to reach out to the island or wait for the island to initiate contact. He decided on the latter course. The others must be consulted to ensure the story would be perfect. A full rendering of the truth would not serve their higher purposes. This much, he knew. How much truth and in what time, those were the issues which had to be considered.

Chapter 4: The Verdict

"Do you have anything to say in your defense?" the King of All Elves Near and Far asked sternly. His wife sat next to him with an equally stony face. Yet Gwendolyn detected a faint wisp of hope in the Elvin Queen's eyes, as if perhaps none of this were necessary. Perhaps she was imagining that, but she'd always been a hopeful Elf-girl.

"I have no defense, Your Majesty," Gwendolyn began, "I have broken your laws with my actions." The Queen's eyebrows raised ever so slightly. The King appeared unmoved. "But I have broken the law because the law is unjust. An Elf is an Elf and a warrior is a warrior. Male and female have nothing to do with it."

"Enough!" thundered King Aethelrud, "This is madness. The Great Spirits have made males and females different because they have each been fashioned for different roles—it has been written in our holy texts by the 12 sacred authors. There are three kinds of Elves. There are two genders. Each has a place. This is what makes us Elves. We are not like the Humans or the vile Morphs, who blur these lines. You have presumed to usurp the role of a warrior, Gwendolyn, and this is the preserve of men, as it always has been."

"She is the best archer in the realm," Griffin spoke up. She knew he would, even though she wished he wouldn't. "Everyone here knows it. Surely, we need her bow to fight the Humans and the Morphs. I have come to believe that the Spirits made her this way to help all of Elvinkind." A gasp escaped the Elvin men and women who had gathered for this trial.

"So you speak for the Spirits, do you, Griffin?" asked King Aethelrud with a derisive laugh, "More likely, you speak for your little sister. We Elves conform to nature. Humans destroy Nature; Morphs pervert Nature. We are the guardians of what is natural and a girl with a bow is unnatural. Gwendolyn has a role prescribed by nature…"

"I am not simply made to cook your food, clean your home, and raise your little Elflings," she blurted out. She did not believe that statement wholeheartedly and if pressed, might admit a certain fondness for cooking and an abiding love of children. But the sentence was death and she was feeling bitter, so her words smoldered. What more trouble could she get in? "I can be a brave warrior and I will serve you, King Aethelrud, and our lovely Queen with my bow. What's more, I am sure that there are hundreds of girls who could take up arms for the cause. We live in dark times... If you would just bend the laws, we could win this long war which has shadowed our land."

"She is right, we are at war," her brother Griffin echoed, "And a crisis can lead to laws being suspended. Let her wield her bow for the cause, your Majesty."

The King said nothing. Somehow, this was far more terrifying to Gwen than if he had raged. Gwendolyn pulled her last symbolic arrow from the metaphorical quiver, begging the one person who she felt could truly protect her, "Beloved Queen, I implore you for your mercy and understanding in this matter." Gwendolyn then did what she swore she'd never do since her arrest: she fell to her knees and let her long blonde hair brush against the grass. The Queen appeared ready to speak, but then demurred. Perhaps it was no different than all those years ago when her first husband had been deposed and killed by his brother who then took her as a wife. The Queen had accepted her fate, then. But then was then and now was now. Gwen fervently hoped the difference between the two mattered. There was a tightness in Gwen's chest and she became conscious of the fact she was holding her breath. The Queen did not speak up. The King looked to her, smiled a satisfied smile and rose from his wooden throne, festooned with flowers and vines.

"This trial is over and the verdict is at hand," boomed Aethelrud, the King of All Elves Near and Far. "There will be no female warriors, even if the Humans burn our woods and the Morphs turn to wolves and devour our people raw. What the Spirits have ordained, no King may undo. Gwendolyn, you have shamed your family and your gender with your bow and your arrows. Justice must be done or the Spirits will grow angry. But you are not alone in your transgression. I order your parents to be imprisoned with your brother for letting things go as far as this. They have neglected their duties to our kingdom and will be punished. And I order you to die. This is my verdict, let it be written."

Gwendolyn expected her death sentence, but she was stunned by the imprisonment of her family. Her lip quivered as she pondered the mess she'd created. "You will not kill her," Griffin declared, "unless you mean to kill me, too." That was Griffin. He was only two Sun cycles older than her, but you would think he had reached the age of Gray Hair and she were still a child who had not put on the green dress of womanhood. He was always trying to protect her from the taunts, from the fights, from herself. The sad part was that after she had reached 12 Sun cycles, she was quicker than him. By 13, no one could fire a bow as quickly or as accurately as Gwendolyn. His protection was sweet but unnecessary. The Sun had risen and fallen for 26 cycles since her birth and she knew her bow was more lethal than Griffin's or indeed any of theirs. She did not need his protection. She hadn't for years. And yet here he was clumsily trying to stand between her and her fate. Gwendolyn bit her lip, as she pondered a way out.

"Your defiance will be met with the same justice, Griffin," the king declared, "I amend my verdict: You will die with her." The crowd chanted "*Let it be written.*"

Clearly, things were spiraling well out of control. Gwendolyn's blue eyes searched the scene for something, anything useful. She saw a bow on the shoulder of a guard and pondered whether she could disarm him, load the arrow, and kill the King before they clubbed her to death. In the melee, Griffin might be able to flee. *If* he were smart enough to recognize the distraction. She looked at his eyes and tried to communicate wordlessly. But he just jutted out his jaw with that noble expression as if he were helping matters. Gwendolyn knew she had less than an instant to make her move. She inhaled deeply and rocked on the balls off her feet, preparing to spring. No one was quicker than Gwendolyn. This, she knew. She inhaled deeply. Then, all of a sudden, something unexpected happened, like a Wizard's thunderbolt coursing through the realm.

The beloved Queen—wife of two kings, widow of one—stood up, smoothed her elaborate dress, and approached Aethelrud. She whispered into his ear and the two began speaking softly. A buzz slowly spread across the crowd as Elves theorized what was happening. It would be the perfect time for Gwendolyn's plan to be put into motion, but her feet were rooted to the ground like the sacred trees and bushes her people worshiped as homes of the Spirits. She was totally caught off-guard. She was paralyzed. The monarchs motioned to one of the Sunset Elves off to the side. The Sunset Elves were all merchants of one kind or another. Many were continually on the move between Elfland and the West, bringing goods to the Wizards in exchange for payment. Some believed these merchant Elves to be a separate race of Elves altogether and even those who felt otherwise believed they dabbled in Wizard magic and had darkness in them. Without question, they looked different from the Sunrise Elves who were marked by their blond hair and light skin. The Sunset Elves' brown skin and black hair seemed a total opposite of Sunrise Elves like Gwendolyn or Griffin. Yet they were part of the Realm and an essential part of the Elves' world, just like the Low Elves with their dark hair and light skin. Three kinds of Elves for three kinds of duties—"Many trees make up a forest," Elves always say.

The leader of this band of Sunset Elves conferred with the king, nodding vigorously. "We have considered the criminal's plea for mercy to our beloved Queen," the King said, as the Queen returned to her throne. "And we have decided on a solution." Whether the "we" signified the King and Queen together or simply the King himself using traditional pronoun conventions was left unclear. "We will not shed Elvin blood at Elvin hands in the midst of the Great War. That would anger the Great Spirits even more than Gwendolyn's unfeminine acts. But Justice must be done. Her life and Griffin's have been spared, but their freedom has not. They are to be enslaved by these Elves of the Sunset to do with as they will. No Elf may free them or treat them as Elves. They are now slaves, owned by Thorbad, captain of this band of Sunset Elves. He may do whatever he wishes with these criminals except free them."

"I thank you for these fine gifts," this Thorbad said, "We shall not be kind to them." He was a thick, barrel-chested Elf with gray in his black curly hair and scars on his brown face and arms from his many trips to and from the West.

Chains were clasped on Gwendolyn before she realized that she needed to resist. The guard who fastened them brushed back her flaxen hair and whispered into her delicate ear, "You may wish you had been sentenced to death when all is said and done." He cackled miserably, his breath reeking of wine. At last, it occurred to Gwendolyn what had transpired. The queen had asked the king to rescind the death sentence, but in some ways slavery was worse than death for a Sunrise Elf. And her parents remained in custody for her transgressions. She saw the guard hustle away her parents to some dark prison. Griffin screamed his voice raw and struggled fruitlessly against the iron chains. The siblings were handed over to the Sunset Elves and marched towards the ancient road to the West, the Via, beaten and spat upon by all the Elves of the Realm, even the Low Elves. Gwendolyn had always prized her life, but only now did it occur to her that she prized her freedom even more. And her freedom was gone.

Chapter 5: Slavery

Griffin never dreamed that he would be here. He was an upright and steadfast Elf. He had earned great marks in the treasured knowledge which only Elves possess. He knew which plants produced fruits to eat and which were poison; he knew which leaves could heal an illness or clean a wound; he knew which flowers were simply beautiful and which could intoxicate; he knew which wood was ideal for a bow and which was better to frame a home. He could move without making sounds or tracks, while also following the trails of an animal or an enemy—even if those trails were hours old. Griffin knew the sacred scriptures by heart and could sing them in a mellifluous voice. He could sing of the days when the Great Spirits created the world, planted the trees, blessed the waters, and invented the animals. Three times the Creator Spirit attempted to fashion beings to populate this land and three times He failed: Morphs were too close to the beasts, Humans too far from the plants, Wizards too quick to control the elements. Then, all the Great Spirits joined hands and sang one beautiful verse in perfect harmony and thus were created the Elves— closest to the spirits, stewards to the natural world, the culmination of the races. Satisfied with their work, the spirits dissolved into the waters, the trees, the bushes, and the clouds. They still sought to guide the Elves and protect them, but no longer spoke to them except through the Great Book, compiled thousands of sun cycles ago by 12 blessed authors.

Griffin had won a prize by singing the Creation story in a competition and he remembered it fondly. On that day, they had crowned him with a wreath of flowers, a prize that revealed everything you need to know about achievement. For a few days, the blossoms were beautiful and fragrant. But by the end of the week, they had withered to make place for new challenges, new competitions, new victories. Griffin absently felt his long blond hair as he trudged along. There was no wreath on his head, now. Elves always wore leaves in their hair to remind them of their role as guardians of the natural world. But that was for free Elves. He and Gwendolyn were slaves.

Their bodies now belonged to Thorbad, Captain of this band of Sunset Elves as they marched towards the West and the world of Wizards, who dwelt in the gray mountains which Elves called the "Tomb of Storms and Sun." The leafy crowns had been torn from Griffin and Gwendolyn's heads as the chains were locked around their wrists and ankles. Chains were made of iron and iron came from the earth, but it was not living, nor ever was. It was cold and heartless like the Wizards to whom the Elvin King had long ago joined the fate of his kingdom. The iron weighed down Griffin's limbs so that he could not leap and run like Elves were created to do. It was amongst the worst punishments imaginable. He looked at his sister.

Gwendolyn's blue eyes were downcast, and her steps were slow. He'd always known she'd cause him trouble. He just never thought it would be trouble like this. As a Sunset Elf cracked the whip over her back, Griffin almost felt the blow himself. Or perhaps, he was just feeling the blows he'd received a mile earlier for going too slow. Gwen was not like the other Elvin girls. When she whittled wood as an Elfling, she had sometimes fashioned them into families of dolls like the other girls. But just as often, they were wooden arrows by the time their mother confiscated them. She'd showed enough interest in making clothes, cooking food, or other pursuits that the Spirits ordained for women, but she'd always showed interest in male pursuits like running and shooting, as well. Gwendolyn received her green dress when she moved out of girlhood and became a woman, but the dress did not change her into an Elvin ideal of a female. As a child, she'd been teased for transgressing the rules governing the tasks of her sex, but children can be indulged. Their father never stopped indulging her as if she were still a little girl, even though five sun cycles had passed since her childhood had been completed. Once Gwen had reached the age of fertility—21 sun cycles—Griffin and their mother expected Gwendolyn would fall in line. But she never put aside the bow and she persisted in wearing pants when she ran through the woods, even though dresses were the only modest choice once an Elf girl reached fertility. Gwen did not hate dresses and actually looked quite fetching in them, but she preferred pants when she ran because she could move faster. O Great Spirits, was she fast! But now, she was hobbled by the chains, by the whip lashes, by the knowledge of what she had done. And Griffin still believed it was all his fault. She was his baby sister, even if she wielded the deadliest bow in Elfland. He should have guided her better, stuck up for her more, stopped things before they went too far. Now, "too far" was where they dwelt. Did his mother blame him? Did she blame his father? Could any of them have stopped Gwendolyn from this?

***

The soft grass bent beneath her small feet and Gwendolyn marveled at the beauty of the forest. As they were heading towards land disputed with Humans, Thorbad had avoided traveling directly on the ancient road called the Via. He preferred the cover of the forest just south of the road, now that they were close to lands that the Humans triumphantly called "the Far South." Fighting was bitter here and fighting interfered with commerce. Taking the caravan through the woods slowed them, but was worth the inconvenience. This was not the first time Thorbad had led Sunset Elves west. It was the first time he had slaves to sell. You must understand that he was not a supporter of slavery, but when the King of All Elves Near and Far gives a command, an Elf like Thorbad cannot conceive of refusing. It was how he was made.

Gwendolyn had heard stories of Elves who had been enslaved. She might spend the rest of her life in the darkness of the Wizard's home, the Tomb of Storms and Sun, swinging a pick to pry more iron out of the earth for chains that other slaves might wear. She might make this trek with the Sunset Elves cycle after cycle with heavy goods strapped to her back. She might be sold to the Wizards to share their bed, a mere pointy-eared toy for their base pleasures. She would never again jump from branch to branch, darting at the top of the world. She'd never again have the freedom to pluck a juicy fruit from a bush and bite into it, as the juice squirted everywhere. She'd never again befriend another deer, race it to the meadow, protect it from a wolf. The warm sun would no longer feel like a blanket enveloped around her—now it would be oppressive while she labored. In her previous life, a warm day might be an occasion to leave her clothes at the shore and refresh her pale, lithe form in the cool waters of the sacred lake, feeling the rush as the holy waters caressed her and the heat became a distant memory. Freedom was as sacred as those waters and Gwendolyn had lost it for herself and for those she loved.

"I should have just played their game," she said to no one in particular.

"If only it were so easy," Griffin responded, "But you are who you are and the Spirits made you who you are."

"Perhaps the Spirits placed you in the wrong body," a dark skinned captor taunted, grabbing his crotch with an exaggerated gesture. "If you were made differently, then no one would have fussed about you shooting your arrows into Humans." He grinned malevolently.

Gwen ignored him. "I am entirely to blame, Griffin."

"I think we can agree on that," Griffin said, smiling through the pain. "The Spirits are just, Gwen. They will provide for us." A rod came crashing down on his back.

"They'll provide this for you, slave," a Sunset Elf shouted, "You angered the king and now you're nothing but a piece of property. You are no Elf and you have no prayers for the Spirits. They help those who follow their commands. Your sister and you angered the Spirits. Now, you'll do as you're told. Maybe, the Wizards will test their potions on you to see if they work. Or maybe, you'll dig deep underground for the metals and jewels that the Wizards love to wear."

"Or you'll grow the food for their bread," another offered, "Or shovel the manure from their horses."

"Maybe you'll end up in their beds and *then* you'll be in for it…" Laughter ensued. "She'll play the part of the proper lady then, won't she, boys?"

Griffin lunged at the dark Elf and knocked him off his feet. Griffin got one punch in before his comrades tore Griffin off and kicked at him. Gwendolyn sighed. Her brother never

35

learned. "Griffin," she said as she knelt by his bloodied body. "They're not lying."

He spat out some blood. "The Spirits…"

Gwen had faith in the Spirits. But for her, divinity could be glimpsed when she was looking into an animal's innocent eyes or swimming in the cool waters. But the Spirits rarely moved her when clerics in solemn robes or books gilded with gold started to make old fashioned pronouncements with no relevance to her life. Sometimes, she struggled with her beliefs due to these things. Yet her brother never stopped believing, even though this might be a good time to lose faith.

"Let's get going," Thorbad declared.

"Give him another minute," Gwendolyn insisted. She knelt down and rubbed Griffin's shoulder and something caught her eye. "Hold on, what is that?"

"What is what?" asked one of her captors.

"Right there in the bushes, it's a bird," Gwendolyn said, "A little robin."

The Sunset Elves were unimpressed. "A robin in the woods, how odd!" Thorbad, sarcastically commented.

"I think its wing is broken," Gwendolyn said, her voice taking on a gentle tone. "It's not flying, but hopping around." Griffin looked up and saw the bird. He always marveled how his sister could be so tender with animals, exceeding even the gentlest Elf with her treatment of them. Given the way the last week of their lives had gone, perhaps there was some wisdom in that.

"If its wing is broken, it's as good as dead. Best crush its skull to end its misery," Thorbad declared, "We have a little more time before we lose the light. Let's go."

"No," Gwendolyn said fiercely, "You said I was no longer an Elf, that I was property. But *you* are still Elves and Spirit-fearing Elves if I'm not mistaken. Free Elves like you protect the creatures of Nature. This bird needs protecting until its wing heals."

The Sunset Elf leader, Thorbad, considered the situation and conferred with an Elf named Ardor, who appeared to be his lieutenant. Thorbad smiled insincerely and nodded, "Very well, we will take the injured bird as you wish, but one of the slave-girl's duties will be to tend to it. You can carry the bird, dig for worms, protect it from predators. If you want to save it, then the robin is all yours. But if you ask me, you have enough to deal with right now, little blonde girl."

"I accept your command to protect this bird," Gwen said fiercely, "I will help it until its wing has healed. Come here, little one, it's okay." The bird tentatively hopped into Gwendolyn's hands and chirped weakly. It seemed to understand what was happening and looked grateful for the blonde Elf's kindness.

With pain pounding in his skull, Griffin didn't fully understand what was happening, but he had an odd sense that something important just occurred.

Chapter 6: Trust

They had walked for days and yet Quintus could still smell the burning flesh. It could be years before that smell disappeared from his consciousness. Or never. Marcus had been right—he was *always* right. They did need to get away from the Ranger camp. There was a Human army looking for all of them. There had to be some Wizards lurking nearby to whom that child had belonged. There was someone or something which slew four of his comrades and tore out each of their hearts. Still, Quintus wanted time to fashion some sort of memorial for them, say words of peace in the name of the Golden One. He wanted to grieve. But there was no time for grief, as the Wizard side of his best friend had counseled. There was just enough time for Marcus's fire spell to consume their bodies, sparing the Ranger men and women from further post-mortem indignity. And then it was time to flee, descending from the Dragon's Teeth at the roof of the world and slowly making their way south-west, as Marcus had insisted. The other 14 Rangers appeared to have dissolved into the wind. It was like the dull beginning of a story too often told and Quintus appreciated that fact much later on in the adventure. The hero returns to his camp to find his comrades gone, sparking an adventure? Truly? Quintus may have appreciated the stale nature of this event, save for the fact that he had never considered himself the hero of any tale and the disappearance of the Rangers was not an overdone beginning of some tired story, but rather his reality with a dizzying set of potential causes that he did not wish to consider.

When they appeared reasonably out of immediate danger, they set up their tents and slept. As the One crested the horizon, the Wizard remained sleeping soundly, as he always did. He didn't even bother to set up his tent, but slept where he had lay down and never stirred, even as the two Humans awoke. "Is this typical of Wizards?" Octavia asked, as she and Quintus shared a flask of watered-down ale and what was left of the rabbits they had roasted last night. She was brushing out her long red hair as Quintus sharpened his dagger.

"Do you know anything about Wizards?" he asked. He was surprised that of the many things she could have taken from the Ranger camp, she chose a brush. Octavia Flavius was more complicated than perhaps he had first considered.

"I know I was brought up to hate them and had an unblemished record of Wizard hatred until the last two I've met," she said in her deep unwomanly voice, "The little boy looked at me with those big purple eyes. I couldn't let them kill him. And this one," she gestured at the sleeping Marcus, "he is good, isn't he?"

"He is more than good," Quintus said, "He is great. No one has seen the tragedies he has seen." His lips pressed together as if he keep any secrets from escaping.

"He has a Human name. That is peculiar. Tell me about him," she said, licking the grease off her fingers.

"Even *he* can't sleep long enough for me to tell all his misfortunes," Quintus laughed, "And some misfortunes are best told by the sufferer. I'll tell you this: He never knew his mother, except she was a Human and she gave him a Human name. He was never sure if his Wizard father regretted his birth. He has spent his life trying to master forces that came harder to him than pure Wizards while simultaneously seeking to strike a balance between being a Human and a Wizard."

"He doesn't dress like a Wizard, that's for sure," she observed.

"He hates jewels and precious metals and fine-spun robes," Quintus agreed, "That is the Human part of him. And he doesn't love like a Wizard would, that's for sure."

"Wizards love?"

"They love in their fashion, but never too much. It's not logical," Quintus explained, "But when Marcus loves you as a friend, he loves like a Human does."

She studied this peculiar man with two natures, as he slept under his dark cloak, his chest rising and falling like any other creature in the Four Realms, "Has he ever loved a woman like a Human does?"

Quintus winced and looked away for a moment. "He has," Quintus said, nodding, "But that is not my story to tell, and I'm afraid like most of his stories, it does not end happily. We both have a history with loving the wrong woman..." He paused to chew and swallow. "I will tell you this: he believes with all of his heart that we are living in dark times and that there once was a better world. If you ever want to get him going, just drop a hint about 'the Great Ancient Civilization of Classical Times' which puts our world to shame." The gray eyes of the Ranger twinkled mischievously in the morning light.

"I take it you don't agree."

"Usually, I try to focus on the present because I don't see how some ancient world—real or imagined—has anything to do with me and my own misfortunes. Still, I have learned that he is not usually wrong...at least not *totally* wrong about most things. It can be frustrating, but it is the price of friendship with a Wizard."

"What about the sleep?" she asked with a broad smile, "What's with that?"

"You know Wizards control the elements, right? They believe there are six: air and earth, fire and water, light and darkness," Quintus explained, "Wizards are taken from their homes at age seven to begin their studies. They learn the ancient dead language which only exists in our world as our Human names and nowhere else. They work on focusing their mind, gesturing just so—I never totally understood it. And that permits him to blow your enemies off of horseback with some crazy wind or instantly create the flames which sent my brothers and sisters to the sky and life with the Golden One. But each spell exhausts the Wizard. Some spells are harder than others and all spells are harder for him because he is half Human."

"He rests to restore his strength, so he can cast more spells which sap his strength, so he can rest some more," she said.

"He rests," Quintus agreed, "But sometimes I don't think he is ever restored." He looked at the soldier-girl, squinting with his steel-gray eyes. Octavia was struggling with a knot in her hair for a moment before successfully threading the brush through her flaming locks. "What's with the hair?"

"What do you mean?" she asked.

"You wear it very long for someone in the business of war," he observed, "Why don't you cut it short like most warrior women?"

"You are a Ranger," she said, "This means you've seen much of the Four Realms?"

"There are few parts of our world I have not lived in or passed through," he admitted. She narrowed her green eyes.

"Have you ever seen a red haired Elf or Wizard?" she asked. He pondered and shook his head. "A Morph with this color hair?"

"Probably not," he permitted himself.

"You are from the south of our realm, right?" she asked impatiently. Quintus nodded. "Did you ever encounter a girl in your lands with hair like mine?" she asked, showing off a lopsided grin as she smoothed her hair.

"I must confess that in my experience the only people with such hair hail from the North of the Human realm," Quintus conceded.

"My hair marks me as a woman of the North," she said proudly, hoping she didn't wake the Wizard with her sudden increase in volume. "I can tuck it into my helmet to ensure no one uses it to their advantage in combat. I will not chop it off. It is who I am and where I am from—this is important, to remember where one is from."

"Octavia, in my experience, where you are from isn't as important as where you are going." Quintus permitted himself a small smile as he looked at the fierce girl. The booming voice and muscled arms were inconceivably bellicose and self-assured, but those soft green eyes told him she was barely more than two decades old. She had much yet to learn of the world, but he did not judge her for that. The warrior girl probably knew more now than he did when he was her age…

She shrugged off his advice and he returned to the sharpening of his dagger. The violet eyes of the Wizard suddenly opened with a snap. "How long?" Marcus asked Quintus, his voice a croak as he emerged into wakefulness.

"The blessed sun is high in the sky, my friend."

41

"Too long," Marcus grimaced. "We must get moving."

"We saved some rabbit for you," Octavia said, pushing the meat towards him.

"You are very sweet," he said, gobbling it up. His words were kind, but his inflection was not. Perhaps his Human and Wizard sides fought over that sentence, Octavia mused. She smiled in spite of herself.

"Sweet? You may be the first being in all the world to say that," she said, putting on her helmet and strapping on her boots. "I swore I'd follow you wherever you led, but where exactly are we going, Marcus?"

"A place no creature would ever dare go," Marcus declared as he got to his feet.

"Sounds enticing," she remarked, sarcastically, her husky voice lightening ever so slightly.

"We seek my teachers," Marcus replied.

"Your old school? How delightful. Care to elaborate?" she asked.

He smiled at the sarcastic edge to her words. She had spark, this Human girl with the peculiar voice and garish red hair. He liked spark. "We are leaving the Dragon's Teeth, crossing the Fertile Midlands contested by Elves and Humans, and heading southwest towards the Gray Mountains at the edge of the western world."

"The Gray Mountains? You mean the Dragon's Claws? Where your people live?" she asked. Marcus peered at her for a moment. It made her uncomfortable and so she said, "I may look and sound like a dumb brute, but I know a little geography." "You don't look or sound dumb," Marcus observed, a faint twinkle in his violet eyes, "Yes, Humans call the mountain range 'the Dragon's Claws' as part of the foolish story about a slain dragon's body parts making the world in a time before history." He paused and looked at Octavia kindly, "Elves are worse. They call the mountain range 'the Tomb of Storms and Sun,' as if the sun dies and is buried in those mountains each night. Wizards usually avoid stories about imaginary dragons or dying suns. The Wizards who dwell there simply call them the 'Gray Mountains' because they are gray."

42

"Curious. What do you call the Dragon's Teeth?" she asked.

"The White Mountains," he replied in an obvious tone, "They are white."

"So those gray western mountains which look like Dragon Claws to me; I presume they are home for you?" she asked, matching his strides with her long muscular legs. Despite the quick pace, she did not once appear to breathe heavily.

Quintus interrupted to spare his friend. "Not for over a hundred dark moons has Marcus called that place home."

"Nor is that where we are headed," Marcus added, "Just south of the Gray Mountains is an enchanted sea, often called the Burning Sea. Because it burns," he lightly mocked Octavia, "In that sea is an island inhabited by three Wizards who were cast out of the Wizard realm, perhaps before you were born."

"This tale doesn't really sound familiar," Octavia said, tying back her long red hair but never slowing down for a moment, "Why were they exiled?"

"They questioned the legitimacy of the Wizard Empress," Marcus shrugged.

"No offense, but Wizards and Elves are so foolish to entrust one person with power," Octavia said, shaking her head, the red pony tail swishing back and forth. "Kings? Emperors? Say what you will about Humans, but a council is the proper way for a free people to live. We choose the leaders and they are accountable to us."

Quintus guffawed. She looked at him sharply. "How many people sit on the Human council?" he asked.

"Fifty," she replied in a tone which indicated he should know this fact.

"How many do we vote for?"

"30."

"So all ten dukes of the realm sit on the council by right, as do five of counts and five of the barons, chosen amongst themselves without a vote, right?" She nodded, unmoved. "So if my arithmetic is correct, 20 spots on the elected Council are unelected."

"It is tradition," she shrugged, "It is history. Your father, the Duke of Aureus, sits on that Council, so why are you complaining?"

"It is an unfair game like one finds in a disreputable gambling den," Quintus said with exasperation leaking into his voice. She stopped and looked at him, his gray eyes piercing her green ones, "The nobles control 40% of the seats on the Council outright. And as for the other 60%, please think about those who seek your precious vote. Are there any blacksmiths? Stonemasons? Shopkeepers? Farmers?" She glared at him. "Who are your elected representatives on the Council, Octavia?"

"Non-nobles," she insisted, "Common folk of normal blood, like me."

"Wealthy merchants, highly placed military officers, and important monks and nuns, correct? They are not nobles, but they are not like you, Octavia. They are rich."

"Council spots are unpaid," Octavia said, "Because public service…"

He cut her off, "Public service should not be compensated. I know. It's a ruse, so that the wealthy stay that way and the nobility maintains a disproportionate amount of power. There are ten dukes in the Human Realm and they have 20% of the seats! What are there, 30 counts and 100 barons? And they get another 20% of the seats? And the whole rest of our realm—thousands upon thousands get to vote for a select group of rich people? 'Tis an illusion, Octavia. Trust me. A council can be just as corrupt as one man or woman, at least in my experience," he noted, "Maybe the Morphs are right to have no leaders at all."

"No leaders, no laws, no civilization," Octavia muttered, "Such bizarre creatures, even if they are allied with my people. Well, my *former* people, I suppose. I don't think I'll be returning to the Human world very soon."

Marcus had patiently held his tongue during Quintus's cynical lesson on Human politics for Wizards relish a good helping of cynicism and he shared his friend's political analysis. Still, if you know Wizards, you know they cannot hold their tongues for too long. He finally spoke up, "I am no supporter of councils or kings. And I have a bad history with the Wizard Empress. She exiled my teachers."

"What was the charge?" Octavia asked.

"A spurious charge of treason," Quintus offered in a flinty voice.

"She spread wicked stories about them, but it was whispered that they questioned her right to rule," Marcus explained. "They had proof she was not a daughter of the dead Emperor as she claimed—she was passed off as such by the *pontifices*, that is, the priests, who are as powerful as teachers in my former world. It was said my three teachers supported the claim of the Emperor's nephew to the High Throne."

"I take it you believe there is more to the story?" Octavia asked.

"I do. She was brought to power by forces who sought the war with Humans. The true heir was murdered and she took the throne—war followed immediately thereafter. Once ensconced in power, she met very little resistance to her plan to fight the Humans and someday bring the Wizards out of the Gray Mountains...or the Dragon's Claws of the West, if you prefer." He paused with an insincere smile. "The Wizards on that island stood up to her and claimed that Humans, Wizards, Elves, and Morphs could live in harmony. This made them dangerous to her," Marcus said.

"Who told you this?" Octavia asked

"My father."

"And you believed your father?" Octavia asked.

"He was one of the ones who brought her to power and supported her until..." Marcus swallowed and paused. Time seemed to stand still as he appeared lost in thought. Octavia saw him close his eyes and wince, as if from an invisible blow. She knew that look, well. Before she could say something, he regained himself, "Yes, I believe my father, Octavia. He told me this just before he sent me across the Burning Sea to live in exile with them. It is my last memory of him, a hazy one at that," Marcus said pausing, "That island was the only place I could be after...events in my life occurred. The three exiles taught me of an Ancient Time when all the races lived in peace in one Realm."

"I warned you," Quintus said softly to Octavia, "Now, you've started it." She giggled in a decidedly girlish way which seemed out of place with the large battle axe she carried and the iron helmet she donned.

"Why did your father send you away?" she pushed. She knew she shouldn't push because she realized that the cause was imbued with a massive dose of pain for the Wizard. Still, Octavia was always clumsy in dealing with other people's emotions—Human or half-Human. This, you have surely recognized by now.

"There was an incident," Marcus said, his countenance changing before her eyes. But before she could beg him to elaborate, Quintus grabbed both their arms. The look on his face was clear, he had heard something and they were not alone. "Story-time must wait," Marcus whispered softly to Octavia, his lips faintly brushing her ear, as he placed his hand on the hilt of his sword. There was relief in his voice which did not match the potential for danger. Was the story that bad? Octavia put away her curiosity and tightened her grip on her battleaxe. Quintus had nocked an arrow in his bow.

"We are still very far north in the Fertile Midlands," Quintus whispered, "It should be Humans. Although Elves or Wizards are possible."

"Or Morphs," Marcus added.

"Best be ready for any of them," Octavia said. Her blood coursed hot through her veins as battle seemed to approach. It was the best cure for the cold of this late autumn day so far north. She was no weakling when it came to cold, but even the cloak they'd given her was not much help in protecting her bare torso from the fangs of the bitter wind. A shirt would have been nice. A breastplate as well. She narrowed her eyes. It did not matter what she was wearing now. Danger lurked nearby and that would keep her warm until she eliminated it.

They crept over a hill and gazed down at a sparkling river. Quintus recognized it as the Blue Lady, a slender river which flowed south into the Great Meridian which bisected their world. Quintus knew they had made good time and could easily follow the Lady to the Meridian which flowed west and could aid them in finding their way to Marcus's destination. Before Quintus suggested this plan, they had to deal with those in the way. Three horses drank from the Blue Lady, as three men sat counting out coins on the shore, laughing loudly. A hodgepodge of possessions were piled up next to them.

"What do we have here?" Marcus asked.

"Outlaws," Octavia declared, "See the banner?" A black sheet fluttered in the breeze. "They are part of the Brotherhood of the Fang. They are Humans who do not recognize the Council and take advantage of the war to wreak havoc on everyone."

"There's a village over there," Quintus said, gesturing to the east. "I presume that's where the heap of coins and loot is from."

"Cowards," spat Octavia, "They terrify peasants and town dwellers but run like rats when armies approach. And so close to Council City, too! It's scandalous."

"They have three horses," Marcus observed logically, with no hint of concern at the scandal of outlaws preying on villagers so close to the administrative capital of the Humans. "There are three of us."

"We would move more quickly on horseback," Octavia smiled.

"I suppose you can ride well?" Quintus asked her.

"Not only can I ride well, but I look *good* on horseback," Octavia shot back, "Hair flowing, breasts bouncing, axe gleaming. I look like something out of an epic poem, boys." She smiled broadly. It was false bravado, but it had served her well for the last two years.

"Good to know. I like epic poems," Marcus said without emotion, although she thought she read his face and that he was slightly amused. "Now let's focus on getting the horses before these three link up with their other Fang friends and we get delayed."

"I presume you think it's perfectly moral that we steal their horses?" Quintus asked, mockingly.

"They are fiendish outlaws," growled Octavia.

"Yes, I am quite outraged," Marcus mocked her as he smiled, "Do you think you're close enough to shoot them, Quintus, or should I cast a spell?" Quintus rummaged through his various arrows: armor piercing arrows, whistling signaling arrows, blunt stunning arrows, flanged horse-killing arrows. He chose a standard arrow and squinted as he pulled back his bow. He held it for a moment and then shook his head.

"No, we need to get closer. Neither an arrow nor a spell is a good idea. We don't want to spook the horses and have to chase them," Quintus explained. He stroked his bristled chin for a moment, "I have a plan if Octavia is not above using that epically poetic chest as a distraction."

***

The Brothers of the Fang looked up from their coins to see an unarmed red-haired girl walking towards the river. She did not seem to notice them or even glance in their direction. She bent over to remove her boots and unfasten her top. Her back was to them, but they were transfixed as the leather top dropped to the ground and they saw her muscular back while she stretched to the sky. She splashed water on her face and chest, her back still turned towards them. She appeared to have no idea they were there.

One of the men chuckled, his gapped smile flashing. "There are a lot of scars on that back, but I still want to see the front. I am fond of white mountains," he said with a leering smile to his two comrades, "I daresay those two are softer than the Dragon's Teeth. And we can help her out her pants, can't we?" They nodded and dark thoughts were shared amongst the three men. Before any could act, their dark thoughts gave way to simple darkness.

Quintus cleaned off his dagger. He was angry that Marcus had killed the other two. He thought for sure he could slit two throats before his friend beheaded one with that glowing orange sword. But as they moved in furtively, Marcus was the quicker—knocking off one outlaw's head and then thrusting his sword into the chest of the only outlaw who'd even had an inkling of what was occurring and even then only for an instant. "You win this one," Quintus declared.

"A good plan, though, Quintus," Marcus conceded, "Points for that." Both men quickly looked over at their companion who'd refastened her top and secured all three horses. If Marcus didn't know better, he'd have thought Quintus had conceived of the plan to sneak a look at Octavia. He would not judge, as the red-haired girl with the winged helmet was quite well-proportioned. But the plan was on the level because Marcus knew his friend only had eyes for Elvin women. Marcus, on the other hand, felt free to gaze at any attractive female in his line of vision, Human, Elf, Wizard, or morph. He did not think he could love, but he could look. Alas, Octavia was too swift for the looking and likely swifter still for the loving. The scars on her back intrigued him and he made a note of them. Marcus tossed Octavia her helmet and axe without even a glance.

"I felt bare without these," she said mischievously. They had both been curious to see her. She knew it. She wasn't sure what she thought about Marcus or Quintus, but she always felt better when others found her attractive. They may find her appealing, but none could have her. It was a pact she'd made several years ago after the darkest evening of her brief life. It was a pact which had held strong ever since. Too few beings in the world had that satisfaction, but Octavia knew she was special. No one could overcome her unless she let them, and every time she pondered that, she could not help smiling. It helped keep the darkness at bay.

They helped themselves to some of the villains' ill-gotten goods, mounted their horses, and made great time as they followed the Blue Lady south. Marcus had used no magic, so they could ride without rest as they kept the river in view. "Why are we going to these exiled Wizards?" Octavia asked, several hours later.

49

"Because whatever happened amongst the Dragon's Teeth was not typical," Marcus said simply. She looked quizzically at him. "I have a theory."

"Will you be sharing that theory?" Octavia asked.

"Not until I talk with my teachers," Marcus said.

"Why?"

"Because if I'm right, they will know what to do," he said.

"Quintus, will you support this?" Octavia asked, "Crossing a burning sea to meet with some Wizard outlaws without even knowing why?"

"I have nowhere else to go," Quintus said softly, "And I trust him."

Octavia looked at the Wizard riding confidently, his eyes focused on the horizon. He was the lead rider and he never looked back to see if Quintus or Octavia were keeping pace. He had a world-weary look on this face, as if he knew much more than he let on. Marcus was peculiar, but she knew Wizards were supposed to be peculiar. He was crazy if he wanted to try and cross a sea which Quintus had told her burned like fire and dissolved anything which touched it. Then, again, she must be crazy, too, as recent events seemed to indicate. And Marcus had saved her from certain death. She also had nowhere else to go. Octavia decided to trust Marcus and she spurred on her horse to catch up with him.

Chapter 7: The Little Bird

The Elves of the Sunset trudged on towards the West with their Elf slaves in tow on the Via, the ancient road which followed the Meridian River as it flowed west towards the Tomb of Storms and Sun. Wizards dwelt in that Tomb, where all storms went to die and the sun disappeared each time dusk fell. The Wizards would have even less mercy towards the slaves than the Elves did—for mercy was not a strength associated with those who lived in the gray mountains. Griffin prayed and planned as the days piled up, trying to figure some way to save his little sister, yet again. But this time, he wasn't looking to stop some harassment on the practice field or to silence the sharp words of an elder. This time, Gwen had really "lost the acorns," as Elves termed it. Griffin had to save her, but also himself. And their parents. He thought of their parents, deprived of the light of the sun and smell of the breeze in a dark, hopeless cave which served as the King's prison. Griffin knew he had to save them, too. But first things first, how to get him and Gwendolyn out of these chains and away from the Sunset Elves? He had counted a dozen dark-skinned Elves, including the leader, Thorbad, who was especially terrifying. Griffin knew the stories about Sunset Elves. He had heard that they'd revered the Wizards and been given magical powers in return for their help. If true, this would not be like fighting 12 normal Elves. In fact, fighting was a distinctively bad idea. Even if he could get a weapon for himself and secure a bow for his talented sister, they could never take down 12 Elves, especially ones with possible Wizardly powers. Certainly, not in the condition Griffin and Gwen were in—half-starved, exhausted, beaten. No, his plan needed to focus on escape, not on confrontation. He pondered and he prayed to the Spirits who saw this injustice, their eyes doubtless peeking out of every tree they passed. He felt that Gwen's decision to save the wounded robin would have cosmic repercussions. The Spirits loved mercy, especially to vulnerable creatures. Surely, this would turn the wheel of fate for the enslaved siblings.

***

Gwen held the little bird in the palm of her hand, stroking its feathers gently, and softly cooing encouragement. Just as her guards had demanded, she dug for worms to feed the bird and held it during the day's marches, even when her arms felt like they would fall off—weighed down by chains as they were. She knew she had ruined her life with her choices and she knew that her life would be briefer than she'd dreamed it might be. But Gwen was determined to redeem herself with one pure act. Unlike her brother, she wasn't particularly pious. Yet deep down, she did believe in the Elvin Spirits and wondered if they had placed the wounded robin in her path as a test. If so, she was determined to pass this test and care for the bird until it could fly away.

They had marched for almost two weeks in their slow slog west, stopping at towns and exchanging wares as was typical of the Dark Elves. Already, Gwen could see the robin's wing healing. The bird was too scared to fly, but it was moving its wing with more confidence. And while Gwen could not actually speak to animals, she often felt they understood each other, and she knew in her Elf's heart that this little bird believed her when she told it that everything would be alright. Everything would be alright for the robin, if not for Gwen. Perhaps that would be enough. When she took a pause from caring for her new pet, Gwen thought of how she was going to get Griffin out of this mess. Not herself. She was young, but she was wise enough to see that the two of them would never escape from a dozen hardened Sunset Elves without a miracle. Griffin was likely expecting a miracle, she mused, allowing herself a half-smile. But she had to be the realistic one. She could not free both of them, but surely she could find a way to get him free. Then, perhaps he could save their parents. Gwen would probably die in the attempt, but she was at peace with that, so long as her little bird had healed and could fly away. Gwen was alert to opportunity, but would not act for Griffin until her bird was whole. It was, she felt, the least she could do.

"We will camp here for the night," Thorbad declared. His eleven minions nodded grimly and began to set up the camp. They unloaded the wares from their little donkeys, began setting up the sturdy tents (ingenious tents conceived by Human inventiveness, if you enjoy some irony with your tale), and gathered wood for a fire. They were very efficient, having made the trip to the Tomb—as Dark Elves usually shortened the name for the mountains—and back together a score of times or more. Thorbad was proud of his Elves and their work. But most of his thoughts were of the rich rewards he would receive from the Wizards. They enjoyed many of the Elves' goods: their sweet wine, well-crafted wooden statues, delicious fruits and vegetables, exotic spices, and well-woven cloaks. This trade had made Thorbad rich enough to retire young. Yet the current trip had brought an unlikely boon—two Elvin slaves who were young and strong. When the Gates of the Wizard Realm opened and they saw these two slaves, they might ask Thorbad to go before the Empress herself. What would she pay for a 28 year old male, healthy and long-limbed? Or a 26 year old female, swift of foot and sharp of eye? The Elvin King had been generous in giving these slaves to Thorbad free of charge. Nothing but profit awaited their exchange for him. And they were *his*. Not the Company's. All other sales were shared 13 ways, one share per Elf and two shares for their captain. But the payment for two lithe Elf slaves at the height of their strength and beauty? All his. This was his final trip and he knew it. Once he crossed the Fertile Midlands, he could retire to his home on the Western fringes of the Elf Realm. There he would live in wealth and luxury that his brothers and sisters could only dream of. Thorbad allowed himself a laugh as he pulled on a mug of sweet wine and tucked into a hearty stew with thick black broth and a sprinkling of exotic spices from distant islands.

Banished to her tent, Gwen sipped the brackish water they gave her and looked at the plate with her dinner: A few unidentifiable nuts, a clutch of purple berries, and a fistful of green leaves. A fortifying snack for midafternoon of a day of exploring, perhaps? But not a dinner by any stretch of the imagination. She ate the berries and nuts, then stared at the leaves. Her robin had gobbled down a fat worm and looked happy. Gwen smiled at the bird. She then returned her gaze to the leaves. A thought hit her and she wove the leaves into her golden hair. For a moment, she felt like a free Elf once again. Behind the fabric of her tent, no one could see that she had emancipated herself.

"They look beautiful in your hair," a soft feminine voice said. Gwen thought for a moment that it was the bird and she turned her head toward the voice, which was emanating from the robin's side of her tent. Except the robin was no longer there. It was replaced by a girl, about her age, maybe younger, with long brown hair, dark almond eyes, and a bruised left arm. It took two complete moments for Gwen to realize that the girl was not wearing any clothes.

With catlike speed, the girl leapt towards Gwen and cupped her hand over her mouth. "Shhh, you don't want to disturb the guards," she said, "Resist the urge to scream. I am a friend."

She released her hand from Gwen's mouth, although her arms still were wrapped around Gwen's body—not in a threatening way, but Gwen was still mildly disturbed. "Who?" Gwendolyn squeaked out.

"My name is Alexia," she said, as if that explained anything.

"You are uncovered." Gwen observed.

"My people do cover our forms," she replied, smiling broadly, her eyes staring deep into Gwendolyn's. Realization crept into Gwen's mind.

"You're a Morph," Gwen said softly. The girl had not yet moved away from Gwendolyn and although it was mildly awkward, Gwen didn't mind it terribly. It had been weeks since another creature touched her in any way other than violently. She knew the truth, but she had to ask, "How did you get in here without being seen?"

"I am your little bird, sweet Elf," Alexia said, her brown eyes dancing with delight. "I have been here the whole time. You saved me. And now I plan on saving you."

A guard tore open the tent flap and stuck his face into Gwen's tent. "Who are you talking to?" he demanded.

Gwen's tongue hung limp in her mouth. She looked at Alexia, but she had morphed back into the bird. It was instantaneous, like a flash of lightning. The guard seemed unaware that seconds before there was a girl where the robin now sat. Gwendolyn steeled herself, "I was talking to my little bird," she declared with a firm voice, "I recall Thorbad entrusted the creature to me and I think she is lonely, so I talk to her."

"How do you know your bird is a she?" the guard guffawed.

"I know things about birds," Gwen retorted.

"Well, lower your voice, slave girl or you'll be the one with the broken wing." He left, frustrated that he didn't catch Gwen doing something wrong. She was delighted that in his huff, he'd not noticed the leaves she'd rebelliously woven into her hair. Gwen then stared at the robin, which remained a bird. What if Gwen had been dreaming? What if the lack of food had led to a mirage offering to save her? That reality made much more sense.

Until it didn't.

After a full minute of self-doubt had passed, Alexia morphed back. She smiled wordlessly. "I thought Morphs could only change into eagles, wolves, or bears," Gwendolyn whispered, not willing to condemn her new friend back to robinhood by alerting the guards again. "I've never heard of a Morph who could become a robin."

Alexia held her gaze for a long, silent moment. She seemed to be looking through Gwendolyn's pale blue eyes. "I am not like most Morphs," Alexia said.

"Is that true?" Gwendolyn asked. She remained transfixed by the creature which minutes ago was a small red-bellied bird and was now a woman with impossibly dark eyes, smooth copper flesh, and a tangle of chestnut brown hair. She had never seen a Morph transform from animal to mortal form. It made her dizzy.

Alexia broke the silence by bounding inches from Gwendolyn's pale face. "Surely you know that Morphs and Elves are enemies. You are so clearly an Elf," she said, curiously touching Gwen's blonde hair as if it were some foreign and exotic substance, "And yet you do not seem to hate me."

"I do not hate you," Gwendolyn said, "But I am not like most Elves."

Chapter 8: Wolves

"Are you sure we shouldn't return the stolen goods to the Human village?" Octavia asked.

"There is no time," Marcus snapped, "We are already late. I can feel it."

"We only took what we needed," Quintus offered, "I sent an arrow with a message towards the village. They'll find it. Most of the goods are still right there by the river for them. Besides, you needed a proper outfit, Octavia."

"I definitely feel better with a shirt and some armor," Octavia agreed.

"I'll miss seeing your stomach," Quintus joked, "It reminded me of a shield I once owned."

"Shields are for sissies," Octavia spat back with zest, "Are you flirting with me, Quintus Agrippa Aureus, son of a Duke? Because I am no maiden and I am not fit for a nobleman."

"He is not flirting," Marcus offered, "His complimenting was chaste. Trust me. I am sure he thinks you're pretty enough, but your ears are too round. He likes them pointy, you see." The Wizard smiled broadly.

"'Tis true," Quintus readily agreed, "But as you are no maiden, I am no nobleman. I was, shall we say, 'unnobled' a long time ago." Quintus paused and smiled sadly if such a thing were possible. "I am glad to have taken more arrows and add food to our stores, but why did you take all those golden crowns, Marcus?"

"Humans perplex me," the Wizard replied, "inscribing their most valued coins with crowns for kings they do not have. I understand the platinum coins with towers because Humans are so proud of their buildings, but golden crowns or silver dragons? Humans have had no king for a thousand years or more and dragons do not exist. Your money vexes me."

"I've never used a coin higher than a copper," offered Octavia, "as that is how soldiers are paid, hence the sword inscribed on the coin. Few Bean-eaters see dragons or towers, let alone crowns." She used the rude term for a Human soldier in the hopes of putting them at ease, especially because she feared the Wizard's wrath if she slipped and called him a "Sorcerer." It was a word often used in her previous life, but seemed inappropriate in this company. Even though she knew this with her head, Octavia was aware that her tongue did not always comply with what her mind insisted was the right course of action. If either man noticed the term "Bean-eater," they did not address it.

"We both know you have no use for shiny, pretty objects of value, Marcus," said Quintus, gesturing at his friend's shabby cloak, beaten boots, and belt made out of rope, "So why take all those golden coins, instead of leaving them for the village?"

"Gold is a lot like Octavia's battleaxe," Marcus said, giving them a moment to process, "You cannot be sure when it will be useful or how it will be useful, but you know that it will prove useful before the journey's end."

"Aye, truer words were never spoken," Octavia declared, spurring her horse to overtake the Wizard.

Suddenly, she was thrown from her mount and landed with a thud on the ground, her helmet taking the force of the blow. Dazed, Octavia looked up to see her horse being mauled by a pack of wolves. Marcus and Quintus's horses both reared in terror. The wolves then turned to Octavia and sprang at her. She was still on her back and her axe was neither in sight nor in reach. She pulled out her knife and braced herself. The lead wolf staggered and fell, an arrow shaft buried in its skull. She glanced up at Quintus loosing his bow with his steel-gray eyes narrowed in focus. She caught sight of Marcus, his violet eyes glowing as he raised his hands, his mouth moving furiously. Suddenly, the next five wolves stood frozen. Literally frozen. It was a beautiful fall day just north of the Meridian and the sun warmed her white skin, but Octavia saw the wolves encased in ice, their jaws still gaping open.

"Get up!" shouted Marcus. And in an instant, Octavia sprang to her feet. A wolf leapt at her but she stood firm, pushing her blade into its throat up to the hilt. A glint of metal sparkled in the sunlight and she saw her axe on the ground. As arrows flew from Quintus's bow and an orange glow emitted from Marcus's unsheathed sword, she fought her way to that axe—ever her salvation. Suddenly, Octavia realized that between her and the axe was the biggest, nastiest wolf. She planted her feet in the ground and returned the animal's snarl.

"Come at me, you dog," she roared, but the animal's reflexes were quicker than her own and its bulk was significantly greater than that of the other wolves. This time she was tackled and found herself pinned to the ground with the dagger-like jaws of the beast inches from her exposed soft throat.

Like a thundercrack, the Wizard's glowing sword crashed down on the animal's spine. Octavia did not know which sound was worse, the death wail of the great wolf or the hissing from the sword as the wolf's flesh sizzled on its blade. Marcus pulled her to her feet and she retrieved her axe. "Thanks. Those wolves..."

"They weren't wolves," Marcus interrupted her flatly.

Octavia turned to see the field littered with Human corpses. 20 or so naked men and women lay rigid with death.

"Morphs," Quintus explained, as he slit the throat of Octavia's suffering horse, stroking its mane as he delivered the final mercy for the animal.

Marcus turned to the wolves he'd frozen and brought his sword down on each one of them with cool efficiency. As he did so, each turned into another dead Human.

"What is with your sword?" Octavia asked.

"It's enchanted," he replied.

"No kidding," she said with a sarcastic smile.

"It will cut sharper than metal and burn hotter than fire," he said.

"Not terribly stealthy in night fighting," Quintus observed lightheartedly.

"Indeed not," Marcus agreed, "But it's not yet night."

"You saved me, again," Octavia said. He simply looked at her. "I sense that you like 'damsel in distress's a bit much for my tastes."

"Do I?" he asked, arching an eyebrow.

"It's a tired character in a boring story," she replied, "I don't do 'damsel in distress,' as I am sure you can understand."

"You are a damsel," he shrugged, "and I am not sure how you would characterize being pinned by a Wolf Morph, if not 'distress.'" He smiled, but then it fled his face, as if in full retreat. Marcus paused and looked at her grimly, "You shouldn't have ridden ahead, Octavia. Do not do that, again."

"Lesson learned," she nodded.

"We are short one horse," he observed without emotion.

"Morphs often cluster together," Quintus noted, "And we crossed the old northern road after we skirted Council City. That means the Darkest Forest of the Morphs is a straight shot from where we are. There are bound to be more. So now that Octavia has learned her lesson, let's move on. We don't want to wait for more wolves."

"Or eagles, or bears," shrugged Marcus.

"Or all three," Octavia added, "I am chastened. I made the mistake. I'll walk."

"That would slow us down," Marcus said coldly.

"Your horse is clearly the strongest, Marcus," Quintus said, wearily, "She may be a strong girl, but she's not that heavy." Marcus pondered for a moment and looked at Octavia.

He reached out a hand and pulled her up to his saddle with strength that surprised her, "Agreed," Marcus said to Quintus, "She is not that heavy."

"Why thank you," she replied bitterly, "You two really know how to make a girl feel beautiful." She sat behind him and put her arms around the Wizard's waist in the least familiar way she could, bracing herself as the horse took off on another ancient road which cut north-south. She saw Quintus on their left, keeping pace and wondered why he wore a stupid half smile. Was he trying to keep up with Marcus's horse? Was this some stupid boy competition? Did he know something she did not? And how in the Four Realms did she get herself into this sort of adventure?

They approached the giant Meridian river. Its current flowed west in a stately manner, so unlike the fierce Blue Lady. The Wizard stopped. At times, Octavia felt that she understood

Marcus and at other times, he seemed like a totally alien creature. She presumed she understood his Human side and was baffled by his Wizard side, but who knew? She couldn't tell if he was mad that she had ridden ahead into the Morph ambush. She couldn't tell if he saved her because they were friends or simply comrades. She couldn't tell if he was bothered by her presence in his saddle, comforted by it, or something more. She wasn't sure which reaction she wanted to be the true one.

"How will we cross the Meridian? There are no bridges here," Octavia said.

"Bridges would be guarded," Marcus said simply.

"How do we cross?" Octavia asked.

"One of us is a Wizard," Quintus said, "Even if he is not as nice to look at as a well-proportioned warrior girl, he has other uses."

"He's not worst looking creature in the Four Realms," Octavia teased, "for a Wizard."

He didn't seem to catch the back-handed compliment, as he was muttering in that ancient Wizard language. He then changed to the common tongue, "Stay close to me, Quintus. The spell is difficult to stretch over two horse-lengths."

The horses needed prodding but the Wizard rode right into the river. Actually, Octavia noticed, they were *on top of the river.* As if the water were solid ground, Marcus and Quintus's horses crossed it and ended up on the other side of the Meridian, in what Humans called the Far South, once the exclusive land of Elves, but now a place of conflict between Humans and Elves.

"What in the name of the Golden One?" Octavia asked.

"Water magic," Marcus said, his voice suddenly exhausted, "I did appreciate the compliment, even if it was in jest." Once again, she could not read his tone.

"That trick seems as useful as a nice figure," she observed.

"It's no trick," Quintus said, "It is a particularly difficult spell if I remember correctly and you have never cast it on the Meridian."

"The Meridian over two horse lengths," Marcus boasted playfully. His voice seemed ragged and Octavia could sense his breathing was slightly labored from her position in his saddle.

"The Golden One is hanging low," Quintus observed, "We should camp."

"So close to the Via?" Marcus asked skeptically, "If you question my strength after that spell, do not. I will be fine."

Quintus pondered arguing, but deftly switched tactics. "We should camp where we will be ignored. There are woods over there and the darkness will help cover us in no time. I won't let you sleep past dawn and I'll take the first watch." Marcus met his eyes and then simply nodded. He dismounted flawlessly and then offered his hand to help Octavia down.

"I can take the first watch, Quintus," she said.

"No, you are tired, too. You fought hard and you need sleep," Quintus said, "You take the second watch. I think Marcus is excused from watches tonight on account of the water magic spell, if you will assent." She nodded.

"It's getting cold," Marcus observed. He looked up at the sky and inhaled. "Winter is in the air, even if the calendar says otherwise. I can feel it. It will be unusually cold this evening, even in the Far South."

"Not for me," Octavia smiled.

"You lie," Marcus said with a weary grin.

"I am a woman of the North…"

"You're shivering," Quintus remarked, "You lost some blood back there. That always makes one colder. Now go to sleep." She hated that he was right about the shivering, but she took off her breastplate and helmet and lay down nonetheless. She closed her eyes and felt a strange heaviness envelop her. Octavia wanted to open her eyes to identify the heaviness but she did not have the strength. All she knew was she was suddenly warmer and she was grateful for the feeling.

Chapter 9: The Elf and the Morph

"How will you save me?" Gwendolyn asked playfully, "When you're just a little bird?"

"I don't need to be a little bird," Alexia replied, "I can be almost anything I want."

"Anything?" Gwendolyn asked, wide eyed.

"Anything with feathers or fur," Alexia replied, "No creature whose blood runs cold. No snakes, no lizards, no bugs, no frogs…"

Gwen wrinkled up her little nose, "No, you'd make a terrible lizard," she agreed, "What about an elephant?" She smiled. "That could save us."

"An elephant is too big," Alexia explained, "Horses are too big, as well. I could be a fox or a lion, a hawk or a hummingbird, a playful monkey or a darling kitten…"

"Show me kitten," Gwen demanded. Suddenly a little gray cat nestled itself in Gwendolyn's lap, purring contently. Gwen scratched behind her ears and then turned it over to tickle its fuzzy belly. The kitten purred and purred, until it was a kitten no more.

"Of course, this is my mortal form and I like this form best," Alexia said, still draped over Gwendolyn's lap.

"You should put on some clothes," Gwen said, pursing her lips.

"Should I? Few beings make such a request," Alexia purred. Gwen felt the heat of the blush crawl down her neck to her toes and she quickly changed the subject.

"What animal form is your favorite?"

"I am partial to robin, now, because that's when I met my new friend," Alexia said, holding Gwen in her gaze for a moment before springing off her lap. "But I feel most powerful when I am a lioness."

"Lioness? That is amazing," Gwen said, "And could be very helpful to our salvation. Are you always a lioness when you change? Or could you be a lion?"

Alexia shook her head. "Always lioness. I can be many things but I am always female," she said, "And that makes me happy for I am beautiful."

"You are," Gwen said softly, too softly for Alexia to hear. Or so she thought.

"Morphs hear as well as Elves do," Alexia explained. Gwen was embarrassed again. "We see better and we smell better than your people. We are closest to the animals—even closer than Elves are."

"I was always taught that you were beasts," Gwendolyn said, "That you lived in a world without religion or laws...or clothes." She wrinkled up her nose.

"Religion makes people inflexible," Alexia said, "Laws get in the way of freedom and I never understood why Elves do not have a healthy love of freedom." Gwen nodded with a thoughtful look splashed across her soft features.

"And clothes?"

"I'd like to tell you it's part of our love of freedom," Alexia declared, "But in truth, it's just practical. If I were wearing some fancy dress like a lovely Elf Princess and then morphed into lioness, how foolish would that look?"

"Pretty foolish," Gwen agreed with a laugh.

"And Morphs often change into an animal to hide from Elves or Wizards, so I'd be pretty obvious as the animal with clothes on."

"You are my first Morph friend," Gwen said.

"You are my first Elf friend, so we are even," Alexia agreed, "Indeed, you are my first friend of any kind." She said the last part softly, perhaps even too softly for an Elf.

"But everything I've been taught about Morphs says they can only turn into an eagle or a bear or a wolf. I have never heard of a Morph who could turn into a robin or a lioness or a kitten," Gwen insisted.

Alexia's dark eyes turned downcast and misted over. Without meaning to, Gwen instinctively put her arm around her, as if she were still a broken little robin. As you have surmised, Gwendolyn could love in the natural way that most creatures could breathe.

"What you say is true," Alexia said, "Of all Morphs but one. The exception. The one who could not be a wolf or a bear or an eagle. The one who could be anything she wanted to be except what her kind expected. The Morph they threw away."

"The one whose wing they broke?" Gwen asked gently. Alexia nodded wordlessly. "She has not been rejected. Her wing has healed and she has found a true friend. You are not what you're supposed to be. Neither am I."

"It is good we found each other," Alexia said.

"It is," Gwen agreed.

"Now, I must find some way to save you and then…"

"And then?" Gwen asked eagerly.

"Let us focus on the saving first," Alexia stated firmly. "Then is for later, now is for now. Only now matters." As Gwen nodded, she heard a commotion outside. There was screaming and a call to arms. "Shhh." Alexia put a finger to Gwen's lips, "I'll find out what's going on." In an instant, a small gray mouse darted out of the tent, unseen by the Sunset Elves.

***

He had watched it all unfold from a distance, due to the helpful magic, and he had guessed at what would come next. Some things had come together through our design, he mused, but much had occurred of its own accord. Such was the way of the world. All of the players were important in a small way, but he saw right away that only one was essential to their goal. This was the shape of things. Of that, he was certain.

Chapter 10: Intersecting Paths

She knew Quintus had fallen asleep during his watch. The minute Octavia felt the poke of a spear, she knew she was doomed because their watchman had given in to slumber. The spear thrust was fierce, but it did not pierce her, for the blanket repelled the blow. The Elf…yes it was an Elf she saw as her eyes opened…seemed monumentally frustrated by the failure of his weapon and he stabbed harder and harder to no avail. The Elf had dark brown skin and darker hair, a Sunset Elf. As Octavia came to her wits, she realized she was sleeping underneath the Wizard's cloak, which was odd enough. The fact that its simple cloth was shielding her from the mad stabs of a spear was odder still.

"Stop it," declared a voice which was clearly the Elves' leader, "Let's not kill the Humans. We can sell them to the Wizards." Octavia's eyes cleared from the sleep and she saw Quintus was bound, his eyes filled with shame. She leaped to her feet and threw her tormentor against a tree, kicking his comrade in the guts, so that he doubled over in pain. But Quintus's captor brandished a knife near his throat and she tossed up her hands.

Marcus slept soundly as all of this was occurring. "Is he dead?" the Elf leader asked.

"He's a very good sleeper," Octavia said acidly, earning her a mailed glove across her face, splitting her lip.

Marcus opened his eyes in time to see the blow. The dark Elf hovering above him stumbled, his jaw wide open. "Thorbad, this is no Human. He is a Wizard." The last word was delivered with a sense of awe characteristic of the dark Elves of the Sunset when Wizards were involved.

"What in the Four Realms is going on?" thundered Marcus, as he sat up, shaking the fog from his head. Thorbad strode up to him, looked at his violet eyes—now opened—and lost all of his confidence in one fell swoop. His face turned downcast.

"You are a Wizard, my Lord," he said.

"I am," Marcus replied, "The name is Marcus."

"Strange name for a Wizard," one Elf observed.

"A long and uninteresting story," Marcus snapped, "And who are you?"

"I am Thorbad the Captain of this band, my Lord, and we thought you were a Human," he explained. Marcus surveyed the situation with cool detachment.

"I am not a Human," Marcus stated, "Humans can't do this." He created a fireball in his hands, then blew and it went out with a wisp of smoke. He knew that Elves went crazy for such silly Wizardry. He also thought it was funny they called any Wizard they met "my Lord." Elves were often preposterous, Dark Elves more so than any other in that regard.

"May I ask, my Lord, why are you traveling with Humans?" Thorbad queried.

"They are not simply 'Humans'," Marcus thundered, "This is Quintus, the Lover of Elves. He was exiled from the Human Realm for his love of an Elf girl. No Human is a greater friend to the Elves in all of the Four Realms of our world."

"Release him," Thorbad ordered, "A thousand apologies, Quintus the Lover of Elves. I did not know you, sir."

"Quite alright," Quintus said as he was unbound.

"And this is Octavia, the brave Human who saved a Wizard child," Marcus explained, "All of the Wizard Realm sings her praises for she risked her life to save a defenseless Wizard boy. Forever will she be shunned by the Human world for this courageous act of mercy." Quintus knew that he was being theatrical because Sunset Elves ate that sort of thing up like a second dinner.

"Octavia? Of course, I believe I have heard her song," Thorbad said nodding, hoping that he was convincing them.

Marcus looked at Octavia's face as a trickle of blood oozed from her mouth. "Where is the Elf who split the delicate lip of this gentle lady?" Marcus asked. He was having fun, now. Quintus could tell. All the men pointed at one of their own, who stepped forward with his head hung and his dark eyes downcast. "It seems you owe the lady an apology," Marcus demanded in false wrath.

"Sorry milady," the Elf stuttered.

"Seems only fair she gets to hit him back," Quintus said, sidling up to Marcus and standing at his friend's right shoulder.

"I quite agree," Marcus said.

"My Lord, a woman cannot hit a man, it is against all laws," Thorbad said.

"Are there laws governing the treatment of a Wizard's companions?" Marcus asked. Thorbad nodded sheepishly.

"*Are there*?" whispered Quintus. Marcus shrugged and smiled impishly.

"She's just a skinny little girl, surely you'll let her hit you in the face to even things out?" Marcus asked. The Elf nodded confidently, his masculinity having been challenged. Octavia smiled and threw a punch. The crack echoed throughout the forest.

"A skinny little girl?" she asked.

"I thought we had established you weren't heavy," Marcus replied.

"I think you broke his jaw," Quintus observed.

"Yeah? Well, my lip's going to be all swollen," Octavia said with mock distress, "However will I show my pretty face at the ball?"

"You'll manage, I'm sure," Marcus replied.

"Thank you for the Wizard cloak," she said, as offhandedly as she could, "I take it that's enchanted, too."

"More than just a nice figure, Quintus. She has a brain in that skull, as well," Marcus said sarcastically as she handed him his cloak. The Elves circled around their leader and muttered to one another.

"My Lord Marcus," interrupted Thorbad, "Will you join us in our march towards your western home where the Sun goes to die each night and even the direst storms always pass from our world into nothingness. We could share our provisions and the journey would be safer and more pleasant if you and your companions were with us."

"Give us a moment," Marcus responded, "Which way is your camp?"

"Just over that ridge," Thorbad said, "I have two more Elves back at the camp, stout Elves like these ones, here. We have two slaves we are bringing to the Empress's Realm, along with many fine items. We would be honored to have you in our company." He left Marcus, Octavia, and Quintus.

"I'm opposed," Quintus declared after the Elves were barely out of earshot. "You keep saying we are running out of time, Marcus. And these Elves don't have horses like us. If they are a trade caravan, we'd be lucky if they have donkeys. They have prisoners, too. It will slow us down. Am I right that time is short?"

Marcus looked at him, his face expressionless. "True. Time flees, Quintus. Time always flees like a defeated army. Hmm." He turned to Octavia with the same blank visage. "Do you agree with him?" She thought for a moment.

"Quintus makes some good points," she conceded, "But they have supplies."

"We have supplies," Quintus blurted out.

"They have more supplies. How far are we from the Burning Sea?" she asked.

"A week or two," Marcus answered, "Depending on a thousand potential variables."

"Our supplies will give out before then," Octavia argued, "Plus, we have already run into trouble—twice, if you count these Elves. If Thorbad there has a dozen stout Sunset Elves, then that will certainly make it easier on us if there are more Morphs around."

"Or Humans looking for you," Marcus added.

"Or Humans looking for me," she agreed, "We could benefit from sharing the journey with them. We are close to the Ruins and they are said to be cursed."

"I do not share your view of the Ruins, but it is the common one. Other than that point, she argues well, Quintus," Marcus noted, "Are you convinced?"

"Perhaps," he said, knowing that the Wizard was convinced, so that was probably the end of that, "But I presume you do not intend to journey with them to the Wizard Gate at the foot of the Claws." His grin spread ear to ear, "My Lord."

"No, I don't suppose that would do us any good," Marcus agreed, "given that I am as beloved by the Empress as you two are with your Human Council. Nevertheless, I think it's perfectly useful to have Thorbad and his Elves believe I am a Wizard of good standing. He seems to have decided this and I am loathe to burden him with the truth."

"So we are agreed?" Octavia asked, "We will share the road with these Elves until we hastily slip away to cross the Burning Sea?"

"We are agreed," Quintus said with a sigh, "So long as we are also agreed that if it turns out to be a bad idea, I was the one who thought so."

"We are agreed on that, as well," Marcus conceded, "Frankly, I am surprised. I had thought Quintus would be keen on spending time with Elves and I had thought Octavia would be bitterly opposed. I believed you hated Elves."

She shrugged her shoulders and turned toward the camp, "I hated Wizards, too, until fairly recently," she said, "Perhaps, I am growing soft…"

Chapter 11: Elf Girls in Chains

"We are so delighted you will join us," Thorbad roared, "My men and I have a ritual dance to celebrate our meeting. Ardor, grab your flute." He was the Elf Octavia had punched and he appeared to hesitate for a moment before following the order and making some beautiful flute music—albeit in obvious pain.

"Dance on," Marcus said, a smile painted on his weather-beaten face in a distinctly insincere fashion. The insincerity was, of course, lost on the Sunset Elves.

Griffin had been brought out of his tent to split wood for a huge bonfire. His sharp blue eyes gradually figured out the contours of what was happening. Thorbad and his men had come upon three figures and captured them. The fire was a celebration for adding more captives. Upon further consideration, this did not seem to fit. The figures were not captives, but honored guests. How did that happen? Griffin swung the axe, wondering if this was his moment. The Sunset Elves were distracted by three new companions—yes, they were definitely companions, not prisoners. Griffin was unwatched and he had an axe. Could he move quickly enough in these chains to free Gwendolyn? The three new companions were moving closer and Griffin's Elvin vision was sharp. He studied them. They looked like Humans. Griffin squinted to improve his view. Why would Elves be excited to meet up with Humans? It was a curious encounter. Just then, Griffin noticed a critical fact. The female Human with the garish hair of the North and one of the male Humans who exhibited no particular uniqueness each led horses. Horses! Yes, this *was* the answer to his prayers. A plan began to form in Griffin's mind. He and Gwendolyn could mount the horses and even with their chains on, they'd be faster than the Sunset Elves and their donkeys. All he had to do was find a way to get a message to his sister, figure out the best use of the axe, and act quickly.

"Keep chopping, slave!" one of his captors bellowed. All heads snapped in Griffin's direction, including the three guests who looked on curiously. This was unexpected and unfortunate; he did not want attention. Not now. Griffin resumed chopping.

"Would you do us the honor, Lord Marcus?" Thorbad asked.

Griffin paused again, but no one was looking at him. All eyes were on the third Human, a dark-haired man with slight flecks of gray in his hair, a powerful jaw, and….purple eyes. Flames leapt from his hands and the bonfire was ignited. He was no Human. He was a Wizard. Now, it all made sense. They were Wizards. Griffin knew that Elves and Wizards were allies in the war, but he never trusted the sorcerers. Elves were the caretakers of the Natural World, enlisted by the Spirits to keep Nature safe. Wizards used the elements as instruments of power. They lived in forbidding mountains where the sun seemed to die, where they hoarded jewels and precious metals while speaking in forgotten tongues. The sorcerers might be necessary allies, but Griffin did not have to like them. The three Wizards's presence changed the situation irrevocably. Even if he and Gwen were able to get past their captors and mount the horses, those three Wizards would simply wave their hands and mutter some nonsense words and the very elements would oppose the slaves. Some horrid gust of wind would blow them off their saddles and they'd be worse off. No, this was not the Spirits's answer to his prayers. As he looked at the strangers in the light of the fire, he noticed that the other man and the woman did not have purple eyes. They *were* Humans. He hated Humans, but they were not as powerful as Wizards, so this might be a blessing. He'd also heard that some of the Humans opposed slavery. That could be useful. He chopped and pondered, remembering that the Spirits always answered the prayers of the patient, although not always in ways they expected.

"How did that one end up as a slave?" Quintus asked, gesturing to Griffin.

"He and his sister opposed the will of the Elf King," Thorbad explained, "They were given to me, so I could sell them to Wizards. A fine price they will fetch." He smiled, punching the arm of his lieutenant who was still absently rubbing his jaw.

"I am sure that my people will be most grateful," Marcus said, catching Octavia's eye as he winked. "It has been a long time since I have been home."

"It won't be long now, my Lord, maybe a week or two on the Via," Thorbad said, "We will make haste when the sun spirit rises tomorrow."

"Yes, I am quite homesick," Marcus said without emotion.

"You said there were two slaves," Octavia said, "Where is the other one?"

"Bring out the other slave," Thorbad ordered two of his Elves, "Our guests should be familiar with the cargo we are hauling."

Gwendolyn was brought out in chains. Marcus looked at her and he knew immediately. The slim Elvin form with soft womanly curves, the pale blue eyes, the blonde hair seemingly fashioned out of lightning, the pointed ears. Marcus cursed in the ancient tongue and looked at Quintus. As expected, Quintus's eyes had grown to twice their size and everything else in the world had fallen away for him. Marcus knew his friend preferred Elves and this one was a pretty one. He also knew that Elf girls in chains were irresistible to Quintus. Surely, this would complicate matters. Marcus sighed audibly.

"What exactly did she do?" Octavia asked, skeptical of how any creature so slight and non-threatening could manage to provoke the wrath of a king.

"I am an archer. I wanted to be a warrior," Gwendolyn answered, "And Elves have very ancient views on what is proper for females."

"Don't drag the Ancients into this," Marcus said, as he scooped out some of the stew from a bubbling pot. "Elves' gender roles are not as ancient as you might think."

"Either way," Thorbad said, "She angered the King and lost her freedom, along with her brother. Now you have seen her. Take her back."

"What is her...what is your name?" Quintus asked.

"I'm Gwendolyn," she said, flashing a smile filled with summer.

"I am Quintus," Quintus answered the blonde Elf. She was deposited back in her tent as his words floated after her. Whether she heard them, he did not know.

Marcus groaned to himself. Anyone near him may have presumed it was his reaction to the stew, but the Wizard actually enjoyed the meal. His groan was for the complication. A pretty blonde Elf girl in chains, he thought to himself. If only Quintus could resist. But alas, then he would not be Quintus, would he? Marcus pondered revealing all to Quintus in the hopes that the truth might shake him of his sudden infatuation with this random Elf girl. But Marcus felt that the truth sounded silly in his head and so he swallowed it with the brown stew. There had to be another way to divert Quintus from this and focus him on the more important matter. Marcus just shook his head as he tucked into the bubbling mutton stew, studded with potatoes and onions, as well as some herb he could not place. The sweet wine paired nicely with the stew. Marcus had to admit that Octavia had been correct in choosing to march with these Elves. Few things warmed a man's insides like a hot stew and several cups of good wine.

As the flames began to die down, the Elves drifted off to slumber, save the one designated as the watch-commander for the next three hours. Marcus knew he had to have the conversation with Quintus, vain as it was likely to be. There are, as you know, some conversations which you simply must have, even if no good can come of them.

"I can see it written on your face, brother," Marcus said sternly, "Just come out and say it."

"Say what?" he asked, not wanting to give his friend the satisfaction so swiftly.

"That your eyes were as big as two pale moons when that little Elf girl pitter-pattered out of her tent," Octavia interjected, draining another cup of wine and feeling very silly and light-headed.

"What do you want me to say?" Quintus asked. "That she's beautiful? I can say that. Do you disagree?"

74

"She's quite lovely," Marcus said curtly, "But I know you too well."

"What do you know, brother?"

"That you want to nibble on those pointy ears," erupted Octavia, laughing hysterically. "You have to be careful you don't get hurt. Elf ears are sharp…"

Marcus inhaled and exhaled with exaggerated effort. "We have seen many beautiful women in our time together, Quintus," he said, "Some we have looked at, some we have lain with, some we have…"

"Loved," Quintus said, the lines of his face creasing ever so slightly.

"Some, we have loved," Marcus agreed patiently.

"I never knew that Wizards loved," Octavia said, refilling her cup, "Can you love, Marcus? Have you ever loved?"

Marcus ignored her. "Quintus, we cannot get involved with this situation."

"What situation?"

"Elf girl in chains? That situation," Octavia explained.

"You don't understand," Quintus said softly, "Not all of you, anyway, Marcus."

"She is very beautiful. She's been enslaved. The world is not fair. You can make it right," Marcus said, "Elf girls in chains, Quintus the Righteous. Feel free to stop me when I am in error…"

"Let me say something," Octavia interrupted, finishing her wine and gently wiping her injured mouth with the back of her hand, "I'm not sure I want to get involved in Elf on Elf slavery, but I am pretty livid that they enslaved her for wanting to be a warrior because she's a girl. That boils my blood."

"Elves do what they do," Marcus said, "They are too strict, obsessed with religious matters, and excessively serious about everything that does not matter. Sometimes they act stupidly and enslave their own. We have bigger issues."

"Do we?" Quintus asked.

Marcus thought for a moment and made a concession to himself. He placed one hand on Quintus's shoulder and one on

Octavia's, drawing them closer. "Let me be clear, nothing short of the world is at stake here." Marcus looked from side to side to see if anyone were listening. "Do you understand me? The world. It's that important."

"Who's being serious now?" Octavia asked slightly slurring her words, "*Nothing short of the world*! What sort of story did you step out from?"

"Enough sweet wine for you," Marcus declared, raising an eyebrow. "Do you comprehend the stakes, Quintus?"

"I do, Marcus. I always assumed the stakes were high from the way you were acting," Quintus said, "And you know I will stand at your side in whatever quest awaits us. However, I can't help how I feel about Gwendolyn. She enchants me."

"She *enchants* you?" Marcus asked, narrowing his eyes and letting out another annoyed sigh. "You don't even know her."

"That is irrelevant to the enchantment, Marcus. Search your Human side," Quintus said with a grin, "I think we should try to free her from her chains."

"Out of the question," Marcus said firmly.

"Okay, I think *I* should try to free her," Quintus said, "And you should not try to stop me. Maybe Red over here will help me."

"Free an Elf?" Octavia said, "I wouldn't hold my breath, my *enchanted* friend."

"What about standing shoulder to shoulder with a fellow female fighting injustice against your gender?" Quintus asked.

"I don't subscribe to that," Octavia said,

"Why don't you try to get to know her?" Marcus suggested, "Before you get us all in trouble by striking off her chains."

"I will make that deal," Quintus said, "I will get to know her, probably fall further in love with her, and free her from her slavery." He grinned, almost taunting the Wizard.

"What about her brother?" Marcus asked.

"If it will make her smile for even a moment, I'll save him in, too," Quintus said.

Marcus sighed. "Can we agree that our number one focus is getting to the Burning Sea as quickly as possible?" Marcus asked, "And any Elvin Emancipation is of secondary concern?" Quintus nodded and smiled. "And if freeing them interferes with our number one focus, you'll drop it?"

"I can try," Quintus said, "But I'm only Human."

"I know," said Marcus, "I know."

Chapter 12: Enchantment

"Quintus is quite taken with you, sweet Gwendolyn."

"You're embarrassing me."

"You do not mind being embarrassed."

"Perhaps," Gwen considered, "Which one is Quintus?"

"The Human," Alexia said.

"With the light brown hair and the beard, the one dressed like a Ranger?" she asked. Alexia nodded. "He merely asked my name; that doesn't mean he is 'taken with me,' Alexia. Only that he didn't know my name." Gwendolyn crossed her arms and wrinkled up her nose.

"If that was all that we knew, then maybe you'd be right," Alexia said, smiling impishly.

"We know more?"

"*I* know more," she said, "How badly do you want to know what I know?"

"Very badly," Gwen insisted.

"Say 'Alexia, I'd do anything to find out,'" the Morph insisted.

"Fine. Alexia, I'd do anything to find out," Gwen repeated.

"Anything?"

"Anything."

"Good," Alexia said with a smirk which could not be described as innocent, "I heard them arguing about you. The Human woman with the Northern hair was sympathetic because you were punished for being a woman who wanted to fight."

"Makes sense," Gwen nodded, "She seems to be a Bean-eater."

"The Wizard kept saying that you and your brother were none of their business and 'let Elves do to Elves whatever they want.'" She imitated his deep voice and exploded in a fit of giggles.

"Sounds like a typical Wizard," Gwen said. "What about *Quintus*?"

"Quintus said you were beautiful."

"Do not deceive me, Alexia," Gwen insisted with a pout.

"I heard it with my own little mouse ears," Alexia said, instantaneously taking the form of a small gray mouse for effect. She swiftly resumed her mortal form. "That is not all he said." She remained on her hands and knees as if she were still a mouse and grinned.

"What else did he say" Gwen asked.

"You'll have to catch me to find out."

"No morphing."

"Why not...?" Before Alexia could finish the "not", the Elf had tackled her and pinned her to the ground. Gwen was lightning-quick. Alexia knew she was stronger than Gwen and could have overpowered her. But she marveled at how quickly this Elf could move. She was like light itself.

"I caught you," Gwen declared, her pale blue eyes burning, "Tell me what else the Ranger said about me."

"He said you were 'enchanting,'" Alexia said, "You've enchanted him."

"Enchanting?" Gwen marveled, "No one has ever said that about me before."

"He also said he wanted to free you, so I think this Quintus might be very useful in our current situation." Gwen nodded hopefully, as she rolled the word "enchanting" on her tongue for the next hour.

***

A week had passed since the Sunset Elves had "captured" the Wizard and his friends and the group had made great progress towards the west on the ancient road. Thorbad was more confident traveling the Via with a Wizard in his company and being able to use that road had shaved days off of his travel. Thorbad wasn't the only one who was pleased. From the singular perspective of Marcus, things were going about as well as they could. The Sunset Elves had willingly shared their supplies, especially the Elvin morning elixir which he adored. The Wizard was certain that this hot and dark beverage was a better way to start the day than the weak tea of the Rangers. To make matters even more delightful, there was their top-quality wine, which Thorbad broke out on day three. The Elves had not slowed down Marcus's journey towards the Burning Sea too badly, despite the fact that they were not mounted. It was impossible to tell if their presence had helped deter any other attacks, but it was irrefutable that no one had hindered their progress since their group of three had swelled to 15, not including slaves.

The slaves. Yes, that was the one portion of the journey which had not gone according to the Wizard's plan. On the first day that they had journeyed together, Quintus had offered to take the rearguard. He'd explained to Thorbad that his horse had been slain by Morphs and that he would be best off in the rear of the company, using his Ranger skills to detect sneak attacks from behind. Marcus was about to speak up that it was Octavia's horse which had been slain by the Morphs and that Quintus's skills were best employed in the front of the company, but Octavia's dark green eyes met his own with a look which implored him to say nothing. He stared at her narrowed emerald eyes for a moment, searching her Humanity and perhaps finding his own. An almost imperceptible nod followed and Marcus spoke, "Quintus can see and hear better than most Humans," he declared, "He would be a great help in the rear of our force. Curse those Morphs for killing his horse." He had not delivered his lines especially well, but Thorbad readily agreed and went on for the better part of the morning about the savageness of Morphs.

Yet Marcus knew that the slaves marched at the rear and Quintus was positioning himself to be close to the lithe blonde Elf. What the Wizard did not know is whether he let this happen because of his Human side's affection for a dear friend or his Wizard side's assurance that allowing Quintus to know this girl would surely break her spell on him. He hoped it was the former, but was resigned to the fact that it was likely the latter. Quintus's infatuation with Gwendolyn was a distraction from their mission. If she remained an impossibly pretty face from a distance, then Quintus would fawn and moon over her. If he spoke with her, perhaps she would simply be another girl, albeit a pretty one. A pretty *Elf* girl, he corrected himself. *In chains!* Marcus clenched his fists and ground his teeth. Still, he consoled himself that this Elf girl could not hope to do anything but fall in Quintus's esteem as he got to know her. That was clear.

Wizards are wiser than most, but they are frequently wrong about Humans. The more Quintus spoke to Gwendolyn, the more he was consumed by love of her. She adored the bow as he did, spoke with passion about the natural world in ways that made his heart leap in his ribcage, and cared for that little robin as if it were her child. Everything she said was uttered in the mellifluous tones of an Elf's normal speaking voice. Quintus did not lose his love by getting to know her, he fell deeper and deeper. Marcus remained annoyed, but he knew Quintus would follow him when their paths diverged from the Sunset Elves' journey. He was Quintus, after all. He was the friend who had saved Marcus all those years ago. He would not abandon Marcus for a pretty Elf girls—chains or not. This was a temporary situation to be endured, Marcus told himself and his fists relaxed. Thorbad had also been briefly irritated by the Ranger chatting up a wretched slave, but Octavia simply explained that Quintus was curious about Elves—all kinds of Elves. Thorbad seemed unsure if he found this defense convincing, but when the Wizard nodded in agreement, it was enough for him. The Sunset Elves were so predictable when it came to Wizards.

Yet Griffin was the most annoyed of all. He loathed Humans almost as much as he loathed Morphs and this Human was certainly getting too familiar with his sister. Griffin had to listen to them blather on hour after hour, knowing full well what the Human's game was. He had confronted Gwen on the second day and told her that the Human meant to seduce her, but she very firmly and very clearly told Griffin to leave her alone. It was typical. He had protected her his whole life, but always from the insults, the jokes at her expense, the dirty looks when she pulled back the bow. No Elf-boy had ever desired his sister. She was beautiful, but she was damaged. She did not adhere to the rules and Elves adored their rules. While other Elf-boys might have found her physically appealing, they found her way of life repugnant. The minute she spoke of archery or some other inappropriate pursuit, she became undesirable for the Sunrise Elves in Griffin's social circles. He had never before protected her from boys's desires because he had never needed to. Now, there was a strapping Ranger, probably ten sun cycles older and an eternity worldlier, walking inches from his sister with flickering desire kindled in his gray Human eyes. To Griffin, Gwendolyn seemed as innocent as some beast sipping cool water while the arrow winged towards its throat. Griffin's desire to free his sister from the dark Elves of the Sunset only became more vital as the Human with a taste for Elves laid his trap for her. And yet as the sun spirit descended into the tomb which was the Wizard's realm, time was short. All too soon, the group would be at their destination, the foreboding Tomb of Storms and Sun. Any hope of freeing Gwen and himself would evaporate once they reached the gray mountains. He prayed to the Spirits because he was helpless to do anything else.

"Why do you let him get his way so often?" Octavia asked Quintus while Marcus was busy amusing the Sunset Elves with some silly magic trick to lift the gloom of the darkening evening.

"You'll find that it is usually easier that way with Wizards," Quintus said, swirling an amber ale around in his cup before drinking it. It was crisp and fresh with just a hint of bite. Elves knew their way around food and drink and Quintus was grateful for that.

"But you are friends, you are equals," Octavia insisted.

"We are friends," Quintus agreed, "But one does not befriend a Wizard as equals. At least not completely." She looked totally perplexed. "Octavia, he loves me, we are brothers, and he would kill or die for me as a Human friend would. But the world is different for Wizards. I don't think I can put it into words. They are not Humans, and if you think of him as a Human, you will find yourself frustrated."

"He is half Human, isn't he?"

"Aye, and that is sometimes the best part of him," Quintus agreed with a slow nod filled with thoughts he did not share, "Or at least, the Human part of Marcus is the easiest part to understand. But you cannot expect a horse to act like an eagle or a dragon to act like a mouse. Wizards are Wizards and must be approached on their own terms."

"They usually get their way?"

"The usually do," Quintus said, "The very elements bend to their commands, Octavia. Yet there *are* times that they don't get their way and it does not kill them." He grinned, ever so slightly.

Octavia nodded and changed the subject, "You love the Elf girl, don't you?"

"I do," Quintus nodded.

"You have loved Elves before?"

"I have. It did not go well, as I am sure Marcus has explained."

Octavia winced and touched his arm gently, more gently than he thought her capable. "He did." She looked at Quintus with mournful green eyes. "And Marcus, you had said he once loved a girl, too? Is that love like Human love? Or is that another example of 'Wizards are Wizards and must be approached on their own terms?'"

"Yes, there was a girl Marcus once loved," Quintus said, failing to meet her gaze, as he stared at the dark, wet earth with a fascination that was unwarranted.

"What happened?" Octavia asked when he did not offer more.

"It did not go well, either," Quintus explained, cutting off the sentence as if he were wielding an axe and the words splintered while he spoke them. He met her gaze, but his look made it clear that he was not interested in discussing the matter any further.

"You are going to find a way to free Gwendolyn?" Octavia asked, as the awkwardness burned the back of her neck.

"I will."

"Marcus is adamant that we have a more important mission."

83

"Aye, he is adamant," Quintus agreed, "And no doubt, he has good reason to be adamant. He always does. Still, he will let me have my way. It will not kill him."

"You do realize you'll have to free her brother, too?" Octavia asked, Quintus shrugged. "And you do realize he hates the very ground you walk on."

"I usually charm people eventually," Quintus said, with a grin, "They just have to get used to me." He got up and retired to his tent.

Octavia looked over at Marcus and saw that he had already succumbed to sleep on the bare ground, wrapped in that magic cloak. She decided that sleep was probably a good use of her time, even if another hour of drinking was far more pleasurable. She walked to her tent, stopping only to push her leather sack under the Wizard's slumbering head. It was a makeshift pillow and he probably would not notice, but he seemed more comfortable and she believed that he would have done the same for her.

She slipped into her tent and began unlacing her boots, when she heard a squeak from the corner. Octavia looked over with bored detachment until the mouse turned into a woman. Without a moment of hesitation, Octavia grabbed her dagger and prepared to kill her. "No no, I am a friend," protested the mouse-girl.

"I have never had a friend who was a Morph," Octavia hissed, her eyes narrow and hard like emeralds.

"Please, just let me talk." Alexia pleaded, "You can see that I am unarmed." She stood in front of Octavia with her hands spread, so that the warrior girl could be certain she was speaking the truth.

"Start talking," Octavia said gruffly, "You don't have much time before I lose my patience and cut you open."

"Shhh, it's okay," Alexia purred, "We're on the same side." She slipped as close to Octavia as she dared and smiled at her. Octavia thought she smelled like exotic spices, the kinds the Sunset Elves sold. Perhaps the legends were true that you could smell a Morph.

"First, do not come into my personal space," Octavia said, "Second, put something on for the sake of the Golden One. You beastmen may have no rules, but that doesn't mean I have to sit here and talk to you like my tent is a whorehouse." Octavia thrust a blanket at the Morph.

"I am happy to cover up if it bothers you," Alexia said alluringly, "But are you absolutely sure it bothers you?" She moved her weight to one foot and held her pose, so that Octavia had the chance to change her mind.

"Your time is running out, Beastgirl, cover up and tell me why you are in my tent," Octavia demanded as her grip on the dagger became tighter. Alexia got the point and wrapped herself in the blanket. All flint and no spark, this one, she thought.

"Gwendolyn is my dearest friend," she explained, "I love her more than anything in the world and the sight of her in chains without leaves in her hair wounds me each and every time the sun crests the horizon. I thought that you might share my sympathy to her plight."

"What made you think that?" Octavia asked.

"She is being punished for being a woman," Alexia said, "And you know what it's like to be a woman. We both do." She let the blanket slip open a little to see if perhaps her original plan might still work. But the soldier-girl did not as much as glance in curiosity.

"I don't know why you keep showing me your body," Octavia said, gesturing at Alexia's uncovered parts, "I have a woman's body myself, so you show me nothing I have not already seen. As far as your little Elf-slave, I have never in any of the Four Realms heard of a Morph declaring she is friends with an Elf."

"Are you not a Human who is friends with a Wizard?"

"A good point," Octavia conceded with a smile. Alexia liked the smile. She could work with a smile. Perhaps, this Bean-eater was not entirely made of steel and stone. "You want to free the Elf-girl, why not morph into some fierce beast and eat all the Dark Elves?"

"You wouldn't defend them?"

"We're just along for the trip," Octavia said, "We have no oath with them."

"I cannot morph into such a beast capable of slaying 12 stout Sunset Elves," Alexia said, pouting, "If I am to free Gwendolyn, I will need help."

"What about her brother? It seems like everyone forgets about him," Octavia said. Alexia shrugged. The blanket slipped, but she caught it and refastened it.

"I do not think he will be much help."

"Do you want to free him, too?"

"Of course, Griffin is her brother and she loves him. Anyone she loves, I love, too," Alexia said, "While we speak of love, I know that your Ranger loves Gwendolyn."

"How do you know that?"

"I sit on her shoulder all day."

"You are the robin!" Octavia declared. Alexia put her finger to Octavia's lips. It definitely smelled of spice from one of the eastern islands. For a moment, Octavia let it rest on her lips. She then grabbed the Morph's delicate wrist in her firm grip and wrenched it away.

"You are strong like a man but beautiful like a woman," Alexia said, blinking her dark brown eyes for effect.

"Do you want my help or not?" Octavia asked sternly.

"I want your help," Alexia said softly.

"Okay, here it is. Quintus would lift the all of the Dragon's Claws over his head if it would free the little blonde Elf slave, and I can be convinced that a girl who wants to use a bow and arrow should not be punished for that," Octavia said.

"This is wondrous news!" Alexia said, jumping up. The blanket slipped off and she was simply herself again, alone in her skin, which felt glorious. Octavia averted her eyes, but did not protest as she knew the conversation was going to end soon.

"But we need to convince Marcus to get involved."

"The Wizard? 'Marcus?' Such a queer name for a Wizard."

"It is a long story of which I have only been told part. The point is that he does not want us to get involved," Octavia explained. "And Wizards can be very stubborn."

"*I* will try to convince him to get involved," Alexia with a fiendish smile filled with seduction.

"No!" Octavia said, her lip curling, "You know nothing of Wizards. From my brief time living in the company of a Wizard, I have learned that you must...approach them on their terms."

"That is my intent," Alexia said, feigning innocence while exuding something darker.

"Wizards are not like Humans or Elves or Morphs," Octavia explained, "You do not get them to do what you want by focusing on bodily desires. You appeal to their sense of logic."

"You want me to *reason* with him?" Alexia asked, "Interesting strategy."

"Just leave Marcus to me."

Alexia considered the offer and shrugged. "Agreed, Fire-Haired Girl of the North, the Wizard is yours to convince in whatever way you deem," Alexia said, "But we must act before we reach the Wizards' Mountains. Speak to your Marcus tomorrow because you must all be ready when the time is right."

"When will the time be right?"

"You will know," Alexia said, "Perhaps, a little bird will tell you." With that, she morphed back into a gray mouse and scurried towards Gwen's tent. Octavia lay down to sleep with too much swirling around her head. A Morph and an Elf were friends? The Morph was the robin? Quintus's dream of emancipating the Elves was possible? And how in the Four Realms would she convince the Wizard to help—by tomorrow? She closed her eyes and gave herself over to sleep because she could do nothing else. Her only hope was that the dark dreams did not invade her slumber as they so often did.

In this hope, she was disappointed.

Chapter 13: Fairy Tales

The Wizard sat alone, drinking the hot, dark elixir. His face was lined with worries and his violet eyes had a faraway look. It almost seemed that all the camp's attention was focused on him while he sipped the Elvin beverage. Hot water strained through dark and mysterious Elvin beans. He'd forgotten the Elvin name for it, but he was certain it was the Elves' greatest contribution to civilization. This was the good stuff, Marcus thought, not like that wretched false elixir the Rangers sometimes used in imitation of the Elves. Or tea. He loathed tea. The steam rose off the dark liquid which tasted rich and slightly bitter, like so much of life. Marcus's mind was always sharper after consuming the elixir. If for no other reason than this morning beverage, he was glad he'd met up with the Elves of the Sunset. They were merchants and merchants knew that product quality was key. A good cup of this dark morning beverage helped clear his head. He'd forgotten the difference it could make. He inhaled the morning. He'd forgotten much. Too much.

Quintus eyed the Wizard while he tended to his bow and sharpened his sword. He trusted that Marcus's Human side would triumph over his Wizard side, but he knew it was a risky thing to count on. As he turned his glance to Gwendolyn, his heart was torn to shreds, watching her pack up the camp— bearing burdens which seemed ready to snap those slender shoulders. Her brother had a sour look. Perhaps it was the slavery or the proximity to mountains that Elves called a Tomb; or perhaps it was Quintus's interest in his sister. Quintus didn't care. Like Marcus, he believed strongly in the equality of all the races, even if he didn't subscribe to his Wizard friend's romantic view of the Classical past when all races lived in peace. There had never been peace, Quintus observed. But there were always broad-minded folks like him and Marcus, who saw through the hatred.

Thorbad's dark eyes fell on the Wizard. For a moment, he thought of joining him for breakfast, but then thought better of it. They were no more than three days from the Tomb and riches beyond riches. Thorbad could finally leave the caravan life and settle at the feet of those mountains, looming stoically on the horizon. This sale would be his last one. Two Elvin slaves for the highest bidder. And perhaps the price would be raised once it was discovered that Thorbad the Sunset Elf kept company with the great Wizard Marcus and his famous Human companions. This would only augment his glory amongst the Wizards and amongst his own kind. Soon, all would come to fruition.

Behind the darting eyes of a robin, Alexia watched the Wizard as well. She wanted to fly closer, so she could spur the soldier-girl into action. But Alexia was careful not to fly too well, lest the Elves demand Gwen give her up—having discharged her Elfish duty. That was unthinkable. The Morph was not sure that she had totally convinced Octavia to help, and she was even less sure that the red-haired warrior could convince the Wizard of anything. Alexia did not know much about the ways of Wizards. However, this one looked lonely and few lonely beings could resist Alexia. She watched Octavia emerge from her tent. The girl's muscled arms and legs did not entirely undermine her femininity and her face was pretty enough, but there was something conventional about her. Her skin was fair, but not too fair. Her body was pleasant, but not too pleasant. And while she was lean where she needed to be lean and soft where she needed to be soft, Octavia was certainly not intoxicating. She did not carry herself with enough swagger to be intoxicating. Her movements were awkward and her voice too rough and deep to be seductive. Perhaps in an army filled with anxious men, Octavia could be appealing. But she was not irresistible as Alexia was. So how was she going to convince the Wizard? Surely, she wasn't serious about reasoning with him...

The dark green eyes of the warrior found their target. She locked on and strode towards him, her powerful legs moving confidently. Well, they appeared confident, even though she dared not stand still, lest her knees knock together. She was nervous about her task, even though Octavia had faced many things more terrifying than a Wizard drinking his morning brew. She did not hesitate for a moment, although she did look back to note the robin watching her movements. Octavia turned her head, her red ponytail sweeping back and forth and she sat down next to Marcus. He looked at her and nodded acknowledgement of her presence.

"What do you know about Morphs?" she asked. If he was taken aback by her directness in dispensing with customary pleasantries like "Good morning," he did not betray any hint of it.

"I know a little about Morphs," Marcus answered flatly, sipping at the steaming cup, as if it were more important than anything in the Four Realms.

"Is there anything you don't know 'a little' about?"

He sighed in his world-weary way. "There is quite a lot I don't know 'a little' about." He paused for a moment and drained his cup. "Elves believe Morphs are the first creations, a mistake of their gods. Wizards think Morphs are simply Humans who have mastered the one piece of magic left to non-Wizards. Humans insist that Morphs are a separate race which stands in between Humanity and the animals."

"Can they turn into any animal at will?" Octavia asked.

"It is said that in Classical Times they could, but that is deep in the distant past—a thousand years or more. In our times, Morphs have the ability to change into an eagle, a wolf, or a bear. Each Morph is born with the ability to do all three, but they must choose one form at their coming of age ritual at 17 years old. Once they choose which of the three they will be, they never morph into the other forms. And no Morph has been seen in any other form for as long as post-classical history can testify."

Octavia considered his words and paused for a moment to drink the steaming cup he'd offered her. "Do you think you can you trust Morphs, Marcus?"

"Most people say you cannot. It is said that the Morphs abandoned the other races when the Dark Lord rose."

"The Dark Lord? That's a fairy tale," Octavia chuckled.

"Perhaps," considered the Wizard, "But even fairy tales can tell us truths. There is always a core of truth in stories, no matter how fanciful they might appear."

"Morphs cannot be trusted?" she pressed.

"They have few laws, no true government, very little conventional religion," Marcus explained, "I am sure you've heard they rarely wear clothing and lie with one another when desire moves them. It is said they abandoned us all for the power of the Dark One and I think that you must accept the kernel of reality which lies at the heart of that old tale. So many Morphs probably aren't trustworthy—at least that is what most creatures think."

"What do *you* think, Marcus?" Octavia asked. He looked at her with those piercing violet eyes.

"I think it depends on the Morph, just as it depends on the Human or the Wizard or the Elf. Some are probably untrustworthy. Others, maybe, are different."

Octavia bit her swollen lip a little as she looked down at the cup she was holding in both hands, "I met a Morph last night," she said, looking up to catch the faint hint of surprise in the Wizard's eyes, "I am pretty sure she wanted to lie with *me*."

"Not surprising."

"But she was a *girl* Morph," Octavia explained, "And if you haven't noticed, I am a girl, as well."

"I have noticed," he said without expression, "That is the way of Morphs. Girls with girls, boys with boys, boys with girls. I had thought Humans cared little about such pairings." He shrugged. "Morphs certainly don't have the obsession that Elves have about who merges with whom." He gestured at the dark Sunset Elves, packing their donkeys with wares.

Octavia was a little mad that the Morph's attempt at seduction was so unsurprising to Marcus. "She tried to seduce me and then morphed into a mouse."

At that, he actually looked surprised. Octavia counted it as a victory. "A *mouse*? Not a bear or an eagle or a wolf? Are you sure?"

She nodded. "She is friends with the Elf girl," Octavia added. This seemed to surprise the Wizard even more. It was all Octavia could do to keep from smiling.

"A Morph and an Elf?"

Octavia nodded and leaned in close to Marcus, so that no one had any chance of hearing them. Her fiery hair brushed his cheek ever so slightly. "The Morph is the robin who perches on the Elf girl's shoulder. She wants us to help free the Elf slaves."

Marcus exhaled loudly through his nose. "Listen Octavia, I do not believe in slavery and I know our friend Quintus is consumed with Human passion for this creature, but let me be clear: if I am right, our whole world is in danger. I do not wish to frighten you with the details until I am sure I am not utterly mad, and for that I need the Exiled Wizards. But it is my firm belief that all of us are in grave peril. We have no time to meddle in the affairs of Elves or Morphs."

"I understand," Octavia said, her lip breaking into a small smile, "But I have never heard of a Morph befriending an Elf, have you? It sounds a lot like the ancient times." She stared into his eyes with purpose. The Wizard blinked and then nodded.

"Yes, it does sound like the ancient times," he muttered, "And she can be a mouse and a robin?" His brow furrowed in thought. Octavia got up to leave and he tapped her arm. She stopped and looked. He handed her the leather bag she had propped under his head last night with a nod that passed for Wizard gratitude. "Octavia?"

"Yes?"

"Let me think on it, okay?"

"On what?"

"The Elves."

"Of course," she said, "Whatever you decide is best, I'm sure." She smiled and turned away, walking confidently back to her tent. Not once did Octavia give in to the temptation to look back and see if he were watching her walk. She wasn't sure whether she was ready to know if he was. Alexia noted a hint of swagger in her walk and slightly recalibrated her assessment of the Northern girl.

It was a hard day's march, but there wouldn't be much more of it. The caravan had made great progress. The Mountains stood steadfast in front of them and it wouldn't be more than another day or a day and a half before they reached the Wizard's Gate. Even Marcus had to admit that from this view, the mountains really did look like a dragon's claws might. He chuckled to himself as the absurdity of the fairy tales creatures told to make sense of their world.

Maybe it was the difficulty of the terrain or the knowledge that their journey would soon be done, but Thorbad broke out the most delightful spiced smoked hog and gave the order to tap the best barrel of wine yet. He had no idea that Marcus, Quintus, and Octavia would disappear when all were sleeping, taking the path south towards the Burning Sea.

Marcus had pondered Octavia's information, and he rarely took his eyes off the robin. His Human side sympathized with the plight of the slaves, punished for crimes which were not crimes anywhere other than in the needlessly severe Elf world. He was also gladdened that a Morph and the Elf girl were friends because it confirmed his beliefs about the universality of all living beings. But his Wizard side could not be placated. He alone knew what was happening. The heartless Ranger corpses. The black blood. The coldness he felt in the earth. He wasn't exactly sure how they fit together, but he was absolutely certain what they all pointed to. It was no mere fairy tale. There had been other signs he'd noticed over the last few years, but none as clear as this. He had to cross the sea and get to his old teachers. If they agreed with his reading of the signs, then dark days lay ahead for the world. In the grand scheme of things, two wronged Elves meant little. Octavia, Quintus, and he had to make their own way tonight and leave Gwendolyn and Griffin to their fates. There was no alternative. Quintus would have to see that.

Thorbad was emptying flagon after flagon, which was not entirely unusual. The Sunset Elves had a reputation for overindulging in food and drink. But the wine which usually

93

made him loud and light-hearted seemed to be darkening his eyes, if that were possible. He grew grim and silent.

"This is the time," Alexia said as she peeked out of the tent.

"Are you sure?" Gwendolyn asked.

"It has to be," she insisted, "Just trust me." She kissed Gwendolyn full on her pink lips. She had never done that before. Gwendolyn turned even paler, if that were possible. "For good luck," Alexia declared, "We might need it. Just make sure you do as I instructed."

"For good luck," Gwen repeated absently, the spicy taste of the Morph's kiss lingering on her lips. She exited her tent.

"Who told the slave girl she could leave her tent?" demanded Thorbad. The other dark Elves shrugged. "Go away, slave. Can't you see we're celebrating?"

"You have nothing to celebrate," she shot back. "You are a disgusting excuse for an Elf. In two days, you are prepared to sell two of your own race to the Wizards." Griffin tore out of his tent when he heard the voices, his chains clanging as he shuffled towards his sister.

"Enough Gwen!" he shouted.

"You are not my own kind," Thorbad remarked acidly, "You have disobeyed the King of all Elves Near and Far. You have forfeited your leafy crown and your Elvishness. You are a thing, now, just like the wine and the cloth that I sell. And after all this time, I am enraged that you do not know your place!" He jumped to his feet and threw his cup at her, but Gwen deftly sidestepped it. Her speed was a marvel, especially as she was bound by chains.

Quintus, Octavia, and Marcus all exchanged looks. Thorbad was pompous and a bit of a buffoon, but they had never seen him act like this. It was as if something had hold of him. "Thorbad," Marcus said, softly but firmly, "It is just the wine firing your heart." He turned to Ardor, the lieutenant, "Get the captain another cup and return the Elf slaves to their tents."

"No!" fumed Thorbad, "This girl has been a thorn scratching my legs since we left the gleaming city of the

Sunrise. Her brother has accepted his lot. She still thinks she's a free Elf. You are a slave, now, and I will make sure you know it." He strode towards her. Quintus put his hand on the hilt of his sword. Marcus gestured to him to remain calm. The atmosphere at the camp crackled, as clearly none of the other Sunset Elves understood what their captain meant to do.

"What is your meaning?" asked Griffin, as he interposed himself between Thorbad and Gwendolyn.

"Seize him," Thorbad ordered and two of his Elves grabbed Griffin immediately. "I am going to teach your sister what being a slave really means." Griffin struggled but was too weak to escape the grip of his captors.

"Thorbad," called Marcus, "She knows she's a slave. Girl, tell him that you know you're a slave and we can return to the merriment of our evening."

"My Lord Wizard," Thorbad spat out, "She does not know she is a slave, do you, girl?" Gwendolyn looked at the robin and then back at Thorbad. She shook her head defiantly. "See what I mean?" Thorbad raged. He turned to two of his men, "But I will teach her that she is a slave and her new master will be grateful for the lesson. Gunther, Ardor, tear off her clothes and pin her down." Thorbad began to unbuckle his belt and the Sunset Elves he'd commanded paused at the order, but then moved to comply with their captain's request. From their looks, it appeared they saw no other choice available.

Things then moved very quickly, even for a Wizard's mind to contemplate. Before Gunther and Ardor could seize Gwendolyn—who looked utterly surprised and terrified— Marcus saw that Quintus was in front of her with his sword drawn. The robin morphed into a beautiful brown haired girl who began cursing at the Elves. Griffin slipped free as his captors were distracted and staggered towards his sister. Octavia was on her feet with her battleaxe gleaming in the firelight, unsure where to stand. She could not let him rape the Elf as she watched. That was unthinkable. Her chest tightened as if to confirm this fact.

Gwendolyn shouted out in terror, "Please, I am a maiden. You must respect that." Tears cascaded down her white cheeks as the Morph comforted her.

"A Morph?" Griffin declared with an equal mix of surprise and contempt.

"This is not the time," Quintus stated, his teeth clenched, his feet spread apart as he held his sword aloft.

"The Human is right, you small-minded fool," Alexia hissed, morphing into a lioness and roaring defiantly.

This was an important moment and Marcus knew it. If he let things play out, the 12 Elves would likely overpower Quintus, Griffin, and the lioness. He was sure Quintus would fight bravely and he expected the lioness to maul one or two, but the Elves would pick them off with their bows. He looked at Octavia. She remained standing next to Marcus, but seemed sure to defend Quintus after the first move was made. She might even things out a bit, but it was still certain that one or both of Marcus's friends would die or be severely wounded. His Wizard side noted that this would be an ideal time to part company with the Elves, openly and without a ruse. Yes, the Elf girl did not deserve to be raped, but the entire world, all Four Realms, might perish if Marcus did not make it to the Burning Sea. And only he knew… To everyone else, it would seem like a foolish story. But he knew.

Marcus looked at Octavia, her steely gaze focused on the contours of what was now a battlefield. He looked at noble Quintus Aureus, ready to be pierced with spears and arrows for the love of a blonde Elvin maiden. Such a living fairy tale, that one! As Marcus looked at Quintus and Octavia, something snapped inside of him and it became clear. What was the point of saving the world for strangers who didn't know or care who he was? He was not concerned about his cold father or mysterious mother. He had no siblings of which he was aware. He cared nothing for the women of various races he had bedded and left. He didn't really miss the Rangers with whom he'd traveled, although he lamented the brutal death several suffered. He only had two friends on the black earth. Quintus mattered. And now, it appeared that Octavia mattered to him, too. He felt a tightness in his chest as he thought about those two Humans. They mattered. And what mattered to them mattered to him. You will be delighted to know that his Wizard side did not get its way, this time. It was an uncommon, but not entirely inconceivable occurrence with Marcus.

"Stop!" thundered the Wizard and a wild wind blew with such force that everyone lost their footing for a moment. "We are comrades and will not cut each other to pieces for this. Thorbad, the juice of the berries has gotten the better of you. You are not an Elf who rapes virgins."

"How do you know what I am?" Thorbad asked darkly.

"I shall solve this," Marcus decreed. He thrust his hand towards his tent, muttered a few words, and two sacks of golden coins flew out of their own accord and settled at Thorbad's feet. "I offer you a fair price for both of the Elf slaves. There is a sack of golden crowns for each Elf. I will buy them from you and this matter will be settled."

Quintus permitted himself a smile which he exchanged with Octavia, but neither of them relaxed their posture an iota.

"I do not accept," Thorbad said, "I will do to my own slaves as I see fit."

"There are rules which govern Elves and Wizards," Marcus said firmly but calmly, "You cannot refuse a deal to which I have offered you a fair price."

"He is right," Ardor added—he had seemed most conflicted about the Captain's orders. Octavia noticed that he was the Elf whose jaw she probably had fractured on the first night. A shame. He seemed alright for an Elf.

"The Spirits have condemned her through the King and he committed her and her brother to me," Thorbad said, "The Spirits's laws overrule any laws the Wizards and Elves may have with one another."

"You wish to appeal to the Spirits?" asked Griffin, "Then consent to combat. Let the Wizard and the Captain fight and the Spirits will determine whose cause is just."

Marcus looked at Quintus and felt the friendship swell his heart, "I will fight you for ownership of these two slaves," Marcus consented.

"There is no way I will fight a Wizard," Thorbad declared, "It is suicide."

"We must solve this," Marcus said, turning it over in his nimble mind, "I will designate Quintus as my agent. He will fight on my behalf. Surely, you do not fear a Ranger, Captain Thorbad?"

"I do not, my Lord."

"Then you and Quintus shall do battle. If you win, you keep your slaves. If he wins, I own your slaves," Marcus explained, "You shall fight until one of you surrenders or is killed, but I hope it will not come to that."

"If I win, I get to kill the Morph, too," Thorbad insisted.

Marcus shrugged. "As you wish."

Thorbad pondered. "I will fight your Human friend, but I do not have the best deal, here," he said, steepling his hands, "If you win, you own two slaves. And now that we know she's a virgin, she is even more valuable. If I win, I get to keep what I already have. This is not a good risk for a merchant. I am a Sunset Elf. I need more to justify my risk."

"You get to kill the Morph," Quintus insisted.

"I'd have done that, anyway," Thorbad sneered.

"You have no hope of that, Dusk Elf!" taunted Alexia, who had resumed her mortal form.

"Be silent, you savage beast-girl," spat Thorbad who always hated the 'dusk Elf' slur, "Listen to me, Wizard, where is my advantage, here? What is my gain? I will not consent to this unless my risk is outweighed by my reward. Keeping two slaves who I already own does not make for a good gamble. What else do you offer if I win?"

The Wizard looked perplexed. Octavia had not yet seen such a look on Marcus's face, as his logical brain searched for ways to resolve this. "I have an idea," Octavia declared, "If Quintus wins, the Wizard owns your two Elf slaves. If you win, you kill the Morph, keep the Elf slaves, and can make me your slave as well."

"Octavia!" shouted Marcus, "No!"

"I accept the offer," Thorbad said. The Human would make a very marketable slave. She was strong enough to do manual labor and shapely enough to warm a bed. What would the Wizards pay to have a Human slave, especially one with such strong limbs and ample breasts? "Do you withdraw, Wizard, or do you accept the terms?"

Marcus looked at Octavia and then at Quintus. "I accept," the Wizard said softly.

As Quintus approached his adversary, Octavia grabbed his arm with more force than any man he had ever known. She leaned in and whispered harshly in his ear, "You had better win this fight, Ranger, or else you'd best pray he kills you, understand?" Quintus nodded, a smile slowly spreading over his face. He tried to share that smile with Marcus, but the Wizard showed no sense of mirth, nor had not taken his eye off of Thorbad for one instant.

Chapter 14: The Fellowship of Outcasts

Quintus stood on the balls of his feet, remembering the training he'd once had when he was Quintus Agrippa Aureus, heir to his father's Dukedom of Vinland in the sunny south of the Human realm. The firstborn boy or girl in a noble family was expected to undergo military training, although some were more successful than others. Quintus had been very successful. He excelled at the bow and at the sword, even at fighting without weapons. He was quick, strong, and smart, a warrior who saw the battlefield well and improvised when needed. Quintus Aureus had been very successful as a warrior, less so as a son. It had all gone wrong when he first lost his heart to an Elf maiden. "Good to see nothing in my life has changed," Quintus thought, as he prepared for Thorbad's initial assault. This Elf girl was even more beautiful than his long lost love, or perhaps his memory of Valeria was simply fading around the edges. But Gwendolyn seemed so filled with life; she excited his pulse as no girl had for a very long time. He knew Marcus disapproved of the emotional slavery of Humanity, but Quintus accepted being Human on his own terms. Humans loved deeply and illogically. It was how they were made. He was at peace with that, even if it placed him in a perilous situation like this one. Yes, fighting for a maiden's salvation was a silly story one told to eager children, but Quintus had always loved those stories and Marcus never stopped reminding him that truth could be found in all tales.

Marcus. He had come through and this gladdened Quintus to no end. If he were full Wizard, he would never have intervened for something as foolish as a friend in love with a near stranger. In fact, intervening for friendship in any matter would have been too much for any Wizard worth his cloak. Yet Marcus was not all Wizard and there was hope in that. He was Human on his mother's side and Quintus believed that portion of him permitted Marcus to love his friend and put that friend's needs above his own. Perhaps it would permit him to fall in love himself someday. Perhaps. But first things first, Quintus needed to defeat the Dark Elf. A Morph's life and the freedom of two Elves and a Human depended on it. In some way, the very existence of Marcus's Human side depended on it, as well. Quintus was all too aware of this fact as he raised his sword.

The bow was out of the question for the combatants were too close and even Quintus couldn't load and fire before being overtaken. He had cast his bow to the side, but not too far away, and focused on sword and shield fighting. He held the sword tightly but not too tightly in his right hand and made an "L" with his left arm as his teachers had once taught him so the shield was balanced and covered most of the body's targets between chin and knee. The Dark Elf had also eschewed his bow and gripped a long spear with a well-crafted point. Quintus assumed the wine which had impaired Thorbad's judgment would also affect his fighting. He should be more predictable and more savage with the wine firing his blood. They danced around, searching one another, and Quintus found himself with his back to the other eleven Elves. He did not give it a second thought. These Elves would respect the process, even if their captain died. It was a religious struggle and Elves were noted for their piety. In the back of his head, he also knew that Marcus would never permit the Elves to tip the balance unfairly if Thorbad began to lose. Quintus glanced at Octavia. She would defend him, too. He'd not known her long, but their bond had been forged in combat and he trusted her completely. She had even offered her own freedom for his cause. Surely, she had won Marcus's friendship, as well, for the Wizard seemed genuinely troubled by her offer to be enslaved. Quintus steeled himself to focus on the eyes of his opponent, even though a simple half turn of his head would put Gwendolyn in his line of vision. There was an unclad Morph with unfathomable angles standing next to her, but he only had eyes for the Elf slave girl. Well, slave girl for not much longer, if he could prevail.

Thorbad's eyes revealed his plan and he thrust at Quintus with the spear. He favored his right, as expected. Quintus danced away and slashed at Thorbad's arm with his sword. Thorbad drew back from the blow, bleeding but undeterred. The wine would also dull his pain, Quintus recalled, factoring that in. Quintus had delivered several blows and the Sunset Elf was staggering, but only growing more and more furious. Yes, the wine cut both ways, Quintus reminded himself. Quintus had hoped the captain would surrender, but the wine had done its work and the pain was clearly not impairing the Elf. Quintus had held back from hurting him too badly, in the hopes Thorbad would give up and keep his life. Quintus did not want to kill him. Too many Elves had died since the war began and Quintus felt somewhat responsible, even if that were ridiculous. It was clear within the first minute of their struggle that Quintus was superior as a warrior.

But this was his undoing, for he was so sure of himself that he left himself open and Thorbad savagely thrust his spear into Quintus's shoulder. The Human stumbled backwards, dropping his sword while blood poured out of the wound. Quintus had been trying so hard to avoid killing his adversary that he had lost his focus and was now in grave peril. Thorbad charged again at the stumbling Human, barely missing him with a second thrust which would have been fatal. Quintus grasped Thorbad's spear with his right hand to prevent another blow. Confused but seemingly impervious to the pain of his many small wounds, Thorbad bashed at Quintus's injured shoulder with his helmeted head. This time, Quintus fell on to his back.

The Wizard raised his eyebrows almost imperceptibly. Alexia was watching him to see if he would intervene should his man get killed. She did not make trusting Wizards a habit, nor indeed trusting anyone. Still, she presumed that if Quintus lost and was slain, the Wizard would call down fire or lightning or ice or some nonsense on the Sunset Elves. Surely, he would not keep his word and permit Gwen to be raped or his red-haired friend to be enslaved. The Wizard could end this all with a few ancient words and a wave of his hands, so why go through this puppet show? Why not simply use his powers to free Gwen and kill the slavers? Yet even with Quintus on his back and bereft of his sword, the Wizard merely raised his eyebrows. Would he let his friend die? Alexia wondered if she should grab Gwen and flee while all eyes were on the battle.

Octavia was ready, unsure about what to do. She looked at Marcus and he simply looked blankly at her. She wanted to wordlessly ask when they should intervene to save Quintus. Octavia was loathe to leave the Elf-girl to her grim fate, but Gwen would live even if Thorbad took her against her will. Quintus would not live if they did not step in. She'd foolishly offered herself as a slave should he lose. That seemed to be far more possible now than it had at the beginning. Would Marcus disrespect the process? Could he stop this? How powerful was this Wizard? His expression became slightly less blank and she almost detected a faint smile creasing his features—not his mouth, which remained in a straight line. But his eyes seemed to smile as if he knew more than he let on. She prayed to the Golden One that this was so.

Quintus realized that he had underestimated Thorbad and the effect of the wine on his pain threshold. He still wanted to avoid killing him, but he needed to decide that killing him was an option should his own death hang in the balance. He rolled over onto his front, stood up, and moved left, all in one fluid motion. Thorbad charged at his bleeding foe, but his spear caught the air where Quintus had been. The Human covered himself with his shield as he knelt to pick up his sword. In this vulnerable position, Thorbad was able to gash Quintus's leg a little but not badly. Quintus struck back, but half-heartedly, as he was still hoping that Thorbad might pass out from loss of blood and put a merciful end to this. But his hope was in vain. In fact, Quintus knew that he was bleeding badly himself and could feel a little light-headedness. He wanted to show mercy, but perhaps that was not to be. Bloodied and raging, Thorbad gambled all on one fierce throw of his spear. Quintus was surprised at the tactic and it flew hard at him, but the Elf was too tired and too affected by the wine to throw it true. The spear stuck in a tree and Quintus called for him to surrender. A merciful end, it would be, thought Quintus.

He regretted his optimism.

As Quintus let down his guard, thinking the battle had ended, Thorbad rushed at him with his bare hands, intent on beating him to death. Caught off-guard, Quintus was driven backwards as the Elf reached for his throat. The Ranger had enough presence of mind to look down, so that his chin touched his chest and the soft flesh of his throat was less exposed. Quintus knew then that the Golden One had sealed Thorbad's fate. Before matters could get worse, he lowered his sword and caught the dark Elf in his belly, ending his time in this world and closing his eyes with doom. Octavia looked at Marcus and saw relief wash over his face, as if he expected the result, but not the intensity of the struggle. Or maybe that was not the expression. She couldn't tell what the Wizard was thinking and she resigned herself to that fact. At least Quintus was not mortally wounded; she could read that. And that was something.

For a moment, some of the other Sunset Elves seemed ready to avenge their captain. But the Wizard walked calmly between the furious Elves and his exhausted friend. "It is done," he said firmly. "Your Spirits have ruled and their ruling is final. I own the two Sunrise Elves. The Morph's fate is mine to decide. And the Human warrior remains a free woman. Quintus has triumphed."

"He is right," declared Ardor, gesturing to his comrades. With Thorbad dead, he was now the leader, Marcus recognized. "Will you let us take our wares to the Tomb of Storms and Sun, Lord Wizard? Or are those forfeit like Thorbad's life?"

"Your wares are your own," Marcus declared, "I am no thief. I take only your slaves per our agreement. And I ask you to leave us Thorbad's weapons and personal supplies."

"For whom?" asked a Dark Elf.

"That is the Wizard's concern," Octavia said, understanding Marcus's intent.

"Yes, I have won his spear and his bow and arrows," Quintus said, nodding, "and all that he possesses by right of the victor."

"You will also take some of my gold, Ardor," Marcus said, gesturing towards a bag. "Thorbad was not a wicked Elf. Tonight was not representative of his life. He deserves a proper Elvin burial and I will compensate you for that." Ardor nodded and the Wizard bid him to come closer. He leaned in and whispered, "The rest of this gold is for your men, so long as they swear on their Spirits not to mention what happened here. The situation was this: Your Elf slaves escaped with a Morph who killed Thorbad. You did not meet a Wizard and his Human companions. Are we understood?"

"Yes, my Lord," Ardor noted, "But why?"

"I have other affairs to handle and wish to never enter your stories," Marcus said, "I have made you a very fair offer, but your men must respect my terms. They are absolute. Do you understand?" Ardor nodded. Marcus looked deeply at him, studying the character of the new Captain. The Wizard must have been satisfied that Ardor was an Elf of his word because he bid them to be off.

The Sunset Elves took their leave immediately, marching even in the darkness to get away from the Wizard and his companions. They bore Thorbad with them, leaving his weapons and supplies as requested. To an Elf, they counted themselves lucky they did not forfeit their wares as well. The gold was unexpected and generous. They would keep Marcus's secrets.

"What now?" demanded the Morph as she stood with her hands on her hips.

Only a Morph, thought Marcus. "*What now?*" repeated Marcus, "Isn't it enough that Quintus has saved your life, Morph? And your Elvin friends no longer have him as master? And Gwendolyn's maidenhood remains intact? 'What now,' indeed!"

"We have traded slavery at the hands of a Sunset Elf for slavery at the hands of a Wizard," Griffin stated wearily. "Though I am grateful that our new Master doesn't want to see my sister raped. Huzzah." Sarcasm dripped off his words.

Quintus had expected Gwendolyn to run into his weary arms. It hadn't happened yet. Life certainly wasn't like the fairy tales, was it? She stood there, unsure of what was happening. The Morph girl clung to one side of her and her brother to the other. There was no room for Quintus. Marcus looked at his friend and smiled.

"It was Quintus who delivered her from the outrage," Marcus said, "I think he deserves both of your gratitude." He gestured to Quintus.

"Thank you," Griffin said, his tone belying his words.

Gwendolyn slipped free of her brother and her friend and ran towards Quintus, encumbered by her chains. "That was a wonderful thing you did for me," she said, embracing him, "I shall never forget your kindness, Sir Quintus."

Marcus enjoyed the scene—whether it was his friend getting the long sought-after embrace or her addressing him as "Sir"—it was unclear which amused him more. The Morph wore a scowl on her pretty face. Marcus couldn't tell if it was meant for him or Quintus. "You misunderstand my character," Marcus explained, "I have no intention of owning slaves. In the names of your Spirits and the six gods and goddesses of my people, I break your chains and end your slavery, here and now. You are free Elves, Griffin and Gwendolyn. That is my right as your new master." As good as his word, he cast an air spell and the chains fell off the arms and legs of the two Elves.

The Morph's smile defeated her frown. Even Griffin seemed filled with mirth. "Is it true? We are free?" he asked.

"Yes," Quintus said, "So fill your hair with leaves and flowers." The Elves did so without delay.

"We are free to go?" the Morph asked, narrowing her fierce eyes.

"Yes," Marcus said, "And by the way, I spare your life Morph-girl. You'll recall that was given to me, as well."

"The name is Alexia," she said, "Thank you so much, Wizard." Her tone was skeptical, but the Wizard expected as much. He studied the brother and sister Elves as well as the Morph. He pondered Octavia's words. He kept his own counsel per usual, and it seemed that he had an idea. Quintus knew the look on his old friend's face.

"So Gwen and I can go?" Griffin asked.

The Wizard nodded. "But I also have a proposition for you."

"I am not interested," Griffin cut him off, "Come on, Gwen. Let's leave them."

"I am going with you," insisted Alexia.

"You are hateful and repugnant," Griffin said, "You will not come with us."

"She is my friend," Gwendolyn shouted, abandoning Quintus and striding up to her brother. "I am not parting company with her."

"She is a Morph," he brother stated.

"She is a friend," Gwendolyn replied.

"Elves!" shouted Octavia with a powerful voice which made all creatures stop and stare, "Enough with your Elvin drama. Marcus had a proposition and I think you owe it to him to listen."

"I, for one, would like to listen," said Gwen.

"He'll enchant you with his magic," Griffin said, "Let's return to our homeland and free our parents."

"I am with you," Alexia said, grabbing Gwen's hand.

"Enough," the Wizard thundered, "Hear me out and then make your choices. There was a time in history when all four races lived in peace. The Classical Times were thousand or more years ago and Elves, Wizards, Humans, and Morphs existed in harmony."

"The Classical Times?" Alexia asked, "Do you mean to tell us some nonsense story about a golden age? Why are you wasting our time?"

"Listen to him," Octavia said menacingly. Her affection for the Wizard had grown immensely in the last hour. He was her friend and she would not suffer some barbaric Morph to mock him.

"It's a foolish notion that times were better hundreds of years ago," Griffin said, "Things have always been as they are, now. Anything else is wishful thinking. I expected more from a Wizard."

"Where do you think the road you've been traveling came from?" Marcus asked.

"Someone built it," Alexia snapped.

"It is the Via. The Ancients built it," Marcus declared, "They built that city you call the Ruins, as well."

"How do you know?" asked Alexia.

"I have been there. There is a dome with a 150 foot span. Do you know any creature who can build something that elegant? There is a stadium which seats 50,000 beings. Could Humans build that, today, Octavia?" She shook her head. "Can Elves?" Griffin just held his gaze. "Do you think that your lifespan is all there is of the world? Is it inconceivable to think a superior world existed?"

"Wanting something does not make it so," Griffin sniffed.

"Why do Elves put leaves in their hair?" Marcus asked, "The Classical people did that. Why do Humans name their children in the old tongue? Why do Wizards use that language for spells? Is that all a fairy tale? This road is perfectly straight and never washed out by rain. How many new roads are so ingenious?"

"What's your point?" Griffin asked.

"We are on the most important quest imaginable and I am inviting you to join us," Marcus said, "In the spirit of those ancient times and cooperation amongst the races. Cooperation which built domes and arenas, perfect roads, and so much more." Quintus might have tried to get his friend to cut out the history lesson (half of which he did not believe), but Marcus had just invited the pretty Elf to join them and he believed in that more than in anything else at this very moment.

"A 'quest?' Truly?" Griffin asked with barely concealed contempt, "May I talk with my sister? Alone?" The last word was directed at Alexia, although Quintus couldn't help but believe it was meant for him, as well.

"Griffin," Gwen said, stamping her foot as if she were still a child, "These people saved us from slavery. You treat them like garbage. Where are your manners?"

"My manners? Who is the one making friends with a savage beast-girl? Is that how you were raised, Gwendolyn?"

"She was the robin I saved," Gwen explained. "We have a bond, Griffin. You may go wherever you like, but if you want me to join you then you'd better get used to my 'savage naked Morph.' She is the best friend I have ever had in my 26 sun cycles."

108

"I cannot believe you are talking like this," Griffin raged, "Elves and Morphs are mortal enemies and always have been, no matter what that crazy Wizard thinks about some fantasy world where all races lived together and built domes. Insanity."

"Again, the 'crazy' Wizard broke our chains and put leaves in our hair. We are free by his hand," Gwen said, "If not for him, I'd have been brutally raped."

"Fine," Griffin spat, "I can tolerate a Wizard. But a Morph and *Humans?* They slaughter our people in heaps, Gwen."

"The red-haired girl volunteered her freedom as a price for ours," Gwen said, "And Quintus..."

"*Quintus,*" he mocked her.

"Quintus risked his life to free me. You cannot get more heroic than that," she said, "He is bleeding, right now. For me. Is that what bothers you? That these people care for me?"

"They are not 'people.' Maybe the Wizard. Maybe. But Humans and Morphs? They do not care for you. They do not know you. The Ranger has his own plan for you and his friends support him. A quest? What an absurd ruse. Open your eyes, Gwen."

"Open *your* eyes, Griffin," she said, her pale blue eyes flashing, "These people helped us for no reason at all and we owe them everything. Whatever *quest* they are on, it is not too good for two Elves who were slaves when the sun spirit last went down."

"What about our mother and father?"

"You don't think the guilt crushes me that they are in some dismal cave?" Gwen asked, "That is on my head. What are we going to do? Return to the Sunrise City and break them out of the King's guarded prison? We are only two Elves."

"But no one has ever shot arrows like you," Griffin offered.

"Agreed," Gwen permitted herself a smile, "But two Elves can do nothing." Griffin hung his head. He loathed that his little sister was right. "But two Elves, a Morph, two

Humans, and a Wizard? That might be something…" She was smiling. He refused the smile, but he nodded in resignation.

"I still hate them," he said, "Maybe the sorcerer less than the others. But you're probably right about their being useful."

"I'm probably right? I've never heard that from you before, brother," she said, "I think you're coming around nicely." They returned to the group.

"How did the Elf council go?" Marcus asked in a light-hearted tone.

"We are interested in hearing about your quest," Gwen said.

"*We?*" Quintus asked, "Both of you?"

"She is interested," Griffin said, "I have conceded that I cannot convince her otherwise. I am staying, but I am staying under protest and I think you are ridiculous to call whatever journey you're on a 'quest.' It is as if you believe yourself part of some story about Ancient times, Marcus the Wizard. I know your game, Quintus."

"You are free to leave," Quintus said.

"Someone has to protect my sister," Griffin replied.

"That is my point," Marcus said, "You may join our fellowship and we will protect one another. I made sure the bow was left for you, Gwendolyn as I know you have talent with it and this got you exiled. The spear is yours, Griffin. Those are suitable Elf weapons if I am not mistaken. Your people may not let you use the bow and enslave you for that, Gwendolyn, but you'll find my friends and me to be more open minded about such things."

"Can we find some clothes for the Morph?" Octavia asked, "I'm sure you boys are enjoying the scenery, but I'm already bored with it." Only in the last few minutes had Octavia felt like she could breathe again without significant effort. The whole situation had been too close. She did not breathe a word of her struggle, but it was all just too close. Octavia gulped down air in as surreptitious a way possible.

"I'm sure we can work something out," Marcus said, "But no one joins our fellowship against their will."

"My brother has forgotten that we are outcasts," Gwen said, "We cannot return to our people."

Octavia punched Marcus's shoulder playfully, regaining herself slightly for that is how it is. In moments of great stress, Octavia—like all of us—regained herself slightly and in small gasps, "This is a Fellowship of Outcasts, Elf girl. I cannot return to the Humans or they'll kill me. The same is true of Quintus. And let's be clear—Marcus had no intention of passing through the Wizard Gates, as he is not welcome in those mountains. We are all outcasts."

"I am an outcast, too," Alexia said, "I am the only Morph in all the Four Realms who cannot do bear or wolf or eagle."

"But you can do everything else," Gwen said, squeezing her hand in solidarity.

"You are especially gifted," Marcus said gently, as he looked into Alexia's dark eyes. "The Morphs were once all like you."

"In the Classical times, blah blah blah," Griffin said, "We've heard it, already. What foolish quest is your Fellowship of Outcasts on? And we are *so* grateful that you have generously offered us spots on this *quest* so we can share your peril." He smiled falsely and folded his arms.

The Wizard half smiled. "We will ask Alexia to wear something when she is in mortal form," he said, "Even though we know it is hard for her and not natural amongst her people." She nodded begrudgingly, intrigued by the gentle tone the Wizard had taken and the fact—or so she hoped from his history lesson—that she was not a total anomaly. "As for our Quest, I believe that a shadow has fallen upon our times. We are headed to meet with three exiled Wizards across the Burning Sea to get some direction, but I believe that nothing less than the world is in danger—everyone you know and everything you see. There is a great evil afoot and I mean to try and stop it."

Griffin laughed deeply. "You are something out of a bad fairy tale meant to scare naughty children, aren't you, Marcus the Wizard?" Griffin asked, "You expect me to share my bread with heathen beast-girls and filthy Nature-mauling Humans to 'fight a great evil which is afoot'?"

"Yes," the Wizard said plainly.

"You should trust him," Octavia said, "We do." She gestured towards Quintus who nodded solemnly, his eyes frozen on Gwen.

"What makes you think this?" Gwen asked Marcus. "About the evil?"

"There is a passage in one of the incomplete histories of the Ancient world which speaks of the coming of the Dark time after the fall of Classical Civilization," Marcus explained, "One sign that I remember reading was the discovery of corpses with hearts torn from their chests." Griffin audibly gasped. "Octavia, Quintus, and I found several of our Ranger comrades dead with their hearts torn out and a black liquid which we could not identify pooled around their bodies. I do not profess to know what it means, but I have never seen anything like it. There must be a greater significance."

"I saw a Wizard mistreated in the same way," Octavia added, transfixed.

"I have seen such things," Griffin said softly. His tone had completely changed. "I never told you, Gwen. But about a half a sun cycle ago, my warrior-band found a stack of Elf and Wizard corpses without hearts. We found the black liquid as well."

"Wizards *have* hearts?" Alexia asked, trying to inject levity.

"Frozen hearts, but hearts nonetheless," Marcus joked back at her. His face then turned grave, again. "Half a sun cycle?"

"That's Elfspeak for six months, right?" Octavia asked.

"Yes," Marcus said gravely. "Heartless corpses in Elfland? It is worse than I thought."

"That sight," Octavia said with a slight hitch in her voice, "The Wizard boy's father with his heart torn out. That's what changed my mind about joining you."

"And I thought it had been my charming personality," Marcus said, arching an eyebrow. His expression then darkened and he sighed heavily. "I so wish we'd found the boy." He looked positively inconsolable, which Octavia found to be odd.

"Me too," Quintus said with a sad expression, as he put his hand on Marcus's back.

"Okay, Wizard with a Human name, tell me then, who would do this sort of thing?" Griffin asked, visibly shaken.

"A great evil which is afoot," Marcus replied with an insincere smile, "And we will know more when we visit the exiled Wizards across the Burning Sea."

"May I have the spear?" Griffin asked. Octavia tossed it to him.

She studied him closely. This one might be all right, she thought to herself.

Chapter 15: The Loves of Gwendolyn

Gwen woke up, unsure if it had all been a dream. The dull brown canvas of her tent walls looked familiar, but she was dizzy with what had happened. *If* it had happened, she corrected herself. Inhaling through her nose, she decided that it probably didn't happen. Perhaps she wanted it to have happened, thus she must have dreamed it had happened. But there was no way it really happened. It had to have been a dream. But what a sweet and intoxicating dream it had been...

A brown bunny hopped into the tent, slipped under Gwendolyn's blanket and morphed into Alexia. "Good morning," Alexia said.

Even her words were bouncy, Gwen marveled, perhaps that was left over from the rabbit form. "Good morning," Gwen repeated. "Alexia, I was wondering. Last night?"

"Yes," the Morph smiled knowingly. Gwendolyn's eyes widened. "You don't remember?" Alexia asked, her bottom lip pouting,

"I feel as if it were a dream," Gwen explained.

"I feel the same way, my darling Elf-girl."

"It is so?"

"Yes, of course," Alexia said, drawing back the blanket and tossing it to the side. Gwen blushed. It started at her forehead and rolled like a pink wave down her body until it reached her feet. Alexia had heard that when Sunrise Elves blushed, their entire body blushed. But she had never seen it. She positively adored the Elfish quirk. She laughed. Gwen laughed with her. It was beautiful.

"I cannot believe this isn't a dream," Gwen said softly in that melodious Elvin voice.

"Believe," Alexia said, pressing her lips against Gwen's.

***

"How far are we from this Burning Sea?" asked Griffin.

"It will be a few days of hard marching south," Marcus explained, "The Classical people about whom you believe nothing did not see fit to build us a road that went the way we need to go. The sea was not poisoned in their times, so it's odd that no road was built."

"Why is poisoned?" Griffin asked

"A curse lies over it," Marcus replied.

"Sorcerers..." Griffin grumbled.

"That's an ugly word," Octavia snapped. She turned to Marcus, "A few more days and we're at the Burning Sea?"

"A few days and we reach a desert," Marcus corrected her, looking at Quintus with mournful eyes, "And if we survive the desert, we reach the sea. We would then cross the sea to reach the island."

"Quite the complicated journey to meet some teachers," Octavia shrugged.

"So let's head south, now," Alexia said with a smile. She seemed especially buoyant this morning, Octavia had noticed. She did not complain. Yesterday, Alexia had been a colossal burr in everyone's flesh.

"In a few hours," Marcus said, his eyes narrowing.

"And waste the light of day?" Gwen asked, wrinkling up her nose.

"We must prepare for the desert crossing," Marcus patiently explained, "It is no ordinary desert. I want Gwen and Quintus to go into those woods and hunt. Kill some critters and leave their flesh to dry in the sun. That will be essential once we are in the desert, for no animal or plant exists there to eat. Octavia and I will ride ahead and scout the best path to ensure we do not have any unpleasant neighbors who might be lying in ambush. This is a dangerous part of our world and we do not wish to blunder into any enemy."

"What about me?" Griffin asked.

"You and Alexia need to fill every container we have with water and guard the camp," Marcus said, "Any creature unfriendly to us could be found in this part of the world: Humans, Morphs, Wizards, Elves. The ground in the southwest is soaked with the blood of all four races."

"'You do this, you do that.' Who made you king?" Alexia asked. At least she was wearing a makeshift dress which

Octavia had sewed for her. Octavia remembered how shocked Gwendolyn had been that a Human woman could be both a warrior and know how to sew. She did not mention that most of her recent sewing experience involved stitching wounds shut on the battlefield, but she'd mended enough clothing for her brothers and father when she was younger. The skill was the same, even if the material was a bit different. Dresses did not cry out for their mothers when you sewed them, Octavia noted to herself.

Marcus's Wizard side was grateful Alexia had the dress on because she was a distraction when she was uncovered. Of course, his Human side missed the opportunity to drink in her exquisite form. "Do you find my duty allocation illogical?" Marcus asked.

"She's right. Why do you get to decide?" Griffin fumed, "Are you the captain of the Fellowship of Outcasts?" Contempt dripped off his words.

Marcus's expression did not shift an iota. "We have no captain. You'd like to know why I instructed as I did? Very well. Our supplies are low. Quintus and your sister are our best archers and we will need food to fortify the desert crossing. Octavia and I have access to horses which will permit us to move swiftly to scout the route ahead. You, Griffin, are still regaining your strength from weeks of beatings and hard labor, so I did you the kindness of gathering water. And I presume the Morph girl can take the form of a guard dog for our possessions and smell danger if it approaches. That was why I chose each person for their task. Simple logic."

"I am not staying with *her*," Griffin stated, crossing his arms like a child.

"I agree," Alexia declared, "Why are you in charge of 'duty allocation?'"

Quintus and Octavia looked at one another. "We can do as my people do," Octavia offered, "We can vote. Surely that's fair, right? All in favor of the duties as Marcus has suggested them, raise your hands." Marcus, Octavia, and Quintus raised their hands. Gwen looked at her brother, at Alexia, and at Quintus. He looked so very handsome in the morning light and the chance to fire arrows with him set Gwen's heart aflutter. She raised her thin white arm.

"That is four of six," Quintus observed, "We would say 'the motion carries in the Human world. Are you satisfied?"

Griffin looked sullen. Alexia was stony faced. "Will you all be mad if the guard dog eats an Elf boy?" she asked acidly.

"I've heard Elf doesn't taste so good," Octavia said, mounting her horse.

"It depends on the Elf," Alexia muttered, a half-smirk slowly emerging on her sun splashed face.

***

"Are Wizards always logical?" Octavia asked Marcus as they rode together.

"So I've heard," Marcus replied without tone, his eyes fixed straight ahead.

"Then wouldn't it have made more sense to have the Ranger scout our route? Given that this is what Rangers do better than anyone?"

"Maybe I thought the best duty allocation put Quintus with Gwendolyn."

"You are a romantic, Marcus," Octavia squealed in high pitched tones so foreign to her normal husky voice, "There is a soft Human heart in that chest, isn't there?"

"Don't be so sure."

"Why not?"

"I would not wish for you to be disappointed, Octavia," he explained wearily, "And trust me, you would be."

She bit her lip and spurred on her horse to keep pace. "And what is the logic behind putting the insufferable Elf and the bitter Morph together with our belongings? I can't see that working out well."

"I believe that the major weakness in our fellowship is their mutual distrust," Marcus said, "They need to learn to live with one another for all of our sakes."

"One of them might kill the other before the Golden One crests the sky," Octavia offered.

"That would also solve the problem."

"Logical," Octavia said as the wind tousled her red hair.

***

"You are the finest shot I have ever seen," Quintus marveled.

"I am? Thank you," she said sweetly. They had walked and talked for two hours without a moment of silence other than when the hunt demanded it. He was so easy to talk to that she found herself telling him everything she could about herself. Well, nearly everything, she mused… "You are a great shot, as well," Gwen said, "and quite good at so many other things."

"Like what?" he asked playfully.

"Saving pretty maidens from wicked Elves," she said, "For openers."

"From the moment I first set eyes upon you, I swore by the Golden One my people worship that I would not leave your presence until you were free," he said solemnly, looking directly into her eyes.

"Well you don't need to leave my presence, so that's all the better," she said, nodding, a blush infiltrating her impossibly white throat and face.

"I could not agree more, Gwendolyn," he said, holding up a hand so she stopped and fell silent. Perhaps there was another quarry to be shot. Instead, he brushed aside the tall grass and found a solitary blue flower. He expertly plucked it and handed it to her.

"For your golden hair," he explained, "To remind you that you are a free Elf, once more."

"I thank you, kindly, noble Quintus," she said, with a mock curtsy.

"This is the bluest flower in all the Four Realms," he explained, "As I am sure you know, it likes to hide behind tall grass and bloom unobserved."

"I feel the very same way about myself," she said, breaking into a slow smile.

"I chose it because as blue as it may be, it is nothing compared to your eyes," Quintus said, "which are the bluest things I have seen in the whole wide world."

She blushed again, but he could only see it creep down her neck and disappear. "What am I to do with you, Quintus Aureus?" she asked, playfully.

"You could kiss me once," he suggested.

"I owe you at least as much for my freedom," she whispered softly. She kissed him on his lips, lingering much longer than proper for an Elf maiden. She noticed that he kissed differently than Alexia. It was firmer and stronger. But it was just as lovely.

Quintus swore to himself and to his One that no matter what happened for the rest of his life, he would never be able to repay the debt he owed to Marcus for engineering this kiss with his illogical duty allocation.

***

"How delightful that you two did not kill each other," Gwen said, long after she and Quintus had returned. The strips of meat were drying in the sun. They had done well in procuring meat for the journey and had also found several healing herbs which might prove helpful. Gwen was amazed at the Elf-knowledge Quintus had. He had spotted the herbs before she had and could identify them as if he were an Elf himself. She found herself quite conflicted.

"If one of us were dead, who would you have missed more?" Alexia asked. Griffin screwed up his face.

"I am her brother," he said, "You are just some little bird on whom she took pity."

"Enough bickering," Quintus said, inspecting the water they had collected and nodding thoughtfully, "Where are Marcus and Octavia?"

"They have not returned," Alexia said, "Perhaps they are engaging in some *recreational* activities." She grinned

119

fiendishly, her emphasis making clear her meaning. "Now I know why the duties were allocated as they were."

"Who are you kidding, Morph?" Griffin asked "That girl is a brute. She's more man than he. If you're right, then I'll lay odds she has *him* pinned down somewhere, unable to use his hands to cast a spell to escape." They shared a laugh—it was an uneasy laugh to share as they still loathed one another, but it was a shared laugh nonetheless.

"You don't know Marcus," Quintus said, pondering the absurd scene for a moment but unwilling to let Griffin and Alexia see his amusement at it. "I find your theory highly unlikely, to say the least." Suddenly, he looked up in the sky. "The blessed sun is descending. This is not right."

"The sun ascends and descends each day, Quintus," Gwendolyn teased.

"Marcus and Octavia should be back," Quintus said, peering into the distance with purpose, "He wanted to leave by now. No more joking. This is not typical of him."

"You are worried?" Gwen asked. He nodded.

"Should I hunt for them?" Alexia asked, tossing off her dress and morphing into a fox. Quintus nodded and she scampered off.

"I cannot believe I have lived to see a Human worry about a Wizard," Griffin marveled, shaking his head in disbelief, "He's a *Wizard*, you fool. He does not need looking after. He shoots fireballs from his hands and all that."

"He does. But I repeat, you don't know Marcus," Quintus said, "He needs looking after just like any of us."

"Fine, but if Alexia finds the two of them together in the way she suggests, he's sure to be embarrassed," Griffin declared, "And then he'll be even more intolerable than usual." Quintus was about to give the surly Elf a stern lecture about the proper time for jokes, when a loud crack stunned them all into silence. Gwen instinctively moved closer to Quintus.

"What was that?" she asked.

"A thunderbolt," Quintus said, scanning the southern sky.

"There are no storm clouds," Griffin observed.

"Do you still think he's fooling around with a girl in the woods?" Quintus snapped as they tore towards the sound of the thunderbolt. Griffin shook his head soberly, clutching the spear as he prepared for whatever lay ahead which had provoked the magic.

Chapter 16: Temptations

Swift Gwendolyn was the first to emerge from the woods with Quintus and Griffin behind her, as quickly as they could keep up. The scene they saw was complex. Octavia and Marcus were standing back-to-back in the center of a full-blown attack. He was brandishing his glowing sword, she was clutching her battleaxe in both strong hands. Their horses were nowhere to be seen. The field was already strewn with naked corpses of dead Morphs and armor-clad corpses of dead Humans. A large number were severely scorched, likely from the Wizard's thunderbolt. Gwen noticed that Octavia's right leg was swathed with blood.

A circle of wolves had enclosed them and at least four large eagles hovered above. Two gigantic bears were each directly confronting the warrior-girl and the Wizard, as about a half dozen well-armored Humans were shouting out orders. Gwen saw a small red fox dart out from where it was hiding in the tall grass and morph in midair into a lioness. The lioness hit the ground running and surprised a wolf, tearing its throat out before moving on to the next. Gwen was shocked and exhilarated by Alexia's savagery.

"Gwen," Quintus shouted, "can you take care of the eagles?" She nodded and drew her bow. Griffin placed a hand on Quintus's shoulder.

"You and I should get the Humans before they see us," he said. Quintus nodded and they moved to where Alexia had opened the circle and began to assault the unsuspecting Humans. Quintus started with his bow and then moved to his sword, hacking and cleaving as if he were an Elf performing a ritual dance. Griffin plunged his spear into those parts where the armor was weakest, shocking the Humans as they fell. At one point, his spear became lodged in a victim and he could not get it out. A comrade raced at Griffin with a mace held high, but Griffin took a dagger from his victim's sheath and expertly threw it at the assailant, catching him flush in the throat. Blood burst like a fountain, he staggered, and lay down dead.

Well done, Quintus thought, as they turned to the remaining wolf Morphs.

The battle had turned, Octavia could see that. Her leg was warm with the blood and throbbing with pain, but she sunk her axe into the bear's chest with all her remaining might. The animal stopped, its jaw agape and then turned into a dark haired girl who crumpled naked to the ground. A fireball emerged from Marcus's left hand and blew up in the face of his bear. The animal recoiled and roared until Marcus's sword cut the roar short by slicing through its neck.

Gwen had needed five arrows to kill the four eagles, each dropping to the ground in mortal form with a sickening thud. She scanned the horizon for more eagles and saw a cloaked hulking figure on a small hill. She could not make out its race, for it was too far away for even her sharp Elvin eyes. But it was an enemy. She could feel that, so she released three shafts in quick succession. It was probably too far to hit her target, but there was only one way to really know for sure, she thought. Gwen squinted and believed she saw one arrow hit its mark, but she could not tell for certain. Either way, the figure withdrew down the other side of the hill—whether wounded or simply concerned by her arrows, she could not tell.

"What about the horses?" Quintus asked as he went body to body systematically to ensure no enemy still breathed.

"They were spooked by the bears," Octavia explained as she sat on a large rock, "They reared and threw us both, then bolted." Her leg bore the marks of bear claws.

"Should we track them?" Gwen asked.

"Can you speak to horses, Alexia?" Marcus asked. She had returned to her mortal form, dirty and covered with wolf blood, yet still radiantly attractive.

"Only if I could morph into a horse," she said, "But horses are too big for me."

"You fought well, Alexia," Quintus observed, "I did not expect you to fight so hard for beings you do not seem to care for."

"Morphs have no king, but we live in clans. A morph would live or die for its clan, as you can see," she gestured at

123

the field, "I have not had a clan since my expulsion. You are my clan now, Fellowship of the Outcasts. I will kill and die for you." Her brown eyes burned. "This does not mean I like you all, but you can count on me."

"Well said," Marcus nodded. He looked at Octavia's leg and surveyed the battlefield. "We'll just let the horses go. They would never have survived the desert crossing, anyway, so we would have had to cut them loose when we reached the edge of the desert."

"They will want to run free," Gwen said happily. Her countenance turned dark. "I saw someone on the hill over there. I may have hit him, but he got away."

"Human or Morph?" Griffin asked. He still delivered those words with a tone of contempt.

"I could not see," she explained, "He was cloaked and the hood was up."

"It could have been either," Alexia said, lifting her small nose in the direction Gwen had gestured. She sniffed and wrinkled up her nose. "I have never smelled that scent before on a Human or a Morph. It is foul. Are you sure you didn't kill it? Because it smells like death."

"There is only one way to find out," Octavia said, struggling to her feet.

"You need to get back to camp," Griffin said, "I assume the bear gashed you and if we don't apply the healing herbs soon, the wound will fester." Her deerskin pants had been shredded by the animal's blow and the blood was still flowing from the injury.

"You and Marcus take her back to the camp," Quintus said, "Alexia, Gwen, and I will crest that hill and try to track the one who got away. If he did get away..." They took off towards the hill, Alexia again as a fox.

"You cannot walk on that leg," Griffin said sternly.

"Will you be carrying me, Griffin?" Octavia asked with a chuckle. She was at least a head taller than the Elf and she didn't see his slender frame carrying much weight, even if she was not heavy.

Wordless, Marcus scooped Octavia up and slung her over his shoulders. He strode towards the camp without saying a thing. Octavia meant to resist but knew she shouldn't. The bear had hit her thigh with all its force and as the fiery blood of battle settled down in her veins, the pain was clearer. She was surprised the Wizard could lift her so easily. While Octavia was not an especially large framed girl and her figure was trim, she was tall and her muscles were dense. Plus, she was wearing armor. Yet the Wizard did not appear to strain at all. She'd never considered how strong he might be, but he clearly had had a hard life and this could strengthen a man or a woman beyond measure. As they arrived at the camp, Marcus muttered something under his breath and held out his hand towards her tent. Without warning, her bedroll flew out of its own accord and unrolled in front of them. Marcus set her down gently as Griffin hurried to get the herbs Quintus and Gwen had gathered.

Octavia rested her head on what passed for a pillow on her military-style bedroll. She bit back the pain from her leg and swallowed, looking up at the Wizard. "Thank you, Marcus," she said without a trace of her usual sarcasm. The Wizard appeared distracted. He motioned towards the woods and an owl flew towards him. It appeared that Marcus and the owl were conversing for a minute and then the owl flew off. Octavia had lost a lot of blood and was unsure if she were hallucinating the conversation. Marcus turned back towards Octavia and knelt down next to her, frowning as he looked at her leg.

"Listen to the Elf," Marcus replied, "He will fix your leg." Then, he got up and turned away, his dark cloak fluttering in the breeze. He put up the hood and began walking.

"Where are you going?" she asked.

"To examine the dead," he said, his eyes suddenly weary, "We need to know more about who attacked us."

"Hurry back," she said, adding, "You've cast a lot of spells. You'll need to rest."

Griffin returned, making a paste out of the herbs in a small bowl. Marcus just looked at Octavia for a moment before saying, "Don't ever worry about me; just let the Elf heal you."

He disappeared into the wood, his dark cloak trailing behind for an instant.

"Let me fix this," Griffin said. Octavia settled back and closed her eyes. He spread the paste on her thigh slowly and methodically. She wasn't an Elf, he thought as he worked on the wound. Her red hair was garish and the sprinkling of freckles on her nose was unnerving for one accustomed to the ivory unblemished flesh of Sunrise Elves. Yet even if she moved like a man, her eyes were the eyes of a woman; he noted this when he looked at the girlish eyelashes of the closed eyes. She had removed her breastplate and he could see her flat belly, as sheer as ice, and he could admire her breasts rising and falling as she breathed. Those breasts were far larger than any Elf girl's and they were alluring in their way. The deerskin pants had also been discarded and she was wearing only her short pants. As he spread the herb paste on her rock-hard thigh, he knew he was a few finger lengths away from an opportunity. A stirring in Griffin's loins was checked by the rules in his head. She was a Human—the only thing worse than a Human was a Morph. "So there is something worse..." he thought to himself. Of course, the mere thought of Morphs brought the image of Alexia's unclad body into his Elvin head. Octavia was the lesser of two evils. An Elf male was not permitted to mate with an Elf female unless they had had a joining ceremony, but such rules did not apply to coupling with a Human woman, did they? "Did they?" he thought. It might be permissible in a situation like this, so long as there were no other suitors who might be angry and could threaten him. What were the obstacles? Quintus was not an obstacle—his Human eyes were always on Griffin's sister. The Wizard? Griffin had joined Alexia's joke about the Wizard, but he did not think that Wizards were interested in such things as coupling with red haired Humans. Yet he needed to be certain before progressing.

"Are you and Marcus?" he asked. She opened her green eyes.

"Are we what?" she asked, as he massaged the healing paste into her leg. "Are we comrades? Yes. Are we friends? Absolutely."

"Are you more?"

"More? Like lovers?" she laughed hysterically and it was like pipe music to his ears, "No, most definitely not." She laughed a little more and closed her eyes again. "Will my leg be okay?"

"You are in good hands," Griffin explained, "I placed first in my Healing courses. It was my best subject." Any Elf girl would melt at this statement of unparalleled success, but Octavia did not seem particularly impressed.

"The bear got me pretty good," she said, her breathing slowing.

"You will be whole again," he said, softly and melodiously, he moved his hand from her wound further up her leg, "It is such a beautiful leg, so I am very pleased I can help heal it." His hand moved further up, finally slipping under her short pants and headed for its target.

Suddenly, pain ruled his world as he felt his wrist being crushed in a grip like the iron chains he once wore, "Let's not do that," Octavia said coolly. She released his wrist and sat up, the muscles of her abdomen tensing in an appealing fashion as she made the move.

"We can go as slowly and as gently as you like," he said, moving to stroke her hair, his voice nearly purring.

"Are you attempting to seduce me?" she asked, raising an eyebrow.

Griffin was not equipped to respond to that. No Elf girl would be so direct about being seduced. Octavia spoke like a man. Yet she was a woman. He was sure of that. "Would you be interested?" he asked, slipping one finger under the waist of her shorts, preparing to slide them off.

Her look was filled with anger and murder. His hand withdrew of its own accord without him even realizing it. He thought she was going to kill him, right there, and he was paralyzed with fear. That look was the most terrifying thing Griffin had ever seen. His only consolation is that the look softened as soon as his hand withdrew and then softened further as she erupted with laughter. Octavia laughed and laughed and laughed. It was not like the laugh she had tossed off earlier.

This one shook her body, her breasts bouncing along with her hair. She snorted as she tried to catch her breath. When she finally finished, she swallowed and said, "That's sweet and you seem like a nice little Elf-boy, but no." He blushed. "Wow, you have come a long way in a short time if you want to merge with a Human."

"I've never slept with a Human before," he said.

"Well, that's progress for your racial views, Griffin, but no, not this Human." There was a flicker of the terrifying look again, but it extinguished itself swiftly.

"Is it that you have no heart or does it belong to someone else?" he asked, trying to strike a light tone in the hopes that the dreadful and murderous look would not return. Octavia swallowed down all of the darkness that this encounter had awakened.

"I'm not sure," she said, forcing a false smile, "22 years I have walked this world and I am still working on the answer to that question." A thought popped into her head. "Your sister is a maiden. Are you a 'maiden', too? Is that was this was about?"

"By the Spirits, no!" he shouted, "Elf girls refrain from coupling until the joining ceremony, but boys are permitted by our clerics to visit the Low Elves and practice for our future wives."

"How nice of the Low Elves!" Octavia remarked acidly.

Griffin thought of the Low Elves and their white skin and black hair, light like the Sunrise Elves, dark like the Sunset Elves, a people apart. "They are paid," he explained.

"I'll bet your clerics visit them, too," Octavia said rebelliously.

"It is said that some do," Griffin shrugged, "But the holy writings permit it. The Low Elves exist for such things."

"Seems unfair Gwen has to be a virgin while the boys get to go play with whores," Octavia observed.

"It is our way. It is fair in its own fashion," Griffin said. He summoned what was left of his courage, "Will you embarrass me in front of the others, Octavia? For trying?"

"No, we can keep it between us," she said with a warm smile, "I am grateful for the healing, as well as the compliment about my leg." She winked.

"You should rest for a while," he said. She closed her eyes and he made sure she was asleep before throwing his arms around an oak tree and falling to his knees. He wept for forgiveness from the Spirits. How could he have considered using his body to bridge the chasm between Humans and Elves in such an intimate way? Low Elves were inferior but they were *Elves*. A Human? From the North? Who fought as if she had man parts? Who had laughed at him? He loathed himself, even as the pressure in his loins persisted.

A lovely cardinal perched on the oak's lowest branch as if an answer to his prayers from the Spirits. The beautiful bird was a sign that he was forgiven his lapse. How incredible was their mercy for an Elf such as him! The cardinal fluttered to the ground and morphed into Alexia.

"Why are *you* crying?" she asked, "Didn't Octavia get hurt?"

He just stared at her blankly, beginning with her dark eyes and then—as if against his will—moving his gaze lower. His Elvin eyes toured her mortal form in all its splendor. She had cleaned off the blood and dirt and stood radiantly and defiantly nude. Alexia was no answer to a prayer, this savage beast-girl. She did seem to be an answer, however.

"When you have finished memorizing my body for your filthy Elf thoughts, we need to talk," she said, bored.

"I wasn't…"

She covered the space between them in a blink and pressed a tan finger to his pale lips. There was no realistic chance she would push it further, but she liked that the righteous Elf desired her. It was intoxicating to be desired even by those who were repulsive. Griffin was not repulsive, in fact he was quite handsome. But even a Morph knew there were times to resist the impulse. Morphs had a well-deserved reputation for living in the moment and eschewing the consequences of their actions. But there were times that they could foresee how an act might disrupt the future. Morphs did not like restraint but they were capable when a situation dictated it. Or a person dictated it. Gwendolyn. Alexia enjoyed sleeping with males and females alike, Humans, Morphs, and Elves, too. She'd never been with a Wizard but hadn't given up hope of seducing Marcus if the opportunity was right. Still, she loved Gwen. That love did not preclude her from merging with other beings as she merged with Gwen, but it did preclude her from sleeping with Gwen's brother. This was love. This was restraint. Still, the way the pale blond Elf looked at her with such hunger covered her body with gooseflesh. It was glorious, but it was not to be.

She removed her finger from his lips and put on her dress, breaking the spell. "You should know that your sister definitely hit something with her arrow," Alexia said.

Griffin shook his head to clear it, "I keep telling everyone she is the best shot in the Four Realms." He stared at the dress, clinging to the curves of her body.

"Whatever she hit, it bled," Alexia said.

"Did it die?"

"No, it escaped," Alexia said, "But its blood was black." Griffin paled, at least as much as a Sunrise Elf could. Suddenly, the thought of an illicit embrace with Alexia fell out of his head, at least for the time being.

Chapter 17: Gratitude

"You know a lot more about the world than I do," Gwen said to Alexia as they embraced in her tent. The walls were flimsy fabric supported by wooden lattice, but they seemed like impenetrable stone whenever they were together behind them. "What creature bleeds black?"

"I have no idea," Alexia replied, "I never seen, smelled, or *been* an animal which bled anything but red."

"Even the Wizard didn't know," Gwen observed.

"Wizards don't know about everything."

"That's true," Gwen agreed. She smiled at Alexia.

"Let us think of other topics which don't involve Wizards or blood," Alexia suggested with a sparkle in her eyes.

"Like what?" Gwen squealed girlishly.

"Like how white your skin is," Alexia said, tracing her finger from Gwen's lips down her throat. Gwen shivered. "I have never seen anything as white as your skin, my darling Elf girl."

"It's just normal Sunrise Elf flesh," Gwen said, her breathing increasing, "Besides, Octavia's skin is very white, too."

"Not this white," Alexia whispered, pressing her lips against the side of Gwendolyn's neck. "Nothing in all the Four Realms is this white." She continued kissing, tracing the contours of Gwen's body so that her stomach tightened.

"There are pale Morphs," Gwen spit out in between short breaths.

"Morphs come in all kinds of colors," Alexia said, "But none like this. It is like kissing snow, but much much warmer…" Alexia kissed her with passion that Gwen had never dreamt possible and she found herself more unable to speak with each successive kiss.

***

"Marcus, try it again," Synthyya instructed him.

Marcus concentrated on the soft brown mud, spoke the ancient words with perfect inflection, and moved his right hand upward with his palm upturned. For a moment, he felt he had succeeded because the earth rose up around her ankles. Then it sunk down into the ground with a gurgle and a hiss. Marcus exhaled and fell on his side, exhausted. "It is no use," he muttered to the Wizard woman.

"It is of use," Synthyya stated firmly but kindly. Her brown hair—streaked with gray—fell about her shoulders with a fancy hat perched on the top of her head, as was her custom. "You will master it, despite your blood."

"Give him a respite, Synthyya," Dariuxx, a rotund Wizard, clad all in black advised, shaking his shaggy beard. "Earth magic is hard for him."

"All magic is hard for him," agreed the third Wizard, Zarqqwell, a tall thin man with darker skin and a trim beard which had gone entirely white. "His Humanity is an obstacle we cannot ignore. He knows that he has challenges which typical students do not." The others looked at him knowingly and all three teachers nodded in silent agreement—whether to the spoken statement or something else, they kept to themselves.

"I can overcome it," Marcus said, struggling to his feet.

"And you have," nodded Dariuxx, the large Wizard in black, his unkempt brown beard bobbing up and down.

"We have all been impressed with your work," Synthyya, the lone female Wizard amongst them, agreed. "You are a marvelous student. But Zarqqwell is correct: you must work harder than any Wizard."

"I do," Marcus said, "I have. Always."

"We know," said Zarqqwell, a frown creasing his trim white beard. He softly placed a thin hand on the boy's shoulder. "But you can never stop. The world will not let you. Not this world. Not these times." He exhaled loudly.

"It is so," Synthyya agreed. "Thus, we try again, Marcus. This time, turn the wrist more sharply. We will get it right." The other two Wizards nodded solemnly in agreement. Marcus drew a deep breath.

***

"Marcus," Griffin shook him, "It is time. Were you dreaming?"

"It was like dreaming," Marcus said as he opened his eyes, "But different."

"You were shouting out names," Octavia said, "Weird names, Zarqqwell and Dariuxx and Synthyya."

"Was I?" Marcus asked, as Quintus handed him a cup of the Elvin hot morning beverage. He knew it was the last of the Dark Elves' store. Just as well. "Zarqqwell, Synthyya, and Dariuxx are not weird names. They are Wizard names."

"Your name sounds so normal," Octavia said.

"That is because he has a Human name," Quintus explained.

"The only request of my mother, or so I was told," Marcus explained with sad eyes. "The three Wizard names are the names of my teachers. They are the ones we seek on the island."

"The exiled Wizards?" Griffin asked.

"Yes," said Marcus, "I have traveled this way before and sometimes such events trigger a Wizard to see the past as clear as if it were the present."

"Can you see the future, too?" Griffin asked.

"Wizards cannot do that. That's a myth," Marcus said, "Although occasionally, it is a useful myth."

"Are your teachers old?" Octavia asked.

"Not for Wizards," Marcus explained, "Wizards live for one hundred, even one hundred twenty Human years, usually. Zarqqwell is in his 90s, Dariuxx and Synthyya their 80s, although we measure time in a slightly different way than you do."

"80s and 90s? Sounds old to me," Octavia observed.

"That's because Humans rarely reach their 70s," Quintus said, "Only Elves live longer than Wizards."

"We can live until 150 or more," Griffin said proudly, "A gift of the Spirits."

"Well, your sister may be 150 before she exits that tent," Marcus observed tartly, "Can someone tell Gwen and Alexia that even the Wizard has awakened?"

Their tent flap opened and Alexia strode out with a huge smile, unclad as always, and stretched out her arms to the sky. Griffin dropped his cup at the sight. Gwen followed her, totally clothed, but equally euphoric. "Sorry," Gwen said.

"Let's go," Quintus said, "We could reach the edge of the desert by this afternoon if I have chosen the path correctly. But I warn you, I have never spent much time in this part of the Four Realms." To Octavia, Marcus looked haunted by the news that the desert loomed near, even though it had been all he'd spoken of for weeks. As the group moved, Marcus lingered towards the rear, an odd place given that the Wizard usually walked towards the front. He seemed in his own world, or more so than usual.

"It's just a desert," Octavia said to Quintus, "We've crossed the known world from one mountain range to another. Why does he seem *scared* of one desert?"

Quintus looked back at Marcus, who did not even seem to notice he'd become the topic of conversation. "It is not just a desert," Quintus explained in hushed tones. The Elves and Morph had heard him with their sharp ears and quickened their pace to hear. Marcus continued his slow, distracted advance from the rear. "It is was not always a desert. It became a desert when spells were cast to curse it. It's a desert of no magic."

"The magic is strong here," Marcus observed, swallowing hard. It was unclear if he had heard them or simply was announcing this.

"What does that mean?" Octavia asked.

"It used to be a meadow and the island was once surrounded by an ordinary sea enclosed by land sometimes called the Horns of the West. But at some point the Wizards cursed the water and the land. The water looks normal, but if any of us touch the Burning Sea, it will consume us like fire— quite simple. The desert will be unpleasant for us, nothing more. But not for Marcus. It will drain him and eventually kill him if he does not make it through in time. And no magic or enchanted object works in the Desert of Despair," Quintus explained, "It is the only way to reach the Burning Sea. Once we cross into the desert, Marcus will have no magical ability. His sword and cloak will be ordinary and he will cast no spells."

"I could see why he's depressed," Alexia said, wondering if this desert would prevent her from morphing. "What about me?" she asked.

"You'll be fine," Quintus assured her, "Its curse only affects Wizards. But it's worse than losing his magic. From the second he steps across the threshold, the desert will rapidly suck all strength from him. He will want to fall asleep, but we cannot let him. He will die a little bit, every hour that he is in that place."

"Wake the Wizard? Easier said than done," Griffin smirked.

"This is no joke," Quintus said in sober tones, "If Marcus falls asleep, even for a moment, he will never wake up. The desert was created to kill any Wizard which tried to cross it."

"You know a lot about it," Octavia observed. Quintus nodded wordlessly.

"No wonder the exiled Wizards stayed exiled," Gwen said.

"Some say the desert was created to prevent prisoners from escaping," Marcus noted, catching up with his comrades, "Others say it was to prevent anyone from reaching them. Perhaps, it serves both purposes."

"Other than the exiles who are imprisoned there, only one Wizard in recorded history has ever crossed the desert and lived," Quintus said softly.

"How many crossed unsuccessfully?" asked Alexia.

"Many…" Marcus replied, his voice cracking.

Octavia's eyes misted, even though she tried to suppress it. "Only *one* other Wizard survived the crossing?"

"That Wizard crossed it twice," Marcus explained, "Although he was a much younger Wizard when he did." A faint smile seemed to crease his features. Quintus put a burly arm around Marcus's shoulders.

"You?" Gwendolyn asked. Marcus nodded. The desert had come into view. The sand started abruptly, as all vegetation stopped. It looked ordinary. But the Wizard froze in his tracks.

"How long a trip is it to the Burning Sea?" Griffin asked.

"Two days," Marcus said, "Maybe more if we get lost. Once you go deep enough in the desert, it is hard to tell East from West and North from South. We want to go Southwest."

"Shall we get started?" Alexia asked.

"Wait," Marcus said, opening the pouch threaded on his fraying rope belt. "We should be clear about something before we enter. In case I do not survive, you all must continue the quest."

"Marcus!" admonished Quintus.

The Wizard's eyes seemed to catch fire, "Quintus! We must prepare for the possibility. I will tell you all that I know, right now, just in case..." his voice trailed off and he inhaled deeply before resuming, "It may sound preposterous, but I believe the Dark Lord is not a fairy tale. He is real. I know little more than that about him. But he is real and he caused the fall of Classical Civilization a thousand or more years ago. For some reason, he has not been seen for centuries—or at least there has been no evidence of him. But in the last few years, I have seen signs. I know that the heartless corpses and the black blood are signs. There are others, too. I cannot put it together, but I think the Dark Lord is part of a true story. He is behind the blood, the corpses, and the coldness I felt in the earth when we were in the Dragon's Teeth. Synthyya, Zarqqwell, and Dariuxx taught me all I know. We must ask them what to do because if the Dark Lord is alive and well, he poses a threat to our world, just as he destroyed the ancient world."

"The Dark Lord. The villain of children's tales? Real? Are you sure?" Gwen asked, squinting in the sunlight, while the orange orb began its descent.

"No," Marcus admitted, "But I am sure that I need to consult my teachers and follow their counsel. Quintus, you will need this if things do not go my way in there..." He gave Quintus a beautiful gem-encrusted ring.

"I have never seen this before," Quintus marveled.

"Even friends have secrets," Marcus said, "This ring is enchanted. It will be a useless pretty bauble in the desert, but when we emerge, it will summon a magical boat. Simply put the ring on and say '*Venite*.' The boat will come. It is the only way to cross the Burning Sea."

"I have no magical powers," Quintus protested, "I am just a man."

"All the magic is in the ring," Marcus said, "If I do not survive my third crossing, you must summon the boat and tell the Wizards what I have told you." He grabbed Quintus by the shoulders. "They will know what to do."

Quintus held Marcus's stare for a moment and clenched his jaw, "I'll hold on to it," Quintus said, "But *you* will summon the boat, Marcus. There is no other possibility." Marcus nodded mournfully, but his assent to the statement was withheld and both men knew that.

"If it is all right with the Fellowship, I would like to rest one last time," Marcus said, "We can enter tomorrow when the sun rises."

***

Marcus sat alone in his tent, studying its construction to distract himself. He'd spent innumerable evenings in a tent like this and still he marveled at the Humans' ingenuity. It was a simple tent with a light wood lattice circle which could be folded up, a center pole topped by a circle of iron, a few rods that connected and a heavy fabric draped over it. He could set it up or take it down swiftly and the collapsible center pole and foldable lattice made it simple for a man or a beast to carry. Yet despite its portability and convenience, the tent was comfortable and relatively spacious. Humans were often unwise, but they were undeniably clever, Marcus mused. As he pondered the strengths of Humans, one interrupted his reverie. "May I enter?" Octavia asked, pushing aside the flap of Marcus's tent.

"Of course," he said.

"How are you?" she asked, biting her lip, which was starting to deflate.

"The last time I was in this very place was the last time I saw my father."

"When you were sent to the exiled Wizards?" she asked. He nodded, closing his eyes.

"I have never been sure if he sent me across the desert and the Burning Sea to save my life or eliminate his embarrassment. He did not make it clear," Marcus explained, "When the Empress ascended the throne, war was declared on Humans. I was the Wizard with the Human name from his Human mother. Much tragedy ensued for me. Much tragedy." He winced and paused for several uncomfortable moments. "Perhaps my father wanted me to live or perhaps he wanted me to conveniently disappear. Or die quietly. I cannot be sure, but I have always had my suspicions. No matter, he took me to the edge of the desert and wished me luck in the crossing..." His voice trailed off into a whisper. There was another long pause. "The day is a fog in my mind. I have few other memories of that day and the ones I have are ones I wish were fogged out."

"Marcus," Octavia began, "I have known you for weeks, but it feels like it has been years."

"I feel the same way, Octavia."

"If you don't survive the crossing..."

"You will continue the mission," he said. She looked so sad and the Humanity within him stirred ever so slightly. "When Wizards part, they do not say 'goodbye' as in the common tongue. Our word is '*vale*' which means 'be strong.' You will be strong if I perish," Marcus said calmly, the calm doubtlessly from his Wizard side. His features softened, as his Human side seemed to emerge. "And if I do perish, Octavia, you should know that I have been so very grateful to acquire your friendship."

She bit her lip, again, "What do Wizards believe happens if you...perish, Marcus?" Her deep voice took on a mildness heretofore unheard.

"Wizards believe there is nothing on the other side of the pyre," Marcus explained sadly, "For most, this life is all we have and when we die and are consumed by the flames, there is no existence at all."

"That cannot be," she insisted, "You said 'most...' What did you mean?"

"A select few Wizards are chosen to walk with our gods for all eternity," he responded, "At least, it is said." He shrugged skeptically. Her green eyes widened and seemed almost to glisten with tears for a moment before drying again and taking on a characteristic hardness.

"But which Wizards walk with the gods?" she asked, her voice flecked with iron as if she were calling into question the beliefs of all Wizardkind.

He met her iron with a twinkling smile. "No one knows," he said, "And Wizards do not like *those* words. Some say achievement in this life permits you to live on with the gods, others insist it is piety and devotion to one of the gods who will grant you this favor, still others favor the belief that the gods save those who use their powers to improve the world."

"I think the last," Octavia insisted with an almost comical finality.

"Perhaps," he allowed as his smile wavered, "But those who espoused that belief also believed that killing the half-Human Wizard with the strange name would improve the world and save them from annihilation. So I think it best to avoid accepting any of the beliefs uncritically."

"I meant the real meaning, not the meaning of the small-minded," she declared, smiling involuntarily as if affected by some charm of his smile, "How many lives in the world must one improve to avoid the nothingness?"

"Maybe one," he chuckled, "If so, perhaps there is hope for me."

"There is not a lot of hope in the world of Wizards," she observed. Octavia had meant to add that he had improved her life, but a lump in her throat seemed to block the sentence.

He nodded. "Wizards are known for many things, Octavia. Hope is not among them. That is yet another way that I do not conform." He shrugged.

"I, for one, believe you will live, despite this desert's curse," she said, "But when you die, your gods will invite you to walk with them."

"Is that so?" he asked, raising an eyebrow.

"I know things about Wizard gods," she teased, hoping to lift the darkness of this moment. It worked. He smiled again.

He placed his hand on hers, "I hope that I live through this ordeal. And if I must die and I do end up walking with my gods, I shall bore their holy ears off speaking for all eternity of you and Quintus and how much I have treasured my time in this world with you both."

"Your gods will be very angry that you wasted precious and rare Wizard love on mere Humans," Octavia forced a smile.

"Maybe, maybe not," he said with a shrug, "But I'd rather not know so soon. Let's presume I will survive and we can add more time to our friendship."

"You have a deal, Wizard," Octavia said. She slipped her hand from beneath his and offered to shake as Humans of equal status do. It was a supremely awkward gesture, she knew. Totally inappropriate to the situation, but the only gesture she could manage. As he shook her hand, he held it for a lingering moment. She believed that she could feel the forces within him and when he released it, the world felt perceptibly darker. Octavia walked out, pausing at the entrance to turn back. "Marcus?" she said.

"Yes."

She held his gaze for a moment and tried to choose the words from the ones swimming around her head. She chose the ones which best summed up how she truly felt and she inhaled. Then, the words died on her lips. "Be strong," was all that escaped.

"I shall," he said, nodding gravely.

Chapter 18: The Desert of Despair

It didn't look any different from a normal desert. Alexia could not sense any wicked magic or curses or evil of any sort. The sand was coarse, there was no vegetation—no trees, no bushes, no grass. It was a desert. The landscape was empty and featureless, but there were no malevolent clouds looming overhead or fierce creatures lurking in plain view. In fact, there were no creatures of any sort. It had taken her the first two hours to figure out what form she should take. She'd heard of humped horses in the deserts of the world, but she couldn't morph into an animal she'd never seen and normal horses were too big anyway, so humped ones would probably be too big as well. She'd tried at least six different forms before settling on a jackrabbit. It seemed odd to be such a fast creature when the group wasn't moving very quickly, held back by the Wizard, who was walking much slower than usual. The desert was fairly unremarkable to Alexia. The wind seemed more biting when it came and it certainly hurled particles into one's eyes and mouth—regardless of form. But otherwise, the only thing odd about this desert was the way it abruptly began, as if an invisible line divided the desert from the normal land of the valley. Grass, grass, sand. Just like that. The only other noteworthy thing was the effect on the Wizard. While Alexia could morph at will with no impediment, the Wizard had cast no spell since crossing the threshold. The heat drained everyone, but it seemed to drain him ten-fold. He walked more laboriously, did not speak at all except with effort, and even his breathing appeared to slow.

"Why don't you let me help you with that," Gwen said to Marcus, pointing at his cloak, which he'd removed and draped over one shoulder.

"It is heavy," he said, breathless. "You are slight."

"It is heavier for you because of the enchantment of this place," Gwen said, "I would be honored to carry it for you until nightfall. You may then have it back, for I hear deserts get very cold in the evenings."

"They do," he said, hesitating and then handing it over. It was heavy, but Gwen knew it was easier for her than for him, so she bore it without betraying a hint of strain. He mouthed "thank you" although the sound did not come out. The others were far ahead, but Gwen matched her stride to his, so that Marcus was not alone.

"I admire you," she said sweetly.

"Why is that?" he forced a smile.

"You saved me."

"Hardly. Quintus saved you," he said.

"He did," she agreed, bobbing her blonde head up and down, "But we both know he had a reason to try and save me. So did my brother. So did Alexia."

"They all love you," Marcus said, "In different ways." His knowing look seemed to indicate to Gwen that he was aware of her ways with the Morph. However, the softness in his eyes seemed to say that he did not intend to tell or to judge. Perhaps she was reading too much into his strained tones and dulling eyes. Perhaps she read what she wanted to read in the face of a Wizard. Many confused thoughts crowded her head and Gwen shook it in a vain attempt to sort them.

"That is my point, Marcus," she explained, "They had reasons to stand between me and the awful intentions of Thorbad. You had no such reason."

"You praise me too much, fair Elf-girl, I did not want to get involved," he protested, stopping a moment to catch his breath.

"That's what was brave," she said, threading her arm through his and helping him forward until he caught his breath. "You stood up for me when you had no reason to. You are not my brother or in love with me, nor were you..." she paused to choose the words, "a friend of any sort. You did not want to get involved and yet you did."

"I did," he nodded. His voice sounded like an echo.

"I am happy that you did, Marcus."

"I am too, Gwen," he whispered in a ragged voice that did not seem his own except as a pale shadow of itself.

Her bright blue eyes sparkled in the sunlight. "And I know part of you may have gotten involved because it was just and all of that," Gwendolyn allowed, "But I also know that you saw that Quintus would die. And you probably thought Octavia would stand with him and that she would die, too. And you got involved because you love them." He raised an eyebrow and nodded.

"I do," Marcus admitted.

She smiled a charming Elvin grin. "Don't you see how it all works, wise Wizard? Quintus loves me, you and Octavia love Quintus, you love Octavia, she and Quintus love you, Griffin and Alexia love me and I love you all. We were a fellowship before we spoke the words." Her smile was as pure as a child's.

"You are the wise one," Marcus said, "And yet your age is so tender."

"I am wiser than I was a few weeks ago," she explained in a serious tone, "And I tell you all of this because the fellowship's love of you will get you through this ordeal."

"It has been seventeen of your sun cycles since I've walked on these sands. I was much younger when I last crossed this accursed desert." He coughed for some time and grabbed his knees, unsteadily wavering as if he might topple over. "I am no longer young," he croaked, "and the magic here is so potent."

"You are so much more loved than you were seventeen sun cycles ago," she said, staring into his eyes with her own small pools of light blue. "Do not despair." He looked at her, marveling at this special Elf.

***

Griffin looked back at his sister and the Wizard. They were lagging, but not too badly. She was carrying his cloak for him. That girl never ceased to surprise, did she? At least she was keeping company with a Wizard. Griffin was not overly fond of Wizards but they *were* allies with Elfkind. It was better than her kissing the Human. *Or a Morph!* He knew about

Morphs and their ways. Gwen and Alexia were the only two who shared a tent and unspeakable thoughts had crossed his mind. He gritted his teeth and tried to distract himself as a gust blew rough sand into his face.

"Quintus, you don't believe the Wizard about the Dark Lord and all that, do you?" Griffin asked. When Quintus did not answer immediately, Griffin went on, "The Dark Lord is a story told to young ones—like stories of goblins." Alexia morphed into mortal form to join the conversation. A conversation to which she was not invited, Griffin noted, trying vainly not to look at her unclad body.

"Or trolls," she added.

"Or dragons," Griffin replied.

"Or trolls riding dragons," she chuckled.

Quintus looked at them severely. "Will I spend my days worrying about a Dark Lord destroying the world? I will not," he said, biting off each word, "But I would believe Marcus if he told me the sky was green and the grass was blue."

The Morph snorted in derision, "Yes, a wicked Dark Lord is scampering about collecting hearts for himself," Alexia said with a smile, "Seems like some awful bedtime story told by an unhinged uncle to his gullible nephew."

"Right," Griffin said, "Don't stay up late or the Dark One will get you! Octavia, what do you think?"

She did not break stride, her winged helmet and breastplate gleaming in the unfiltered sun. "I just want to get through this horrible place with our Fellowship intact," she said in booming tones which only seemed to deepen her already too-deep voice. Griffin walked more briskly to try and keep up with her long strides.

"Right, but you don't seriously believe…" His question was interrupted by a loud *thwump*, followed by several more. Arrow shafts began falling all around them.

Instinctively, Quintus looked for cover. There was none. They were as naked as the Morph in this desert. He and Griffin held their shields aloft as they tried to discern the direction of the arrows. "We are under attack," he said, as if no one had noticed.

Alexia morphed into a tiny hummingbird and flew off. "Alexia?" Octavia called.

"Typical Morph," Griffin observed bitterly, "Just like the stories."

"Fall back to Gwen and Marcus," Quintus shouted as the arrows kept falling. One stuck in his shield. "We have to protect Marcus. He can't take a hit in this place."

Gwen had already dropped Marcus's cloak and whipped out her bow, firing at the direction of the attack. She saw no one, as the wind was blowing sand in her eyes, but she knew the direction the arrows were traveling and was sure that a few going towards that direction might hit their mark. She was livid that the wind was knocking them down, costing her some distance. Marcus had drawn his sword but it was a dull gray instead of glowing orange and it seemed a struggle just for him to hold it aloft. Quintus thrust his shield to Octavia.

"Protect Marcus," he insisted, as he pulled back his bow to try to match Gwen. Octavia dutifully stood in front of the Wizard, using Quintus's shield to keep him safe. Defense was not her favorite part of the battle, but Quintus was right about Marcus. This place was killing him every moment that went by. Griffin joined Octavia and attempted to use his shield to help protect Gwen because she was so vulnerable for that moment when she pulled back the tense bow. But she did not notice him. She was in that special place where her entire world was "load, pull, aim, release." Yes, she was a woman and the bow was not her proper instrument, but Griffin marveled at her artistry with it. The Spirits had not placed such skill in a female's body for no reason. He was certain of that.

As suddenly as the attack had begun, it ceased. The fellowship waited a few tense moments before allowing themselves to believe it was over. Quintus looked around. Octavia and Griffin had each caught three shafts in their shields, but no one else looked hit. Marcus looked pale and drawn, but there was no evidence he had taken an arrow. There was a buzzing sound and all looked up at it, Quintus and Gwen with their bows pulled back. But her Elvin eyes were sharper and she identified the object first. "Don't shoot, Quintus," she said,

"It's a hummingbird." The bird hovered and then morphed into Alexia.

"Thanks for all of your help," Griffin shouted sarcastically.

"You are very welcome, Elf-boy," she purred. "There were five of them. But Gwen hit one, so I only deserve credit for killing four."

"You killed them?" Octavia asked.

"Yes, they did not think a hummingbird was much of a threat," she shrugged, "A puma is another story."

"What in the Four Realms is a puma?" asked Quintus.

She morphed into one and then back. "It's like a lion, but I think they may live in deserts. I saw one near a desert once. Anyway, our foes did not have a chance."

"Who are 'our foes'?" Marcus asked weakly. Octavia helped him to his feet.

"They look like Elves," Alexia said, "Come and see them."

"Elves?" Marcus asked, "In the Desert of Despair?"

"The 'Desert of Despair?'" Octavia guffawed.

"That is what Wizards call it," Quintus explained.

"Seems awfully dramatic for Wizards," she snickered.

"Few things make Wizards dramatic," Quintus offered, holding up a hand to signal to Marcus that he need not speak, "The wicked magic of this desert is one of the few things which qualifies. Why would Elves be here? That's very strange. Almost as strange as seeing Octavia wield a shield."

"Shields are for sissies," she said, pausing as if thinking it over, "Although occasionally useful in the right situation."

"I can't believe Gwen hit anything with that wind in our face," Quintus marveled. Gwen blushed and smiled sweetly. Her smile suddenly disappeared when they reached their assailants.

"They are Low Elves!" Griffin and Gwen exclaimed at the same time.

"Low Elves?" Quintus asked, "Here in the Desert of Despair? Alone? *Attacking?*"

"It is unheard of," Griffin said, staring at the bodies.

"There has never been a recorded instance of Low Elves using violence on anyone," Marcus said, sitting on the ground. He looked drained of all life.

"The Low Elves have been oppressed forever," Octavia observed, "They don't even rise up against the Sunrise and Sunset Elves. Why would they attack us?"

"They're not really oppressed," Gwen said, "They simply do the work that is assigned to them." Quintus began examining the bodies.

"So they enjoy being whores and whatever other jobs you leave for them?" Octavia asked.

"They clean streets, dispose of our dead, work iron," Griffin explained.

"Sounds like slaves," Alexia shrugged.

"My father was an iron worker," Octavia raged, "Humans consider him an artisan." She narrowed her eyes and it was terrifying to behold. Griffin shivered involuntarily.

"They are not slaves," Gwen insisted, "They are paid for their work."

"How do you know these are Low Elves?" Alexia asked.

"They have light skin as the Sunrise Elves, but dark hair like the Sunset Elves," Gwen explained.

"Sounds to me like they are the offspring of the two," Octavia said, "Is that why they find themselves in these jobs?"

"No, no, no," Griffin protested, "Sunrise and Sunset Elves can intermarry as they wish. It is not typical, but there is no law forbidding it. Our grandfather was a Sunset Elf."

"Don't the babies come out like this?" Alexia asked.

"No, Elves always resemble their mother's skin and hair. If a Sunset Elf-boy marries a Sunrise Elf-girl, the children will have fair skin and blond hair. The Low Elves are different," Gwen said.

"They cannot intermarry," Quintus said, looking up. "And generally they do not seem unhappy, at least when I was briefly in the Elf world. Nor do they wield weapons. Ever." Gwen and Griffin readily agreed. "So why would they be here, firing bows at us in the cursed Desert of Despair?"

"You don't know?" Alexia asked.

"Of course not," Quintus replied, standing up. "Isn't it obvious?"

"Isn't what obvious?" Griffin asked.

"The smell?" Alexia asked.

All sniffed. "I smell nothing," Octavia said, "Other than sand and sweat."

Alexia shook her head. "They have the foul smell on them that I smelled at the last ambush," she explained, "The smell from the one who Gwen hit but he got away?"

"The one who bled black," Marcus said, as Quintus helped him to his feet. It was as if all the color in his voice had been washed out.

"Yes," Alexia said nodding. She pointed at the dead Low Elves. "It's not as strong, but it's there. I don't believe you can't smell it."

"What does it mean?" asked Gwen, shivering despite the heat.

"It means we must get moving," Marcus said, his voice a hoarse whisper.

Chapter 19: The Burning Sea

Day was bad, night was worse. Octavia preferred the cold to the heat, but not by much. She was accustomed to bone-chilling cold, for she was a woman of the North, where one became acclimated to frigid temperatures before being weaned. Yet the desert's cold had a hollowness to it which made it entirely different from the cold of the North. In addition to the hollow cold, Octavia could not make peace with the ragged winds whipping up the sand, which attacked her exposed flesh like a million biting insects. The fellowship had no chance to light a fire with such winds and they knew the Wizard would not be able to start one with his fire magic. Of course, there was no wood, even if they could create a spark. All they could do was huddle under blankets and hope for the first faintly warm rays of morning before the heat became oppressive and they yearned for the cold. Octavia had drawn second watch, her least favorite. First watch meant simply delaying her sleep, third and fourth gave her enough time to get some rest in before waking. But second watch meant two hours of sleep followed by two hours of watch. She'd barely had enough time to fall into sleep when she was awoken by Alexia. When second watch was over, she'd never been able to fall asleep and then it would be morning and she'd be tired. Still, at least she'd be able to grab a few hours of rest if not actual sleep. It was more than she could say for miserable Marcus.

Quintus had made it clear: not only did the person on watch duty have to look for more Low Elves or other threats—he or she had to keep Marcus awake. Octavia shuddered to think what Alexia might have tried to accomplish this feat. She laughed to herself. The Wizard was too tired to even show any attention to the alluring Morph and that must have simply deflated her. She slunk back into the tent she shared with Gwen with a pout on her face. Octavia had some theories on what happened in that tent, but the only person with whom she wanted to discuss those theories was Marcus and it would be a pity to tell him when he couldn't make a witty reply. Wit was far from him now, as she strode over to where he was sitting.

***

"Take my hand, son," Zarqqwell said.

"I should have anticipated it," Marcus snarled.

"No," the teacher shook his head, a slow smile piercing the craggy dark features, "You were more powerful than I expected. More powerful than you expected, as well. This is good." Zarqqwell's dark skin was offset by his neat white beard. His eyes were a dark purple as he looked at Marcus. Marcus liked that he called him "son."

"I thought it would simply come when I cast the spell," Marcus said, "I did not expect it to come that fast."

"The wind is as fast as it wants to be," Zarqqwell explained, "Air magic can be tricky because you cannot see it or feel it like water or earth or fire or light."

"The rock did come to me when I summoned it on the air, *magister*," Marcus said, rubbing his forehead, "It just came too quickly." The Wizard word for "master" and "teacher" was one and the same, which you probably do not find surprising.

"You will learn to master it," Dariuxx said loudly with an enormous grin, his hands resting on his ponderous belly, as he joined the teacher and student. "I, for one, believe you could master all five of the elements." Zarqqwell gave his colleague a piercing look and Dariuxx hung his head as if there were an unspoken agreement between them which he had breached.

"You give me too much credit, *magister*," Marcus said, "No one masters all five, not even you. Even one element is hard for me as a half-Wizard."

"Magic is hard for everyone, *discipulus*," Dariuxx replied with a furtive glance towards Zarqqwell, "Don't fool yourself into thinking it is easy for pure Wizards. Magic is work, but you work like no Wizard I have ever seen. You have talents and we believe in you. You are a fine student."

"Your knowledge of Classical Civilization makes us proud," Zarqqwell said.

"You will do great things," Dariuxx agreed. "Let us find Synthyya and have lunch." He smiled through his tangled beard.

"Synthyya...."

***

She shook him by the shoulders as violently as she dared. "Marcus! Marcus!"

"Synthyya..."

"Wake up this instant or I swear to the Golden One, I will..." Octavia shouted, a trace of worry coloring her tone, "You cannot sleep. Not here, my friend."

Marcus's eyes focused on Octavia. "Octavia?"

She fell to one knee and embraced him with a sigh of relief. "You are awake?"

"I have been awake," Marcus said, "I was just seeing the past again."

"You kept shouting 'Synthyya'."

"Jealous?" he asked weakly, trying desperately to banter with her, despite the fact that his powers were being sucked dry by the desert.

"Terribly jealous," she replied sarcastically, taking the hint, "Why, you look so darn desirable right now, it's all I can do to keep my hands off of you." He nodded, wanting to go on with it—the back and forth—but knowing he could not. She took that hint, too. "Tell me about Synthyya, Marcus."

"She is one of the three exiled Wizards. She was a teacher, a *magister*, which means 'master' of earth magic," Marcus said, "Zarqqwell was the master of air magic and Dariuxx of fire magic. They were the best in their Element and sat on the *Curia*, the advisory body for the Emperor before..." He gulped at the air for a breath.

"They taught you their special magic?"

"They each taught me their element, but all three worked with me on Water and Light Magic, too," he answered hoarsely. Octavia offered him a drink of water and he drank it greedily.

151

"I thought there were six Elements," she said, trying to keep him awake by following the conversation wherever it led.

"The 6th is Darkness," Marcus said, his voice reedy but stronger after the water, "We do not study that magic. There are six gods of the Wizards: We believe the God of Air and the Goddess of Earth created our world and populated it with Humans, Wizards, Elves, Morphs, and animals. It is said they had two children, the Fire God and the Water Goddess who then had twins, the Dark God and the Light Goddess. The story says the Light goddess was born first and they had trouble getting the Dark God to be born."

"Perhaps he liked the darkness of the womb?" she suggested.

"Perhaps," Marcus smiled, "But the Fire God was forced to slice open his wife's belly to get his son. It is said she never forgave him the scar and used her magic to obstruct her husband for the rest of time."

"And her husband was also her brother?" Octavia asked.

"So it is with gods," Marcus said, "'Tis a story anyway. From that point on, water would always quench fire—that's the lesson for children."

"Sort of the answer to why the tiger has stripes?" Octavia asked. She knew she needed to keep him talking, so that he stayed awake.

"Indeed," Marcus said, "But I always felt the story explained how Darkness can bring hatred even to those who should love one another."

"Do you believe in your gods?"

He shrugged. "I believe in the power of the elements," he said, "And in the power of love." He winced. "And in the power of hate, I am afraid." He closed his eyes and breathed rapidly as if he were being stabbed repeatedly. "The gods?" His voice trailed off, but his glassy eyes remained open. That was a victory.

"We will be out of here soon, Marcus. I promise," she whispered softly as she held his hand. Her own breathing became ragged, but not due to magic.

***

"He won't survive another night, Quintus," Octavia said impatiently.

"I do not know how much further we have," Quintus replied. "I only know we have to walk until the desert ends and we see the water and the horns of land which enclose the Burning Sea. I have never been here. I rely only on what I remember from his stories."

"This place is killing him," she insisted.

"I know," he said softly, "And that is killing me."

"Me too," she agreed, putting her hand on Quintus's shoulder.

"I know," he said, looking at her with a warm smile.

Marcus had stumbled twice already, falling face-first into the sand. Griffin had helped him up both times. Gwen still carried his cloak. No one could see Marcus in this condition and not feel pity, or anger at the wicked magic which did this sort of thing to a Wizard. Even Alexia was moved, for she licked the sand off his face in her puma form, an act of unselfishness unlike so many of her acts. They trudged on, terrified to speak about the real possibility that they had turned the wrong way and were not coming to the end of the desert, but simply the end. Octavia was right. Another night in this desert and Marcus would die. He had not spoken for the last several hours, as he needed all his remaining strength to put one tattered boot in front of the other. The sand was now up to their knees. Alexia had to revert to mortal form just to keep her head above the sand and she kept looking back at little Gwen, trudging on with the Wizard's cloak slung over her shoulder. Marcus would die first, but none of them would linger on much longer unless the desert ended soon.

It was Alexia who first saw it.

"Look!" she shouted, "See how it sparkles!" The others could not see like a Morph so they looked at her queerly. "The water is close," she explained. After a few more minutes, the Elves could see it, too, but Octavia did not believe it until she saw it with her own Human eyes. Quintus let out a joyous yelp.

Marcus collapsed a third time, his eyes squeezed shut. Griffin and Quintus wordlessly marched over to him. Each grabbed an arm and dragged the Wizard across the invisible point where the desert ended and lush green grass and trees sprouted around the Burning Sea. Marcus opened his eyes with considerable labor.

"You did it," Quintus said, his eyes bleary.

"*We* did it," Marcus corrected him. His voice was still a whisper, "Put on the ring and say the word. The boat will come to you." He gasped a little but it sounded less desperate.

"It doesn't look like enchanted water," Alexia said.

"Morph into a fish and find out," Griffin said sourly.

"I don't do fish," Alexia replied, creeping closer, a curious look on her soft features.

"Stay back," Marcus shouted hoarsely and then crumbled to the earth from the effort of shouting.

"Listen to him," Gwen warned, grabbing Alexia by the shoulders.

"What happens if I put a stick in it?" Octavia asked. Marcus's gesture indicated she could. Octavia grabbed a long branch and placed it in the cool water. "Doesn't look like anything happened." She drew the stick back and the part which had touched the water was gone. "It disappeared!"

"It disintegrated!" Griffin marveled.

"Nothing touches the Burning Sea and survives annihilation," Quintus explained, "It's enchanted by wicked magic, too." Marcus nodded in assent.

"What about our magic boat?" asked Gwen.

"It will hover several inches *above* the water," Marcus explained, his eyelids leaden, "It is enchanted with air magic by Zarqqwell himself."

Quintus held the ring aloft and yelled, "*Venite.*" The ring glowed, and the fellowship was enraptured with the way the gems pulsed with energy. "Where is it?" asked Quintus.

Marcus lay against a tree. "It should be here," he said. "It does not take long. It is a short trip to the island, albeit a treacherous one."

"What's that?" Gwen asked, pointing to a faint glow behind tall grass.

Marcus peered intently. "Help me up, please." Quintus pulled him to his feet. They drew back the grass and found the enchanted boat…smashed into several pieces. It was faintly glowing as if it had heard the ring's summons but could not answer the call.

"Someone destroyed it," Griffin said.

"Who?" Alexia asked.

Marcus shook his head. "Something is not right," he said, "Zarqqwell created this enchanted boat. It cannot be broken. It is the only way I have ever crossed the Burning Sea." His head was spinning and he lay down.

Quintus knelt next to him. "Rest, my brother, we will figure this out." Marcus looked like he was going to resist, but he gave in and fell immediately into sleep. Griffin stood with his hands on his hips, gazing strangely at Quintus. "What is it, Griffin?"

"Why do you call him 'brother,' when Humans and Wizards are at war?" Griffin asked.

"Humans and Wizards *are* at war," Quintus said, "But Quintus and Marcus are not. Do you not understand the difference?"

Griffin shrugged, "No matter, it appears our journey is at an end. We cannot cross the sea without the magic boat."

"We will *not* return to the desert," Octavia thundered, "He will not survive." She gestured at the unconscious Wizard, as his chest rose and fell.

"Unless someone knows how to cross a sea which dissolves sticks, then we have no other choice," Alexia said. "I hate to agree with Griffin, but I am not going to try to swim that poison water." For good measure, she threw in a stone which disappeared on impact. "What else do you suggest we do?"

"I do not want to see that desert," Octavia insisted belligerently, putting her face inches from Alexia's, "That is for sure."

"Stop fighting," Quintus said, "We must work together."

"I have an idea," Gwen said softly. All eyes turned to her. She pointed at one of the trees where a songbird was serenading them—not that they noticed amidst their bickering. "Alexia can fly over the sea."

"I can," she said, "But that only puts *me* over the water."

"It's a start," Quintus said. "How big a bird could you be? Can you carry us?"

"I cannot do eagle," she pouted, her eyes misting. "Let me think for a moment. What about this?" A great white bird appeared where Alexia once stood. It called to them with a squawk and all looked puzzled. But Gwen understood and nimbly climbed on Alexia's back. She spread her wings and flew, disappearing for several minutes before returning. Alexia morphed into mortal form with Gwen still astride her back.

"Is it far?" Griffin asked, "We cannot even see the island."

"If you could walk across the sea, then it would be a ten minute hike," Alexia said, "I flew there in a couple of minutes."

"That is closer than I thought," Quintus offered.

"I can fly Gwen, but she is very light," Alexia said, "It is close enough to carry her, but I am uncertain about much more weight."

"You can get Gwen there, so that's two people we can get to the island," Quintus said, rubbing his chin, "What about Octavia?" Alexia looked at her up and down.

"Maybe if she takes off the armor," she said, "Strip it off."

Octavia thought Alexia's tone to be lewd, but she understood the logic. She tossed aside her arms and armor until she was clad only in her short pants and the leather top she used to support her breasts. The Morph studied her half-clad form for a moment and grinned. Octavia, who—despite her protestations to the contrary—had never been entirely comfortable in a state of undress, wriggled with awkwardness and blushed. Satisfied, Alexia morphed into the bird again and Octavia gently climbed on her back. She flew but only briefly before she returned. Octavia leapt off her back before Alexia resumed her mortal form.

"No good?" Griffin asked.

"Too heavy," Alexia said, panting.

"Is it the muscles?" Gwen asked. Octavia blushed and stared at the ground.

"It's not just the muscles," Quintus said, "She's a head and a half taller than Gwen, that's the difference."

"It was close, but I would not risk it over that evil water," Alexia said.

"But if Octavia is too heavy, I might be, as well," Griffin said, "We're likely close to the same weight. And Quintus and Marcus would be far too heavy."

"I might be able to get Octavia or Griffin over," Alexia allowed, "But it's too big a risk if things go wrong halfway through the trip. I can take Gwen for sure. You and Octavia are too heavy to chance it. And the Ranger and the Wizard are too large for this form. I wish I could become a larger bird, but I know no larger bird."

Quintus slammed his fist into the ground where he was sitting. "Okay, we need to open our minds to all possibilities," he said.

"We know we can get Gwen and Alexia over," Octavia offered, "That's something. Maybe they can ask the Wizards to come."

"If the Wizards haven't come already and the boat has been destroyed, something is wrong," Quintus observed. "Let us discuss all possibilities. Everyone, suggest whatever comes into your head and surely we can find some way to solve this. There are five of us."

Much discussion ensued with ideas that ranged from fixing the magical boat to tunneling under the enchanted sea. All suggestions crashed on the shoals of reality until Griffin's eyes lit up.

"Quintus, do you know that tree?" Griffin suddenly asked, springing to his feet. Quintus shook his head. "There is some Elf knowledge the Rangers lack," he said with a satisfied smile.

"It's a Ferrum tree, isn't it?" Gwen beamed.

"Yes," Griffin said, pointing to a large tree with long drooping vine-like leaves. "The leaves feel like regular leaves," he said shaking them, "But try to slice them." He held one taut for her. Octavia swing her axe and recoiled as if she'd hit stone. "They are supple like vines," Griffin explained, "But they are as strong as steel. There is a trick to plucking them out."

"Nice plant knowledge," Octavia said, "But I don't get it."

"Can you tie knots like an Elf, Quintus?" Griffin asked.

"I most certainly can," he replied.

"Good," Griffin said, smiling. "If we tie several of these together, we can make a long and sturdy rope." He looked at Alexia, standing there with her mouth agape. He thought he'd impressed her. He wasn't sure if he was delighted or repulsed at that.

"What can we do with that?" Gwen asked. Griffin's face fell.

Quintus picked him up. "Hold on, I have it. If we tie one end to this tree and Gwen could tie the other end onto a tree on the other side, then we could work our way across the sea on the vine. If it will hold..."

"It will hold," Griffin promised, "You mean hand over hand?"

Quintus nodded. "You said a ten minute walk if there were no sea, Alexia?"

"Ten, fifteen minutes at the most," she guessed.

"It could work," Griffin said thoughtfully, "But it would have to be taut."

"It would also have to be a perfect knot, Gwen," Quintus said.

"Then, I'll tie a perfect knot," Gwen promised sweetly.

"Once she ties it on the island, we'll tie our end to the tree on our shore, so it will be plenty taut," Griffin said, "Then we have to make sure we go one at a time, grasping it as we hang over the sea. It is strong, but I would not risk more than one person at a time for the vine is supple and will hang low with the weight. Too low and..."

"Don't look down," Octavia observed.

"Right," Griffin said, "One question, and we may need to wake the Wizard. Are there any trees on that side of the sea? For Gwen to use?"

"Interesting wrinkle," Alexia nodded.

"Yes," Quintus answered, "There was a pear tree Marcus used to sit under and read. He has spoken of it to me. There must be trees."

"I will pluck out the vines, you start tying them together, Quintus," Griffin said, "Are you sure you can tie knots?"

"As good as any Elf," Quintus shot back.

"We'll see," mock-snarled Griffin.

"Marcus would be proud of the cooperation," Gwen said to Octavia, gesturing at the sleeping Wizard. Octavia nodded, feeling useless. She wasn't plucking vines or tying them, nor was she turning into a bird. She was just standing there, still in her undergarments, feeling like a half-naked and useless fool.

Within an hour, there was a long Ferrum leaf rope for Gwen to bring to the other side and tie an Elvin knot.

"You will have to tie the best knot of your life, Gwen," Quintus said, "As high as possible on the tree." Gwen nodded and mounted the great white bird. "Let me know when you've succeeded by pulling on it," he said to Griffin, "Then we can tie it off on our end." Octavia just sat there, still barely dressed, her eyes blank, feeling utterly worthless. A few minutes went by.

"There it is," Griffin said, pulling. "She did it!"

"Do you want to tie the knot?" Quintus asked.

"No, you've done so well," he replied gracefully, "The honor is yours."

***

Alexia and Gwen waited on the other shore, seeing the vine tense up. For a moment, Alexia dreamed that the others all perished in the Burning Sea and she was left alone with Gwen. It was a silly romantic dream, but she felt no guilt. Guilt was for other beings. Impulsively, she pulled Gwen close and kissed her. Alexia could sabotage the vine and make her dream

159

a reality. The Morph demurred. For what reason, she was not sure.

"Not now," Gwen said, pulling away from the embrace, "We must get everyone across." Alexia pouted but obeyed. Love had mastered her impulses and that had never happened before.

***

"Wake Marcus and tell him the plan, Octavia," Quintus said, "I will try it first. If it can hold me, it will hold any of the rest of the fellowship." She dutifully woke Marcus and told him their idea. He seemed glad and his color had returned slightly, but he was still clearly weak from the desert.

After Quintus had crossed, he pulled the vine as prearranged to signal the next to cross. "Quintus did it!" Griffin shouted, "Marcus, do you want to go next?" The Wizard got to his feet and grabbed the vine, beginning hand over hand. Normally, he would have done it with relative ease, but the desert's magic was clearly not through with him. His arms shook and his fingers unlatched and he fell to the ground before he got two feet.

"He's still too weak," Octavia said, helping him up.

"It can take a day or more to recover from the desert," Marcus said mournfully. "Go without me. Quintus has the ring; it will prove you are my friends. I have sent them a couple of messages about you. I'll follow when I can in a day or two."

Griffin shook his head. "We have to stay together."

"I can try again," Marcus said, struggling to his feet.

"No," Octavia said, "You were not strong enough a moment ago. You are not stronger now. Last time you fell on the ground. What if you fall into the sea? There is another way."

"What do you propose?" Griffin asked.

"Get another vine and tie him to my back," Octavia said, "I'll carry him."

"Octavia," Marcus said, "What if you're not strong enough? We'll both perish."

"Better hope I'm strong enough," she said with a smile, "Or we'll be taking a very brief swim. Do you think the vine will hold us both, Elf?"

He pondered. "I do," he said, "Quintus's weight barely moved the vine. It may bow a little, but it is high enough up that you ought not brush the water. Still, it is a very big risk, Octavia."

"It is my risk," she said. "Tie him to me."

Griffin tied them together as asked, frowning in dismay. Octavia's eyes narrowed, "You had better take my axe over, Griffin. I may need it on the other side." She inhaled deeply and grabbed the vine. He was heavy but her arms were strong. She began placing hand over hand and crossing the sea. She refused to look down. She refused to let go. She refused to be death of Marcus and herself. She was useful.

He clung to her, his arms knotted around her bare belly, his head buried in her thick red hair. He allowed himself a dream for a moment—but only for a moment. Her arms were like iron as she crossed the Burning Sea. This was a warrior, this daughter of a blacksmith. This was a friend. Several times she paused to catch her breath, her arms shaking with strain. But they made it to the other side and collapsed on the ground together.

"We're even," she said.

"What do you mean?" Marcus asked.

"You carried me when my leg was hurt," she said, panting, "So now we're even."

"I wasn't aware we were keeping score on saving each other's life," he said with a faint touch of playfulness.

"Maybe we are," she said, her green eyes twinkling ever so slightly.

He considered for a moment. "If so, I am still winning." he said, "By three, if I count correctly."

"The day's not over yet" she said and walked away towards Griffin who had just arrived. "Elf boy, where is my battleaxe?"

The six members of the fellowship marveled at the island. Marcus, however, seemed unnerved at the strange fact that no one had come to meet them. He had managed to send word, but there had been no response. This was odd. Still, his old teachers would be delighted to see him. He looked at his beloved pear tree and remembered how this place of exile felt like home more than any other home ever had. He had been called "son," here. Marcus opened the door of the Wizards' dwelling with a smile. The smile evaporated immediately. The floor of the dwelling was littered with dead owls, unmoving and hideous unidentified creatures, and his three teachers. All three lay lifeless. Black blood was everywhere and the entire room was smashed to pieces.

"They're dead," Marcus said, stunned.

The whole Fellowship went mute. Quintus and Octavia assumed battle stances and began to scan the room. Gwen put an arrow in her bow. Alexia morphed into a lioness and Griffin moved towards the dead Wizards. Marcus simply sank to the ground. They examined the room for threats, but none were forthcoming. Finally, Gwen relaxed her bow and Alexia morphed back to mortal form. Marcus looked on with a blank expression. Suddenly, Griffin raised his voice.

"The woman Wizard," Griffin said, "She's not dead." Marcus rushed to her.

"Synthyya?" he asked, "Can you hear me?" She opened one violet eye. "Who did this, Synthyya?" Marcus demanded.

"*Dominus maleficarum,*" she whispered.

All the blood drained from Marcus's face and he sat down as if hit with a hammer.

"Some of us don't speak your ancient Wizard tongue," Alexia reminded him.

"She says 'The Dark Lord'," Marcus translated.

Chapter 20: The Dark Lord

Marcus summoned up the strength to get a hold of himself. He had to. There was no logical alternative, given the situation. He had to put out of his mind the dead owls, unidentified creatures, and motionless Wizards which were arranged on the floor. He had to put out of his mind the unthinkable tragedy which had once touched him and sent him to this place so many years ago. He had to put out of his mind the revelation that he had been right—the Dark Lord was no fairy tale, but a real threat. He had to find a way to do what Zarqqwell had always taught him: to let go of things beyond his control and focus on things within his power. It was the wisdom of the Ancients. He needed it now. Marcus inhaled and exhaled with purpose as he turned to the task at hand and the slender reed of hope on which he placed his wishes.

"Will she die?" he asked the Elf-boy firmly.

Griffin narrowed his eyes until they were slits, as he stared at the prone Wizard woman. "It is hard to tell," he said, trying to stop his voice from quavering but failing miserably in the endeavor. "I am not sure."

Marcus placed a hand on Griffin's slender shoulder and spoke softly and gently, "I need you to be sure one way or the other," he said calmly, "Will she die?"

Griffin looked at the female Wizard. She was in terrible shape, worse than Marcus had been in the desert. Whoever— *Whatever* had done this… He looked for the hopeful signs from her body, as he had once learned from his instructors. "She could live," he squeaked, "Did we bring the healing plants over the Burning Sea?"

"I didn't bring any," Gwen said, deflated.

"Nor I," said Alexia. Of course, she wore nothing, so the lack of healing plants was clear enough.

"I had a Wizard to carry," Octavia winced.

Quintus was rummaging through every pouch on his belt. "Here, this is a healing plant, isn't it?" he held it aloft and ran over to Griffin. Griffin inspected it and nodded approvingly.

"Yes, it is a very good one. Well done, Quintus. What is her name?" Griffin asked Marcus.

"Synthyya," Marcus said.

"Does she speak the common tongue?" he asked.

"Of course," Marcus said, as if the question were preposterous. As if any question could be preposterous when Griffin found himself trying to heal a Wizard on some island of exile in the midst of an enchanted sea, surrounded by creatures which looked like... He put it out of his head.

Griffin addressed the wounded Wizard, "Synthyya, I need you to chew these two leaves slowly and swallow them. Can you do that for me?" She opened both eyes with great effort and nodded almost imperceptibly. He pressed the two leaves into her slightly open mouth and proceeded to tear the other ones into small pieces.

"Can I do anything?" Marcus asked.

"Pray to your gods," Griffin suggested, "Success is very unlikely."

Marcus's face remained stoic but anyone could have detected how his eyes turned downcast. Octavia stepped forward, "You are in good hands, Synthyya," she said, "Griffin was the best healer in his class."

"Yes, he was," Gwen said with a warm smile.

"I do not know what could have done this to her..." Griffin began.

"Yes, you do," Marcus said firmly, "The Dark Lord."

"Right, the Dark Lord," Griffin said in a tone which betrayed his struggle to believe that this was so, "Anyway, I will try my best to clean and heal her wounds but it looks to me that she was gravely injured, perhaps days ago, and simply left to die."

"She is a very powerful Wizard," Marcus declared in a tone which left no room for dissent on the matter.

"That could help," Griffin allowed.

"She is a hundred times the Wizard I am..." Marcus whispered.

"You should thoroughly check the other Wizards," Quintus advised, "If she is near life then they might be, too. We cannot afford to neglect them if they are still with us in our world and not with their gods." Griffin dutifully looked at the other two Wizards. Alexia had morphed into a dog and was sniffing at the strange creatures lying face down. Gwen went from owl to owl, hoping one might be okay. Octavia just sat down, rubbing her sore arms.

"I've examined them both," Griffin said, after a few minutes, "They have both been dead for at least a day."

"You cannot revive them?" Marcus asked.

"I use herbs and treatments taught by Elvin wisdom," he explained, "I leave magic to others."

"There is no magic which raises the dead, is there?" Octavia asked.

"There is," Marcus said, "But it is not our magic. Zarqqwell and Dariuxx are dead, then? You are certain? You have used your Elf skills to be *absolutely certain*?" There was fury in Marcus's eyes which frightened everyone in the room. Griffin nodded meekly and returned to Synthyya. A shadow fell over Marcus and he winced as if suffering a physical blow. Quintus put a hand on his shoulder and said nothing. Octavia wanted to speak, but thought of nothing to say. The creatures on the ground seemed familiar to Octavia, but there was no conceivable way it was so.

All of a sudden, Synthyya's eyes fluttered open. She muttered several incoherent things before they heard her mumble, "I can see why you were first in your healing class, Elf." Her eyes closed and then opened with some effort. She tried to bring herself to a sitting position. Marcus helped her.

"What, in the name of the Spirits? No, it can't... You were so near death. My herbs couldn't have...so quickly," Griffin stuttered.

"I told you she was an uncommonly powerful Wizard," Marcus said, permitting himself a tiny smile. "What happened, here Synthyya?" She seemed dazed and was on the precipice of falling over, but she braced herself unsteadily.

"I can tell you everything in a moment," she said softly with much effort, peering around the room with dazzling violet eyes. "What about Zarqqwell and Dariuxx?"

"Dead," Marcus said, swallowing audibly after he uttered the syllable.

"What day is it?" she croaked.

"Dies Terrae. When were you attacked?" Marcus asked.

"Dies Incendii. It has been two days," she said. Her voice was still ragged like a quilt which has worn threadbare, but it sounded better than it had a minute ago. Griffin pressed the rest of his healing herbs at her and she ate them. Synthyya muttered several words in the Ancient tongue still spoken by Wizards. She closed her eyes and took several long breaths. "We did not expect the attack," she said, gazing downwards, "The desert is meant to keep us in, but it also keeps other Wizards out. He is not like other Wizards. His power is terrifying."

"Who?" asked Alexia, back in mortal form.

"The Dark Lord," Synthyya said, looking at the Morph, as if studying her body. "Where is my staff?" she croaked weakly.

"Is this it?" Octavia asked, handing a long carved stick to her.

"Yes, thank you," Synthyya said, running her fingers along the wood. She summoned strength, as if she were preparing to stand. Instead, she nodded to no one in particular, muttered some words, and gestured towards a closet. A dress flew out and landed in Alexia's arms. "I am not dead. This is my house. When you are in my house, Alexia, I will ask you to maintain some modesty. I am sure you are proud of your…um…assets. But those assets appear to be distracting most of your fellowship. You are my guest and so you may have this dress as a gift. It should fit you." She gestured again and a large hat flew out and landed in the Wizard's hands. Synthyya examined it and then put it on her head.

"How do you know my name?" Alexia asked, putting on the dress without as much as a sharp comment towards the Wizard woman.

"I know you all," she said, studying their faces, as she leaned on her staff, "The Fellowship of Outcasts, you are calling yourselves, right? It is an honor to finally meet you, Quintus—I have heard so very much about you over the years. And this must be Gwen? Adorable, just as I expected." The voice was tired, but not quite so threadbare. Synthyya looked at Octavia and broke out into a broad smile. "I adore your hair. You are surely Octavia. A lovely shade of red."

"Just like yours," Octavia blurted out, shocked to see a Wizard with Northern hair.

"Today, dear. Today," Synthyya said mysteriously, "And of course, this is Griffin. I owe you my life, kind Elf." She was still very weak, but recovering quicker than any being Griffin had ever seen.

"My pleasure, my Lady," he said with a bow he thought appropriate.

"How do you know us, ma'am?" Gwen asked, "Is it magic?"

Synthyya laughed heartily, "Gwen, Gwen, Gwen, there is no such magic. Why is it when Humans and Elves don't understand, they presume it's magic?" she asked Marcus. He shrugged. "Marcus owled me to tell me he was coming. I would have liked to tidy the place up before you arrived, but *events* intervened..." She seemed far more light-hearted than the situation seemed to require. It did not take long for the others to conclude Synthyya was a bit odd, but in a thoroughly charming way.

"He owled you?" asked Octavia, screwing up her face as she repeated the words, "What does that mean?"

Synthyya nodded knowingly. "Of course, you don't know," she said, gesturing towards the front door which opened at her command. A small ball of dirt flew in and landed in her hands. She took a moment to sculpt it into a tiny but realistic owl and then she blew on it. The clay owl took flight. "The Wizard gods created owls as special companions for Wizards. They will listen to a message from any Wizard and fly to another Wizard to deliver it, no matter where in the Realm the recipient may be."

167

"The owl will sound like he is hooting to you, but the words of the sending Wizard will sound clear to us as if he or she were there with us," Marcus explained.

"All these poor dead owls. They were your friends," Gwen said sadly, a tear escaping her pale blue eye and trickling down her soft white cheek. Quintus put his arm around her in comfort and she nestled her head on his chest.

"Yes, I am afraid so," Synthyya said, "Many Wizards have personal owls with which they form a bond. If it is close enough, the Wizard can see through the owl's eyes, so he or she can see what the owl sees, even if it is far away."

"Do you have an owl, Marcus?" Quintus asked, wondering if there was yet another secret of which he had been unaware.

"I never met one who liked me that much," Marcus shrugged, "Story of my life."

"You see through its eyes? What does the owl get out of this deal?" Alexia asked.

"You'll never hit a Wizard's special owl with arrows," Synthyya explained, "If the Wizard is alive, the owl is magically protected from arrows, which will never find their target, even at close range. It is part of the bond. Although the magic does not protect the owl from other weapons." She scanned the room grimly. "I don't see Dariuxx's owl. Perhaps he escaped."

"What if I morphed into an owl?" Alexia said, "Could I deliver messages?"

"Have you ever tried?" Marcus asked. She shook her head. "You can't because owls are not animals. They are magical beings which look like birds. They are special."

Alexia slipped out of her dress and closed her eyes. Griffin marveled at how quickly she could get out of her clothes. After a few moments, she opened her eyes, astonished. "I cannot become an owl," she said, unbelieving.

"No, you cannot, sweetheart," Synthyya said, "Can we stay dressed, please? It's a lovely dress and you're still very pretty with it covering all of your parts." Her tone shifted from light-hearted to deadly serious, "I cannot believe that we were surprised by the attack. We should have seen it coming. Zarqqwell *and* Dariuxx? Dead? This is horrible." Her tone was serious, yet it didn't sound very mournful to Quintus, but then again, he knew that Wizards rarely betrayed too many emotions.

The clay owl dropped out of the sky and fell to the earth. "Is it dead?" asked Gwen, staring at the lump of dirt as if it were real.

"It was never alive, my little blonde friend," Synthyya said sweetly, "It is just some earth magic. I find it helps with the telling of tales."

"What are those?" Quintus asked, gesturing at the huge, hulking creatures which lay prone all over the floor. They were the most horrifying things Quintus had ever seen with scaly skin covering muscled arms and legs. Their powerful hands ending in sharp claws were still grasping crude weapons. Their mouths hung open in death, revealing row after row of sharp teeth punctuated by four fangs at the front. Black tongues lolled from the gaping mouths and yellow horns protruded from their skulls.

"You call them 'orcs,' Quintus," she said, "Wizards call them 'ogres.'"

"They look like the drawings we have for goblins," Griffin said, poking one with his foot.

"Yes, Elves call them 'goblins,'" Synthyya explained, nodding, "Morphs call them 'trolls.' They are the same beast, no matter what you call them. They are wicked, regardless of their name." Gwen buried her head deeper into Quintus's chest.

"Total carnage of orcs, that's for sure," Octavia observed.

Alexia squinted, "But trolls aren't real," the morph said, "They are a nightmare that young ones have."

"Nightmares sometimes are true," Marcus said.

"Goblins?" exclaimed Griffin, "Alexia is right. We tell stories of goblins to frighten naughty children. They are fiction."

"They look real to me," Quintus observed.

"Do they bleed black?" Marcus asked, knowing the answer, as it was pooled all around them.

"They do," Synthyya said, "We killed several of them. Not enough, clearly."

"Are *they* animals?" Gwen asked.

"No, not in the strictest sense of the word," Synthyya explained, "We believe animals are natural creations of our gods, just as they created Wizards and Humans and Elves and Morphs. Ogres are not natural. They are made by other hands, borrowing the life force of natural creatures by way of dark magic."

"I don't understand," Alexia said.

"Few do," Synthyya said, "But we uncovered the secret after Marcus managed to convince an owl to send us a message several weeks ago. He has come a long way if he can convince owls to carry his messages. They used to just peck at him." She smiled.

Marcus seemed to suddenly understand. "Yes, yes, of course..."

"What?" Quintus asked.

"He needs hearts, doesn't he?" Marcus asked Synthyya.

"Yes, a Wizard who has mastered the magic of Darkness can create ogres," she explained, "But the magic needs the hearts of other creatures to perform the spell."

"What kind of hearts?" Gwen asked, trembling.

"Humans, Wizards, Morphs, or Elves," Synthyya said, "At least that is what we believe. Ogres are horrifying creatures, even more so when alive. Their eyes glow red when they are not dead. You should never look directly at those eyes. Understand?"

Octavia wanted to scream out, "No, you crazy Wizard, I do not understand!" but she mutely nodded as did everyone else.

Alexia was trying not to smell the horrible stench, which judging by others' non-reactions was something only she smelled. She tried to concentrate on her hearing to distract herself from the trolls' scent and she heard a faint rustling. "What is that sound?" Alexia asked.

"I hear nothing," Synthyya said.

"Over there, where the dress came from." Alexia said. Swords, axes, and bows were brandished by the Fellowship as they grimly pondered the chances a live ogre might still be lurking. "Come out!" Alexia called as she prepared to morph into whatever animal might be best for troll-fighting. A small brown owl flew out and landed on Marcus's shoulder.

"It is Dariuxx's owl," Synthyya said with euphoria, "He survived!" The bird blinked and hooted. Synthyya's face betrayed a hint of surprise, "I sense that he likes you, Marcus." The bird stared at Marcus with its large eyes.

"That would be a first," Marcus said, eyeing the owl suspiciously. "As you've made clear, I have historically been very poor at convincing owls to carry any message to any Wizard. They hate me."

"There is a piece of Dariuxx in him," Synthyya said, her voice taking on an unusually kind tone, "Dariuxx loved you deeply, Marcus. He would want you to take care of his owl, now that he is walking with our gods." Marcus seemed uncomfortable, but nodded dutifully.

"You think he walks with the gods?" he asked. Synthyya nodded in the most serious fashion of which she was capable. "I will take care of it...for Dariuxx," Marcus said, and he spoke ancient words to the owl. It stared at him, unblinking. Marcus was thoroughly unconvinced that anything good was going to result from this bird.

"We should take something from Zarqqwell as well," Synthyya said, "For you, Marcus. You were his favorite student in all his years of teaching—both before the Exile and after. Perhaps, he never told you with words, but it was so. He always believed in you and would want you to have something of his before we leave this place."

"Leave this place?" Marcus asked.

"Yes," she said, as if it were the most obvious thing in the world. While still limping, she hurried around the room purposefully. "Aha! His staff. Here, take his staff." She gestured and the gnarled wooden pole flew towards Marcus. He caught it and the owl began hooting.

"A staff?" Marcus asked, raising an eyebrow, "Isn't that sort of old fashioned? A Wizard and his staff? I don't think anyone under six *decems* still uses a staff."

"Oh, you no longer like old fashioned things?" Octavia remarked sarcastically, "That is a new layer in the personality of Marcus the Wizard."

"Do not doubt the power of a good staff," Synthyya said, "I know that younger Wizards find them unfashionable, but a good staff can amplify your powers. If you direct the spell through the staff, it can be more powerful than if you just use your hands."

"I don't know if I believe that," Marcus said.

"I didn't believe in the Dark Lord an hour ago," Gwen offered.

"Take it," Synthyya said, "To remember Zarqqwell by. We should leave this place. There is a darkness here which cannot be eradicated." She walked towards the closet. She was muttering about how hats had gone out of style, too, and lamenting the foolishness of several generations of younger Wizards whose views on hats she found thoroughly vexing.

"Are you looking to see if any other owls survived?" Griffin asked.

"No," Synthyya said, "I wanted to see if any more of my hats survived. It would appear I am stuck with just one. I feel naked without a hat. And don't you say a word, pretty little Morph. I know you want to." Alexia had opened her mouth to speak, but shut her lips tight.

"Hats?" asked Quintus. He felt that the situation seemed far more urgent than hats, given the two dead Wizards and return of the Dark Lord.

"Hats, Quintus Agrippa Aureus," Synthyya snapped, "I like hats and those monsters destroyed all but one of them. This is very concerning."

"Is it?" Octavia asked, as perplexed as Quintus.

"It is," Synthyya said, looking deeply offended. "Let us be off, now that we know the hat situation is what it is."

"Why are you so eager to abandon your home?" Marcus asked.

"We are going to burn this dwelling to the ground," Synthyya said, matter-of-factly.

"It's our only shelter. Why would we do that?" asked Quintus.

"We must honor the bodies of our fallen friends by giving them back to the god of Fire," she said, "Perhaps there will be immortality for them or perhaps their book is closed forever. I, for one, believe they walk with the gods for eternity. The Fire god will also consume the bodies of the wicked ogres and that will purify this ground. Darkness was here. The Dark Lord's feet walked on these floors. My floors—freshly swept! We must not stay here any longer. His darkness lingers long after he has left."

"So *he* was here?" Marcus asked.

"He was," she said softly, "I feel that he could have killed us all in an instant, no more than two instants. But he wanted us to suffer. So he wounded us so deeply that we were sure to die, but only after days of agony. We lay here through the day of Fire, the Day of Light, and now the Day of Earth. I'd have been dead tomorrow, as well on the Day of Air. He meant for us to die after suffering."

"Why did this creature want you to suffer?" asked Alexia.

"Because he's evil," Octavia replied, gripping her axe.

"Perhaps," Synthyya said, "But I believe Alexia was asking 'Why you?' Why did he want *us* specifically to suffer, right?"

"Yes, Synthyya," Alexia said, "Why you?"

"That is a longer story which I will tell you after we burn down this house," Synthyya said, "But before we leave this island."

"You are leaving the island?" Marcus asked, incredulous.

"Matters have gotten quite out of hand," Synthyya replied, straightening her hat.

173

Chapter 21: The Origins of the Strife

The flames seemed to lick the sky. They dwarfed the small island while their orange fingers snapped all night long. Gwen did not think it was wise to burn the dwelling, for night was falling and they had nowhere else to sleep. What if the fire consumed the trees on the island? What about the animals? Were there animals? She had seen none on the island, save the owl. What if the conflagration attracted the attention of this Dark Lord? Yet Gwen was now in the company of two Wizards and they didn't seem to want counsel from the rest of the group on this or any other matter. Synthyya had taken a few items out of the dwelling, further lamenting the destruction of her hats, but otherwise she was intent on destroying it with the bodies of the other Wizards and the goblins. At least, there had been food which was rescued. Synthyya had provided them with fresh bread and other delicious foods unlike anything Gwen had tasted since she'd left home as a slave. She was no longer a slave, but somehow she felt less safe as a free Elf. She could not believe that goblins were real, that some Dark Lord existed, that Marcus had been correct when he predicted that everyone was in danger. She thought of her parents. She thought of her brother. She thought of Alexia, her Morph infatuation. She thought of Quintus who she just might love. Gwendolyn shivered. But it was not cold so close to the fire. She shivered in fear, although she was not sure which of her many fears was most immediate. At least the fire was not spreading, she noticed. Clearly, the Wizards' powers were coming back and they could control such things without an Elf's advice on the matter.

"I have a question," Octavia said as they sat near the flames, greedily eating their fill from the exiled Wizards' pantry.

"And what is that, my red-haired warrior girl?" Synthyya asked.

"What exactly *is* the Dark Lord?"

"I was wondering the same thing," Griffin stated.

Synthyya smiled, it was a tender smile like a mother's. "No one knows for sure, friends," she explained, "Some of my people say he is the god of the Darkness himself, son of the Fire god and Water goddess. Others say he is simply a Wizard, nothing more. Many believe he is somewhere in between a god and a Wizard."

"I feel like I understand none of what you just said," Octavia said with a smile, "But after all, I am just a dumb Human. I know little of Wizards, save Marcus."

"You know one of the best of our kind," Synthyya said, her pink lips creasing into a smile, "For your friendship with Marcus, I am most grateful. As for my answer, we know little about *Dominus Maleficarum,* as we call him, except that he is very powerful and has mastered the sixth element—the one most Wizards avoid."

"The Darkness," Marcus said. Synthyya nodded. "Wizards recognize six elements: Air and Earth, Fire and Water, Light and Dark. The first five we worship as gods and seek to master in our spells. The sixth we worship and respect, but we do not meddle with the Darkness. We leave that be."

"Why?" Alexia asked.

Synthyya began sculpting the mud and it took life once again. "In the beginning, there was the Air Father and the Earth Mother. They mated and brought forth Fire and Water, who then had two children of their own: a daughter, the goddess of Light and her twin, a boy, the god of the Darkness. The Fire god had to retrieve the son by cutting his wife open. The god of the Dark was born, but husband and wife's love was never the same. This was the beginning of the Strife which always follows the Darkness."

"You told me this story," Octavia whispered to Marcus. He nodded.

"Everything in the Wizard world revolves around the Elements," Synthyya said, "Our days of the week are named after the five we worship: Earth day, Air day, Water day, Fire day, Light Day."

"No Dark day?" Gwen asked.

"No, dear, only five days per week," Synthyya said, "We are Wizards. We have a logical calendar with 73 five-day weeks per year. Every 20 years, we add a week of five Dark Days to the end of the calendar. Those days are unlucky. This year is such a year." She sighed.

"I've always wondered, which days are your rest days?" Griffin asked.

Marcus chuckled darkly. "Wizards have occasional holy days to rest, but generally do not take days off from our labors like Elves or Humans do. Another feature of the Wizard world which I do not miss. I've always thought Humans are wise to take the seventh day for rest. Most Wizards do not understand such notions, nor would they comprehend a seven day week when five divides more neatly into the 365 days of the cycle."

"Humans are illogical, but Elves are lazy," Octavia shrugged. "How many days do Elves have in a month?"

"30, just like Humans do," Griffin said.

"Like some of Humans' months," Marcus noted, "Other Human months have 31. Quite illogical." Octavia stuck her pink tongue out at him playfully. She turned to Gwen.

"You Elves have 12 months with 30 days," Octavia agreed, "Quite similar to Humans. But we rest about four days off per month and you rest ten. Am I right?"

"You view it all wrong," Gwen said, "We work ten days, we rest five days. Then we work ten more and rest five more."

"That's ten days of idleness per month," Octavia insisted, "Lazy. And if I am not mistaken, you take five *more* days off at the end of the year."

"We call it the 'sun cycle' but yes, those days are for carousing," Gwen said. She thought for a moment, "And a sixth day is added every four sun cycles," she added sheepishly.

"That's the Unday," Griffin said, "An old tradition."

"Wasn't Synthyya talking about Wizard gods?" Quintus asked, "The calendar comparison is lovely and I am sure Morphs have their own ways to mark times, too. But I want to know more about what Synthyya was talking about."

"Yes, six Elements and six gods," Griffin said, "Synthyya, do you really believe all that stuff about six gods and whatnot?"

"I do," Synthyya said, "Just as you believe in your Spirits and the Humans believe in their Golden One which shines in the day." She turned to Alexia. "And the Morphs believe in the eternity of life-force." Alexia nodded, awe-struck. "Morphs mark time with the moon, in case you care." Alexia gasped.

"What about you, Marcus?" Gwen asked, "Do you believe?"

"I am complicated," Marcus said, changing the subject swiftly, "But let's presume that the enemy we face is not one of the six gods. He must be a Wizard. If he is a Wizard, he can be killed, right?"

"I don't know," said Synthyya, "As I once taught you, we believe that he alone destroyed Classical Civilization a thousand or more years ago and clearly, he still lives today, long after any normal Wizard should be drawing breath. The Dark magic can do much that seems impossible. Many find him to be a fairy tale and no doubt this works in his favor. I may have doubted the continued existence of a Dark Lord until he showed up at my home and destroyed my hats."

"And killed your friends," Gwen added.

"Yes," Synthyya allowed, "And ended a great civilization long ago…"

Alexia rolled her eyes at Gwendolyn. Gwen smiled at the silly gesture.

"Don't roll your eyes," Quintus said, sternly to Alexia. "Respect the history."

"It is not her fault," Synthyya said, removing her feathered hat, "Let me try to explain." More sculpted figures arose and took life in the space around the red-haired Wizard woman. "A thousand years ago—some say two thousand—all the races lived in relative harmony in the ancient world. I am sure some did not get along and hatred existed—as it always has—but for the most part the Classical Civilization was a golden age for peace and advancements. We do not know how the Dark Lord destroyed it, but he did. Like the god of Darkness, he spread strife between the races and their world collapsed. For centuries, the world lay in the darkness while the Lord brutally ruled the races and all shared the misery. His ogres roamed the world and death was ubiquitous."

"Even if this is true," Gwendolyn offered, "This has not been our world. What happened? When did this stop?" She looked at Marcus.

"I do not know and neither does Synthyya," Marcus said, he paused and closed his violet eyes, "Nor did Zarqqwell or Dariuxx. All we do know is that at some point during the Dark times, Humans and Wizards worked together to stop him."

"That sounds strange," Griffin said.

"Perhaps," Marcus allowed, "But they found a way to make the Dark Lord disappear and he was gone."

"Although the strife, the hatred, remained long after they made him go away," Synthyya said, with sad violet eyes, "The world was free of the Dark Lord, but it was not free of the hatred he unleashed. Hundreds of years have not erased the mutual distrust among the four major races of our world. They have lived in a cold peace but they have seethed at one another for reasons I do not fully understand."

"What has changed in our time?" asked Alexia, delighted no one had mentioned the old story about the Morphs abandoning the other races and joining the Dark Lord. She hated that stupid myth. She would never abandon her friends, especially Gwen.

"If the Dark Lord was imprisoned, then he escaped. If killed, he has risen. If bound, he is unbound," Synthyya said, "He is back—that much is clear. I cannot tell you why, but I can tell you when." She stared at the fire for a moment, "I must have had 50 hats in there and only one survives." She seemed genuinely sad about her hats, Octavia noted. Quite odd. She decided not to linger on this but to pose the obvious question.

"Okay, we can leave aside the 'why.' When did this happen?" Octavia asked.

"The Empress," Marcus said, his eyes aflame. Perhaps, Octavia observed, it was the flames from the burning home reflected in his eyes. Or perhaps his eyes were on fire. She could not tell. She just marveled at it. "Is that right, Synthyya?"

"It is," she said, as a clay woman in a cloak appeared and floated around her. Even though it was just mud, the eyes looked malevolent to Griffin. "It was 26 years ago. The Empress stole the High Throne of the Wizards and unleashed her plan to clear the world of Humans and Morphs. The Dark Lord is connected, somehow. The signs began a few years thereafter, although we were blind to them until very recently. "

"You opposed her, didn't you?" Octavia asked, "That is why you were sent here?" Synthyya nodded.

"Her claim to the throne was illegitimate and her plan was wicked," Synthyya said, "I would rather spend eternity on this island than be part of that hatred."

"This is when the war between Wizards and Humans broke out," Quintus said, "And Marcus became a target because of his Human blood."

He nodded. "The war was the fault of us Wizards," Marcus said glumly.

"Do not be so sure," Synthyya gently chided him, "The Empress wants the Wizards to come out of mountains and fill the world. This is true. To do this, she needs Humans and Morphs dead, but…"

"What about Elves?" Gwen interrupted. Clay elves appeared.

"Elves? Your voice is so soft and sweet and innocent. More so than any other Elf I have heard," Synthyya said, "There is something special about you, Gwendolyn." Synthyya smiled and her eyes rested on the Elf for a moment. "The Empress calls the Elves 'allies' but her true intent is to reduce them to slavery." The little clay Elves lost the leaves in their hair and stooped under unseen burdens.

"We have tasted that bitterness," Gwen said, "But Marcus is right, it is the Wizards who did this."

"Not quite," Synthyya said, "The King of the Elves has joined her because he wants to regain the land Elves used to occupy north of the Meridian. Humans reproduce more quickly

179

than any other race and they have pushed the Elves deeper and deeper south, taking their land. The Elf king is greedy for the land his ancestors once ruled. We firmly believe that he has guessed at the Empress's plan and expects to double cross her at the end."

"You know a lot for a lady confined to an island," Octavia observed.

"Things are not always what they seem," Synthyya said, with a twinkle in her eye, "not unlike the alliance between the Wizards and the Elf King."

"He has done us wrong," Griffin spat. Gwen nodded.

"So Humans are victims?" Octavia asked, trying to hide her delight.

"Sorry, my dear," Synthyya said, "The Human Council wants the Wizards' wealth and the Elves' land. Humans believe they have a duty to populate the world and they need more land to feed themselves. Elves have been pushed further and further to the margins but they still control the most fertile land we know. The Humans covet that. The Council also knows that Wizards hoard gold and gems in our Gray Mountains and while we are powerful, we are few. They presume they can overwhelm us with numbers."

"They are probably right," Marcus offered, "Although the Human casualties would be staggering."

"Not really the Council's concern," Quintus tartly observed.

"Where do I fit in?" Alexia asked, "I mean, my people?"

"The best part of Morphs is that they live in the moment," Synthyya said, as clay eagles and wolves and bears turned into mortal men and women and then back, "The worst part of Morphs is they rarely think long-term. The Humans use them in their war because the Morphs really just want to fight. Too many Morphs simply enjoy the killing, the raping, the pillaging, but they do not consider the consequences."

"All the races share the blame," Alexia said firmly.

"Maybe," Synthyya said, "But I believe that the root of this is with the Dark Lord. He is using them all for a bigger purpose. He plays the longest game of all, as he has lived a

180

thousand or more years. He must know that we guessed at his plan and that is why he paid us a visit." She muttered several things of which the only discernible word was "hats."

"The more we all fight, the more hearts he can harvest for orcs," Octavia noted.

"I think that is part of it," Synthyya said.

"You think there is more?" Griffin asked.

"Much more," Synthyya said.

"Tell us," Gwen pleaded.

"I have told you all that I know," she replied, "For now, I must rest." She suddenly looked terribly weary. "The Elf-boy has saved me, but only rest will restore me to what I was."

"We should all rest," Gwen said.

"Must we cross the Burning Sea, again?" Quintus asked, "You know the magic boat is broken, right?"

"I know it is broken," she said, "I am sure Marcus and I can fix the boat. It will be a good chance for him to practice with Zarqqwell's staff."

"What about that horrible desert?" Octavia winced, looking at Marcus, "We cannot do that again!"

"We will not," Synthyya said, "There is another way which I can explain in the morning. I am suddenly very weary."

"What happens when we leave this place?" Marcus asked, "If you and I don't know anything more, how can we stop *Dominus Maleficarum?*"

"We must find someone who knows more than us," she said simply, brushing the feathers on her hat.

"Who?" Quintus asked.

"Tomorrow, we will seek the Historian, leader of the *Custodes,*" she said, her tired eyes sparkling for a moment, "He knows more than anyone in the Realm. You'll love him. He's a wonderful host."

Chapter 22: We can all dream

Their rest was fitful, but restorative, and the Fellowship of Outcasts, with Synthyya added to their number, woke when the rosy fingers of dawn emerged over the horizon. Well, the non-Wizards all awoke... Quintus opened his eyes and saw Synthyya and Marcus deep in slumber, no doubt recharging their spent powers—Synthyya from combating the orcs and the Dark One; Marcus still reeling from the treacherous desert crossing. Quintus did not know how his friend would survive another crossing so soon, but Synthyya seemed unperturbed about traversing the Burning Sea and Desert of Despair. In fact, she seemed monumentally unperturbed about the fact that the Dark Lord was real and lurking somewhere in the Four Realms. Hats, on the other hand, appeared to vex her to no end. Perhaps it was just a case of Wizards being Wizards, he shrugged to no one in particular. Even the threat of some diabolical force with the power to destroy the world did not rise to the level of justifying emotion for a Wizard. Such a strange race, Quintus mused. There was something especially peculiar about Synthyya, but he could not put his finger on it.

Gwen was already up and chatting with Alexia. Quintus wondered at the nature of their relationship. Their tents were all on the other side of the Burning Sea, so the fellowship had slept in the open air under the watchful stars. His religion told him that the stars were the souls of everyone who had died since the beginning of time, shining brightly in the embrace of the Golden One who ruled the day. Quintus was not always sure what he believed, but then again he hadn't believed in orcs or the Dark Lord prior to yesterday. Still, he was grateful they'd slept in the open because he had questions about what happened behind the thin walls of Gwendolyn's tent. Could Alexia be a rival for Gwen's love? He could not believe Gwen would prefer Alexia to him. But then again, he could not believe the Dark Lord was a real Wizard and not some spooky tale to frighten children. Gwen and Alexia were chatting lightly while Griffin glumly sat by himself. He was also an obstacle to Quintus's love, although an entirely different kind of obstacle.

Quintus was not sure whether to try and win him over or undermine his credibility. He needed more time to plan his strategy. On one thing Quintus was certain: he would spend the rest of his life loving Gwendolyn—even if his life and everyone else's might be shorter than expected based on yesterday's revelations. A powerful hand clamped down on his shoulder and Quintus leapt—quite nearly out of his boots.

"Calm down, Quintus," Octavia guffawed, "You are awfully jumpy in the morning, aren't you?"

"You startled me, that's all," he said, sitting back down and trying to regain his composure. He saw Gwen and Alexia giggling and wondered if it was at his expense.

"Daydreaming about your Elf-girl, no doubt," Octavia teased.

"No, I was just trying to figure out what was odd about Synthyya," he said, gesturing towards the sleeping female Wizard.

"She appears to be a blonde," Octavia said, "Whereas yesterday, she was flame haired. I'm not sure how or when that happened, but I take offense."

"As a flame haired Northerner, yourself," Quintus mused, as he looked at Octavia's hair, a shade of orange like the licking flames of a fire.

"Exactly," Octavia said with a grin, "She was the first being with such hair I have seen since leaving the North. I thought I'd found a friend, a red-haired comrade, and now she's blonde and gone over to Gwen's side. Wizards!"

"Would you prefer if I go with a light brown instead?" Synthyya boomed. Now, it was Octavia's turn to jump. Quintus laughed at *her* expense.

"No, I was just making a jest, Synthyya…"

Synthyya opened her eyes, sat up, and smiled warmly. "I know, sweetheart, so was I," she said, "I didn't realize you took hair so seriously." With that, she muttered some words and smoothed back her blonde hair. In an instant, it became a sandy brown. "Would this keep your shortpants from getting into such a twist?"

"It looks beautiful, Synthyya," Octavia said with a nervous smile.

"Of course it does, dear," Synthyya said, "We ought to get going."

"You'll need to wake Marcus," Quintus said.

"Easier said than done if I remember correctly," Synthyya said, poking Marcus, who was wrapped in his cloak.

"I don't think he'll feel much through that cloak," Octavia advised, "It saved me from several spear thrusts. I believe it's enchanted."

"It had better be, Octavia," Synthyya said with a smile, all dimples and teeth, "I gave it to him. I am glad it has served him—and you—well."

Marcus's violet eyes opened. "Too long?" he asked Quintus.

"No, you slept the right amount," Quintus replied.

"We were discussing the cloak I gave to you," Synthyya said, "Apparently Octavia is very fond of it." Octavia blushed.

"It was quite useful when we encountered the Sunset Elves," she said.

"Interesting," Synthyya said, "Marcus, why don't you eat something and then take out another gift, Zarqqwell's farewell present from all those years ago."

"What is that?" Quintus asked.

"The ring," Marcus said, motioning to the platter of muffins studded with fresh berries they had rescued from Synthyya's pantry before torching her home. Two muffins flew to his hand. "Zarqqwell excelled at air magic and the boat was his creation. I presume Synthyya has a plan to fix the boat so we can cross this sea without Octavia doing any heavy lifting."

She scowled at him, half-jokingly. "Why did you get all these presents, Marcus?" Octavia asked, "Was it your birthday?"

He laughed. "Wizards don't celebrate birthdays. One year is nothing in the Wizard world. We recognize a *decem* which is ten years for Humans, although there is no celebration except for each *viginti* which would be 20 years. A *quindecem*, that is 15, is the age of adulthood, but that's not really a celebration. The gifts to which she alludes were those given to me when I left the exiled Wizards. Synthyya gave me the cloak, Zarqqwell the ring, and Dariuxx gave me the sword. It was I who should have given them gifts for their teaching me."

"Such a nice boy," Synthyya marveled.

"So you didn't celebrate a birthday until you were 20?" Octavia asked.

Marcus's face fell. "I turned 20 in the midst of the Empress's ascent and the onset of the war. I assure you that there was no celebrating the half-breed with the Human name. Four years later I crossed the Desert of Despair after my father left me there," Marcus said. "There was no merriment I can remember."

"You were only 24 when that happened?" Octavia asked.

"You do not fully understand Wizards," Synthyya cut in, "Wizards are fully grown by 15 and most are married and start trying to have children by that age, even though they continue to pursue their studies. 24 is not all that young for Wizards."

"But you live so long, I would have thought you'd only be an adult at like 40 or something," Octavia said.

"Is 40 impossibly old for you?" Marcus asked, raising an eyebrow.

"How old are you?" she asked.

"How old do you make me to be?"

She studied his powerful body and noted the threads of silver woven into his black hair. Young, but not too young. Old, but not too old. "30?" she asked. Marcus, Synthyya, and Quintus all laughed heartily.

"Marcus is about 46 according to Human years," Quintus explained.

"Still early in his life for a Wizard," Synthyya added, "But he has not been young for a long long time." She gave Marcus a knowing look as if the two of them were sharing a thought to which Octavia was not invited. Dariuxx's owl swooped down and rested on Marcus's shoulder. "He still likes you," Synthyya insisted.

"He has poor taste in Wizards," Marcus replied.

Griffin walked over from his self-imposed exile. "I presume you have a plan, Synthyya," he said, suddenly screwing up his face, "Weren't you red haired yesterday?"

"I think it looks gorgeous," Gwen said as she and Alexia joined them. "How did you do it?"

"It wasn't authentic, only Humans from the North have red hair. I use a little Earth magic to make life interesting," Synthyya said, "This color will last a day or two, no more. I confess that I can't remember what my original hair color is. It's too much fun to keep changing."

"I can agree with that," Alexia said with a sincere smile. Quintus noticed her hand was by her side, but it was ever-so-slightly touching Gwen's.

"What *is* your plan, Synthyya?" Marcus asked. "You said something about 'the Historian' last night."

"Did I?" she asked.

"You did," Griffin insisted.

"Hmmm. I don't remember doing that, but I am sure you're right. He is half Elf and half Human, the keeper of ancient books, chief of the *Custodes*. He knows the history of our realm better than anyone…"

"Four realms," Griffin corrected her.

"What did I say?"

"You said 'our realm,'" Alexia explained.

"There are Four Realms," Gwen said gently, "Humans, Elves, Wizards, and Morphs."

"And I said 'our realm'?" Synthyya asked. All nodded. "Well, I must be right. Anyway, he dwells in a secret hall, but luckily I know how to get there. Well, I have a good idea about how to get there. Or close to there, anyway. He must be informed about the latest developments, and I am sure he will help us plan what to do next."

"What about the boat?" Octavia asked.

"The boat?"

"To cross the Burning Sea," Marcus said patiently, brandishing the ring.

"Of course, *the boat*," Synthyya said, mock-seriously, "We probably need the boat unless you want to take a very unpleasant swim in the sea."

"I would do anything to get a chance to wash in a sea, right now," Octavia said, "But I don't think this one would be good for my complexion."

"No," Synthyya agreed, "I'd hate to see you end like that, Octavia. We've got to stick together as the flame haired women in this group."

"Isn't your hair brown, today, Synthyya?" Octavia asked.

"Oh, I quite forgot," she laughed.

"She is right in the head, isn't she?" Quintus whispered to Marcus. He nodded. "We can trust her?"

"She's eccentric," Marcus whispered back, "But do not underestimate her." The Elves and Morph heard them with their sharp ears and seemed to all breathe a sigh of relief, although Gwen's relief was several shades stronger than that of Alexia and Griffin.

"Marcus, pick up the staff," Synthyya said, sounding very much like a teacher.

"I loved Zarqqwell and appreciate the memento," Marcus said, "But I've never felt comfortable with a staff. There is no one under three *viginti* who uses one."

"That is because young Wizards are stupid," she snapped, "A proper staff will make your spells more powerful. Zarqqwell and Dariuxx are gone forever, but the staff and the owl contain parts of their magic which live on. Your work for today is to experiment with both. By sundown, I want you to be comfortable with casting through the staff and seeing through the owl's eyes. No excuses." Marcus hung his head in resignation.

"Finally, someone who tells *him* what to do," Alexia whispered to Gwen, who giggled in response.

"Fine, what should I do about the boat?" Marcus asked.

Griffin was on edge. If she said "What boat?" again, he would go completely mad. This whole quest had gone horribly wrong. How in the *Four Realms* were they going to reassemble

187

a boat smashed by goblins? Goblins!? And even if they crossed this accursed sea, did they really want to go back through the desert with its desolation and heat, where the Wizards slowly died, and more Low Elves possibly lurked? This was madness. If only he could convince Gwen of this. He looked at his sister and saw her hand touch Alexia's. Dear Spirits, let it only be immature flirting and nothing more, he prayed. His thoughts came to a halt like a rearing horse: was he concerned about his sister or was it that Griffin desperately wanted to merge with Alexia himself, to kiss her full on the lips and press his bare body against hers? His skull pounded as his tried to clear the terrible thoughts from his mind.

No one else seemed to notice. Synthyya was telling Marcus to put the ring on a certain finger on his right hand and to hold the staff with that hand with a particular grip. Wizards! Griffin had had enough of them to fill a lifetime. Marcus held Synthyya's right hand in his left and they chanted some of that nonsense ancient language. Nothing seemed to happen. Synthyya then adjusted Marcus's grip on the staff and instructed him on his breathing. This all seemed so stupid to Griffin. Why hadn't he gotten Gwendolyn out of this madness when he had a chance? Now they were stranded on an island for exiles with the only shelter burned to the ground as some evil sea surrounded them. The Wizards tried again and again, failing each time.

Until they didn't.

Finally, something went right—whether the grip, the ring, the breathing, the words, who knew?—and a glow appeared in the far distance on the other side of the sea. The pieces of the boat were floating towards them. Marcus and Synthyya raised their staffs in unison and the pieces miraculously fused together. The reassembled boat floated several inches above the Burning Sea, as if waiting for the party.

"Can we board?" asked Quintus.

"We can," said Synthyya, pointing her hand at a tree. A pear flew into her hand. "For you, Marcus. From your favorite tree. A reward for your good work with the staff."

"I know you never get tired of hearing it, Synthyya, but you may be right about the staff's power," Marcus grumbled. His owl hooted as if in agreement.

"Pretty fascinating magic," Octavia said, as she stood next to Marcus on the boat. He offered her a bite of the pear and she bit into it, the juice staining her lips and trickling down her chin.

"Thank you," Marcus said as they hovered towards the far side of the sea. Her green eyes sparkled as the sun danced off the water and her lips glistened with the juice of the fruit. For a moment, she looked like she was going to say something inviting, but as quickly as the look had appeared, it disappeared.

"It's unfair," Octavia mock-pouted, "Wizards alone get to play with magic."

"You fail to grasp the reality," Marcus said with an embarrassed smile, "There is much magic beyond Wizards' control. The glance of a pretty girl, the touch of a friend when you are despondent, the rush of a river in flood, the color of the sky at sunset. It is all magic of a sort and not at all in the hands of Wizards." She met his gaze for a moment, swallowed, and felt her breathing change. Just as swiftly, Octavia broke the shared glance and punched him on the shoulder.

"You were pretty impressive there...for an old guy with a staff," she teased, "Keep working and you might someday be as captivating as me."

"You're very confident in yourself, aren't you?"

"I've spent the last four years being the most attractive thing for miles," she said with a shrug. The bravado and confidence was all for show, but Marcus seemed to believe her, so she swallowed down the pain and smiled broadly.

"I thought Human armies were filled with women," Marcus said, "You know, equality and all that in the name of the One?"

"Human armies *are* filled with women," Octavia agreed, "But half of them look like boys with breasts."

The Wizard raised an eyebrow. "And the other half?"

"The other half are flat."

"So they just look like boys?"

189

"Exactly," Octavia said with a smile, "In that climate, I feel that I look like a beautiful duchess who could knock your teeth out."

"An alluring combination to be sure…"

"A girl can dream, right?"

"We can all dream, Octavia," Marcus said, a little too seriously for the tone of the preceding conversation.

***

"The Dark Lord?" he chuckled to himself as he watched unnoticed by the friends due to the power of the magic. The Dark Lord was a fiction of sorts, although a useful one. There was just enough truth baked in to make the meal palatable. Wise as he was, he knew it would be best not to reveal too much to too many lest he imperil the real mission. Let them have their Dark Lord for now. It would suffice to bind them together and so he could justify the lie. When to tell them the truth and how much truth to serve them? Those were the questions which occupied his mind for the near future.

***

They reached the other side of the Burning Sea and disembarked, gathering their belongings which they'd left on the shore. "That was well-cast magic, Wizards," Alexia said, although her tone was not entirely sincere, "But now we have to face the desert which sucks the life out of your people. It seemed like such a nice day, too…"

"There's no way around the cursed desert?" implored Octavia.

"No," Synthyya replied, as if that were a foolish question.

Marcus inhaled deeply through his nostrils and exhaled. "Marcus," Gwen said, "It will be all right. Just like last time, okay? I will take your cloak, again."

"Aren't you the sweetest thing, Gwendolyn?!" exclaimed Synthyya, "Why I'd take you and frost a small cake with you, you are so sweet. But we will not be crossing the Desert of Despair. No, no, no." She laughed.

"I thought there was no way around it," Quintus insisted.

"There isn't," Synthyya replied in a tone which seemed to say that he should know better.

"I'm confused," Octavia said. The others echoed her.

"We can go *under* the desert," Synthyya said, joyously clapping her hands. "I just have to find the door. Zarqqwell was always so good with this." She looked more peculiar than usual as she began knocking on thin air with her staff. She was mumbling to herself. Just when everyone's patience appeared ready to give in, she let out a triumphant sound. Synthyya bent down and clutched a handful of dark soil—so different from the stark sand only two feet further. She threw the dirt into the air and a door appeared out of nowhere. It was a standard wooden door with iron hinges and a handle. She tugged on it. It didn't open. "Hmmph, that's odd," Synthyya said to no one in particular. Of course, a random door which appeared out of thin air was also odd, but clearly, not to her. Synthyya tugged two more times before she smiled knowingly. She then pushed and the door open. "Push, not pull," she chuckled to herself, "I should have remembered."

The magical door opened and revealed a small ledge which ended in a rope ladder. Without a word, Synthyya walked through the door and started to climb down the ladder. Marcus followed her and the rest of the fellowship did the same. "I have never heard of a tunnel under the desert," Marcus said, as they stood in darkness. Synthyya hit her staff on the ground, muttered a word and her staff glowed. Marcus followed her lead again and did the same.

"The tunnel didn't exist the last time you were here, silly boy," Synthyya said, "We have worked on it for years and years. Maybe a *decem*, I'm not sure. It took the three of us a long time in exile to realize the anti-magic spell worked above-ground, but not underground."

"You dug this?" Griffin asked, incredulous.

"Not with shovels, my Elvin friend," Synthyya giggled, "With magic. Very quiet magic." She lowered her voice. "If the Empress knew we had a way out of exile, she'd have put a stop to this. She's really quite intolerable, and not at all pretty, either."

"You've used this tunnel before?" Gwen asked.

"Oh yes, quite often," Synthyya said, "We went into the world to gather necessary items like hats and pastries, as well as to learn more before returning to our exile home."

"And the Empress never knew?" Marcus asked.

"She has been quite distracted with her little war to eradicate Humans and Morphs," Synthyya explained, "This worked in our favor—at least insofar as it let us build a tunnel. The wholesale death and destruction…not so much."

"It might have been nice to know about this tunnel before we crossed the desert to see you," Octavia said in a scolding tone, "Marcus quite nearly died."

"Aren't you kind to care about him?" Synthyya said, her smile never wavering, "Such a sweet freckle-faced girl who could disembowel several men in less than an hour! That's so you, isn't it? How you worry about dear Marcus. It's touching for an old teacher to see. Sweetheart, I sent my owl to Marcus with the information when I knew you were coming, but the ogres killed it before it could reach you."

"How long will it take to cross this tunnel?" asked Griffin.

"We'll camp two-thirds of the way through and then finish tomorrow," Synthyya said, "And there is a lovely lake not far from where we emerge so that all of you can bathe. You smell like a horde of ogres if you don't mind me saying so. I should have offered my bath to you before we burned down my house. So foolish of me. Sometimes I get a touch forgetful about such things." She then began to sing to herself while she led them through the tunnel.

***

"It will be nice to be in our tent again, won't it?" Alexia asked Gwen as they took the first watch in the tunnel.

"Sometimes, I feel like it is the only safe place in the world," Gwen said.

"How I have missed you, sweet Elf."

"Wait a moment, Alexia," Gwen said, her nose wrinkled up, "I have to ask you something."

"Anything."

"Do Morphs get jealous?"

"What do you mean?"

"I mean, you and I have been... well, we've...you know." Alexia waited to watch the full-body Elf blush before answering and letting Gwen off the hook.

"I know," she said sweetly.

"Would you ever merge with another being? Other than me?" Gwen asked.

"Yes, it is how I am made," Alexia explained, looking perplexed, "I will always cherish you and will never say no to an invitation to your tent. But Morphs do not mate for life. We follow our desires. You and I are of this moment. I hope you understand."

"I do, I do," Gwen protested, "But what if *I* want to be with someone."

"Someone named Quintus?"

"Yes," Gwen said, blushing all over again. "What if I wanted to *be* with him?"

"Would I be jealous? No, Morphs don't get jealous," Alexia said, "You can be with him, although it would be different for you than being with me."

"How?"

"Are you truly a maiden like the good little Elf-girls are supposed to be?" Alexia asked. Gwen nodded. "Incredible!"

"I have a Morph's pretty head resting on my shoulder, right now," Gwen said, "So while I may be a maiden by the rules of my people, I think I left 'good little Elf-girl' a long way back in my journey."

"Yes you did," Alexia purred.

"So it's all right if I love Quintus?" Gwen asked, "Because I think I may."

"It's all right," Alexia assured her, "No more talking, okay?" Gwen nodded.

***

The fellowship emerged from the tunnel into a dazzling day and sure enough, the glimmering lake was a brief walk from the tunnel's exit. "Why don't we let the ladies wash first?" Synthyya asked. "I had a bath two nights ago, so I am still fresh as a flower. The gentlemen will wait here and give the girls their modesty. I have several things to which I must attend alone. I will be back in a few hours."

"Like what?" Griffin demanded.

"I have errands to run and I will likely take time to pray," she said with a smile, "Surely, *you* don't object."

"You pray?" Griffin asked.

"Yes, Elves are not the only beings with religion," she chuckled, "I have some tasks to accomplish, but I will come back. When I return, we will head for a most delightful inn on the road to the Historian's. I know the innkeeper and he will give us soft beds and the most delicious pork pies."

"Are you going to pray with Synthyya, Marcus?" Griffin asked, "To your gods?"

"No," Synthyya answered for him, "Marcus will spend the time with his owl. That is his assignment."

Octavia, Gwendolyn, and Alexia headed towards the lake. Synthyya went into the forest. Marcus went in the opposite direction after asking Quintus and Griffin to refrain from killing one another. He spent several minutes trying to establish a rapport with Dariuxx's owl. "I've never been good with owls," Marcus said to the bird, which simply stared at him. It spread its great wings and took flight. Within a moment, it was a speck in the sapphire sky. And then it was gone.

"Perhaps, for good," Marcus observed to no one in particular. Then he heard Synthyya's scolding voice in his head and he sat down on a tree stump and closed his eyes. He saw nothing but blackness. He ground his teeth and accelerated his breathing. It almost seemed as if the darkness was slightly less dark. Harder and harder the Wizard concentrated before a blue light seemed to enter his head. Within a few minutes, the figures sharpened and he was aware of what was happening.

Marcus was seeing through the owl's eyes. He had done it. He had made Dariuxx's bird his own. Uncomfortably, the owl's eyes were focused on the lake where the girls were bathing. Marcus knew he should break the connection, but he was so ecstatic he had made it work, he could not. He had never once in his life managed to see through an owl's eyes. He tried to survey the scene as a cool emotionless Wizard. He could see the light reflected off of the water and he could appreciate the aesthetic beauty of a woman's body, whether Morph, Human, or Elf. The curves were so well designed and delightful to the eye—nothing more, he told himself. He simply could not let his Human side come to life in this moment and he would be fine. Wizards treasured beautiful things and Marcus had never been Wizard enough to share their appreciation of precious gems, lavish cloaks, or shiny metals. Females, on the other hand... He could admire their beauty in a detached Wizardly way. So he told himself...

He thought of trying to stop, but he could not bring himself to break the connection with the owl. There was Gwendolyn, her body impossibly white and impossibly smooth as was typical of Sunrise Elves. The owl must have turned its head because now Marcus saw Octavia, freckles wildly dancing on her bare skin. Thin pink ribbons could be traced on her back and her left side, scars which were doubtless souvenirs of her combat experience. Fortuitously, the owl must have flown to another branch, because now he saw only Alexia, her tan body gliding through the water. At least, her body was familiar for she had revealed it routinely since they'd met. There was no mystery, there. No magic. No desire. He may very well have said this last part aloud to himself, as if to convince himself of it. The owl's eyes were so clear that he could see the little droplets of water cascading down their bodies. It was wrong to steal the privacy from these three lovely women. He knew this to be so. He was a Wizard and above the slavery of such desires. Yet the Humanity within Marcus stirred. He was disappointed in his lack of self-control. His Wizard side reasserted itself and Marcus broke the connection. But he had to know it was too late.

Chapter 23: Hope

"I feel better," Quintus said. "I know a Ranger shouldn't admit that, but I was a nobleman once and more accustomed to frequent bathing."

"Quintus Agrippa Aureus, the only nobleman Ranger in the world," Marcus said with a smile, "This lake was definitely a stroke of fortune." Quintus noticed something different about Marcus's tone when he mentioned the lake and wondered if something more was behind it, but let it drop. He thought it prudent and Quintus was always good at reading a situation.

"The Elf boy seems especially sour, today," Quintus said, gesturing towards Griffin who had bathed hurriedly and gotten dressed without speaking to the Human or the Wizard. "I believe that if you cut him, he bleeds vinegar."

"It may be so," Marcus chuckled.

"But if vinegar flows in his veins, then perhaps honey fills the veins of his sister," Quintus offered, "How two as different as they can spring from one womb baffles me."

"Veins coursing with honey? I am not quite sure of your anatomy theory, but she is different from him, and from Elves in general. He is typical of his kind. It is lost on you, my friend, but Elves are a bit odd," Marcus allowed, "I like his sister much more than I like Griffin."

"As do I," Quintus concurred, "But you knew that already."

"I did," Marcus said, pausing for one of those long intervals of uncomfortable silence so characteristic of Wizards. They both sat down on a log. Quintus felt like Marcus was going to tell him something about Gwen, but he didn't. "Griffin is not wicked, though, Quintus, though we may wish to judge him as such."

"He is narrow minded," Quintus said.

"He is, but you know that Elves are rarely known for their broad mindedness, even the pretty ones," Marcus said, "I believe that Gwen is different from most Elves. Very different, if I judge her correctly. Griffin is normal for his kind."

"Gwen *is* pretty."

"I do not disagree," Marcus said without inflection.

"She's not a filled with hate of other races like her brother is."

"Indeed not, but there is good in Griffin," Marcus said, "*He* saved Synthyya, not you. Not me. If he hadn't, where would we be, right now in our struggle with the Dark Lord?"

"True," Quintus allowed, "The Dark Lord is real? Truly? In the name of the Blessed One, I remain astounded. I can't quite get my mind around that truth, Marcus. Is he as powerful as the stories say?"

"I know very little about him other than he was the unparalleled master of the Dark magic which we avoid in our times," Marcus answered.

"Is such magic evil?"

"The Dark magic is not evil, but it delves into matters which are very very…" He seemed at a rare loss for words.

"Dark?" Quintus asked, Marcus smiled warmly in the way that only an old friend can muster, even at a difficult moment.

"Yes, there is a lot of such magic concerned with the mind, with life and death and with the well…as you say, 'darker' elements of our being. If Synthyya's lessons are right, then he has lived ten times the life-span of a normal Wizard, if that is what he is. And he was powerful enough to overthrow an entire civilization, although I do not know how one Wizard alone could do this sort of thing. I presume this Historian is an expert on that. At least I hope."

"Hope is good."

"Hope is something the Dark Lord destroys in all the fairy tales in which he appears," Marcus said softly, "The Classical world was unified and advanced—much more so than our world. You have looked upon the Ruined City with me. You know what they were capable of doing. If he could devastate their civilization, there is no telling what he could do to ours."

"Do you think he means to kill us all and use our hearts to make orcs?"

"I cannot guess at his plan, but it seems he is using the leaders of the races like one of those entertainers who amuses children with puppets."

"He plays off their fears and their hatred," Quintus noted.

"Which is why Griffin gives me hope," Marcus said, "He seems to be losing a little of that hatred."

"Not enough for me."

"Nor for me," Marcus agreed, "But he is better than he was. We can agree on that." Quintus nodded. "He was brought up with this hatred. It was not in his heart when he was born."

"And what beings can do, beings can undo," Quintus observed.

"Exactly," Marcus said, "Quintus, I have been lost for so very long. You know that, brother. My life has never had meaning since…"

"I know," Quintus cut him off so he wouldn't have to articulate the tragedy.

Marcus hung his head for a while. "Quintus Agrippa, you know how I have lived. I have drunk too much, warmed a bed with too many, and cared for too few."

"I have been much the same, dear friend," Quintus said.

"But now, I feel like I have a purpose in my life," Marcus said, "I cannot hope to defeat the Dark Lord. I am a mere half-Wizard and not very powerful, even for my own kind. But I can help and if I do, then I feel like there was a reason for everything I have endured. Isn't that true?"

"I would say it is," Quintus agreed, "I too have a purpose. I will help you with this goal. If I had not met you, Marcus, I would be dead. You know I believe the Golden One sees all and directs all. You saved my life for a reason nearly a *decem* ago. My purpose in this world must be to assist with your quest." Marcus smiled. Whether it was at Quintus's correct use of a Wizard term or for some other reason, Quintus could not tell.

"You have an even more immediate purpose, Quintus."

"More immediate than helping to save the world?" the Human asked, his gray eyes twinkling ever so slightly.

"Gwendolyn," Marcus said, "Your love for her gives you direction and purpose. Your love for Gwen is more important to me than anything, including our quest. It enriches you both and gives hope to everyone, including me. If I may descend into the dramatics of my Human side, I would say your love could save our world."

"You too can love again, Marcus."

"I hope that is so, my friend," Marcus said, trying to ignore the forces twisting inside of him, "But love is complex for Wizards."

***

Oh yes, the "Dark Lord" was certainly the road to choose, he noted to himself, as he watched them, unseen. If only he could conjure up a damsel in distress or a dragon, then the hook would be so buried in the half-Wizard's cheek, he would be certain to do all that needed to be done. "Dominus Maleficarum." He smiled to himself. While this weakness for such tales was especially pronounced for Marcus, it was no less true for the others. This could all work, he hoped to himself. If presented properly, this could all work. A world threatened by "The Dark Lord!" He smiled again and a thousand ideas scampered about in his brain.

***

"How did your prayers go?" asked Griffin, not entirely sincerely.

"Quite well," Synthyya said, not appearing to notice the edge to his words, "I think that a spiritual life is very important to one's happiness." Her hair was red again, but no one bothered to point it out, anymore.

"I think you Wizards do not recognize enough gods," Griffin said, "The Spirits are everywhere and in everything. I cannot see why you reduce them to six elements."

Synthyya just smiled broadly. "Gods are like dinners," she said cheerfully, "You may love roasted boar whereas it gives my insides an ache. I might walk for days to have a fresh fish dinner cooked in wine by the Sea Peoples. Alexia might enjoy a freshly killed striped horse when she's a lioness. Different tastes but all food."

Octavia didn't fully understand Synthyya's extended metaphor, but wanted to stand up for her, especially as she had returned to red hair, so she said, "Wizards have more gods than Humans. We have the One, does that irritate you, Griffin?"

"I think that you are deceiving yourselves, that's all," he said glumly, "The sun is not one true God watching over you. It is simply one spirit amongst many."

"Oh Griffin," his sister chastised him, "There is so much to learn in the world. Why can't you use your Elvin ears to hear and to learn about everyone's traditions?" He gave her a sour look but remained tight lipped.

Quintus spoke, "I do not think belief in the Golden One limits things. I believe worshiping the One makes things limitless. The One is male and female, young and old, rich and poor. To me, all races are united in the Golden One because the Sacred Circle encompasses everything." He absently fingered the iron circle which hung around his neck, representing his faith. Gwen seemed impressed and gave him a fawning look. He blushed a little.

"That's not what your barren monks and nuns say as they burn their incense and memorize their texts," Alexia said, "They call the rest of us 'heathens.' You Humans talk about the equality in the One, but then you have dukes and duchesses, counts and countesses, barons and baronesses. 'Equality' seems a slippery term, hardly extended to all of your people." She spat as if to judge all of Humanity.

"I take what I want from monks or nuns and leave what I find distasteful. I have never given any man or woman exclusive rights to tell me about the Golden One," Quintus said, gazing at the bright yellow sun which hung in the sky as a fiery orb of hope, "I do not necessarily disagree with you about the

201

hypocrisy of a hereditary nobility, either. As we all know, I would not have made a good duke."

"What about you, Octavia?" Gwen asked, "You are Human. Do you pray to the sun? And if so, do you think like Quintus?"

"I believe in the One," Octavia said, looking down at her own iron ring around her neck, "I do not think quite like Quintus. My father brought us up to go to the holy places and pray with the monks and nuns and I always have. Quintus sounds like quite the original thinker, so perhaps he would make a better duke than he thinks. At least a more interesting one." She smiled girlishly. It was an odd look for her, but not as odd as you might have expected if you saw it. "What about you, Marcus? You are split between the Human and Wizard worlds. What do you believe?"

"When I was young, I prayed to the gods of my father," he answered, "However, we were not a good fit, me and my gods. They stopped answering my prayers and so I stopped giving them the satisfaction of praying." His eyes hardened and his lip curled into a scowl. Quintus touched his arm and nodded sympathetically. Marcus sighed and winced. "I left my gods many miles ago, so you will have to pray without me."

"You do not pray?" Gwen asked, "For anything?"

"I do not," he said coldly and the little Elf saw the darkness, as it fluttered about the corners of Marcus's eyes.

Synthyya regarded Marcus for a long Wizard moment with something of a mother's mix of sympathy and judgment. She shook her head and her face changed, "Marcus has his reasons and they are good ones, even if he and I part company on issues of theology. Nevertheless, the Historian will give us a new focus. He can help us understand what has come to pass." She smiled confidently.

"Is he far?" asked Gwen.

"Yes," said Synthyya. She paused again in Wizardly fashion for a short eternity. "Oh, you wish to know how far? Too far for today. We will come upon an inn soon. I know the innkeeper, a Human named Septimus. A very kind man with the best pork pies in all the wide world. He harbors one inconvenient hatred, but we will have a nice warm bed and those divine pork pies to get us through the night."

"What do you mean?" asked Octavia.

"I mean the nights are growing colder as autumn wears on and a warm fire and a decent bed will aid us," Synthyya said cheerfully, "Perhaps a piping hot cup of tea, too." Marcus grimaced and Synthyya stuck out her tongue at him. She knew he hated tea.

"No, that's not what I was asking about," Octavia replied graciously.

"Oh, you mean the pies? They have this flaky crust and are stuffed with a delicious combination of pig flesh which he cooks with onions and some spices he will not reveal..."

"I believe Octavia—and the rest of us—were curious about the 'inconvenient hatred' of which you spoke," Marcus explained patiently.

"Of course, of course, Marcus," she said with a chuckle, "He hates Morphs."

"Nice," said Alexia.

"Aren't Humans allied with Morphs?" asked Griffin.

"They are, but Septimus does not care for alliances or wars. He will board Elves, Wizards, and Humans so long as they pay, but never Morphs," Synthyya explained.

"Why not?" asked Quintus.

"A pack of bear Morphs killed his wife several years ago," Synthyya said, "Septimus hates them all. He is uncannily observant for a Human. He can spot a Morph in Human form. I've seen it. He'll kill the Morph on sight no matter who he or she is with. Alexia will have to morph into something typical like a dog or a cat. If it's dark and he's distracted, he might not notice."

"Morphs haven't been able to be dogs or cats for centuries," Marcus said, "It would be a good cover. He'd be looking for a bear or a wolf or an eagle."

"I can pass for Human," Alexia insisted, "I assure you I have passed many times before. It won't be a problem for me."

"Oh no, sweetie, he will spot you and kill you," Synthyya said merrily, "And I am growing to like you, so that would be a pity. If you can become a pet, we'll sneak you a pork pie."

Alexia pouted for several minutes, then took off her dress and handed it to Gwen before becoming a very average-looking dog. A little while later, they came to a small village and Synthyya strode up to the Hawk's Talon Inn and knocked on the bright red door. It opened halfway and was then flung open as the innkeeper smiled.

"Synthyya, I did not know you were off the island again," Septimus bellowed. He was a large man with a thick beard, a bald head, and a huge belly which shook every time he laughed, which had been frequently in the brief time since he'd opened the door.

"Septimus, I am on Wizard business again," Synthyya said, "I am a lady of leisure, all this work is killing me." She smiled broadly, her white teeth contrasting with her red lips.

"You have quite an army with you," he said, pretending to be impressed.

"I mentioned your pork pies and people kept joining my group," she chuckled. Septimus laughed heartily, his belly quavering this way and that.

"I shall try to live up to your gracious description," he said, turning to the fellowship, "I was just starting a batch of pies, now. They will help ward off the chill. Ale can warm a being up, as well. I must confess that I did not expect you, Synthyya."

"Wizards have a habit of showing up when you least expect them," Octavia blurted out. Septimus put a huge hand on her shoulder and laughed again.

"Very true, Red, you are most welcome," he said, "I only have three rooms available, so you will need to share. I apologize for the inconvenience, but if Synthyya had let me know, I'd have held all my rooms for her. She is the best Wizard I know. I know the Council has condemned you Wizards, but the Council has little sway here. We are far from the lawmakers and a wise innkeeper makes a living by boarding all kinds. That goes for the Elves, too. I welcome you, so long as you pay."

"You are very kind," Synthyya said, studying the group, "And you know I have coin to pay for all. Wizard coin will do, won't it?"

He thought for a moment. "Yes, that would be a copper per room, so three stars will get you dinner, three rooms, and a breakfast."

Synthyya fumbled around and gave him three copper coins with a closed eye inscribed upon them, honoring the youngest god, that of Darkness. She fingered a silver coin with a river and handed that over, too.

"You mistakenly gave me a half-silver with your payment, old friend," Septimus said, "I love to see the Water Goddess's coin, but am too honest to take your overpayment."

"This is for another matter which you and I can discuss after my party is settled," Synthyya said with a smile, "Gwen and Octavia can share a room, so can Marcus and Quintus. Griffin, I would love to spend some time discussing spiritual matters with you. Would you mind sharing my room?"

"But you are a woman and I am a man," Griffin said.

"Elves," laughed Septimus, "you are so strict about such matters."

"I promise I won't seduce you if you make the same promise," Synthyya said cheekily.

"Fine," he said, "but I hope the pies are as you promise."

"There will be barrels of ale as well," Septimus said, "Just one thing." He barred the entrance just as Gwen and Alexia were stepping through. "No animals."

"She's my precious little dog," Gwen said sweetly, "She sleeps at the foot of my bed."

"You are a beautiful little Elf," said Septimus, "And I am partial to Elves, more so than most Humans are." He elbowed Quintus and his tone became lewd, "I bet you don't know that Elves are smooth all over, eh?" Quintus kept his composure and forced a smile. "But as pretty as you are, you cannot convince me. Your dog is not allowed."

"The dog gets very frightened of the night," Marcus explained, "She will be no trouble at all." Alexia barked in as friendly a way as she could.

"Your dog will be very safe in the stable with the horses and other animals," Septimus assured Gwen, "I lock the door and have only one key. But no dogs in the inn."

"Even for an old friend, Septimus?" Synthyya asked.

"I only have two rules," Septimus insisted, "The dog sleeps in the stable."

"I do have the coin of the Fire God with which I could part, for your trouble."

"Synthyya, even a full silver in the coin of Wizards cannot relax the rules I ask of you," he said, kindly but firmly, "Animals in the stable and Morphs never darken my door. Those are my rules and I will not suspend them, even for such a pretty little Elf with the boundless sky in her two eyes." He smiled at Gwen.

"It is a fair rule," Synthyya agreed, putting away the full silver, "We are grateful for your hospitality." She whispered to Marcus, "See that she gets a pie."

***

"Octavia, will you do me a favor?" Gwen asked.

"Of course, Gwen," she said. Octavia had been taught to dislike Elves much as Wizards, but she had grown as fond of Gwen as she had of Marcus. Her world was much different than she had expected it to be.

"Do not tell my brother what I am going to do tonight."

"What are you going to do?"

"I am going to sneak into Quintus's room," she said with a knowing look, "He will leave the door unlocked. We arranged it at dinner."

"A fine dinner. The pork pies were as good as Synthyya said they were," Octavia chuckled, the ale had loosened her tongue, "You will head to his room, will you? Do you think that Alexia might get jealous?"

"How did you know about that?"

"I have brains, brawn, and beauty, Gwen," Octavia said with a smile, "I am the complete package. Be not afraid, your secrets are safe with me."

"You are such a friend," Gwen said, throwing her delicate arms around Octavia's neck. "Alexia and I spoke. She will not be jealous."

"She is a woman like us, even if she is a beast from time to time. We do not always mean what we say, you know that," Octavia cautioned her.

"Octavia, my heart has been on fire since that night Quintus freed me," Gwen said, "I can think of no other way to quench the flames."

"You are a maiden...with a man, I mean?" Octavia asked. Gwen nodded. "I can tell you what I know if you are interested." Gwen nodded all wide-eyed. "Before we turn to that, tell me: what will Marcus do while you are in there with his roommate?"

"Quintus said he'd go somewhere. He was sure Marcus wouldn't mind."

"Do you think he'd come *here*? I mean trade rooms with you?" Octavia asked.

"Would you want that?" Gwen asked. Octavia swiftly changed the subject and gave her all the advice she could, based on what she knew and what she had heard. Four years as a professional soldier had certainly informed her about the act.

***

The Wizard had left the room just in time to pass Gwen in the hall way, her pale face a deep crimson. Quintus would soon see her head-to-toe in that shade. Good for Quintus, Marcus thought as he walked. Even if the world they knew was going to end, Quintus would have his moment of joy, tonight. He deserved no less. What of Marcus himself? That was a thornier issue. He knew he had several options for the evening to give Gwen and Quintus their privacy. Some of Marcus's options were safer than others. One was markedly unsafe. Logically, it was not the one to choose. Were Marcus a full blooded Wizard, it would be unthinkable that he'd have chosen that option when others were available. Still, he was a Human, too and Humans are noted for being pulled by their emotions. If only he had failed with the owl, he would not be opening this door. But as he had looked through that bird's eyes, he had seen things. Beautiful things. Desirable things. He knew that his choice to open this door would have consequences. His Wizard side warned him that there would be no going back to the way things were if he opened the door. If the others found out, there would be repercussions. All this was clear. Yet being Human meant living with feelings. Those feelings might be inconvenient or even potentially dangerous, but they were no less real.

The door opened of its own accord after he waved his hand over it. Few Human doors could be easily barred against a simple spell of air magic which could unlock locks, unbar doors, turn knobs, etc.

"I sort of expected you," she said as she stood there, unsurprised.

"Did you?"

"I had a feeling, that's all."

"Yes," Marcus said, "So did I. A feeling."

"That explains why you're here," she said, smiling.

"I suppose that it does," he agreed.

"I have long wanted to do this," she admitted, "To be with you in this way."

"I have long fought this urge," Marcus said, "But my fight was in vain."

"This is not uncommon," she said, her eyes twinkling. She removed his cloak. "Undress, Marcus, there is no one here but us."

"You're wearing a dress?" he remarked.

"I want you to remove it with your magic," she replied with narrowed eyes, her voice crackling with energy. He paused for a moment and chanted the words. The dress flew over her head and the Wizard drank in the image of her bare body, its soft curves framed by the moonlight coming through the window.

"As requested..." he said gesturing towards her unclad form, giving a slight ridiculous bow. She looked deep into his violet eyes and saw what she wanted to see. She had him. He was hers.

"Please tell me you saved me one of those pies for me," she purred.

"I did," he said, "You can enjoy it when we are done, Alexia."

"Excellent." Then she pounced on him as if she were one of the jungle cats she could be in a moment. He was equal to the task, his strong arms embracing her tightly as he pressed his mouth against hers. Alexia parted her lips and slipped her tongue into his mouth. She had never tasted a Wizard before. It was unlike an Elf or a Human or a Morph. His breathing grew heavy with fierce desire and she reveled in this flare of passion of a Wizard, even if he was half-Human. She dug her nails into his bare shoulders and he did not flinch. Alexia knew he could wave his hand and speak some word and she'd be thrown all over this barn if he wanted that. She loved the fear that he could do this to her. But despite his powers, he was hers. Only when she was certain it was time, did she allow it all to come to completion.

The moment the euphoria faded, he knew he should not have visited Alexia. It was a moment of desire brought on by his illicit viewing of the lake. All three women were lovely to behold, but Alexia seemed to be the most likely to reciprocate with a minimum of post-act drama. This was his logical side, telling him that merging would Alexia would lead to the least amount of complications.

As he left the stable, Marcus knew in his logical Wizard way that this was completely wrong.

Chapter 24: The Coldness of the North

"Weren't the pork pies divine?" Synthyya asked, adjusting her hat over today's hair color—a mousy brown.

"Like nothing in the world," Quintus said, his gaze falling on Gwen.

"And after dinner when Septimus sang and the ale flowed?" Synthyya cheerfully recounted, "Some of the best nights of my life have been in the Hawk's Talon."

"I certainly had the best night of my life," Gwen said, smiling sideways at Quintus. Alexia had been right, it was very different with a man. But even though Quintus was so strong, he had been unfathomably gentle with Gwendolyn—almost as if he feared he would break her with his bare hands if he did not check himself. Of course, Quintus had been with Elf girls before and this should have bothered her. But he was surprisingly tender and kind and the joy she had felt was so complete and so absolute that she was certain she loved him. Gwendolyn had never loved any boy romantically. She shot arrows with the boys, but they never seemed to look at her in that way and usually they lost interest when she beat them at target practice. Briefly, when she had 15 sun cycles, she toyed with the idea of letting the boys win. But something stopped her. If she were Griffin, she'd have thought it was the Spirits, but she was not Griffin. Whatever it was—even if it was simply a voice inside her—she refused to bury her gift. No one shot arrows like Gwendolyn and she was adamant that the whole of Elfland knew it. They did not like it. But they knew it. Quintus let her be who she was. He did not need her to be what her people thought she should be. In many ways, Gwen wished she had been interested in things that other Elf girls loved—her life would have been so easy. But easy was not exciting. And Quintus Agrippa Aureus was exciting. When he touched her, it was like the Wizard's thunderbolt had hit her. And when he embraced her, her knees went weak. No one had ever done that to her.

"We are in a swamp," Alexia observed with distaste.

"Oh, I hadn't really noticed," Synthyya said, "It *is* a swamp. That's good."

"Why is that good?" asked Octavia as she breathed in the thick air with effort.

"It means we're on the right path," Synthyya replied, "I think."

"You *think*?" asked Griffin. "You're not sure?"

"I don't get out as much as I'd like since my exile," Synthyya said with a full measure of unwarranted cheer, "And when I do, things change over and over again. I do recall a swamp, so that's good." Alexia shook her head and morphed into a bird, so that she didn't have to march through a swamp. She chose a robin.

Octavia had noticed Marcus was speaking to no one. He was striding along with the owl on his shoulder, avoiding eye contact with the Fellowship. There had been no banter between them this morning and that was odd. Perhaps he had something weighty and Wizardy on his brain. He alone amongst the Fellowship of Outcasts had guessed at the Dark Lord's existence. Of course, his melancholy could simply be that he was an outcast—thrown out of the western mountains by an indifferent father, never knowing his mother, suffering some unspoken travesty to which he and Quintus constantly alluded but never fully articulated. Maybe the pork pies didn't agree with him or he hated swamps. She knew she should just leave it alone and accept a Wizard on his own terms. But something gnawed at her, dogging every step she took. It was a question sitting in the pit of her hard stomach. It was one of *those* questions. You knew you should not ask it. You knew you should just let it sleep in the darkness where it dwelt. You knew there was no answer you would like. You should leave it alone. Octavia Flavius, youngest child of an iron worker, an exceptional warrior, and a thoroughly decent Human knew it was not a good question to ask. Yet she simply had to ask it.

Octavia took a deep breath of thick, soupy air and quickened her pace so she caught up with the lonely Wizard, his dark cloak hanging on his broad shoulders, the hood pulled up over his head against the autumnal chill. The brown owl sat mute upon his left shoulder, so she approached him on his right to avoid disturbing it.

"Good morning," she opened. He did not break pace, using the staff as a walking stick. It made an unpleasant sound as it landed in the mud. The air smelled of rotting plants. The Wizard did not look at her.

"Good morning," he repeated.

"Gwen ended up in your room last night with her prince, didn't she?" Octavia tried to keep the tone light, but knew she was clumsy in handling people, especially Wizards.

Marcus looked back at Quintus and Gwen walking along merrily. Quintus was adding fresh flowers to her flaxen hair. Where he had found flowers in this noxious place, who could guess. Marcus's eyes narrowed. "Yes."

Octavia could sense the way a battle waxed and waned. She could feel when to attack and when to defend. Was conversation so different? She knew this conversation would lead nowhere good, and yet she could not stop herself. "I was quite lonely," she joked, "when Gwen left. But at least I didn't get kicked out of my room for their tryst." Marcus did not take the bait left for him. He was stony silent. "Did they kick you out?" she asked directly.

"I left of my own free will."

"Where did you go?"

He looked at her for the first time in the conversation with pain in his violet eyes, as he struggled to meet her green ones. His mouth moved several times, but no sound came out. He stared at the sky for a long long time.

"I went out," he said simply.

***

"Who is the Historian?" Griffin asked when they stopped to rest after the vile swamp had finally ended. He sought to break the silence, for he wondered why the rest of the group was acting so oddly this morning. Only Synthyya—the bizarre hair-changing Wizard, who had spoken to him half the night about religion after she'd returned from some secret

212

errands—seemed normal. Well, not normal but at least *herself.* The other five were all acting queerly this morning, as if they were all in on a joke he'd missed.

"He is half Elf and half Human and he knows so much about the world," Synthyya said. "He is very very old and very very learned."

"Why do you think he can help?" Griffin asked.

"He knows more about the last few thousand years than anyone in any of the races. He is always learning new things about old events," she gushed, "My hope is that he has more details about what the Dark Lord did to the Classical civilization."

"And perhaps what the Dark Lord is doing now," Griffin added.

"Exactly," she said, "I could not help but notice that you seem to have acquiesced to us that *Dominus Maleficarum* is more than a fairy tale, Griffin."

"It was hard to explain the dead goblins, otherwise," he explained.

She studied him with piercing purple eyes. "Yes, you are coming along quite nicely," she said with an impish grin.

***

"Do you know how much longer this Wizard woman is going to take before we get to the Historian?" Alexia asked Octavia while both were gathering wood for a fire. Conveniently, Quintus and Gwen had been sent off to hunt as if Synthyya hadn't a clue about what they were likely to do together when alone and deep in the cover of the woods. Marcus was brooding under a tree. Griffin and Synthyya were engaged in conversation, so Alexia and Octavia were picking up fallen branches.

"I have no clue," Octavia said.

"You should ask Marcus," Alexia said, "He's also a Wizard. Maybe he knows." She felt a slight twinge at dropping his name. There was no need to throw it all in Octavia's face. She was a nice enough girl, if a bit awkward. Alexia wasn't sure why she had done it. Was it because Octavia had rejected her in the tent that night? Was it simply because she could not help reminding other girls that they did not have what she had? Did it have to do with Alexia's parents? Was it Gwendolyn? *Gwendolyn.* The name danced on Alexia's tongue. She had told her she would not be jealous of Quintus. It was the truth when she'd spoken it. Alexia had never been jealous of any lover when he or she took on another one. Even lovers for whom she had a genuine affection did not stir jealousy in her breast when they sought a new embrace. Alexia always had the next embrace to look for as well. And in those embraces, bare bodies entwined, lips pressed against one another to stop the pain—she had always found redemption. When Gwendolyn had seemed particularly bouncy this morning, Alexia had asked why. It was one of those questions. Alexia hadn't even expected an answer. She hated herself for caring. She *knew* Gwen would sleep with Quintus. They had spoken about it. Alexia had encouraged Gwen to pursue it. And once Gwen had decided to do it, there was no other force in the Four Realms that could have prevented the burly Ranger from such an outcome. Perhaps, the end of the world triggered by some Dark Lord may have stopped him—but perhaps not. The scent of desire was thick upon Quintus Agrippa Aureus. Alexia did what she had always done—sought a new lover to wash away the old. This time she'd entranced the Wizard, who she'd believed was immovable. And yet there he was last night, shedding his clothes and acting like a Human. It was an astounding conquest for Alexia. Yet for the first time in her life, it wasn't enough.

Alexia almost regretted dropping Marcus's name and half-hoped for an instant that Octavia would let it pass. She did not. "Marcus hasn't been very talkative today."

"Is that so?" Alexia asked. Octavia's eyes met hers. Both women knew in that moment. But Octavia had to be certain. Surely, you understand.

"Do you know where he went last night when Gwen visited Quintus?"

The Morph paused. She could have lied without guilt to spare the awkward Human girl. But she didn't. "He came to visit me," Alexia said. It wasn't fair and it wasn't kind, but the pained look on Octavia's face helped soothe Alexia's hurt, if only for a moment.

"Why would he do that?" It was a stupid question and Octavia knew it, but she couldn't stop now. The cart was already careening down the hill, heading for a crash.

"I had something he needed," Alexia said in a barely audible voice.

***

Octavia was sitting alone, hugging her knees at the edge of the forest when he approached. "I had thought Griffin was taking first watch," Marcus said.

She knew he would come. His stupid owl had been circling her for an hour. He probably was watching her. That's why she refused to weep. Not if he could see. "I couldn't sleep, that's all," she said coldly, "Shouldn't you be recharging your sorcerer powers and all that?" She knew Wizards hated being called "sorcerers" and she had pointedly refused to utter the ugly term since she'd met him until this very moment. It was a slur designed to hurt and she wielded it like a knife.

He let it pass. "Are you angry with me?" he asked.

"Why in the Four Realms would I be angry with you?"

"You seem angry."

"I'm just cold."

"But you are a woman of the North," he said with a wan smile.

"There is something different about this fall," she observed, "Something biting in the wind which has never been there."

"I agree," he said, "You may take my cloak if you are cold."

She recoiled. "No, thank you, I am just fine without your cloak."

A hard silence endured between them. "I regret it."

"What?"

He was going to have to say it. "What I did last night."

"You mean sleeping with Alexia? Why would you regret it?" Octavia asked, her voice rising in pitch, "The girl exudes so much desire, she is virtually aflame. If I were a man, I'd have visited her last night myself." He winced.

"It's not like that," he said, "I just…"

"I get it, you're half Human. She's desirable and you desired her," Octavia said, "What's the big deal? Why are you out here in the middle of the night talking about it with me? Do you think I care?"

"Do you?"

"No."

"Is that true?"

"It is," she said firmly, "You saved me from my own people and I am grateful for it. There are times I regret what I did on that day, but it is done."

"Don't regret it."

"Don't tell me what to regret," she snapped with terrifying fury, "We are comrades, Marcus. I do not care if you choose to merge with a Morph or anything else, although I'd appreciate it if we could not talk about it any longer. It does not interest me." She looked at him with stony eyes.

"I am very sorry," he said softly, "I just wanted to say that."

"You have said it, now please go to sleep," she said coldly, "I have the second watch."

***

"That is inconceivable!" Griffin exclaimed. "There is no way. She would not. She could not. It cannot be so."

"It is," Alexia said, "And it is only because I think so much of you that I tell you." She ran her fingers through his pale yellow hair. His indignation brought her joy. It was not deep or pure joy, but it was a frisson of joy nonetheless.

"Gwen is rebellious, but she would never do such a thing," he insisted.

216

"Why not?" Alexia asked as she put her face right in front of his and stared deep into his light blue eyes. "Surely you know what Gwen did with me."

He turned paler, if that were possible. "I suspected," he said, "But this is worse."

"Because he's a Human?"

"Because he's a man," Griffin said.

"You are a man," she cooed, "Perhaps we can explore that a little in this tent of yours, right now. No one is awake. It is still my watch for another hour. Maybe, I could watch you. Or you could watch me." She stood up and slipped her dress off effortlessly. It dropped to her feet and she stepped out of it. Griffin sat up and stared. She stood confidently a finger's length away from him and she knew that she had only to grab that blond head and pull it a little closer for the Elf to belong to her, entirely. Alexia had resisted this move previously, but her feelings for Gwen and recent events had left her no other choice.

Griffin was caught between his desire and his wrath. If Alexia were right, Gwendolyn was playing a dangerous game. The Ranger was a man and a man could put a baby in her belly. Alexia was alluring and her beauty clouded his head. Yet desire could wait, as tempting as it was, so close and so available. His fury could not. With some effort at self-control, he brushed past Alexia and exited his tent, screaming Gwendolyn's name.

After several minutes, she emerged from her tent. "What is wrong?" she asked innocently. She was so innocent, he observed. Damn her. "Are you okay?"

Quintus Agrippa Aureus, disgraced son of a nobleman, emerged from the very same tent. It was so. Just as Alexia had reported. Octavia was looking on. Even the Wizards awoke at the ruckus. "I am not okay!" roared Griffin. "You and the Human? Together? Like this? Elves and Humans cannot be joined together like this. There can be no sacred joining ceremony between Elves and Humans. And without the ceremony, you are just his…"

"My what?" hissed Quintus through clenched teeth.

Griffin did not flinch. "She knows what I mean."

217

"Say it," Quintus demanded.

"No," said Gwen, "*I* will say it. Elves believe an Elf maiden can only merge with an Elf man after the clerics have said the words and their right hands have been bound together with the leather made from hide of a one year old calf. Or else I'd be a whore."

"It is the way of our race," he pleaded.

"It is not my way," she said.

"It is your way. You are an Elf. You are my sister," he declared, "You must stop this behavior with the Human. It is not too late."

"You don't own me," Gwen said, more fiercely than he had ever heard her, "The Elf kingdom does not own me. No one owns me." She narrowed her eyes and looked at her brother and all of the spectators. Gwen took the leaves out of her hair and threw them on the ground, "These belong to the trees—they are not mine." She tossed aside her bow. "This was a gift from Marcus—it is not truly mine." She met her brother's gaze with a steely look and then proceeded to strip off her garments. "These are not my clothes. I have borrowed them from leftovers and generous friends since we were freed."

"Cover yourself, Gwen!" he shouted.

"Are you shamed? *This* is all that I truly have in this world," she thundered, gesturing at her unclad body, "It is mine to do with what I please." With that, she turned sharply and returned to her tent as she left everyone staring with their mouths agape.

Chapter 25: Fiercely Alone

"Her hair is blue, today," Alexia grumbled under her breath.

"She's completely mad," Griffin agreed.

"It's like she's not totally with us, but that part of her brain is somewhere else."

"Yes, buying hats or something frivolous," he whispered back.

"Do you think this is the way to the Historian?" she asked.

"Do you think there actually *is* a Historian?" he retorted.

"Let's say there is," Alexia said, "Just for the sake of it all. How is he going to help a band of misfits destroy the Dark Lord? This whole thing is just absurd."

"So you believe in the Dark Lord?"

"I don't know. It is hard to argue with the dead trolls we saw," Alexia shrugged, "Although our only eyewitness to the Dark Lord's existence happens to be a completely insane Wizard, whose hair is currently blue. I am so finished with all of this."

"I should be rescuing my parents," Griffin grumbled.

"Why?"

"Are you serious?"

"My parents mean *nothing* to me," she growled, her eyes downcast.

"My parents mean everything to me," he replied, "And they are the only ones who can straighten out Gwendolyn."

That was the word both were avoiding. Their conversation about Synthyya's possible insanity was meant to skirt the topic of Gwen's unexpected tantrum.

"I don't like her with Quintus," Alexia said. She didn't think she could bring herself to think it, let alone say it. But this was a desperate situation and Griffin was her only natural ally in it.

"I feel the same way," he said, "Humans cannot be trusted."

"He is much older than she is," Alexia offered, "I make him to be at least 35 of your sun cycles, maybe more."

"He has a hardness in him," Griffin suggested.

"She is so innocent of the world, isn't she?"

"She is," Griffin agreed with a sigh, "And Elf girls apparently have a poor history when Quintus Agrippa Aureus loves them."

"She is too special to come to that end," Alexia said softly.

Griffin looked deep into her dark eyes. This was a bad bargain and he knew it. Alexia would help him break Quintus and Gwendolyn apart because *she* wanted to be with Gwendolyn. This would be no better. Elves had rules about two women acting in such a way and it was absolutely forbidden for an Elf to befriend a Morph, let alone... Alexia was a Morph and a woman. O Spirits, what a woman! He shook his head to try and clear it. If he succeeded in removing Quintus, it would only clear a path for Alexia. Which would be more immoral? Which would be worse for his little sister? He stared at Alexia intently. Clearly, Quintus was the most immediate threat. He was the being whom Gwen had convinced herself that she loved so dearly. He had to be expelled from her graces. Alexia would be a future problem and the present always came before the future. Alexia was a problem, but not the most pressing problem. Still, as she nodded a wordless consent to their project and walked away, he stared at her body and wondered if he was being motivated by issues other than his sister's complete welfare.

***

Octavia had not said one word to Marcus since the sun had crested the hills of this sloping landscape. They were heading east, that much was clear. The sun had been in front of them when they began, but other than that, even Marcus had no idea where they were. He had spent little time in the Far South, as the Humans termed it. They were south of the great River of Hope, the Meridian, which bisected the world they knew, of this he was certain. Once in the recent past, he knew that Humans were north and Elves were south of the river, plain and simple. But Humans had reproduced far more quickly than Elves and had pushed across the river many generations earlier, calling the lands they conquered the Far South to distinguish it from the previous South, where Quintus grew up. Marcus presumed they were walking somewhere on the border between the Humans and Elves, as there were fortifications in the distance, great stone towers, serpentine walls, and the solid castles so beloved by Humans. Such bellicose building marred the landscape and reminded him of the bitterness of the war in these parts.

Synthyya had studiously avoided the Via or indeed any major roads, so they hadn't seen many Humans or Elves. Marcus trusted Synthyya. Her hair changes were odd, as were her hat choices, especially back when she'd had a veritable arsenal of hats. But she was a great Wizard. The rumors about her madness were untrue and always had been. Of this, as well, he was certain. He knew the others were struggling to trust her and so he tried to hold up his own example to guide them. He glanced back at Octavia. She strode on, all sinew and muscle in her legs, fiercely clutching the battle axe. There was a grim look of determination on her face and her green eyes were narrow with focus. She did not deign to look at Marcus more than twice today. And both of those times, all he saw was cool detachment. She was not consumed with a boiling hatred, which might have been better. She simply looked disappointed and disgusted. That was worse. But if she was so upset that he had visited Alexia, what did that mean about how she once felt about him? Did she simply expect him to be a better man? Or was her coldness a result of some tenderness she had in her heart for the Wizard? "Once had in her heart," he corrected himself in his head. Clearly, it was no longer there. Was that for the best? Probably. But he did not truly know. Not for certain.

"Can you see ahead for us, Marcus?" Synthyya asked. He nodded, somewhat startled. Dariuxx's owl had outstripped them and Marcus stopped to concentrate. Octavia walked right by him without breaking stride or acknowledging his presence.

Marcus closed his eyes and concentrated until the black turned to gray. The gray would not let up and turn to light, so he redoubled his efforts, clutching the staff of his old teacher, Zarqqwell, in the hopes it would help him. Finally, the scene unfolded in his head and he saw with the owl's eyes. This magic had been his downfall, of course, and that fact was not lost on him.

"It is still clear, if we continue this way," Marcus said, "There are a few Human shepherds and sheep, but nothing else."

"Good," said Quintus, "Are we near our destination, Synthyya?"

"Hard to tell," she said, "The landscapes are familiar, but I've not visited him in a *decem* or so. We are a probably a few days away. Or closer. Or further." She shrugged.

"Very well," Quintus said, totally placated. Of course, this was not the way that Quintus Agrippa Aureus generally conducted himself when he was trying to get to a destination. He was unfailingly impatient about where they were going and insistent about scouting ahead himself. He trusted no one's skills as he trusted his own. That was the usual Quintus, anyway. It would have been quite strange for him to let Synthyya guide them, especially given her apparent problems with navigation. He would have chafed at letting Marcus and some enchanted owl determine the right path, as well. Nor would Quintus ever march in the center of any line of Rangers. And yet there he was, his arm locked around Gwen, following along, blithely unconcerned. She looked radiant this morning when the sun caught her blonde hair, which she had pinned up with fresh leaves and flowers. She walked as gracefully as a deer, her very movements seemed musical. No one could fail to notice that Quintus rarely went more than a few minutes without turning his head to gaze upon his love. She blushed every single time her icy blue eyes met his grey ones. In some ways, Marcus's heart swelled to see his friend's joy; in others, he felt that heart crushed beneath the weight of what he had done and what he had failed to do.

"Yes, this is the very place," Synthyya said.

"So we've found the Historian?" Gwen asked.

"No, my sweet little Elf girl," Synthyya said, "We are not yet there. We are here."

"Where is here?" Octavia asked in a monotone.

"Here is where we are," Synthyya said cheerfully. "We must split the fellowship for a little while, so some of us might follow this ancient road south."

"Split? With trolls lurking around?" Alexia asked, "Are you mad?"

"Some say so," Synthyya chuckled.

"She knows what she's doing," Marcus insisted.

"I don't think all of us agree," Octavia hissed through clenched teeth.

"We will get to the Historian," he said firmly.

"I am not really sure about that," Octavia spat back, "And I know I am not alone." Octavia adored Synthyya and it crushed her when the blue-haired Wizard's face fell at the challenge. Octavia wasn't even sure she believed her own words. All the same, she had to utter them. It was important, and you can probably sympathize.

"You all need to trust her," Marcus said.

"I'm not good with trust," Octavia replied.

"Nor am I," Alexia jumped in, "Where are we?"

"And don't say 'here,'" Griffin added.

"Stop," Gwen said, "We are where we are because of what we have done. We are outcasts but we are a Fellowship of Outcasts. She is part of our fellowship, now. Be good to Synthyya." Quintus nodded in agreement.

"I was an Outcast before most of you drew your first breath," Synthyya declared, with a grin, "And I know the tensions amongst you and all that weighs you down as we seek the path we should take. That is why we must split, here."

"Can you explain to everyone what you mean?" Gwen asked.

"Yes," Octavia said, staring darkly at Marcus, "because we don't all know the mysterious ways of Wizards."

"There is a sacred place not far from here," Synthyya began.

"Sacred to whom?" Griffin asked.

"Sacred to all," Synthyya replied, "All four races have come to this grotto and drunk the cool springs therein since history was first told. It is a place where the holiness can be felt the minute you descend. It is a place where the One of the Humans, the gods of the Wizards, the Spirits of the Elves, and the beliefs of the Morphs coexist and commingle."

"The Morphs have beliefs?" Octavia asked.

"We do," Alexia said, stepping closer to the warrior with a fierce look.

"You want us to go to this place?" Quintus asked.

"Not all of us," Synthyya said, "Four of us will go to seek aid from divinity in whatever form it takes. One representative from each race and an equal number of males and females. Perfection. With just four of us, we will encompass all the realm and our prayers will be powerful."

"How should we choose which four?" Alexia asked, "Although I presume I am your token Morph."

"We will not choose, child," Synthyya said with a grin, "I have already chosen."

"Just like that," Griffin snarled, throwing up his hands.

"Not just like that," Synthyya said, her eyes twinkling. "I have thought about this for some time. The combination has to be perfect and then the impact will be tremendous. I will take Quintus and Griffin to represent Humans and Elves. Alexia is our Morph and I am the Wizard. Two men and two women. All four races. A perfect offering of unity to whichever deities you worship."

"I can go," Marcus said.

"Not today, dear," Synthyya said, "You must stay here and wait with our supplies. Octavia and Gwendolyn will assist you in protecting them."

"This is the worst plan ever conceived," Octavia sighed, biting off every word. "I'll take Quintus's place as the Human, so he can be with Gwen."

"The genders would be off," Synthyya explained.

"I've never exceled at being a girl," Octavia said, nearly pleading, "Don't leave me here with…"

"With your friends?" Synthyya asked, arching an eyebrow.

Octavia drew closer and spoke softly. "I don't want to be here with *him*."

"I know, my sweet Red," Synthyya said quietly, changing her hair color to match Octavia's, "But you will stay and it will be okay. All things fade with time except love. Your anger will pass, maybe sooner than you expect."

"You don't understand."

"Don't I?" she whispered back, "I do not take for him in this instance because he is in the wrong. I do not make excuses for him because of the tragedies he has suffered, although they are so terrible that they must be entered in the ledger of whatever he does. Still, he knew what he was doing on that night and he knew the consequences." Octavia said nothing. Synthyya's eyes turned tender. "But dear Octavia, we will all need to work towards ending the strife between us for the struggle ahead. Marcus is not evil."

"He means nothing to me."

"We have a saying amongst my people," Synthyya said, lifting up Octavia's chin with her finger and staring deep into her green eyes, "*Quisque vita sacra est.* Every life is sacred. His life and yours have become entangled. Try to find the sacredness."

"Will you be mad if I don't find it?"

"I will be mad if you don't look," Synthyya said, sternly. "Gwendolyn will be with you, as well. Seek her counsel as if she were your sister."

"I never had a sister," Octavia said.

"You do now," Synthyya declared, nodding towards the Elf, "There is a light within her which does not dim. It is a marvel. She is joy and hope. Speak with her. Embrace her light. Let go of your anger with Marcus. It does not help you, him, or the fellowship." For a moment, Synthyya's stern teacher eyes focused on Octavia. After a moment, they softened again and were filled with empathy for the warrior who had been wounded by a weapon sharper than those forged by smiths like her father.

"I wish I'd had a mother like you," Octavia blurted out, "I never had a mother. Not even for an hour, Synthyya." Her eyes misted over, blatantly against her will.

"Shh. There there, dear," Synthyya said kindly, embracing her stiffly for Wizards struggle with such moments, "If you need a mother, you have found one in me. But mind your mother's wisdom, then. Forgiveness is part of what makes Humans so special amongst the races. I have always envied them for that." Octavia gave an almost imperceptible nod of assent.

Synthyya went off with her unhappy companions to seek holiness or at least aid for the Fellowship. This left Octavia, Marcus, and Gwen to guard their possessions and it was hard to say who felt the awkwardness more. Octavia had a sense that Synthyya had chosen her "perfect" group on purpose to put Octavia and Marcus together in the hope they'd patch things up. But she had not counted on my anger, Octavia thought. He had left his room and sought out the Morph. It was an awful thing for Marcus to do. He was no different than every other man she ever knew—no matter the race. She wasn't sure why it vexed her so thoroughly, but it did. Was it that he was supposed to be better than that? Was it that she had created a persona for him which was neither fair nor true? Was it that she felt that he could have come to *her* room and yet he chose Alexia instead? Was it Octavia's ego that was bruised? Did her own dark history color her judgments? Or was there something else? Something she refused to think about? Something gnawing and nagging at her from the far edges of her emotions? Was it that? It could not be that, she concluded. No. Simply, no. Not Marcus. No.

"I am going west to the pond to get water," Octavia announced.

"Alone?" Gwen asked.

"Yes," she said, "Alone. Completely, totally, and fiercely alone." Her tone brooked no objections and allowed no discussion. By the time one of them called "Be safe", she was already well on her way. She was so far away that she wasn't even totally sure it was Gwen who had wished her well. What if it was Marcus? What did it matter? She had every intention of being safe and words written on wind meant nothing. She had thought she'd remembered a friend telling her that, once. A little further on, she'd remembered that friend had been Marcus—quoting some fragment of an ancient poem. Octavia spat bitterly and doubled her pace to the pond. Synthyya was not master of Octavia's fate. Octavia need not deal with Marcus if she did not want to. Perhaps she'd return to find him merging with the Elf girl, too. That would be just perfect, she thought.

***

"She is angry with me," Marcus answered.

"I can tell she's angry with you, Marcus," Gwen said sweetly, "I was asking if you knew why she was acting this way."

He held her gaze. "Alexia…and…me," he said, his eyes downcast.

"Truly?" Gwen asked—her tone was neither surprised nor judgmental. He nodded. "It is delightful, isn't it?" she giggled. He nodded again.

"You are not mad at me for merging with your lover?"

"She is a Morph and she has made it clear to me that she will not stop swapping partners," Gwen said, "Morphs don't mate for life, she told me. Although I cannot imagine any magic which would permit the two of us to actually *mate*." She smiled. It was the most life-affirming smile Marcus had ever seen.

"It did not hurt you that she and I…"

"I was hurt when she first told me she'd seek out others," Gwen admitted, "But as I searched my heart, I knew I loved Quintus. Alexia is a dear friend and what we have together is unlike any friendship…"

"Because of …?"

"Not just because of that," Gwen said devilishly, "Our bond goes back to when she was the robin and I saved her. We are bound together by that. If not for our friendship, one of us would be dead and perhaps both of us would be."

"I understand," Marcus said.

"Do you?"

"It is like that with Quintus and me," Marcus said, "Although our friendship is completely chaste." He smiled merrily, his eyes twinkling. "The other difference is that I am *sure* we would both be dead were we not friends. I shall tell you that story at some point. You would like it."

"And what of Octavia?"

"It is complicated, I suppose," Marcus said, "And I complicated it further."

"You did," Gwen agreed, patting his thigh, "How do you feel about Octavia?"

"I am torn as I am about so many things."

"'Tis your nature, Marcus. You are half Human and half Wizard," she observed, "I am impressed you are not torn about everything under the life-giving sun spirit."

"It suddenly seems a warm sun today," he mused, "Not for much longer."

"Winter approaches in more ways than one," Gwen said, her pale blue eyes looking past Marcus as if she were in a trance, "Death hangs over us all now that we know with whom we are dealing. We should fix things in our lives while we are afforded the opportunity."

"She hates me."

"Ask yourself why she would react that way."

"Maybe I don't care," he said coolly.

"You are a terrible liar," Gwen said firmly.

"What Elf speaks like that to a Wizard? You're awfully brave for a creature who is so small," Marcus scowled.

"How is Octavia right now? Is she safe?"

"How in the Four Realms would I know?" Marcus exclaimed.

"Where is your owl?"

He narrowed his eyes as if to resist but gave up. He nodded. Then he closed his eyes and saw her. "She is approaching. She is safe."

228

"Perhaps you ought to give Octavia and me some time when she returns," Gwen said, "It will give you a chance to uncomplicate your thoughts." She smiled warmer than the sun.

"I have never thought much of Elvinkind, Gwendolyn. I previously presumed their only purpose in this world was to create that hot beverage you brew in the morning," he said, "But you may be the best thing Elvinkind has produced. There is more to you than meets the eye, isn't there?"

"I am certain you have seen all of me already, haven't you?" she winked.

***

"I've never been so disappointed to be left off a mission to some stupid holy temple," Octavia grumbled as both women gulped the refreshing water she had procured.

"Did she say 'temple' or 'shrine?'" Gwen asked.

"Is there a difference? I've never completely understood religion—it's all magic, if you ask me, and magic is just something Wizards use to deceive everyone."

"You don't believe that, Octavia. Wizards have been good to you," Gwen said, "And to me."

"Speak for yourself," Octavia said, draining her cup. "I am happy he's off playing with his owl. I am thoroughly sick of him."

"Because he slept with Alexia?" Gwendolyn asked. Octavia looked surprised that Gwen knew, but that was stupid. Everyone knew. The Northern warrior girl looked down at her boots and said nothing. Gwen finally broke the silence, "I slept with Alexia. Do you hate me?"

"Of course not," Octavia said, "Who could ever hate you? I still can't believe you wanted to be a soldier. You are the nicest little Elf I can imagine."

"You are changing the subject," Gwen said firmly, "Why do you care whose bed he warms?"

"I don't care."

Gwen smiled. "Neither you nor I believe that," she said, "I think you have tenderness in your breast—vulnerability

229

which you try to drive down. But it's there and it scares you. And I think the tenderest part of you is the part concerned with the violet eyed Wizard."

"Just because you've gone all weak in the knees for Quintus doesn't mean I have to join you," Octavia said, "We can still be friends even if I don't follow you into your sweet Elfish loveland. I don't care about Marcus and I promise that he doesn't care about me."

"If you ask me, I think you two are madly in love and neither of you has the bravery to say it first," Gwen sang, smiling sweetly.

"I didn't ask you and I think you're completely mad," Octavia declared, "This is not Elfland where everyone is in love and the very trees sing to you because the world is alive with joy."

"Elfland is not like that," Gwendolyn said, "Although Quintus did give me the bluest flower and compared it to my eyes."

"You are not helping change my view of Elves," Octavia said, "I am pretty sure I punched the last boy who picked a flower for me."

"You punched him?"

"I was 14 and it seemed like the right thing to do. We can agree that I am not built for love."

Gwen took Octavia's hand in friendship and looked up at her with those flower-blue eyes, "Everyone is built for love, dear Octavia," she said.

"Can we please change the topic before I vomit?" Octavia asked.

Both girls laughed, but then their laughter was cut terribly short. Six hulking monsters emerged from the woods. Octavia screamed "Orcs" just as Gwendolyn screamed "Goblins." As calmly as the situation would permit, Octavia donned her winged helmet, tucked in her red hair, and gripped her battle axe. Gwen pulled back her bow and slotted in an arrow. This was possible, Gwen thought, she just had to take out three of the monsters before they got too close. Octavia was a powerful warrior, she could deal with the other three. Maybe if Gwen got off her arrows quickly enough, she could take out four and relieve the pressure on her Human friend. She looked at her first target with its open mouth dripping with fangs and its eyes, red and glowing. She dropped the bow and the arrow clanged off the ground. How did that happen? Gwen had never dropped her bow in any situation. She told her body to pick it up quickly, but it did not answer her commands. She just stood there, transfixed by the eyes, incapable of moving or speaking. Just shivering in total fear...

Octavia heard the bow fall and wondered if Gwen had been hit. She appeared unharmed, yet looked terrified. How could that be? They were horrible but there were only six of them and Gwendolyn was no coward. What was wrong with her? Why did she have to be like this, now? Octavia clenched her teeth and prepared to fight all six. As she turned to fight them, she saw one of the orcs smile. She could not wait to cleave that smile in two with her axe. Octavia met his gaze and her legs felt like they were made of stone. Sweat poured off of her and her hands went numb. She saw the axe fall out of her grasp but did not remember loosening her grip. All Octavia knew was that her insides were melting and her breathing was burning. She had never been so scared in her entire life. She tried to scream, but only little pathetic moans came out. Death was imminent and it would be welcome if only because it would end the unspeakable terror she was feeling.

Chapter 26: Heroism

"I have always been vexed by a question, Synthyya," Quintus piped up, breaking the silence, which had thickly enveloped them since they'd parted from the rest of the fellowship.

"I do not always have answers," she replied merrily.

"It's about the Desert of Despair. Marcus has no memory of his first crossing when he came to you, although he must have crossed and survived…"

"He did," she replied, her tone losing its cheerfulness, "There is much about that day which Marcus does not fully remember." Her merriment cracked ever so slightly, the crack rapidly spider-webbing through her joy until it became noticeable.

Quintus noticed, but did not address it, for he judged that to be the wise course. "Given the events as he has reported them to me, that makes sense," Quintus simply said.

The Wizard looked very sad, and she turned her violet eyes to the Human. "More sense than you know," she whispered. Her tone indicated she would go no further in explaining her meaning. "What do you wish to know about the desert?"

"Why did you and the others get placed there?" he asked, "Why didn't the Empress just have you all killed?"

"I have wondered the same," Griffin added, "There must be more to your story than you have told." Alexia did not appear to be listening, but with Morphs and listening, what appeared to be might not be so.

"The Empress felt we three were part of a larger conspiracy," Synthyya explained, "And she desperately wanted to uncover it. She is so desperate in so many ways. For example, her choice of cloak. Utterly tasteless…"

"Why didn't she just kill you and the other two Wizards?" Griffin refocused her.

"Synthyya was an important member of the Imperial Council," Quintus noted, "All three of them were."

"Council is not the term we use, it is *Curia*, but yes, there are ten principal advisors to an Emperor or an Empress and as distinguished teachers at the University, five of us held that duty. It wasn't our power which frightened her; it was her desperation which fueled the exile. She presumed one of us would turn and confess the names of those others who opposed her," she explained, "The desert would break us and we'd tell her what she wanted to know. This was 26 of your sun cycles ago, Griffin, just as your sister was drawing her first breaths." He nodded, wondering how one event had anything to do with another.

"Given its effect on Marcus, that makes sense to me," Quintus offered.

"We did not break," she said fiercely. "We would not. When we had passed through the desert—more dead than alive—something curious occurred. The Empress was already there on the shore of the lake. By what magic, I have never learned, although I have my suspicions."

"Did she pass through the desert?" Griffin asked.

"No chance of that," Synthyya shook her head, "But she was there nonetheless and she demanded we confess our traitorous allies. We refused again, even though we were barely living. She then touched us and before we could draw a breath, we found ourselves across the Burning Sea and on the island."

"I have never heard of anything like that," Quintus said.

"Nor had I, and much have I heard, Quintus Aureus. Much more than you," Synthyya said with a smirk, "She told us we could leave the island at any time by revealing the identities of our allies. We need only send her an owl and she would appear. I imagine she expected us to starve, go mad, or kill one another, or break. But we made a life on that island, growing food, gathering fruit, carefully managing the animals which inhabited the land, so we did not run out of sustenance."

"And none of you ever thought of confessing?" Alexia asked.

Griffin muttered something about Morphs, but Synthyya appeared to take no notice. "Confess what? There was no great conspiracy," she explained, "Many opposed her, but none as openly as the three of us. The Empress suffered from dark dreams of well-organized rebellious subjects and we had no desire to puncture such dreams." Synthyya smiled a wicked smile. "As the years rolled on, she grew stubborn and probably felt the torture of being so imprisoned was a worthy substitute for our failure to comply with her wishes."

"As more years rolled on, she likely lost interest," Quintus said, "As her power became more secure and her gaze turned to her wars, she became distracted and that distraction permitted you to teach Marcus four years later when his exile began."

"Indeed, and to construct the boat, and later the tunnel," Synthyya said, "Distraction has its benefits, although many disagree with me on that topic and feel I am fatally biased. Oh, look, we are finally here!"

"It looks like an ordinary cave," Quintus said, looking back for a moment as if he was seeking to catch a glimpse of fair Gwendolyn in the direction from which they'd come.

"It is more," Synthyya said.

"Not much more," Griffin remarked acidly.

"I can feel something," Alexia said. It was a lie, but she was sick of the two men bickering. She was willing to help Griffin deal with Quintus, but their constant masculine put-downs gave her a headache. Synthyya seemed blissfully unaware of their spat. No surprise there…

"How can a place be holy to all the religions of the four realms?" Griffin asked.

"Synthyya prefers 'the realm'," Quintus said, "It's more inclusive."

She looked on, bemused. "Some places are simply special and we do not know why," she explained. "This place has an energy which I cannot put into words. But if you open yourself when you go in, you can feel it."

"Like me," Alexia said proudly.

"Like you, dear," Synthyya said, meeting her gaze and using her violet eyes to make it clear she did not believe her even a little.

"So is there a sacrifice required?" Quintus asked, "Because I could suggest an Elf." His gray eyes smoldered and he cast a withering glance towards Griffin.

"Suggest is all you could do," Griffin replied belligerently, "Anyway, Synthyya, whose gods are in here? Are there mute statues of your element gods? The foolish circle of the One? And what exactly do Morphs believe in?"

"We believe in ourselves," Alexia said, "And in the undying spark of creation which is within our people."

"That doesn't even make sense," Quintus said.

"Belief in the divine rarely makes sense," Synthyya said with a smile, "Even Wizards must put aside our logic. Before we go in, Alexia should explain what Morphs believe, so you can understand."

Alexia was embarrassed and a little perturbed by being placed on the spot. "Some say Morphs have no religion," she said, "Just because we do not appoint priests or monks or clerics doesn't mean we have no religion."

"Then what do you believe?" Quintus asked.

"We believe that when the world was born whatever gave birth to it split into innumerable pieces and that these sparks reside within us," Alexia explained, "The body means nothing. It can get sick or wounded. It can change into an animal and back to a Human. It can feel pleasure and pain, but that doesn't matter. The body can be male or female, but that doesn't matter. The body can waste its time building or writing or painting, but that is of no consequence to us because everything is temporary. If you are a bear Morph, you will be a bear some of the time, but you will die and be a bear no more. If you are a male, there is no reason to be particularly enamored with that because you will die and be a male no more. If you write something or build something, it doesn't matter because you will die and it will perish. This is why Morphs don't separate men and women into roles like Elves do. Being male or female is temporary. This is why Morphs don't get emotional about merging bodies like Humans do, because the bodies we use are temporary. This is why Morphs don't write or build like Wizards do, because all that will pass away."

"Seems like a recipe to ignore the world and focus only on you," Quintus sniffed, "Which is why the Morphs joined the Dark Lord first. He probably promised embraces and food to them, which is all they really care about." You know Quintus by now. He was more open-minded than all that, but he was angry and viewed both Alexia and Griffin as obstacles to his love of Gwen. When you are angry, you say things. Although if you are wise, you can return to yourself with just a word from another.

"Quintus," Synthyya said sternly, speaking such a word. He hung his head.

"The point of our belief system is that we all die," Alexia said, "But unlike the Humans who believe they'll be stars in the night after death or the Wizards who think a select few will walk with their gods in some faraway land or the Elves who think they will enjoy some peaceful Elvin paradise in a forest above the clouds, we think we return to the world again and again. We die and then are reborn."

"Can you be reborn as another race?" Griffin asked.

"No, Morphs alone have the spark of creation which is why we can become an animal at will," she said, "But we will continue to be reborn in a new body with no memory of our previous body."

"How does it end?" Griffin asked.

"It doesn't," she said, "Synthyya, I know I lied before. But I really feel something now. May we enter the cave?"

"We may," Synthyya said, "And you may enter in the way a Morph would enter, Alexia. I will not make you wear the dress in there. Just be sure to hang it on a branch so it does not get wrinkled, please." Alexia nodded and slipped off her dress.

"Real respectful," Griffin muttered under his breath. He shook his head.

"We worship in the way we were made," Alexia snapped, "Shame about the body is an Elvin emotion. It's one of the few things Humans and Elves share."

Alexia walked down the carved stairs into the cave. Griffin and Quintus made to join her but were held back by a fierce wind which suddenly arose. They then noticed their feet had been swallowed by the earth and they could not move. Synthyya's eyes glowed fiercely. "Leave your hatred out here," she said, "Whatever differences you have over Gwendolyn's well-being cannot be taken to the shrine. Leave the anger at the entrance. Pick it up when you return, if you must, but under no circumstances is your disagreement to pass into this shrine. Am I clear?" They both nodded meekly.

Their feet were released and her eyes returned to normal. A broad smile spread across her face. "This is going to help us with our mission," she beamed, "I am certain of it."

***

Nothing had ever frightened Octavia so much. She felt like she was going to pass water any moment like some pathetic child. They would find her corpse with her shortpants wet, another indignity to add to her cowardice. Her muscled arms hung limp by her side and she was shaking like the leaves on the trees above her. She could not even turn her neck to see Gwen, but she could hear her sobbing like a small one who has awoken from a nightmare. The orcs were closing in slowly, almost tasting the fear from the two girls. We are brave warriors. Octavia knew it to be so. She and Gwen were not quivering little princesses in uninteresting fairy tales, and yet the orcs were so terrifying. They seemed to laugh but who could tell? Please let it be over soon, Octavia silently wailed inside her own head. She stared at the tree and saw the branches shaking in the autumn wind. Perched on one of the branches was a lone owl. It hooted at the orcs and one of them fired an arrow from a strange looking bow at the bird. The owl spread its wings to fly but was not quick enough, the arrow seemed to strike it, but then it bounced off harmlessly. The bird appeared unaffected, which caused a lot of roaring and barking amongst the orcs.

A flash came out of the woods and incinerated two of the orcs where they stood. Their blackened lifeless forms crumpled to the ground. His cloak swirling around him, Marcus emerged from the forest and stood grim-faced with his staff pointed at the dead orcs. The live ones were surprised long enough for the Wizard to race in front of them and put himself squarely between the four remaining monsters and the frozen, terrified women.

Why don't the girls arm themselves? he thought as he pointed his staff at the closest ogre, chanted the words, and a fireball erupted in its face. Its death-screams were almost pitiable, if they were not so horrible. Still, neither girl moved. Both looked frozen with fear.

The ogre with a crude bow shot an arrow at Marcus and it bounced harmlessly off his enchanted cloak. The next arrow froze in mid-air, encased in a spell of ice. Angry, the ogre threw his bow to the ground and pulled out a large jagged dagger. He seemed to be the leader and he beckoned the others to join him, so they closed in on Marcus.

The Wizard was magnificent, Octavia had to admit. Most of her hated him for what he did with Alexia, but as the wind caught his cloak and it billowed about him, he seemed like a figure from one of those poems she'd never really learned in school. She'd hated them, too. She wanted so badly to stand shoulder to shoulder with him, but she could not move. He shifted the staff to his left hand and pulled out the sword with his right. It gleamed orange in the falling light of the day. He caught one monster in the belly with the sword as he parried a blow from another with the staff. The staff then lit up and blinded the orc, who had seen his blow deflected. Marcus expertly used the orc he'd stabbed as a shield against the leader who pierced his own soldier in error. Octavia could only watch and pray Marcus would prevail or Gwen could help.

Gwendolyn was trembling all over in terror. She had fallen to the ground, cowering behind the Wizard. Even in her abject fear, she'd known he wouldn't be far. She wasn't certain how he loved Octavia, but she knew he loved the girl. Gwen was quite sure she was also loved by Marcus, although she had a better grasp on the nature of that love. She noted to herself in between the cascading blows of her fear that Marcus was truly a great Wizard; a hero, in fact. The goblin leader struck again and this time it caught Marcus with a dagger in the Wizard's exposed chest, unprotected by his billowing cloak. Gwendolyn's heart dropped. What if he didn't save them? What if this was it? What if this was her reckoning and she had not even loosed one arrow in self-defense?

Marcus staggered, the staff knocked out of his hand by the clawed hand of the creature. The monster smiled a horrible sharp smile and went in for the kill. As he raised his arm to bring down the final blow on the wounded Wizard, Marcus's owl swooped in and pecked at the scaly arm. It did no harm, but distracted it long enough for Marcus to get off a spell—he had pointed at the remaining water in the jug Octavia had brought from the river. It rose up and froze into an icicle which pierced the ogre's throat like a spear. Black blood gushed out and polluted the grass around it. Only the one blinded ogre remained. Marcus picked up the staff and pointed at the ground while muttering the words. He seemed monumentally frustrated when nothing happened. He tried again as the ogre stumbled around, still blinded by his light spell. Nothing. Marcus growled in frustration. He then gestured at the monster with his hand and spoke different words in the ancient tongue. A fierce wind blew and pinned it against a tree. The creature slumped until the Wizard pointed the staff at him and it appeared to be choking, even though Marcus was three feet away and not touching the ogre. The Wizard relented and Gwen and Octavia heard him mutter something while the creature gasped for air. It said nothing in response and so Marcus thrust his sword into its belly, but only part of the way. There was still half of the orange-glowing blade to be seen as Marcus spoke louder to the blinded creature.

"*Dominus Maleficarum ubi est? Nunc, indica mihi, Monstrum!*"

The creature turned those terrible red eyes to him, having clearly regained some of his sight. "*Numquam, veneficus,*" it uttered in a horrible, guttural voice.

Whatever all of that meant, it clearly upset Marcus. He withdrew his sword and then stepped back and pointed the staff at the creature, clearly constricting its throat. It clawed at its own neck for air and finally toppled over dead. Both Gwen and

Octavia slowly regained the ability to move and instinctively grabbed their weapons for a battle that was already won. But for Gwen, as heroic as the Wizard had been in battle, he was infinitely more so in the aftermath. Marcus calmly walked over to them as they stood, their legs still wobbling slightly.

This is it, Octavia thought. He has seen me cower in fear and now he will gloat that he killed six orcs as I played the helpless little girl, a damsel in distress—of all things, for the love of the Golden One! For an instant, she even wished she'd been killed so she didn't need to endure the humiliation he would inflict. He sheathed his sword and rested his staff against a rock, then fell to one knee.

"Are you both unharmed?" he asked in a soft, gentle voice.

Octavia said nothing. Gwen answered for them, "We are, Marcus. Thanks be to the Spirits that you came when you did. We could do nothing. We were terrified."

"Of course," he said with mournful eyes, "Fear happens to everyone in battle at some point."

"It has never happened to me," Octavia said.

"I am sure it will never happen again," he said soothingly, "I do not doubt either of your bravery. It was just one of those things. It is over. We will not speak of it again." His eyes were filled with kindness and empathy. He appeared to pay no attention to the wound he had suffered, but focused on his two comrades exclusively.

She fought herself, but could not resist the urge. "Thank you, Marcus," Octavia said with some effort, as if it were a difficult thing to say. And sometimes, of course, it is.

"You would have done the same for me," he replied, "Wouldn't you?" There was a pause. She nodded. "I am glad that neither of you got hurt."

"And I am glad you were not far from us," Gwen added, "Who would expect to see goblins in the daylight?"

"Perhaps our comrades's prayers were misunderstood," he smirked. "Sit down for a while. They cannot harm you, now." Gwen marveled at how soft his voice was and how kind he had been, as if he were a father comforting his children after a fright.

A fox emerged from the woods which morphed into Alexia, who looked around and sniffed. Crashing through the woods behind her were the others, "What happened?" Quintus asked, rushing to Gwen's side.

"I smelled troll when the wind changed," Alexia explained.

"We have been running ever since she told us," Griffin gasped.

"What happened?" Quintus insisted again, cradling Gwen in his arms.

Octavia opened her mouth, but felt a warm hand on her shoulder. "Six ogres attacked us, but the three of us fought them off," Marcus said.

"Six goblins against three of you?" marveled Griffin, "Was anyone hurt?"

"I took a scratch, but the girls were unharmed," Marcus said, "We fought them off. They were awful, but together, we were stronger."

Synthyya's purple eyes darted from the corpses to the girls and back. She pondered for a moment. "How many did you shoot, Gwendolyn?" Synthyya asked.

"We need not keep score," Marcus insisted, "Let's burn their horrible corpses and get out of here."

"I see no axe wounds," Synthyya said, "Peculiar, wouldn't you say, Octavia?"

"This is not the time, Synthyya," growled Marcus. "Daylight is failing and surely we must go farther tonight. Perhaps there is another inn for us?"

"There is another inn towards the east," she said, "I know many innkeepers in this part of the world. I just want to be sure I understand what happened."

"What is there to understand?" Marcus asked, his pitch rising, "The ogres attacked and we were undermanned because you were praying. Gwen, Octavia, and I held the line as you communed with gods. Not the correct choice for the fellowship if you ask me." He scowled as he met Synthyya's gaze.

"I am not sure that is what happened," Synthyya said, flippantly. Marcus continued to glare at her.

"Why?" Alexia asked.

"Yes, why indeed, Alexia," Synthyya said, "Why are there no arrows in any of the ogres? Why is Octavia's axe clean and shiny? Shouldn't there be blood on it?"

The girls were mute. Marcus tried again, "The ogres are dead, why are you asking how they were killed? You should be asking how they found us! And whether there are more of them close by..."

"There is very little chance that either the Elf or the warrior did anything once they saw the eyes," Synthyya said.

"What are you talking about?" Marcus snapped.

"You never learned anything real about ogres because they did not exist when you were being educated," Synthyya snapped back, "Zarqqwell insisted it would be a waste of our time to teach you the lore of creatures long vanished. Not the correct choice for the fellowship if you ask me." Her tone was mocking, but light.

"Can someone translate for me?" Griffin demanded.

"I am as lost as you, Elf-boy," Marcus said.

"Ogres are made with dark magic," Synthyya explained, "When Humans, Elves, or Morphs see their eyes, they are bewitched with fear. Maybe one in a thousand can resist. I find it hard to believe either of these brave women did anything other than stand here shaking. They may have soiled themselves or fainted from fear. They did not fight."

Marcus opened his mouth to speak, but it hung open because his brain had not yet formulated a new lie.

"It's true," Gwen said, "I have never felt such fear."

"It's their magic," Synthyya said, "It is not your fault."

"You said Humans, Elves, and Morphs. What about Wizards?" Alexia asked.

"We are immune to that spell, although ogres can still kill Wizards, as we know all too well," she paused to dwell on thoughts of her two colleagues.

"So Marcus killed all six orcs by himself?" Quintus asked, applying some healing plants to his friend's wound after he and Griffin had a wordless struggle about who would help the bleeding Wizard.

"Did you, Marcus?" Synthyya asked.

He looked at Gwen and Octavia. "I did," he said averting his gaze, "Now let's burn them and be off. They may have comrades and I can feel the exhaustion creeping into my limbs."

"You did use a lot of magic in saving us," Gwen said.

"So it wasn't a reflection on us?" Octavia asked, "It was dark magic?"

"Of course, sweet Red," Synthyya gushed, "You are as brave as brave can be. You just need some help. I know an earth spell which should protect you. Just let me sit and think of it."

"Earth magic failed me," Marcus said to Synthyya, "I wanted to make the ground immobilize one of them, but I couldn't do it. Even with the staff."

"You struggle with the earth magic," she said, "You always did. How was your water magic? Did you use it?"

"I did," he said, "'Tis the right time of year for that."

"Aye," she said, "Now use the fire magic to burn these monsters and let me think of how to draw the sign on our friends."

"What sign?"

"The one to protect them," Synthyya said, "Aren't you paying attention?"

Chapter 27: Life

They marched east at a hurried pace. Synthyya kept looking over her shoulder. Marcus's owl hovered in sight, but in front of them, scanning the ground immediately ahead. Even Quintus was distracted. "I cannot believe that orcs attacked you and I was not there to help," he lamented to Gwen, "I am so angry with myself."

"It is not your fault," Gwen said generously, "You were helping the cause."

"I drank some underground water and said some words to the Golden One," he grumbled, "Not as helpful as if I were there to fight."

"Perhaps the prayer to your One saved me," she replied with a smirk.

"I should have been there…"

"Your friend was there and he saved us," Gwen offered, "He was there because he is your friend. Thus, you saved us."

"Marcus saved my life, once, did you know?" Quintus sighed.

"That is how you met?" she asked. He nodded gravely. "He says you saved one another's lives. You'll have to tell me the tale when we have more time."

"I fear that we do not have as much time as we would like," he muttered.

"You are so sad, Quintus Agrippa Aureus," she said, locking her arm in his, "You must look to the light and not the darkness. The goblins did not hurt us. Synthyya will remember the sign."

"You think too much of her."

"And you think too little of her," she replied sharply.

***

"How was the praying?" Octavia asked Synthyya, who had insisted on marching in the rear, even though she was supposedly the only one who knew where they were going. She continued to glance over her shoulder every few paces.

"I think it helped, Sweet Red, let's say that," Synthyya said, "How were things for you while we were away?"

"Other than wetting my shorts a little and nearly dying a horrible death at the hands of no-longer-fictional monsters, it was just lovely," Octavia guffawed.

"You sound more like Octavia, now," Synthyya allowed, "I mean how were *things*?" Her knowing look translated her meaning.

"I hate him less, I'll admit that."

"You hate him not at all," Synthyya said with a certain sharpness, "He failed you, once. True. Has he not saved you, as well? Does that even out?"

Octavia paused and thought. "No, it is not about evening out. I am still furious with him, although do you know what is really strange, Synthyya?"

"That you do not fully understand why you are so furious at him?"

"Yes, exactly. How did you know?" Octavia asked.

"The 'mysterious ways of Wizards,' is what you called it," Synthyya chuckled, "But in truth it has nothing to do with Wizardness. I know because I am like you."

"The only daughter of a blacksmith who fights better than she loves?" Octavia chuckled right back at her.

Synthyya smiled. "Not quite, dear. But I am a being and I do understand that sometimes other beings make us feel things we don't comprehend—for good or for bad. If it makes you feel better, we make others feel such things, as well."

"He is a great companion in the fellowship," Octavia allowed, "A brave warrior, who has aided me on the field several times. We are comrades and I can live with that."

"Comrades?" Synthyya sniffed, "What about 'friends?'"

Octavia paused and searched her heart. "I think that is too much. Marcus and I cannot be friends, Synthyya."

Her words were colder to Synthyya than the fanged wind which was blowing from the north, biting any piece of exposed flesh and holding it fiercely.

***

It dawned on Griffin first. "This is Elfland," he said, beaming.

"You sound very delighted to be in a place which expelled and enslaved you," Marcus offered.

"Not to mention your sister," Quintus added.

"I recognize where we are," he said, "We have been moving south as well as east. This is the edge of where I had been before the enslavement. I think we are quite close to the holy city of the Spirits. Perhaps, three days from the city of the King."

"How delightful," Gwen said flatly, "Perhaps he can enslave us all over again."

"He means that your parents are not far," Alexia said, "Isn't that right?"

"Yes," Griffin said, "We could find them and free them."

"No detours," Synthyya said from the rear without so much as breaking stride or tossing off a casual glance in Griffin's direction.

"Excuse me?" he demanded.

She stopped, inhaled, exhaled, and fixed her purple gaze on him. "We do not stop for anything," she said, "The inn where we can rest safely is very close and the Historian is likely one more day away. No detours."

"Am I still a slave?" he asked.

"There are leaves in your hair," Marcus observed, "So you know better than us." Gwen recognized that Marcus was targeting Griffin because he knew Quintus felt he could not. Such friendship, she marveled, even if wrongheaded.

"I am free. So I may come and go as I choose?" Griffin asked.

"Are you seriously contemplating leaving our fellowship to try and free your parents? Whose whereabouts you know nothing about?" Marcus demanded, incredulous.

"Some of us loved our parents," Octavia said, "You may not understand." Gwen frowned as she saw Octavia was still jabbing at Marcus. She had thought she'd heard Octavia pronounce an "S" as if she meant to add "Sorcerer" at the end of the statement. But that word had not escaped her pink lips and perhaps that was something good, Gwen concluded.

"My parents mean nothing to me," Alexia said bitterly, refusing to elaborate, "But if you want to save your parents, you can count on me, Griffin."

Marcus eyed the Morph suspiciously. What was her game? "You are discussing the breaking of the fellowship," he said coldly.

"You mean the Fellowship of *Outcasts*?" Griffin asked, "I was not aware we were bound by sacred oaths. We have all helped each other. It has been good. I wish you well, but I am going to save the people who birthed me and then clear our family name."

"I did not know you had a family name," Quintus marveled. Griffin simply held his stare.

"You think you're going to free your parents and what, return to a normal life?" Marcus asked, "Pure folly."

"If a free-born Elf who has been enslaved escapes and makes it to the King's city, there is a passage in the sacred writings which declares the slave is free," Griffin said.

"Some clerics read it as that," Gwen replied, "Others believe the translation is that he should be killed." Griffin looked surprised. "I listened to the preachers just like you." She looked at him with those pale blue eyes, shimmering like the sea itself.

"Surely, you cannot be considering anything else," Griffin pleaded with her, "*You* put them in that prison, Gwen. You can right that wrong. Alexia will come with us and we will return to our lives."

"Have you forgotten the Dark Lord?" Quintus asked.

"This creature is so powerful he destroyed an advanced civilization and you think a band of seven outcasts can stop him? Only in a silly story, Ranger. Let the kings and empresses and councils deal with it. I want to save my parents and that is something I can do. Stopping some thousand year old super-Wizard is not in my power."

"You underestimate yourself." It was Synthyya's heretofore unheard voice in this conversation.

"Stay out of this, Wizard Woman," Griffin warned her, "This is family. Gwendolyn, we must go back to our world."

"When will you understand, dear brother? *This* is my world," Gwendolyn said, gesturing around her, "Quintus is my world. Octavia, Marcus, Synthyya, Alexia, and you. Yes, you. I do not want to go back to Elfland. They will take my bow, place me in some horrible dress, marry me off, and reduce me to nothing. That is not my destiny."

"Your destiny?" he asked, incredulous.

"Is with these people," she said firmly, "And their noble quest."

"*Quest?* You use epic words like the Wizard, here, and it is ridiculous as he is. You will stop some Dark Lord, little sister?" he mocked.

"I will fight him beside people who love me for who I am."

Alexia whispered. "She cannot choose them over us, can she?" He agreed.

"We part here," Griffin bluffed. "I wish you would reconsider, Gwendolyn."

A tear rolled down the Elf girl's ivory cheek. Quintus comforted her. Alexia cursed under her breath. Marcus and Octavia looked at one another, then looked away. No one knew what to do.

"Stop!" demanded Synthyya. Even Alexia looked terrified at the tone which had invaded Synthyya's voice. A storm rose in her eyes which would not be placated. "Griffin, you listen to me and you listen, now!" Her real voice seemed buried beneath layers upon layers of fierce anger. "You are part of our fellowship and we value you for who you are and what you do. Make no mistake about it; you must accept the deed we seek to do to the exclusion of everything else. Nothing is more important."

"But..." he stuttered.

"Elfland is here," she thundered, as she pointed her staff all around them, "Go now if you cannot accept my terms. Stay

248

if you can love these people—all of them. Stay if you believe in our cause. Otherwise, go and never return to us."

He stood rooted to the ground for a moment, even though she'd used no earth magic this time. He swallowed. He looked at Gwendolyn, still weeping. "I'll stay," he croaked.

"The same goes for you, Alexia," Synthyya added angrily. Alexia nodded.

No one said anything for a long time.

"She probably scared away the ogres," Marcus whispered to Octavia with a vulnerable smile. She looked at him and involuntarily gave his joke a brief smirk before returning to the hard gaze she'd been fixing on him. He was brave and he was witty, but he was also flawed. Deeply flawed. Even friendship seemed too much a risk with a Wizard. She would fight beside him, but nothing more. He would learn to accept that.

"Weapons out," Quintus interrupted. He nocked an arrow in his bow.

The fellowship came to arms, but it became clear in a matter of seconds that there was no threat. "We are too late," Octavia said grimly, her hard stare suddenly appropriate to their situation.

A dozen Elves had been nailed to trees, including two Elf children. Their pale corpses sent a shudder through Gwendolyn's spine. "Goblins?" she asked.

"Humans," Alexia said with a snarl. Quintus returned his arrow to his quiver and nodded in agreement.

"But these ones are just children," Gwen whimpered, touching their cold cheeks, trying to memorize the faces frozen in death.

"This is the borderland," Marcus said, "Human-Elf fighting is cruelest in these parts. We need to move quickly before we are caught up in it."

"This war has gone on too long…" Synthyya said softly, "Senseless. Utterly and completely senseless." There was no tone in her voice, but you sensed from the softness that even a Wizard could be moved to pity by the sight.

249

"Might we bury them and say the prayers?" Griffin asked.

"It is too dangerous," Quintus muttered, "Those who did this cannot be far. The Elves have not been dead for long." Alexia looked at Gwen's sadness and something stirred in her heart.

"Tell us about this inn," Alexia said to Synthyya, hoping to change the topic as quickly as possible for Gwen's sake, "What is the delicious meal from this innkeeper? Will it be the best roast beast of our lives?"

"Lives? Aha. Yes! Life!" exclaimed Synthyya, "That's it. Stop here."

"Stop?" Marcus asked, "We just went over this. The sun is dipping low and we know that Human soldiers and the ogres are about. I can see the inn through the eyes of my owl. You promised we'd be safe there."

"I can never promise that you will be safe. This cannot wait," she said simply, pouring her water jug into the dirt and mixing it with her staff.

"Marcus is right," Quintus said, looking back, "We cannot bury the Elves, we are exposed out here in the borderlands. The Humans could attack us, and I feel like the orcs would be worse in the night than in the day."

"Oh, you are quite right," Synthyya said, "As fierce as ogres are by day, they are worse in the darkness. Such good instincts from the grim gray-eyed Ranger! But I have remembered the spell. Everyone but Marcus, expose some flesh for me."

"This spell sounds like it has potential," Alexia said lewdly.

"I will make a mark upon you with the ancient word for life," Synthyya said.

"Vita?" Marcus asked.

"More ancient than even our words," Synthyya explained, as she wrote in mud on Quintus's right shoulder, "This language was ancient even for the classical civilization. I only know some of the symbols in this tongue, but these symbols will protect them from the stare of the ogres."

Marcus looked at the symbols as she traced them in mud on the Ranger's shoulder and then touched the word with her staff so that it glowed, as if it were being burned on his flesh. Ζωη. "What does it mean?" he asked.

"In this archaic language, 'Zoe' means 'Life,'" Synthyya declared.

"And with this mark on us, we will never be scared of the orcs?" Octavia asked.

"I cannot promise that," Synthyya said, "I cannot even promise I am doing the spell correctly, for it has not been cast in centuries or more. But if I am right, their gaze should not terrify you. Of course, even without magic, they are still fearsome beasts."

"I just want to face them with none of this silly magic," Octavia declared, as the burned word faded into invisibility on her flesh. She wondered if the spell had failed, but Synthyya seemed to expect the letters to disappear, so perhaps that was normal.

"Silly magic?" Marcus asked. Octavia refused to answer for fear of it descending into a back-and-forth banter, as it might have before Marcus had visited the Morph. Marcus let his words float there for a moment and then abandoned them. The small town came into view. Gwen cast a look back at the dead Elves and decided that while she could not forget them, she needed to continue with her life. It was hard to do; especially in an instant, but Gwendolyn was not like other Elves. This, you have likely suspected.

Alexia sighed and turned to Synthyya. "Tell us about the inn," she repeated her question as they approached. "Is there a soup? More pork pies? Some sweet after-dinner dish?"

"The food is horrible," Synthyya said, "The Elves who run it delight in serving the worst food imaginable to their guests. It's a pity because the Elf girl is actually a fine cook. She and her husband serve barely edible and usually burned food to the customers. It's a joke for them. We do not sleep here for the meals."

"I can see why you chose the place," Alexia said, sarcastically, "I may just morph into a predator and catch my own dinner."

"Too dangerous for that," Marcus said, closing his eyes, "My owl sees something coming towards us from behind and it may be ogres. I cannot tell for sure."

"Padrig and Molly will protect us," Synthyya said, "They are the most discreet innkeepers in Elfland. Many times I have come here and many times I have been sought by those who would do me harm. These two Elves will never let any creature know we are here. Regardless of their race, they treat all their guests like they took a sacred oath."

"Except the food," Quintus observed.

"No one is perfect," Synthyya said. She paused and looked over her fellowship before rapping on the inn's door. A smile crept onto her lips. "The other thing is that Padrig will decide where you sleep and with whom you share a room. Often he likes to board strangers with strangers just to see if they become friends or get into a fight. I will speak with him and see if he will let us pair up amongst ourselves." The door opened and Synthyya spoke softly to two gray-haired Elves at some length. Everyone nervously tried to listen, but even the Elves and Morphs could not hear, which was odd and seemed to indicate magic of some sort. Synthyya pulled out her purse and pressed some more Wizard coins into the innkeepers' hands. It was all too quick, but Gwen's sharp eyes spied a gold coin, which meant it was either a full gold, honoring the Earth Goddess or a half gold, honoring the Air god. She could not see whether a mountain or a cloud was inscribed and she knew little about Wizard currency, but knew well that even seven rooms would not cost either coin.

"All is well," Synthyaa said as she came back to the fellowship, "Padrig wanted us in seven rooms with seven strangers, but Molly prevailed upon him. Only I will share a room with a stranger, which is just as well because I have an errand to run for much of the evening."

"Another errand?" asked Gwen.

"Tut tut, no worries," Synthyya said, "Molly convinced Padrig that you six will room with one another. I made it clear that our presence must be as secretive as possible. Padrig assented, but he chose your roommates."

"What are the rooming assignments that they have decided?" asked Quintus, "And did you get any input?"

"You will be with Gwendolyn, Quintus," said Synthyya as she drank in their mutual delight, "Griffin and Alexia will share a room. As will Marcus and Octavia."

"They insisted on girl-boy rooms," Marcus observed suspiciously, "How odd for Elves."

"They are unusual Elves," Synthyya said with a knowing smile, "This is the only safe place to sleep, so we are bound by their peculiarities."

"You didn't answer Quintus's question," Alexia said.

"No time for more questions," Synthyya smiled, "Help yourself to the terrible meal and I will see you when you wake."

"This could not be worse," Octavia groaned.

***

Quintus was getting more confident of her durability, she had noticed. His embraces were firmer, his kisses fiercer, and he took her with more force. It was as if he was noticing that Gwendolyn did not break as easily as her slight figure might suggest. Still, even though Quintus was acting more like a man (as Alexia and Octavia had explained it), he still was very careful. Beyond careful. Often, Gwen felt as if she were an object of worship and his hands the instruments of his blessings. There was almost a reverence for her pale smooth figure. Quintus treated Gwen as if she were the most valuable item in the Four Realms and her joy was his only calling. She wanted to tell him she was simply a girl and that he could treat her like one, rather than some sacred object in a temple. But she loved his adoration and could tell he loved the adoring, so she let him be and marveled in their love.

***

It was close to the moment, he knew. Up until this point, he could watch them safely from afar without grappling with the complexity of their situation. The way forward had been decided and it all made sense to him when the deciding had been done. Yet now as it all came so close, he wondered about the deceit. Would it work? Was it justified? Was it wrong to tell false things to them, even in the service of something else, entirely? Inhaling deeply, he sang an old song to himself:

"The lies of autumn may wither when winter's cold blows,
ill stories may crack and freeze when buried beneath snows,
but a pretty lie can see us through a wicked storm,
for now, it's enough that the lies of autumn keep us warm."

Satisfied for the moment, he tended to other matters, leaving this one be.

***

Griffin did not loathe himself when he awoke. He looked over and she was unclad, of course. He ran his hand down his own body and discovered the same state. It all came back to him as if it were a dream, but it had clearly been reality. He had given in. Finally. He should have hated himself. This was not like it was with the Low Elves on those trips he and his friends had made. That was sanctioned by the clerics as a necessary release. This was forbidden. What was true for Gwen was also true for Griffin. Elves did not consort with Morphs. Morphs were never to be trusted. They abandoned the other races in the old tales to ally with evil. They were beast-men who acted like animals but were not truly animals. In the Elf world which was so consumed with Nature, the Morphs were an abomination—an affront to nature. Neither Human nor animal. And he had merged his Elvin body with a morph. With a beast-woman.

She slept on and he studied the tan color of her flesh and walked his eyes up and down the curves of her body. Not just

254

any beast-woman, he consoled himself. The most alluring beast-woman in all the Four Realms. Everything about her exuded desire, from her long dark hair to her impossible curves to the enticing way her lips moved when she spoke. No creature could resist her. Even the coldhearted Wizard had succumbed to Alexia's charms, so why should Griffin feel bad? Point of fact was that he did not feel bad. This in itself was alarming. He had slept with the enemy. A gorgeous enemy. But the enemy. He would be disgraced if he were home. But Griffin was not home. He knew that. And he did not feel bad about what had happened. And that frightened him more than anything.

Chapter 28: The Awkward Daughter of a Nobody

Marcus lay on the floor of the uncomfortably quiet room, using his cloak as a place to rest his head. He had not spoken to her nor had she spoken to him since they had discovered the pairings. Marcus saw Synthyya's obvious and unveiled hand in this. "Put them together and perhaps they would resume their friendship"—this reeked of Synthyya's clumsy meddling. But Octavia had made it clear that resuming their friendship was not possible, even after he had saved her life and had tried to save her reputation. Wizards despise the drama of Humans and Marcus was physically exhausted on top of that. He was tired of Octavia's drama and tired from all his spellcasting. Spellcasting—he might add—which had kept Octavia alive...again. He was done with trying. He would simply lock away any care he might hold for this Human and treat her like she wanted to be treated—as a comrade in arms, no more. Their mission was too important. It transcended her refusal to forgive him for a transgression which—the more he thought of it—was not much of a transgression. He and Octavia had no romantic relationship. They had been friends. How had his evening with Alexia irrevocably changed the nature of his friendship with Octavia? Humans. Drama. The only cure for the cold silence of their shared room would be the sweetness of sleep. Octavia hadn't even thanked him for letting her have the one bed in the sparse room. He had stretched out on a cold hard floor and she hadn't even nodded in gratitude. Typical.

"I suppose you are just going to sleep," Octavia said, annoyed.

He was so tired, he didn't even want to expend energy on talking. He opened his eyes with some effort and grunted an affirmative. Then he shut his eyes and drifted, his consciousness descending in swift spirals into the blessed darkness of rest. She sat on the bed and looked at him for a long time. He wanted so badly to recharge the magic within him, which had been drained in the ogre battle, but something nagged him. He felt like he was being watched, and his eyes snapped open again. Sure enough, she was staring at him. Her face was a mixture of contempt and awe. It was the strangest expression he'd seen her make in the time they'd known one another. He wasn't sure whether she was preparing to stab him or caress his cheek. He wondered which would be better. He decided the stabbing. It would end this Human drama.

"What?" he asked, his impatience laced with fatigue.

"Nothing," she said quietly.

"I am very tired."

"I know you are."

"If you have something you need to say, just say it, so that I can sleep," he said.

"Thank you."

"For the bed?" he asked, inhaling deeply to try and stave off his slumber, "I may be a horrible villain in your view of the world, but even villains can be gallant to a lady."

"I am no lady," she said, "I am the awkward daughter of a nobody who has never truly fit in anywhere." She seemed ready to cry. He wondered whether he should permit himself to care. His Human side called out to him. His Wizard side tried to hold firm.

Marcus sat up with some effort; the room swam, but he concentrated and his eyes put everything where it needed to be, so the room stopped moving. "I hope the bed is as comfortable as Synthyya promised it would be." His delivery was stilted.

"I should be the one on the floor," she said, "You are more tired than I am."

"I will not take the bed," he stated, "You are welcome." There was an uncomfortable pause, "It was kind of you to thank me," Marcus added without inflection. He lay back down, satisfied that her hatred had been dulled and so he had made the situation better. Darkness began to close in around him.

"I wasn't thanking you for the bed," she said, "I was thanking you for...I don't know...everything." He fought himself. If he just let it go, she might stop talking and he could rest. If he continued this conversation, however... He lifted his heavy eyelids.

"The orcs?" he asked. She noticed he used the Human word.

"The orcs, the Morphs, the Elves, the Humans—you've saved me from all of them. Every race seems to want to hurt me, except the Wizards," she half laughed-half cried.

"Wizards have hurt you, too," he said mournfully, "Just not with swords or arrows." They looked at one another and simply breathed in unison for a moment.

"I always break everything which is delicate, Marcus. It's just who I am," she explained, "I try, but I am not good with people. I never fit right." The sentence was delivered with her husky voice which so mismatched her womanly body, that it seemed as good a confirmation of her words as any. Marcus looked up at her. She was as lethal as any creature he'd known in all the Realm, but she seemed so vulnerable at this moment.

"It is the same with me," he said, "I never fit right, either."

"The Wizard with a Human name," she said, evincing the slightest grin, "Why didn't you just change your name to something less obviously Human, Marcus?"

"My name is all I have of my mother," he said quietly, his eyes downcast, "I don't know who she was, what she looked like, whether she fought my father when he took me to the Gray Mountains, or even what happened to her. Did she leave? Was she killed? Did my father abandon her? Did she not want to raise me? All I know is she insisted I be given a Human name and—for the only time, I imagine—my father relented. To change my name is to kill her, to erase her from existence."

"I killed my mother," she said quietly as she hugged her knees.

His Human side forced his body up, so that he sat beside Octavia on the bed. He delicately placed his hand on her back, taking care to avoid the areas beneath her shirt, which he knew were crisscrossed with pink scars. At least *those* scars were visible and easy to avoid, he mused. "What do you mean?" he asked.

"When I was born," she said, giving in to small pathetic sobs, "She had given birth to four strong boys with no difficulty, but when I passed into the world, she passed out of it. My birth was the death of her. I never knew her."

"Women die in childbirth for reasons we do not comprehend," he said, daring to rub her back, "All we can understand is that it is never the child's fault." Once again, he sounded like a father consoling his child. She nodded.

"Many women died in birth that year," Octavia said softly, her lip quivering.

Marcus appeared unusually pensive for a moment. "How old are you, Octavia?"

"Two *decems* and two years."

He noticed she used the Wizard word for a ten year period. He thought for a moment. "You were born 22 years ago?" he asked. She nodded limply. "I lived amongst the Humans at various points since my exile…Wandering Wizard and all that…22 years? I know that many Human women died in childbirth during that year. No one knows why. People say there was a sickness in your realm."

"So I have heard," Octavia replied, "Many children, newly born, died, as well."

"But not you," he whispered tenderly, putting his hand over hers. "For that kindness, we are all grateful." She held his gaze and then looked away.

"My father was so good, Marcus," Octavia said, choking a bit on her emotions, "He loved me so much and never once blamed me for her death. He tried to raise me, but he had no idea how to raise a daughter by himself. He knew how to forge weapons, but not how to forge a motherless girl."

"But he raised you well," Marcus said, "So says a motherless boy."

"Do you think so?" she wiped her eyes, "He raised me to be hard and that has made me successful on the battlefield. But I am no good anywhere else."

"It is hard to grow up without your mother," Marcus said, placing his hand under her chin, "I do not fully understand you, Octavia Flavius, but I do understand that part of you. At least you know your father loved you and did the best he could…" For a moment, she thought she detected some moisture obscuring his violet eyes, although perhaps she saw what she wanted to see. Octavia did not know that Wizards are unable to weep. When she later learned this, she was certain she saw what she wished to see. Regardless, for some reason, the appearance of moisture in his eyes affected her and she let loose a violent torrent of bawling. He held her wordlessly.

"I cannot believe I am letting you see me weep," she said, "*No one* sees me weep."

"Not your father?"

"Especially not my father," she said, "Nor my brothers. Nor any creature who walks the black earth."

"How exclusive. I have always been lucky," he joked, trying to reel her back.

"You must think so little of me," she said, her eyes now redder than her hair.

"You know I don't," he replied, "And I will tell no one that you are really made of flesh rather than steel. Your secret is safe with me."

"My secret that I really am just some pathetic little girl?"

"Your secret that you actually are a real Human and not simply a statue of a warrior," he said, "Perhaps, I will have better luck protecting this secret than the one that involved the orcs' eyes." He used the Human word again.

"I have been hard on you," she said.

"We have been hard on each other," he replied.

"But we are both motherless children put in one another's path by fate. Or design?" she mused, "Perhaps we can be kinder to one another." Her eyes looked so helpless, he noticed.

"We have much in common," he said. His eyes suddenly looked so heavy, she noticed.

"Synthyya will be delighted to learn we have not killed one another," she chuckled, trying to reclaim herself from this moment.

"I presume this was her goal in setting us in this room together," he said. "'Padrig insists,' such a lame ruse..." His words were slurring, as he was so exhausted.

"Gwen thinks we're in love," Octavia blurted out.

"Just like an Elf...always in love...birds and trees sing to them," he grunted with obvious effort, his head beginning to bob up and down.

"That's exactly what I said," marveled Octavia. He seemed to be working very hard to smile, but his eyes were half closed and his breathing had changed. "She does not understand. We are just friends, Marcus." She placed her hand atop his.

"Just friends," he repeated, his eyelids fluttering.

"Marcus, I will try harder to be..." she struggled for the words.

"Just be you, Octavia. That is all I want..." His words trailed off and his head fell back on the bed. She put the blanket over him and watched him sleep. They were at peace with one another and she was content.

When Marcus awoke in the morning, he was mildly vexed to find Octavia sleeping on the floor.

***

As they made their way to eat, Octavia and Marcus shared a hope that Padrig and Molly were kinder to their guests with breakfast. "Surely, the food can't be as bad as last night," Octavia said as they left their room.

"Please gods, let them have the dark morning elixir of Elves," Marcus added.

"You appear well rested," she observed as he closed the door.

"My friend refuses to play the girl," Marcus shot back, "She took the floor and left me the bed."

"I don't do damsel in distress," she shrugged, "Never have. We've been over this. Was the bed as good as advertised?"

"Wouldn't you like to know..." He stopped short because he almost ran into the occupant of a nearby room, a Sunset Elf who had emerged through a doorway with no sense that someone might be coming. "Excuse me," Marcus said in a tone which indicated that he had expected the words should have come from the Elf.

The Elf put his hand on the hilt of his sword and turned towards the Wizard. Octavia's eyes narrowed and her dagger was already out and ready before she realized it was entirely unnecessary. A look of recognition washed swiftly over the Elf's face. "My Lord Marcus," the Elf suddenly said with a grin.

"You are Ardor," Marcus declared, "Thorbad's lieutenant."

The Elf removed his hand from his sword and embraced the Wizard. Marcus was so surprised, he did not return the hug at all. Octavia sheathed her dagger and laughed at the Wizard's expression. "Lord Marcus, greatest of Wizards," Ardor marveled, "You look well." It suddenly occurred to Octavia that she had either broken this Elf's jaw or had come very close to doing so. Best to leave quickly in case he remembered that.

"All seems well here, I'll scout breakfast, Marcus," she said as she slipped away.

Ardor looked at Octavia as she walked away and then at Marcus. He smirked. "So you and the fire-haired girl, eh? She acts like a man, but is built like a woman. I'd prefer an Elf girl every time, but as we always say 'many different trees make up a forest.'" Ardor elbowed Marcus in the ribs. Marcus thought of protesting the Elf's misunderstanding, but presumed it would only extend a conversation which he wanted to end quickly. He simply played along so he could escape.

"You and I know there is no Elf in Elfland with breasts like that," Marcus said.

Ardor howled. "So true, so true," he said, "What can you tell me about those rumors which surround Humans of the North?" His look was lewd.

Marcus stopped him with an upturned palm. "Enough. Tell me, what are you doing here, Ardor? Business?"

"Always business, Lord Wizard," Ardor said, "Wizards and Elves; goods and gold, that is my life."

"I regret the circumstances of our last meeting," Marcus said.

"No no no, it was Thorbad," Ardor said, "He'd never acted like that before that evening. I'd never have thought he would have become so unhinged about that pretty Elf girl. It was almost like he was under some powerful magic."

"It wasn't my magic, I assure you."

"Of course not," Ardor said, "You were very fair. More than fair. Most Wizards would have confiscated our goods. Many Wizards would have killed us all. None would have given us gold on top of our goods."

"Did any of your men speak of our meeting?" Marcus asked.

"No, my men do what they are told when gold is involved," Ardor said.

"Good, I cannot be spoken of by anyone," Marcus explained. Ardor nodded. "Well, I must be off. I need breakfast. The redhead kept me up all night, you know how that can be." He faked a lewd grin of his own.

Ardor nodded. "The breakfast here is terrible," he said. Marcus nodded and walked away. "Marcus! Lord Marcus. Wait." Marcus turned and looked queerly at the dark Elf. He seemed to be trying to decide whether to say something. "You were good to me and I wish to repay the kindness. You should know that there were several Elves here last night asking about a Wizard, a blonde Elf, and a red-haired Human. They told the innkeepers they were seeking you and that their master was more powerful than even the Elf King. I do not know who they were working for, but I got a very cold feeling when they were in my presence."

"What did Padrig and Molly say?"

"They had never seen a Human with red hair in all their lives for we are far from the North," he said, "And they couldn't imagine a day that an Elf and a Wizard would be in league with a Human, no matter what color her hair."

"Was that the end?"

"These Elves badgered and threatened the innkeepers for quite a long time," Ardor said, "I come this way often and am fond of Padrig and Molly. I did not like the way these Elves spoke to the innkeepers, so when they finally left, I took several of my men and we followed them. I had a notion that we could correct their rudeness by having a discussion with their 'master,' as they termed him. I could not see to whom they gave their report, but this master was a hooded figure with glowing red eyes. A Wizard, perhaps? He seemed tall for an Elf. Very peculiar. My men were utterly terrified, and so we did not pursue the matter. A shame, if you ask me. Elves ought to treat other Elves with more respect than that. I would have spoken to this master about such things if my men had been braver."

"Interesting," Marcus said with a blank expression.

"I thought you should know, given your need to not be spoken of and all."

"You saw the eyes?" asked Marcus. Ardor nodded. "Were you afraid?"

"Not really," he said with a shrug, "I found it odd that my men were so terrified. They were paralyzed with fear. Of course, it did not occur to me until I saw you that you and the warrior girl were the ones being sought. The blonde Elf must be Gwendolyn, the slave girl, right?"

"Ex-slave," Marcus said, "You were not afraid, that speaks well of you, Ardor. I thank you for telling me. While this news is not welcome, it is better to know than not to know. Thank you, my friend." Marcus placed his hand on Ardor's shoulder.

"We do good to others and good is done to us," Ardor insisted.

"Well said," Marcus agreed as he turned away.

"I'll say a little more," Ardor called out.

"I am listening."

"Never make the fire haired girl angry," he said, "She hits like a man." He rubbed his jaw for effect.

"I shall try to avoid angering her ever again," Marcus agreed with a nod.

***

"Did you hear what I said, Synthyya?"

264

"Yes," she said, nodding. "This is not unexpected, but it is most unfortunate."

"What does it mean?" Quintus asked.

"He knows about you," Synthyya said.

"He knows about Marcus and Octavia and me," Gwen said.

"He has tracked us here," Octavia said.

"By 'he,' we mean who I think we mean, right?" Alexia asked.

"The Dark Lord," Marcus said. It was hard to tell if his grimace was the result of the news or the simply dreadful eggs which lay on his plate. He was displeased that the inn keepers only served weak tea, rather than the morning elixir he would expect at an Elvin inn. He did not care for tea and he cared less for weak tea.

"Are we in danger?" Griffin asked.

"We have always been in danger," Synthyya said, "We are in more danger, that's all. But danger is danger. A difference of degrees is irrelevant."

"I am not sure I agree," interrupted Quintus, "If the information is correct, our enemy knows three of us by description and had a notion that Marcus, Octavia, and Gwen were in this inn. He could be close."

"Yet he did not discover we were here," Synthyya said jubilantly, "The innkeepers kept their word."

"It almost makes up for the horrid meals," Octavia observed.

"How wonderful were the beds!?" Gwen interjected, "I haven't slept so well since I left Elfland. Wasn't it delightful, Octavia?" Octavia put a forkful of leathery eggs in her mouth so she could simply nod. It almost seemed a sin to lie to sweet Gwendolyn.

"What is our move, now, Synthyya?" Marcus asked.

"Am I your leader?" she asked, "What do *you* think?"

Marcus looked instinctively to Quintus to hash it out. Quintus offered, "We should leave while it is day. His powers are weaker during the day, right?"

"That could be true," Synthyya allowed, "Although his powers are still more than our whole fellowship, no matter the time of day or night. And he appears to have Elves working for him. That is a pity."

"Why would an Elf help a goblin?" Griffin asked. "Ardor said they went up and spoke to a hooded goblin? That's unbelievable!"

"Elves, like all creatures, do what is in their best interest," Alexia observed.

"How did your errand go, Synthyya?" Gwen asked.

"Oh yes, I almost forgot," Synthyya said, "Very well. I met with the Historian's right hand man. We are only a half a day away and he is expecting us."

"Unless the Dark Lord has already gotten there and is waiting for us," Quintus said. Synthyya laughed hysterically. No one else understood what was so funny.

"It would be *amusing* if the Dark Lord got there first?" Octavia asked, "I'm a little lost at what's funny, Synthyya."

"Adorable little Red," Synthyya said to Octavia, "Super-serious Ranger," she said, turning to Quintus, "The Historian is the latest in a long line of those who caretake the books which survived the fall of the Classical World. The Dark Lord has been looking for the Historian or his predecessors for hundreds and hundreds of years. He will never find him. His home is hidden from sight by magic of unfathomable power. Let's just hope I can keep straight the directions that were given to me. Like the Dark Lord, I have trouble finding his home, too, sometimes." Once again, she laughed but no one else did.

Chapter 29: The Historian

Marcus seemed more burdened than usual, Gwendolyn noticed. He was worried. Of course, he'd be worried because the Dark Lord had identified three of them and tracked them to the inn. But there was something more. What was it? She gazed at the beautiful green hills of south Elfland and marveled at the animals scampering about—none aware that an evil force had risen and threatened them. Deer pranced, rabbits hopped, squirrels scampered in complete ignorance of the potential for doom. In many ways, the Elves they saw were the same. Sunset Elves, Sunrise Elves, Low Elves all went about their business, whistling and singing. Few took any interest in the fellowship. Griffin and Gwen looked like they belonged and it was not unusual that Elves would be in the company of a Wizard or even two. Alexia was flying above them as a robin, outpacing Marcus's owl as she darted to and fro. Both Octavia and Quintus had tucked their hair into helmets and drawn cloak hoods over their ears. They were both tall, but some Elves grew as tall as Humans and it wasn't entirely uncommon. As long as they weren't seen up close, they wouldn't attract attention from Elves. If this were the Human or Wizard world, they'd have all been stopped multiple times. Humans and Wizards were curious. Elves preferred to not bother with strangers, focusing on their tasks or looking with vacant wonder at the falling multicolored leaves.

She would never admit it to Griffin, but she missed this place. Gwen missed the charm of an Elf's life, lived so close to nature. She missed the many animals that played near her dwelling, whom she'd counted as friends in her peculiar way. She missed long silent hikes in the dense woods. She missed the way groups of Elves would simply break into song for no reason. Yes, she knew how Octavia stereotyped her people and it was not always true. But sometimes it was. She missed her parents. She missed the innocence she had had before leaving this idyllic world. However, Gwendolyn did not miss everything about Elfland. She missed neither the extreme piety, nor the strict laws. Gwen did not miss the way she had been treated because of her gender. Her wish would be to return to Elfland, but be permitted to use her gift with the bow as the Spirits had no doubt intended. That was a wish which she knew would go unfulfilled. A pity, for Quintus would love this place! He adored the natural world and she caught a glimpse of him watching the animals frolic in the late autumn sun. Gwen looked forward to a long life of loving him and then a dark thought entered her head.

What if their time were limited? What if the Historian had no counsel? What if no one could stop this fairy tale monster? Her fears were not abstract—they centered on her friends and especially Quintus. She was grief-stricken by the idea that she might never grow to love him because of the doom which hung over them all—unbeknownst to the Elves picking flowers or the chipmunks gathering nuts. Gwen glanced again at Marcus. She felt that he was feeling the same thing. She looked at Octavia. Yes. It had been clear at breakfast that they had decided to no longer hurt one another. They had made up in their strange fashion. No doubt this had been Synthyya's plan and it had come to fruition. In fact, at breakfast, Octavia had remarked to Molly about her husband's odd habit of pairing up guests and the Elf woman looked thoroughly perplexed by the statement. She'd told Octavia they'd had plenty of rooms and didn't understand why Synthyya only insisted on four. Synthyya simply raised her eyebrows and shrugged with an impish grin.

Yet Gwen couldn't help but think there was something more to Marcus's countenance. Perhaps, his gravity was because he was mourning the time he might lose with Octavia if the Dark Lord succeeded. Perhaps, Octavia felt the same way. Perhaps they had taken a step towards acknowledging this. Perhaps, Gwen acknowledged, she was guilty of being the stereotypical Elf—blissfully presuming that love was everywhere and "trees sang to her" as Octavia had joked. But about one thing Gwen was certain—whether Marcus and Octavia were to be simply friends or more—they were running out of time. "We all are," she thought to herself.

***

Lying to Gwendolyn hurt most of all. She seemed such a kind-hearted and virtuous creature that all of this deception troubled him. Still, he could not tell one, unless he were prepared to tell all. He was not prepared to tell all, so that was that. At least for the moment, he consoled himself... Moments could change. This, he knew.

***

Synthyya stopped sharply as if she had found some jewel-encrusted necklace, Griffin thought. Wizards were unhealthily obsessed with colorful gems and shiny metals. So unlike Elves, he mused to himself. Synthyya said nothing, but slowly approached a shimmering lake where light danced on the surface. She smiled, her red lips pulled back to reveal white teeth.

"It is done," she sighed, as she plucked a flower and tossed it into the pond, her throw assisted by a gentle breeze which could have been fortuitous or could have been magical— it was impossible to tell.

"Are we here?" Marcus asked, looking around. Synthyya nodded.

The robin fluttered down and morphed. Griffin dutifully handed Alexia her dress, laboring to avert his eyes. "You'll pardon me, Synthyya, but you mean we are at the Historian's home?" Alexia asked.

"Indeed," Synthyya said, clasping her hands around her staff with obvious satisfaction. Marcus and Octavia exchanged a glance. Gwen smiled involuntarily; at least they were sharing glances once again, she mused.

"Is it invisible?" Quintus asked.

"What?" Synthyya asked.

"The home?"

"No, it's not invisible," she said, as if that were a silly question only a child would ask, "It's hidden."

"I am not sure I know the difference," Gwen said sweetly.

"O sweet little blonde creature, there is a world of difference," Synthyya said, her tone syrupy sweet, "You can see his home, if you know where to look. If it were invisible, you would not be able to see it." Synthyya laughed.

"I presume you know where to look," Griffin said anxiously.

"I do," she said, "I met the Historian's assistant and he reminded me of a few important things."

"For example?" Marcus asked.

"The flower, Marcus," Synthyya said, "See how it floats on the water?"

"This water is not poisonous, is it?" Alexia asked.

"No, my gorgeous shape changer, it is normal water," Synthyya explained, "Well, mostly normal."

"'Mostly normal.' Of course," Quintus said with a sigh, squinting his gray eyes as he gazed at the shimmering surface of the water.

"The serious Ranger is surprised," Synthyya said, mocking Quintus's voice, "The flower tells the Historian we are here, Quintus. He must check to see if we have been followed or if there is anyone who might be around by accident. There can be no witnesses."

"He can do that?" Octavia asked.

"Yes, with the bowl, of course," Synthyya said impatiently, rolling her eyes at the ignorance of her companions.

Marcus was curious about this bowl, but figured it was best to keep his old teacher focused on the most immediate task. "If we are alone and unwatched, what happens next?"

"The flower will glow, which will tell us the door is open," she said.

"Where is the door?" asked Gwendolyn.

"You'll see," Synthyya smirked.

The other six members of the fellowship scanned the area, as did Marcus's owl, now perched on his shoulder. They saw the lake, several large trees whose branches shaded the

270

lake, a few rock outcroppings, dazzling arrays of wildflowers, and soft mossy grass. "Magic being magic, I suppose the house could be anything," grumbled Griffin, "I thought you said he was an Elf."

"Half Elf, half Human," Quintus corrected him.

"Yes," Synthyya agreed, "He is no Wizard, but many Wizards have befriended him and his illustrious predecessors for a 100 *decems* or more. His backers, the *Custodes* count several powerful Wizards amongst their numbers. There is very powerful magic here. He does not cast the spells, but he caretakes them. He is the face of powerful and mysterious allies and his duties are essential to the world continuing to exist. Perhaps I am being too dramatic. Let's say 'continuing to exist in a way that we cherish.'"

The solitary floating flower glowed, its deep scarlet petals taking on an otherworldly beauty. Synthyya clapped excitedly. "It has been so long since I have seen him," she said.

"Where is the door?" Gwen asked.

"Oh it could be anywhere," Synthyya said, "The rocks, the trees, the grass, the water."

"How will we know where it is?" Marcus asked.

"It will be obvious," Synthyya said, "He wants us to come, so he won't make it difficult." Suddenly a golden oval shimmered in the trunk of a pine tree. "There it is!" Synthyya gathered up her dress and put one hand on her hat as she stepped through and disappeared. Everyone looked at one another, trying to decide whether to follow.

"I'll go," Octavia said, putting her hand on her winged helmet in imitation of Synthyya and stepping into the oval. She took one step and there was no more ground. Suddenly, she felt herself falling. Well, not actually *falling*. She realized after a few seconds that she was sliding, as if on ice that was not cold. The air rushed past her but with no light, she couldn't tell how fast she was going. Her helmet shifted and her red pony tail escaped, trailing her as if it had a mind of its own. The cool wind felt refreshing on her face. Her heart was leaping in her chest. Octavia felt so much better than she had yesterday and now as she slid, she felt like a child at play. Then, it was over.

She landed on firm ground and saw Synthyya. Synthyya smiled and pointed up.

Octavia looked up and saw water. The roof of wherever they were was made of water. She thrust her axe up and it got wet. Yet the water remained suspended there as if held by magic. "What is this?" she asked.

"You are as smart as you are fierce, strong limbed warrior girl," Synthyya said, "Look closely and open your mind."

Octavia looked closely while she heard the thud of another friend landing behind her. She saw the water and detected light above it. Against the light was silhouetted the branches of trees. A little speck darted across as the water undulated. It occurred to Octavia that the speck was a bird. "It's the lake," Octavia declared in awe, "We are underneath the lake."

"How in the world?" Gwen asked in wonder from behind Octavia.

"Magic," Marcus said.

"Magic," Synthyya agreed.

Nine small men with white beards and peculiar hats came forward, chattering in some nonsensical tongue. They greeted Synthyya warmly and nodded in a courtly fashion to the others. "What are those?" asked Alexia.

"Gnomes," Synthyya said.

"Gnomes are fictional," Octavia said, "Like unicorns or dragons or…"

"Orcs?" asked Quintus.

"Good point," Octavia agreed.

"There is much in this world that we do not comprehend," Synthyya said, "The Historian comprehends more than most. What we cannot comprehend, we must accept."

They followed the Gnomes on a curving path until a huge mansion appeared and a large eagle shrieked from one of the towers. "Hello, Hermes!" Synthyya called out. One Gnome climbed on another's shoulders and opened the huge brass door.

The others bowed low and indicated that the fellowship should enter.

"Is this place real?" Griffin asked Gwendolyn.

"It must be," Gwen replied, with a shrug "because we are here."

An old man with a shiny bald head and a thick white beard met them in the entranceway. He was tall for an Elf, but short for a Human, with pointed ears and a stooped posture. He leaned on a polished cane and squinted at them with small eyes. His broad smile had many gaps where teeth no longer dwelled, but his cheeks were rosy red and his smile was infectious.

"Titus!" Synthyya exclaimed, embracing him.

"Synthyya, it has been far too long since I set my bleary eyes on you," he said. His voice was stronger than one would expect from such an ancient-looking creature and it had a gravelly undertone. Yet despite the roughness of his voice, it was cheerful.

"It is a pleasure to meet you, Honorable Historian," Quintus said, walking up to him and bowing low.

"Quintus Agrippa Aureus, the true heir of the Dukedom of the Aureus family," the Historian said with a chuckle, "I am no nobleman and it makes me uneasy if you bow to me. Let us grip one another's hands as Humans of equal rank do." Quintus looked befuddled, but shook the old man's hand firmly. He was surprised by the Historian's iron grip. The Historian's eyes wandered to Octavia. "And you must be Octavia Flavius. My my, how your hair burns like a roaring fire in mid-winter. I promise you all that there is no warrior in the realm with a greater heart than this woman, here." Octavia blushed. "And of course, it is Marcus, Synthyya's finest student."

"I am sure she has exaggerated, sir," Marcus said, "We have all been eager to meet you."

"Oh, I feel as if I know you all," The Historian said, "I have watched your comings and goings since you came together. I have been as eager to meet you, Marcus, as you have been to meet me." He smiled and turned to Alexia. "Ah yes, Alexia the Morph who has powers like your people once did in ancient times..."

"Please, do not remind me of why I am an outcast," she said.

He laughed and hit the floor with his cane, "Outcast? I live under an enchanted lake with nine Gnomes, dear Morph! Who is the true outcast?" He studied her. "You are as beautiful and intoxicating as I had expected, but your treasure has nothing to do with your beauty." She wanted to ask him what he meant, but he had moved on. "And this must be Griffin. You are taller than I had thought. Do not worry, it is meant as a compliment. Forgive an old man his manners. No sister ever had a better brother than Griffin. Oh, how he loves you." He was speaking to Gwen.

"I know, sir," she said, sweetly smiling to Griffin. Both Elves blushed.

"And Gwendolyn, Gwendolyn, Gwendolyn," the Historian said in awe, shaking his head as if he had never dreamed he would make her acquaintance.

"Yes?"

"Gwendolyn," he said, closing his eyes, "it is you I have most wanted to meet. Your arrow is always true and your spirit even more so. May I look into your eyes?"

"Of course," she said, blushing head to toe. She sank to a knee to make it easier for him, as he was bent over and leaning heavily on his cane.

He looked into her eyes for a long time. "Yes, yes, yes, Synthyya, she is so lovely. She is. She is. She is more than I could tell from a distance. Now up close, it is clear. Gwendolyn, Gwendolyn, Gwendolyn. I thank the Golden One and the Blessed Spirits both for this sweet creature." He straightened up and looked at the Ranger with a jovial smile. "Don't worry, Quintus, I have no designs on your fair Elf girl. I am 248 sun cycles old and do not have the energy to fight you for her love." He winked. Quintus, who had involuntarily tensed up, relaxed. "But we can agree that Gwendolyn is special, isn't she?"

"She is, sir," Quintus agreed. He looked at Gwen, her exposed skin all pinkish with embarrassment.

274

"Friends, you are welcome in my home," The Historian bellowed, "My staff will help you get settled. There are seven rooms for my seven friends with basins for you to scrub the dust of the road off of your bodies, fresh clothes to aid your comfort, and a seat at my table for a feast in your honor. Fires will burn in all of my rooms tonight to ward off the chill of this late autumn evening."

"We have many questions, Historian," Marcus said.

"I shall endeavor to answer them all," he responded kindly, "But now, please go to your rooms and change for supper. I must speak to my assistant about the preparations."

"Will we speak of the Dark Lord, tonight?" Quintus asked.

The Historian winced. This was the crux of it, he thought. Ought he tell them the truth or some shade of the truth? He looked at Synthyya. She thought she knew so much, but he knew better. What would be the correct choice? This evening would be critical for the *Custodes*. What to do about the Dark Lord story? It had all been so easy when they were far away. Now, matters were different. Now, they were in his presence and he had choices to make. He could not delay those choices any further.

The Historian sighed heavily, "I have much to tell you, Duke Quintus," he said, "And I am afraid very little of it is hopeful. But while my advice will be dark, there is a light that follows you. And while I am the 11th of my line, heir to the venerable Historians of years gone by, I am also a simple old man. And as an old man in his own house, I cannot conceive of telling you my tales without offering you a bath, a change of clothes, and a delicious dinner. When your skin is refreshed and your bellies are full, we will discuss those grave matters." This would buy time, but the decision needed to be made. He would consult the others as a matter of necessity. He had doubts. They needed to know that.

Titus then muttered something to the Gnomes and they scattered in every direction. After smiling at his guests, he turned and hobbled away.

The hobbling ceased immediately after the fellowship was safely out of sight.

Chapter 30: The Story of Lucretia

Marcus was shown to his room by one of the Gnomes and he opened the thick wooden door. Inside was a large soft bed, a basin of steaming water with a bottle of white liquid and a towel folded next to it, and a desk with a chair. Hung on the chair was a formal Wizard outfit—black boots, scarlet pants, a scarlet shirt with a stiff collar and gleaming gold buttons, and a dazzling cloak, the color of deep water with intricate golden stitching. The Gnome was tugging on Marcus's dark and tattered enchanted cloak, but the Wizard would not let it go. The little creature jabbered on in its unintelligible language, violently gesturing at the replacement blue cloak with the elaborate needlework draped over the chair. He clearly wanted Marcus's magical cloak and would not yield. Finally, the little creature marched up the basin of water and pointed at it and at Marcus's cloak. "You want to wash my cloak?" Marcus asked. The Gnome nodded and clapped his hands. Finally, Marcus relented to get the creature out of his room. He had probably acquiesced because his eye caught sight of a thick book sitting on his desk with a cover inlaid in jewels and silver. "The Last Council of the Classical World" was written in looping letters on the cover. The jewels did not call to him for his was not a typical Wizard, but he was plenty Wizard enough to be entranced by a book. This, of course, was known and so it was no coincidence.

***

Octavia sank into the steaming basin and stretched out. The water covered her body and loosened the knots in her arms and legs. It caressed her stiff back. It seeped into every part of her. She examined the bottle of white liquid. It smelled fragrant. Was she supposed to drink it? She put it to her lips. The door to her room crashed open and a little Gnome scurried in. Octavia stood up and tried in vain to cover herself. With one arm across her breasts and one hand obscuring her womanhood, she was in an awkward position to fight. But the little Gnome did not seem a threat. He was chirping in his high pitched language and jumping up and down. "I am bathing!" she scolded him. He continued in his gibberish. "Do you really want to glimpse my body so badly?" she asked wearily. He chirped and chirped. "In the name of the Golden One, calm down little creature," she said. He pointed at her, his voice rising in pitch, the nonsense words coming out thick like arrows. "The rumors about Northerners penetrate beneath this lake and make you curious, do they? Fine, if it will get you out of my room, then look upon my form." She pulled her hands away from the parts of her body Humans keep covered for all but their beloved. The Gnome stopped for a moment and he gazed up at her well-toned form, speckled with freckles and sculpted from training. Then, he resumed jumping and pointing at her right hand. "What now?" she asked, monumentally frustrated. He pointed at the bottle. "The bottle?" she asked. He nodded, then mimed drinking. "I should drink it?" she asked. He shook his head violently. Then he mimed rubbing it on his body. "I should rub it on my body, but not drink it?" Octavia asked. The Gnome smiled, nodded, and left. He turned and winked at her before closing the door. Octavia poured the liquid into her hand suspiciously and it foamed up as if by magic. She rubbed it on her body and then sank back into the water. The white potion felt luxurious and her pale skin felt restored and refreshed, especially those scars on her back and her torso. Astoundingly, the water had not cooled an iota since she'd stood up. "More magic," she mused.

***

With the blade which had been left, Quintus scraped off the whiskers he'd been neglecting and better sculpted the sandy beard on his chin, so that it contrasted with the smoothness of the rest of his weather-beaten face. His face was neat, his body was clean, and he was dressed as a nobleman. He could not imagine where the Historian had found a Duke's ceremonial outfit in his size on such short notice. But perhaps the notice wasn't so short. The Historian had alluded to watching them.

Could he see through owls like Marcus? Or perhaps something else was going on. They were under a lake, for love of the Golden One! There was a reflective glass in Quintus's room and he tightened his belt in front of it. Sure, his hair was thinning and there were creases around his eyes, which had not always been there. But the man staring back was what he could have been. Rather than the scruffy Ranger, this was Duke Quintus of Aureus—freshly shaven and washed, wearing a crisp nobleman's costume, and looking every bit the person he was supposed to be. The person his father and mother wished he would have been. The oldest son and heir to the Dukedom. A brave warrior for the Council. A worthy husband for a beautiful noble bride. He had thrown it all away for an Elf girl once. Would he do it again if he could? He had loved his Valeria so many seasons ago, but that love seemed faint and shallow, now. Gwendolyn had become his world, crowding out Valeria and so many others. He longed for a reality where he could be Duke for more than one evening and Gwendolyn could be his Duchess. But Quintus Agrippa Aureus had lived long enough to know he did not live in that world. Perhaps, he could create that world, but that would require more time and more effort.

***

"O Spirits!" Griffin exclaimed as Alexia paraded in. She had on a formal gown which accentuated her curvaceous body and her neck was dripping with jewels.

"I feel like this thing is going to choke me to death," she remarked, tugging at the sparkling necklace.

"I had thought that even the finest clothing would only obscure your beauty," Griffin whispered, "But you look more desirable now than I've ever seen you."

"That is because I look like a proper lady," she whispered back, narrowing her brown eyes, "But we both know things are different without the dress. Don't we?" She puckered her plump lips on the 'w' of 'we' and held them in that position longer than was necessary. Griffin nodded, stunned. She smiled, satisfied.

Gwendolyn came in shortly thereafter, positively radiant in a golden dress which caught the light just perfectly and reflected the color of her sunny hair. In her ears and around her neck were blue gems, which perfectly matched her pale azure eyes. Quintus stood at attention and then took her ivory hand and kissed it. Her skin tasted like flowers. Gwen marveled at how tall and broad her love appeared in the dress of a nobleman. He looked like something out of a dream she might have had long ago. Most of her dreams which had thus far come true were the bad ones. But he was real. He grasped her bare arm and she could feel the rough calluses of his hands. They scraped her arm slightly, but she loved it because it was real. So very real.

"Where is Octavia?" Marcus asked. Synthyya nodded behind him. Octavia had on a red formal gown such as Humans would wear to address the Council or celebrate a wedding. It clung to her firm body and the cut of the crimson dress focused everyone's attention on her chest. The dress bared her shoulders, but covered her legs, ending only at her ankles, thus leaving the viewer to imagine her shapely legs without the benefit of seeing them. One had to take so many of her concealed body parts on faith and fill in the blanks, but the dress consoled the frustrated viewer with the clear fact that she had a lovely figure. All in all, it was a dress concocted by a genius and suited to her unique body. Still, she moved awkwardly in it, as if it were the wrong size. It wasn't, but Octavia was clearly uncomfortable.

"You painted your toes and fingers," Alexia marveled, "There may yet be a woman under there, even if the muscles are too strong and the voice is too deep."

"If the orcs find us under this lake and a fight breaks out, I will rip this dress to shreds and fight unclad like you do, Alexia," Octavia promised, "I feel so absurd in this thing." She sat awkwardly, seemingly unaware that she was enticing to the others when clad in such a garment. You might have believed it was enchanted if you were there, but you can be assured, on good authority, that is was an ordinary dress.

"Let's hope the orcs don't find us," Quintus said, "It's a nice dress."

"You look like a princess," Marcus said, his tone impossible to read. Was it sincere or a joke? Wizards were so inscrutable, Octavia cursed to herself. She wasn't sure if he was sneaking glances at her during dinner or checking the doorway for an imminent attack. Her cleavage was undeniably sublime, so she presumed the former. But Wizards could not be easily read. Morphs on the other hand... Alexia made no pretense about staring at Octavia and she half-expected the Morph to start a fight to see Octavia tear off the dress. There had never been any moments like this in Octavia's life where she got glamoured up like some idle noblewoman and overplayed her femininity. When had she last painted her nails? At age seven? When had she last worn something other than pants? 12? It seemed so strange and yet it did not feel entirely bad. Did Marcus really think she looked like a princess? Or was it a joke that the girl who talked and fought like a boy had no business wearing a gown or painting her toenails?

"I know none of you feel entirely comfortable in such fancy clothing," the Historian said, "But this is an important meal and our clothing should reflect it. I am grateful that Alexia has consented to wear what was laid out for her because I know that dining while clothed is not typical of her kind. Of course, we respect that, here. We respect all views, because we believe that improving the world begins in a room."

"I try to make allowance for lesser beings who cannot stand to see such beauty exposed during mealtime," Alexia said with a wicked grin, "Although I've been told I wear this outfit very well."

"Indeed you do, dear," The Historian chuckled, "My household and I get visitors so rarely that it lifts an old man's spirits to share his table with you all." The meal then commenced with the nine Gnomes in stiff outfits bringing out course after course until the hungry Fellowship had eaten its fill. There was a savory soup filled with fish and potatoes which seemed to combine all the flavors of the world in perfect harmony.

"The soup was extraordinary," Gwen beamed, "And the bread you served with it must have been baked just before dinner."

The Gnomes smiled and giggled as they pointed to her. "My staff is delighted at your compliment, Sweet Gwendolyn," he said, "And let me say that the sound of your voice drips into our ears like honey. So the Gnomes say, anyway..."

"Gnomes are real," Griffin said, unbelieving.

"Obviously," Quintus retorted, gesturing at them.

"They are real but not for much longer," lamented the Historian, "These nine are the last of their kind. Gnomes have survived from the time before history was recorded. They can live for 500 years or more, but the Dark Lord hates them. He hates so much." His voice trailed off and the Gnomes seemed ready to weep. Titus had received his orders and he was determined to carry them out. The truth needed to be spiced to match the tastes of this crowd. It was the only way. "The Dark One thought he'd killed all the Gnomes, but a few survived. Now, these nine are the end. They are safe with me. Alas, there are no more female Gnomes, so when these nine men die, the Gnomes will pass into fantasy as Griffin hints. So they are real for now, but not forever."

"So it is with all of us," Synthyya said.

"True," the Historian said, stroking on his beard, "But it will be more true if you and your friends cannot complete the tasks set before you."

"Finally," Marcus said, "Tell us of the Dark Lord and how to kill him."

"That is quite a mouthful," laughed the Historian, although much lurked behind that laugh, "If you think killing the one we call 'the Dark Lord' is your quest, you will be very surprised. It is not quite like that, brave Wizard. Let us begin at the beginning, Marcus. Let us focus on how those who overthrew Classical Civilization were once defeated before we move on to more ominous things." There was room in this meal for a generous helping of truth, Titus determined. He simply needed to blur the edges just so.

"We are eager to hear your wisdom, pardon my impatience," Marcus said.

"Oh, I pardon you a thousand times over because I know what awaits you and your fellowship," The Historian said, "But if you knew what I knew, you would not be eager. You have all heard that Classical Civilization existed a thousand or more years ago and it was a time that Humans, Elves, Morphs, and Wizards coexisted reasonably well. We call it a Golden Age, but I am sure there was still hatred and disagreement because such is the world. However, it seems as if—overall—the different religions were respected, the diverse racial customs were embraced, and occasional intermarriage was acceptable in those blessed days. A council representing all the realms met in the place we now call 'the Ruined City' in the center of our world, and that council chose an Overking or Overqueen to rule with their advice and consent. Each race put forth one or more candidates and the council chose the best being in the realm by a vote. The system worked very well at ensuring all voices were heard and the races cooperated and shared their gifts, as much as one has the right to expect. So many advancements date from this time, I could bore you all night, but as you have heard, that civilization failed many many centuries ago."

"The Dark Lord," Marcus said. Titus swallowed. Here it was.

"Yes, most of us who study the era use 'Dark Lord' as short-hand for the destruction of the civilization, although the one of which you speak is certainly not the only one to blame."

"Who else shares blame? Is there another Dark one?" asked Octavia, incredulous.

"No, no. We all share the blame," the Historian explained, "Despite what you have heard, some powerful Dark Lord did not overthrow a civilization by himself. Many were complicit with this one whose name has been erased. He is powerful—more so than you can even imagine. But I, for one, do not believe he is a god, even if a few scholars are convinced of it. He is a Wizard—perhaps the greatest of the Wizards in a manner of speaking. But one Wizard cannot topple a world unless he has much assistance."

"The Morphs," Griffin interrupted, "The Morphs abandon the others in the old stories we once thought were myth."

The Historian looked at Alexia with sad eyes. "We do not know where truth ends and myth begins because we are trying to reconstruct ancient events from mere scraps and crumbs," he said, "Yes, it seems as though the Morphs as a whole joined the Dark Lord first. But that does not mean *all* Morphs did."

"Nor does it mean any Morph living today bears the blame," Gwen spoke up. Alexia looked longingly at Gwendolyn and the kindness in her sky-blue eyes.

"I quite agree, my golden Elf," The Historian said, "But while the Morphs may have been first, Humans and Elves and Wizards all followed. Many were seduced by power and promises. That is how they operate."

"They?" Quintus asked. Titus respected these beings too much to ladle out excessive untruth. He acknowledged the question with a nod.

"Let me explain: I strongly believe that the Wizard we call 'the Dark Lord' is simply the leader of a significantly sized group of like-minded beings who overthrew the civilization together." That was as close to truth as he dared to tread.

"Why would anyone overthrow a civilization?" Octavia asked, "If Marcus is to be believed, it was a wonderful time."

"I am sure it felt a lot like any other time and did not feel special to those who were there," Titus said, "But in any world, there are those who want power for its own sake—not as a tool to improve the world, but as a way to improve *their* lives. At first, this shadowy *Dominus Maleficarum* was one of them—probably their leader. Our histories point to him as the one who destroyed that world, but if you read between the lines, there were many who participated—some purposefully and others unwittingly. The former disappear from history when he was defeated. In fact, the hole in our history is so big that we don't know the leader's name, so we make up terms like 'Dark Lord.' I find it doubtful he used that name. Can you imagine anyone styling himself a "Dark Lord?' Preposterous. Elves and

Morphs often call him the 'Nameless One' because his name had been erased from history, whether by design or by accident—who can tell? So much of our world is pulled by forces which may be design or may be accident; I, for one, can never be sure."

"But what erased him?" Quintus asked, "If he has recently *arisen* then something must have put him down."

"Yes, good Duke, something did," the Historian said, "The Elves and the Humans had a horrible estrangement soon after this Wizard first rose to power and any chance of stopping the Dark One disappeared for many many sun cycles. Perhaps, he ruled this world of ours for a century or for several centuries—we cannot know, as the sources are thin. But it is clear that suffering fell like rain. Many were enslaved, almost no art or writing has survived, we can only guess at the pain. It seems that murder and rape and hatred hung thickly about as the races merely hoped to survive, nothing more. All the while, the Dark One showed no signs of aging and his power did not wane an iota. This is the power of the Dark magic, which is what has made him more than just a Wizard. As for those around them, we cannot know if they shared this longevity or were simply replaced as the generations multiplied."

"But there was hope," Gwen said, "Isn't that so?"

"Yes, Gwendolyn, hope remained in the breasts of a few," the Historian lectured, "My people. The *Custodes*. They caretook the hope and nurtured it until a plan hatched. Long after our enemies took the world as their possession, several Wizards and Humans came together with an audacious plan to lure the Dark Lord to the land west of the Dragon's Claws."

"West of the Gray Mountains? *West*? There is no such land," Synthyya said. Marcus nodded.

"Even Wizards would do well to listen," the Historian smiled, "For there is much of this world about which even the wisest of your kind is ignorant, but we who caretake the knowledge—we know... West of your Gray Mountains is the Wasteland where darkness is eternal and cold omnipresent. It seems as if the world ends after the mountains but your eyes can deceive you, or else you'd have never have found me, here.

You cannot see the Wasteland, but it is there. The Wasteland is separated from our world by powerful magic which those Wizards gave up their very lives to create. The power of the wall between us and the Wasteland drained them of all their life force but when complete, it was powerful enough that it could keep even the most formidable Wizard imprisoned. Hundreds of Wizards or more died in the casting of those spells."

"I thought Humans were in this tale," Octavia said.

"Oh, they do enter the tale, brave Octavia," The Historian said, "All the braver for agreeing to don an evening gown." He smiled, his tiny eyes twinkling in the candlelight as she blushed so that her face matched her hair and her dress. "Can you imagine if hundreds of Humans and Wizards got along like you and Marcus and Quintus and Synthyya? Oh, the things they could achieve! The prison was set and the Dark One knew nothing of it or its power, but the fact remained that they needed to lure him there."

"How does one lure a monster to its doom?" asked Griffin.

"Love," the Historian replied, "Even monsters can love. The Humans searched and found the most beautiful woman the world has ever seen. No creature could look upon her without falling to the ground in awe. Her name was Lucretia and every step she took was a miracle according to the books. The Humans convinced her to help and she played her role to perfection. She was taken from her husband and daughter and presented to the Dark Lord as women often were, as an offering. So many women of all races were given to him, that he might utilize them for his whims and cast them away, broken or worse. But Lucretia was more than just a beautiful woman. She was like a poem taken flesh. And all the Human arts of beauty were used to enhance her natural radiance. Humans enchant better than Wizards in this realm; they know what to paint, what to cover, what to expose, how to style, the ways one can adorn so that a woman's body becomes irresistible. There are a thousand tricks to make a beautiful woman seem even more beautiful and the Humans of this time knew them all. The ladies who eat with us this evening exhibit many of these

286

Human-invented enhancements, and you are lovely. But Lucretia's appearance defied any words they had then or we have now. By the time Lucretia was dressed and presented to the Dark Lord, he conceived an immovable hunger for her, a love..." He paused and closed his eyes. "Perhaps 'love' is too strong a word for me to use. Perhaps a creature such as him is not capable of an emotion we would call 'love.' But it was more than simply desire that invaded his chest—that much the sources agree upon. With their world hanging in the balance, they presented Lucretia to the Lord. The plan was unfurled like a banner, for at the moment he glimpsed her in all of her glory, a very brave Human—as it had been planned—suggested he marry her."

"The poor girl!" shrieked Gwendolyn.

"She entered all of this willingly," the Historian explained, "She could have refused at any point, but she knew it was the only way to save her husband, her daughter, her world. I am sure the plan started in a room, like this one, as all plans to improve the world do. Lucretia was the very picture of courage and poise in a situation no one could endure. She smiled when the situation called for it. She called attention to her most alluring features when it was required. She seduced the Dark Lord, an act no one could fathom then or now. The Human flatterers convinced the Dark One that he could sire a son with this extraordinary woman which would only amplify his power, so—intoxicated with her loveliness and consumed with a desire to mar it, perhaps—he consented to the marriage. After the words were spoken and dear Lucretia was joined in marriage with the Dark One, the surviving Wizards who were in on the plot approached the couple. They told the Dark Lord they had fashioned a wedding gift which would be unsurpassed and they brought the married couple to the edge of the mountains at the west of the known world. At this point, the sources say the Dark Lord suspected that all was not as it seemed. His counselors were uneasy. They whispered into his ears. The plan seemed ready to be undone. Yet brave Lucretia stepped across the enchanted threshold and bid her new husband to follow. He followed and the prison was complete."

"What about Lucretia?" asked Alexia.

"She was never meant to be imprisoned with him," the Historian said sadly, "She was supposed to let him go first, so he would be trapped alone. She could have returned to her family, once he was imprisoned. He had promised on his very magic to spare her husband and daughter. She was to lure him, not join him—the plan unraveled."

"Why did she go?" asked Octavia.

"Because there was no other path forward," the Historian explained, his face then fell into a sadness, "Humans and Wizards immediately fought over who had made the bigger sacrifice. The Wizards argued that hundreds of Wizards died to create the enchantments which would keep the Dark One in the Wasteland. Humans argued that sacrificing such an innocent and beautiful girl was worth hundreds of lives—especially as she alone would be trapped with the vengeful evil creature in the prison. His weaker followers were likely executed, but many of his inner circle likely eluded justice. I suspect that those shadowy figures have passed down their beliefs from generation to generation, so that they are like salt in soup—it cannot be seen, but you know it is there."

"Why do you think this?" Marcus asked.

"The Dark Lord was gone, but his legacy of hatred and division remained, lingering afterwards in the minds of the allies who defeated him," Titus answered, "Humans and Wizards never fully repaired the break and such it has been to our own time, manipulated by many, especially the Wizard Empress, to achieve their ends. Those who supported him passed down that inheritance and bided their time while poisoning the races against one another both subtly and explicitly."

"And now, *Dominus Maleficarum* has escaped," Marcus said.

"He has."

"How?" demanded Griffin.

"We do not know, dear Elf, although I am inclined to agree with Synthyya who has long held that both the Wizard Empress and the Elf King have had roles to play. Of course, the

Morphs have been all too willing to fight and countless Humans are his willing tools, again. Some are tools, others are the hands grasping the tools. Such it is, my friends, the world is divided and the races fail to perceive the universality of all living creatures. This is how the Dark Lord and his loyalists thrive. Of course, every death can lead to a goblin—I prefer the Elf words of my mother for such beasts—and once they have enough goblins for an army, I am sure they will reveal themselves. But not too soon, lest they jeopardize their plans."

"What will happen, then?" asked Marcus.

"I do not know," the Historian said, pausing, "If I had to guess, they would pit all the races against one—perhaps the Morphs, and wipe them out as they once tried to wipe out the Gnomes. Then, they might use the Elves and Wizards with their goblins to reduce the Humans to a scattering. Once the Humans, Elves, and Wizards were reduced in numbers, the Lord and his counselors might enslave them or simply eradicate them. I cannot read such twisted minds. All I know is that those who support such things cherish the power and feed off the hatred. The world remade in their image would be a terrifying place to exist. The Dark One knows that hope, dear Gwendolyn, must be snuffed out like a candle. I presume he has learned that lesson during his imprisonment." Had he said too much? It was too late for that concern. This, Titus knew to be so.

"Dire news indeed," Synthyya observed in a toneless fashion.

"Is there no way to stop them?" asked Marcus in a demanding tone.

"Surely your books tell you a way," Quintus leapt up.

"A way to stop them? You wish to kill the Dark Lord and bring his supporters to justice?" asked the Historian. Yes, this was what they wanted. He wanted to be completely truthful, but he did need to give them what they wanted. He knew this, as well.

"We do," said Gwen.

"You are not afraid?"

289

"We are not afraid!" insisted Octavia so fiercely that Marcus thought she was going to tear off the gown and reach for her axe.

"You should be profoundly afraid!" the Historian bellowed with a voice so loud the Gnomes scattered and the plates on the table shook. The voice had carried so far that they could hear the eagle's shrieks responding in the distance. "Understand me, friends? *Profoundly afraid*! This Wizard—if he is simply a Wizard—is the most powerful creature which has ever set foot on this land. He will cut your lives short as if you were no more than a piece of string. He is the worst collection of nightmares you could imagine if you lived a thousand lifetimes. You mean to stand against *him*?"

They looked at one another, terrified of the words and the tone of the old man. After a long silence, Marcus stood up and clasped hands with Quintus on his right and Octavia on his left. They met his gaze and rose with him. Gwen stood and clutched Quintus's hand as well as that of her brother. Griffin stood and took Alexia's hand and she came to her feet and joined hands with Synthyya. Synthyya stood and reached across the Historian to grasp Octavia's hand. "We are a fellowship. We do mean to stand against him and we seek your aid," Marcus said, his words forged of steel. The Historian smiled and steepled his hands. He had read them rightly. They loved their epic drama.

"Yes, you are all quite nearly a prophecy," he muttered, "We can fix that. Make it complete. Yes. There is still hope. You all are the hope. The best hope. Perhaps, the last hope."

"We will slay him," Octavia roared. Titus could not resist. The Historian—quite oddly—laughed.

"Sweet Red, it's not that kind of story," he said. He felt he had to say it.

"What do you mean?" she asked, her eyes narrowing.

He knew what he was supposed to say, but he had to retreat from the plan somewhat. Slay the Dark Lord? Titus sighed heavily, his lips creased in a wide smile, "This is not some grand epic where you slay the monster and peace returns to the realm," he chuckled, his eyes twinkling, "If only..."

"We are not meant to kill the Nameless One?" Alexia asked.

"Oh, you must kill him," the Historian said, his features hardening, "But the stories are always so much simpler than reality. In truth, killing him is part of your quest, indeed, it is at the center of your quest. But that is not your only goal."

"I am afraid I don't understand," Marcus said.

"A Wizard who admits he doesn't understand! Ah, you are so brave to say so, Marcus," Titus said, his features softening again, "The one we call a Dark Wizard is the leader of those who will mar our world, but there are many who stand with him. And we do not know who they are. Perhaps, they are descendants of his earlier supporters or perhaps his dark magic has kept them alive for centuries against the rules of nature to which we all must bow. We don't know. You will need to kill the leader, but also discern who is friend and who is foe. To me, that will be harder than killing this powerful Wizard. You must gather them up in a finely crafted net, so that they do not slip away as they once did. If that is not enough to overwhelm you, please know that we must also undo all the evil they have done in the world—remake hearts which have been twisted. If only the goal was just to slay the monster and be done with it all! As I said, it is not that kind of story."

"So there is a way to kill him?" asked Synthyya, "Because the magic he wields seems to have made him impervious to any conventional magic or weapons. You can trust me on that. He has stood inches from me in my own home. He killed two of the greatest Wizards who have drawn breath and appeared to suffer no harm himself."

"There is a way to destroy him," The Historian responded, "And those of us who follow such matters believe that if he can be killed, then the others can be stopped. He is *their* hope and we must snuff that out. Nor can we let them scatter again. Let me be clear, those who stand with me believe we must kill the inner circle as much as we need to kill their leader. We must keep their hatred from infecting more of the world."

"Kill the Dark Lord, kill his willing collaborators, I'm in," Octavia said.

"And end the strife between the races," Gwen said gently, "Transform the hate into love." Octavia would have laughed in her face if she didn't think Gwen was completely sincere.

"Tell us what you need us to do," Octavia demanded.

"This is a subject best left for the morning," the Historian said, eager to end this conversation before he ruined the plan with too much truth, "You will all get a good rest and so will I. There is much left for us to discuss in the morning."

"But..." insisted Quintus.

"In the morning," stated the Historian and his tone indicated that there would be no further debate on the subject, "We will discuss when your fellowship is complete."

Chapter 31: The Bow and Arrow

Marcus was leafing through the book when she arrived, framed in his doorway and more alluring than he could anticipated. Octavia was clad in a sheer nightdress which ended prematurely mid-thigh and was festooned with lace. It hung off her strong shoulders by two narrow ribbons and her red hair tumbled down upon her shoulders like a fiery waterfall.

"Octavia?"

"You barely recognize me," she guffawed, "I think the Historian wants me be more feminine." Her deep voice served as a contrast to the ultra-girlish nightwear and was a joke unto itself. "I feel so foolish, but it is the only thing that was in my room other than the gown. I hope my normal clothes are being washed."

"Agreed," Marcus said, "They took my enchanted cloak, presumably for washing. Do you think the Historian can be trusted?"

"If not, then I am battling the Dark Lord of nightmares wearing this little pink night dress, which is far better suited for wrangling invitations to the bed of a lecherous Duke or Baron," she said with a snicker.

"You look just fine," Marcus said, "Even if it is a change for you."

"It's quite a change," she said, "I don't think I've worn a dress since I was 12."

"You look nicer than you will let yourself believe," he said quietly.

"What's with the book?" she hurriedly changed the subject as the darkness of that old catastrophe began to manifest itself in nausea.

"I believe the Historian left it for me," Marcus said, "It appears to be a history book about the late Classical Era."

"Sounds so exciting," she said, sarcasm in full force, "If only I had gotten the book and you had gotten lacy nightwear." She smiled devilishly. He arched his eyebrow. Octavia was joking with him again and that was one of the few good things which had occurred over the last day.

"I was on my way to bed," she said, "dressed like a tart selling her nether parts for gold in a house beneath a lake." She smiled at the absurdity of it all. "And I just wanted to stop by your room, so I could tell you that you were right."

"A Wizard never gets upset at those words," Marcus grinned, "But what do you mean?" Octavia tried to swallow down the nausea. She stood against the door in a way she imagined Alexia might, but instead of exuding sultriness, she lost her balance and simply looked clumsy and oafish—an event all the more comical as she stumbled in a very brief and completely uncharacteristic pink, frilly dress. Marcus very kindly refrained from laughing at her expense. It clearly took a lot of the famed Wizard self-control.

She regained her footing, abandoning the attempt to be seductive and feeling the nausea subside. "For weeks, you alone believed that our world was in danger and you alone guessed that the Dark Lord was real. And everyone mocked you. Except Quintus."

"Good old Quintus," Marcus beamed.

"We thought you were quite mad."

"And yet you followed me."

"You can be quite persuasive and occasionally charming," she said, "But mostly we didn't want to upset the crazy Wizard. Fireballs and lightning bolts and all." She looked at him, clad in a simple shirt and short pants, no doubt left by the Gnomes for his bed wear. He didn't look like some powerful Wizard. Erase the violet eyes and you'd have mistaken him for Human and not a particularly impressive one. Sitting at the desk with an old book, wearing ordinary clothes, he was a long way from the great Wizard who turned back her Human comrades, or the wolf Morphs, or the six orcs whose images still made her break out in a cold sweat. He had no cloak flapping in the wind, nor a sword which glowed orange, at this moment. He was muttering no ancient words and his eyes were not narrowed in concentration. He just looked like a man. An ordinary one. She reminded herself of the Historian's words: that the eyes lie to us.

"Why are you saying this, now, Octavia?" he asked.

"Because it's all true, just like you said," she replied, "And no one else seems to have admitted it, so I thought you might like it if I did."

"Thank you," he said, "We can do this, Octavia." He held her gaze.

"I fully agree, Marcus," she said, not knowing exactly what he meant by 'this.'"

***

"Quintus."

"Griffin."

They had bumped into one another in the hall and each took the measure of the other with fierce eyes. "Where are you heading?" Griffin asked.

"I wasn't aware that you cared for my comings and goings," Quintus replied.

"I care very much, Quintus Agrippa Aureus," Griffin said, using Quintus's full name as a taunt. "If you are headed for my sister's room, I would ask you to remember your manners. We are guests and I presume coupling under a host's roof is as rude in Human society as it is in Elvin society. The Historian is both."

"How strange," Quintus said, "And you seem to be headed towards the Morph's room with desire written all over your face. How important are manners to you, truly?"

"I do not approve of you and Gwen," Griffin stated.

"I couldn't tell," Quintus said with an insincere smile.

"I will fight beside you, disgraced nobleman, because I recognize the threat we are facing," Griffin declared in clipped tones, "But if we both come out of this, please know that even then, I will not approve of you and my sister."

"I will love her, nonetheless," Quintus replied. Both men paused and stared. After a minute, they each turned around and returned to their own rooms.

***

Griffin never came. Alexia lounged about on her bed for a little while longer, laughing at the night dress which the Gnomes had laid out for her. "They can make me dress up for dinner, but in my own room, I shall be as I was made," she said to herself. She gazed down at her body, wondering how Griffin could possibly be late when she awaited him. She reveled in her own beauty. There was, she felt, nothing else good about her. But she had this, she thought, as she stood in front of the reflecting glass and examined herself. She had always had this, even when she'd had nothing. This body was something. It was worth more than empty titles or shiny gold. This body could get her what she wanted. She exhaled. Griffin was not coming. Perhaps, his foolish religion had found a way to numb the desire in his loins for one evening. His loss. She morphed into a mouse and scurried out to seek some adventure. If excitement was not going to come to her, she would come to it—wherever it might be.

She scurried down the hall, past all the closed doors. Not a sound escaped any of them, as if chastity had suddenly become the rule. How odd that Gwen and Quintus weren't embracing one another. How bizarre that Griffin did not come to her room, seeking release. She even listened closely at Octavia and Marcus's doors. Octavia did look stunning in that dress—the creamy whiteness of her cleavage deliciously contrasting with the deep red of the fabric. She knew the Wizard had noticed because she could smell desire on him. She was well aware that he was not as good with self-control as most Wizards were. She knew that first-hand, she chuckled to herself, although all that came out were squeaks. Quintus and Gwen's chastity was surprising, yet relieving to her for obvious reasons. Griffin's was disappointing, but not really bothersome, because he had begun to bore her already. But Octavia and Marcus? Alexia had spied her padding down to his room earlier in that brief little night dress, her long smooth legs, enticing in their awkward way. Sure, her voice was too deep and she had no sense of how to be seductive, but she had a body. Why didn't the Wizard use some of his air magic to relieve Octavia of that short little nightdress and have at her? Why did other creatures not act on their desires? Alexia did not understand why urges were not satisfied in other races. Why did they think urges were there in the first place?

She scampered down the stairs and crept into a dark room where she saw a strange greenish light. She was curious, so she slipped in unseen. She saw the Historian with his back to her, gazing into a large bowl of water from which the greenish light emanated. She crept a little closer and saw images of Elves in the bowl of water. They looked real enough to touch. Their voices sounded as if they occupied the room with the Historian. What sort of sorcery was this?

"Alexia," the Historian said without turning his head. She remained completely silent and backed her little mouse body into the shadows. "Alexia, I know you're there." He didn't even turn his head. "There is no mouse in this home."

She dutifully morphed into her mortal form. "How do you know?"

He turned to look at her. "I think I know my own house, Alexia," he said, "And I promise you that I know every living creature under this roof. It would be difficult for a mouse to swim well enough to get here." He smiled kindly.

"What is that bowl?" she asked.

"It was a gift from long ago," he explained, "It permits me to see the world beyond my house."

"What can you see?" she asked, walking closer.

"I see what it lets me see," he said, "Sometimes I can concentrate and it will show me someone I want to see. But mostly, I simply let it show me what it wants me to see. Sometimes, it is best to not fight things, but to simply let them be."

"With magic bowls of water?"

"With many things," he said, smiling through his snowy beard, "Sometimes, things happen which we do not want. Sometimes, people choose to take us at our words and love other people because we told them we were moving on to other lovers."

"I don't know what you're talking about."

297

"I am sure you do," he said gently, "Sometimes, we must let things happen and not try to undo that which is done. I believe the world makes sense, Alexia, for me and for you. Try to think about that."

"Why are you looking at my eyes when you speak with me?" she asked.

"Isn't that the polite way to engage another in conversation?" he asked impishly.

"You are old but you are still a man."

"I am."

"With desires?"

"They are more muted than when I was say, 100 sun cycles, but yes, they are still there."

"I am completely unclothed and I am stunning. Would you agree?" Alexia asked.

"No one with blood in their veins could dispute that, dear Alexia," he said.

"When I am like *this*, no one ever looks at my eyes," she explained, "They look everywhere else, depending upon what they like, but no one looks at my eyes."

"Is that so?"

"Men, women, Elves, Humans, Wizards, Morphs," she said, "None of them can stop their eyes from wandering. What is wrong with you?"

"It is a lesson for you, sweet dark-eyed, unloved little Morph," he said, "You sell yourself short when you conclude you are only beautiful because you are desired physically. There is more to you."

"Silence," she said, the word smoldering as she uttered it, "If you want to have me, old man, you may."

"I will not because I think too much of you," he said.

"You're rejecting this," she struck an alluring pose, "Truly?"

"You are rejecting yourself, Alexia," he said, "Listen to me. Things will get harder when your fellowship leaves this place. Those who oppose us, the unmentionable ones, will find your weaknesses and exploit them. Let things be with

Gwendolyn. Learn to love yourself. Much more than you can imagine rests on this."

"You will wake up regretting that you passed up an evening with me," she said with a scowl. In an instant, she was a mouse and then she was gone.

"She is very beautiful," a deep voice rang out in the darkness.

"More than she knows," the Historian answered, "We must hope she realizes before it is too late. If they find out what is in her heart..."

"They will use it to break the fellowship to pieces," the voice said.

"And all will be lost, my friend," the Historian lamented.

"You revealed too much to them at dinner."

"You would have me reveal too little," Titus replied.

"We have a plan," the voice insisted, "Nothing you have said to them is a lie."

"Nor is anything I said to them the whole truth," Titus sparred, "*'Some scholars believe him to be the god of darkness?'* Truly?!" He shook his head.

"Your embellishments serve a purpose," the voice insisted, "He is a formidable Wizard, even if he is not all that they imagine. We have all agreed that these seven are eager for all the epic material, so give them what they want."

"I am to do that, so that we get what *we* want," Titus muttered, "Indeed..." He pondered for a long time and shared the silence with his friend. Finally, the silence was broken by the other man.

"Even a group such as this will not be able to stop him, let alone the *nefandi*," he offered, "He is greater than all of them combined. How will you approach this?"

The Historian looked up and opened his eyes. "There is a weapon."

"Is there?" the other man's eyes grew large, "One that can destroy him?"

"Yes."

"You have spoken of this with the others?"

"I have not," Titus said, "It is a secret for a precious few, lest he hear of it. I will tell our guests tomorrow and you will learn all that they will for you will complete the prophecy. The prophecy is not a lie. There is that, I suppose."

"A weapon? Is it so? An enchanted weapon? Tell me."

"Go," Titus said, "You will know the facts tomorrow."

The other man thought better of resisting, bowed to the Historian, and left the room. A few minutes later, there was a popping sound and a Wizard girl's outline could be seen against the darkness.

"*Magister,*" she addressed him.

"*Discipulus.*"

"You called for me. What is your bidding?" she asked.

"Keep my secrets," the Historian replied.

"Of course," she replied, "Tell me whatever you need and I shall lock it away."

"I also need you to attend to several tasks which are essential to our cause," he instructed her, "You must act swiftly and without detection. Only you and I must know the complete truth of things. Do you understand?"

"Yes, *magister*. All will be done, as you wish."

He permitted himself a smile. Much was occurring which was beyond his powers and quite a bit which was beyond his desires. About this matter, however, the Historian was determined to keep his own counsel. This was the way. A pang of fear struck his heart that perhaps he was foolish to believe he knew better than all of the others. He banished the fear and explained his plan to the Wizard girl. Much would occur without his consent, but about this matter, his choice was immovable. She would carry out his wishes and hold back the truth from all. Even Titus was unsure about who exactly could be trusted.

***

The breakfast far exceeded anything any of them could ever remember. Thick slabs of bacon, hot buttered rolls, exotic fruits, dark Elvin morning elixir. "I feel like you are fattening us up for the slaughter," Synthyya chuckled as she bit into the soft bread.

"In some ways, I am," the Historian said with a sad smile.

"Oh Titus," Synthyya said, casually waving her hand, "It is never as bad as all that."

"Except when it is," Griffin said, nervously eyeing the eagle which was perched in the corner of the room. *"That* wasn't there, last night."

"I thought it was a statue at first," giggled Gwen, as she took a piece of fruit from Quintus's plate and gobbled it up. Quintus gave her a look of mock anger and she girlishly stuck her pink tongue out him.

The eagle seemed supremely unconcerned with the fellowship. Octavia piled her plate high. "Keep eating like that and you'll never fit back into that gown," Marcus teased Octavia, who was back in her regular clothing which had been washed, no doubt by the Gnomes. He had been relieved to find his clean, but still enchanted cloak neatly folded outside his door this morning.

"The next time you see me in a gown like that will be my wedding day," she laughed, "And even then, it's split odds that I actually wear a dress."

"I am sure your groom will be delighted to see his lovely bride marching towards him in military-issue boots and a breastplate," Marcus snickered, devouring the bacon, "Naturally you'll wear the helmet your father made for you for the ceremony."

"Naturally," she chuckled, "Whoever the groom is should know what he's getting into by marrying me."

"Poor bastard," Marcus bantered.

"Where is Alexia?" Gwen asked.

"She was up late," the Historian said, "I am sure she'll be down soon." He seemed to tremble a little, but no one noticed. This was the moment. He knew it.

"Last night, sir, what did you mean when you said 'completing our fellowship?'" blurted out Quintus.

301

"Once Alexia comes down, I'll explain that and more," he said, "Until then, please have another roll or some bacon."

A few minutes later, Alexia stumbled in, her eyelids half closed, her dress slightly askew, and her hair a tangled mess. "Difficult night?" asked Marcus.

"I did not sleep easy," she said.

"None of us did," Gwen smiled empathetically, as she turned her sapphire eyes to her friend.

"I can help with that," Synthyya said, gesturing towards Alexia's hair. After a few words and a flick of the wrist, Alexia's hair was straightened out, as was her dress. The eyes would only open after two mugs of the Elvin elixir—magic of another sort, to be sure.

"This is our last meal together," said the Historian, girding himself for the story he would tell, a story which would walk a narrow path between truth and untruth, "I should tell you all I know, my friends." They all turned to him. He knew that this was a risk. When the others discovered his choices, there could be dire consequences. Still, Titus saw no other path forward, so he swallowed hard and told the tale he had invented, "Back when the Dark Lord and his supporters first arose, there was a fellowship which came together to stop them. This was a thousand years ago, although some insist two thousand. The fellowship was perfectly balanced: Two from each remaining race on the council, a male and a female banded together. Eight brave souls. They alone saw the threat he represented and recognized the powers he wielded."

"No one else saw that he was a threat?" Marcus asked, "That's hard to swallow."

"You must remember that he was simply a Wizard, or appeared to be so, no different than any other. We do not live in an epic poem where the antagonist is so obvious," the Historian explained, "*Dominus Maleficarum*, as you call him, probably looked quite ordinary and few suspected he had mastered the magic of the god of darkness. But these eight companions did. They discovered what he truly was and sought out all the available knowledge on how to destroy him. So many books still existed back then which have been lost." He winced. The audience thought it was about the lost books. He alone knew the real reason for his wincing, but he pressed on. "This fellowship of eight used their knowledge to fashion a weapon. They created a bow and an arrow unlike any other. The Elves cut down one of the last Magna trees, which no longer grow."

"That is so sad" Gwen wept.

"Indeed," he said, "The Morphs turned into beasts—it is unrecorded what kind—and let thousands of hairs be plucked from them for the string."

"Were they bears or wolves?" Alexia asked.

"Probably neither," he replied, "Back then, Morphs could choose any form. That power disappeared until a special girl came along in recent times." Alexia almost blushed. "The Humans forged the arrowhead with iron techniques we no longer understand and assembled the bow and string as only Humans can. The two Wizards cast spells to aid the archer who wielded it, amplify the weapon's powers, and render it indestructible and inviolable. This artifact was the last great achievement of the Classical Civilization, an enchanted bow and arrow which—when fired by an unmatched archer—could destroy this wicked Wizard. They believed that despite the dark magic which had made him virtually invincible and undying, if this special arrow shot from this unique bow pierced his heart, he would cease to exist."

"Did it work? I mean obviously not," Octavia corrected herself, "Why not?"

"It was never fired," the Historian said, his bleary eyes sad, "One of the Humans and one of the Elves fought over who would be the one to loose the arrow. Both were fine archers and neither would admit the other was superior. In their struggle, they broke the weapon so that the string was torn from the bow. No one could prevail upon them to bury their anger, so the Humans took the bowstring and the Elves took the unstrung bow and they left the cause. The fellowship was broken. Many say that Humans and Elves began their mutual hatred at that moment." He looked at Gwen and Quintus. "But

303

there is new hope in every generation that the races will come back together. As my parents would attest."

"Were you raised as Elf or Human?" Griffin asked.

"As both," he said, "My parents moved around, so I got to know so many Humans and so many Elves. I never learned to hate. Perhaps that is why I was made Historian by those who caretake our hopes. Gwendolyn, I knew your grandmother from my time with the Elves. She was a fiery Elf-girl and not at all like your parents tell the story. Gwen, you have a touch of rebelliousness in your blood and that is not a bad thing."

"What is a grandmother?" Alexia asked.

Titus nodded with sympathetic understanding. "Morphs use the common tongue, but not all of the words," he explained, "As they only live 30 or so sun cycles, there is no need to use words for one's father's father or mother's mother. A grandmother is the mother of your father or mother, Alexia." She nodded. Gwen placed a kind hand on her friend's shoulder.

"The bow snapped, what about the arrow?" asked Marcus, redirecting the conversation impatiently.

"The Wizards and Morphs did not know what to do next," the Historian explained, "They knew the bow and arrow could not be destroyed but they were surprised it could be torn into pieces. They were distraught about the breaking of the fellowship."

"What about the protective spells?" Synthyya asked.

"The magic did not anticipate a foolish argument between friends," he said, "The bow cannot be destroyed, but it can be dismembered. So the Wizards and Morphs broke the arrow in two, so each race had a piece. The arrowhead went with the Wizards and the shaft with the Morphs. Soon thereafter, the Dark Lord and those who stood with him completed the overthrow of Classical civilization and went on to rule the world we know until the coming of Lucretia. The whereabouts of the bow and arrow quietly drift out of most histories, much as those who escaped justice when he was later imprisoned."

"So where does that leave us?" Alexia asked.

"In a prophecy," he said, his eyes sparkling with joy, "There is a prophecy that a new fellowship will arise to stop the Dark One. four men and four women, two Wizards, two Humans, two Morphs, two Elves—just as before. And that they will reassemble the bow and arrow and end the Dark Lord's existence once and for all. Without him, his followers will collapse, so long as we identify them and annihilate them." His voice had taken on a flinty quality.

"Nice story, but we are short one morph by my count," said Octavia.

"There is a second morph in the room, right now," Alexia said.

The eagle morphed into a tall man with impossibly dark skin. The Historian helped him into a robe to hide his nakedness. "This is Hermes," the Historian said, "He has been my right-hand for several years now and he is both a Morph and a male, which helps you fit the prophecy."

"I have never cared much for prophecies," Marcus said.

"They are as often false as they are true," the Historian agreed, "But this one is our only chance, so I am inclined to believe it true." He swallowed to keep his throat from constricting.

"Titus is right," the Morph said in a deep voice, "I will join your fellowship and we will reassemble this bow and arrow. Then the Dark Lord will be no more."

"You are an outcast like us?" Quintus asked suspiciously.

"I am a Morph who works for a half-Elf," Hermes replied, "Let us say that I am unwelcome in the Darkest Forests of the Morphs."

"But how are we going to find four pieces of a bow and arrow which were lost a thousand—maybe two thousand—years ago?" Octavia demanded.

"Oh, Octavia Flavius..." Titus began. The words then caught in his mouth.

After the brief awkward silence, Octavia spoke up to fill the void. "Oh, Titus..." she mocked him gently, "Titus *what*? Do you have a last name?"

305

The Historian regained himself. "I do not have a Human last name like Flavius or Aureus. I took my mother's last name, which was Elvin," he explained.

"Elves don't have last names," Quintus said.

"No, they do not," Griffin added quickly.

The Historian fixed a stare onto Griffin. He refused to break the stare. It went on for 30 seconds or more until Gwendolyn said, "Yes, we do."

"Gwendolyn!" Griffin exclaimed.

"Stay calm, Griffin," said the Historian, "Elves do not reveal their last names to non-Elves under any circumstances for any reason. Even if you were friends for 100 sun cycles, an Elf would never tell a Human or Morph or Wizard their last name."

"I have known so many Elves," Synthyya marveled, "I presumed they just had first names like Wizards."

"It is strictly forbidden to reveal your name," Griffin said.

"Perhaps, it is for you," said the Historian, "But I am old and I cannot imagine the Elvin King's law runs down beneath this lake. And you are friends. More than friends, you are my great hope. So Octavia, let me tell you that my name is Titus *y Goedwig* which means something like 'Titus of the Woods.'"

"You have revealed your secret name!" Griffin shouted, astonished.

"He told me several years ago," said Hermes, "If that makes it better."

"It does not," Griffin spat.

"Our family name is *y Bryniau*," Gwendolyn said suddenly, "It means that we are from the Hills."

"It's beautiful," Quintus said, "It suits you."

Griffin was speechless in his fury. "Gwendolyn! Our parents told us…"

"Our mother and father are in a cave by order of that wretched king," she said, "This is our family now. If we are to free our parents and save the world together, I think we can tell them our family name. Griffin, can you not let the old rules go?"

He pouted in silence. The male Morph spoke up. "Titus tells me that he has left a very important book with you, Marcus, which should help point us in the right direction," he explained, "We know that each race has one part. We will find the pieces and reassemble them."

"Sounds like that's the easy part," muttered Marcus.

"Maybe," the Historian allowed, "But each of you will need to go into your former world. You will need to enter places which have rejected you, made you outcasts. Many challenges will arise from this for you as individuals and as a fellowship. But you cannot let your fears overtake you, or your temptations consume you. Those who stand against us will be watching and will seize his opportunities to break you."

"The Dark One already knows who we are," Gwen said, "He tracked us to the inn."

"The Nameless One does not know you exist," Hermes laughed, "Or else he would be here with us now and we would all be dead."

"What about the Elves?" Marcus asked, "They were working for an ogre."

"Surely, the ogres found their burned dead where you left them," Synthyya rationalized, "Perhaps there was a witness who gave a description. It would be better if Hermes is right."

"I am sure he is right," Titus said, "I trust him with my life. But even if the Dark One does not know who you are, he and his followers will try to stop you as you get closer. We call his followers the *nefandi* or 'unmentionable ones' in the ancient tongue. They are faceless and unnamed to us, but they are out there. You must support one another and put the fellowship first. I believe that your love of one another is the only true weapon we have against this evil."

"That and the bow," Quintus said. The Historian shook his head. He had gone this far and turning back was impossible, but still, he held these creatures in the highest of esteem. He could not simply tell them fairy tales and leave them with nothing.

"The bow is simply the means of delivery," Titus said, "The love is what matters. As I said yesterday, you must remember that you are not in some epic story where you must go on a quest to reassemble the bow, kill the Dark Lord, and live happily thereafter."

"Sure sounds like that kind of quest," Octavia said.

The Historian steeled himself as he struggled to strike the right balance, "Looks and sounds can deceive, Octavia. Yes, you must kill him because his magic is key to their success, but slaying that creature is the simple task—albeit not an easy one. Gathering up his faceless supporters will be harder, as many may pose as ignorant. Some will pose as your friends. And repairing the damage is the hardest task still. A great Classical overking once said that winning a war is easier than winning what comes after. I repeat, so that you cannot mistake me: the love is the key. You must put aside your disputes and leave them here. Your quest is a dangerous one. The prophecy is clear that eight will begin the quest but eight will not be living when it is complete."

"Someone will die," Gwen asked softly. Titus nodded.

"Perhaps several someones in this very room," he replied. There was an uncomfortable silence at that statement.

"Let us not focus on that," Hermes boomed, "We have four pieces to find. One is in Elfland, which is closest, so that is where Titus and I think we must begin."

"We are looking for a bow without a string," Marcus said evenly.

"In *Elfland*, where we are known to be criminals?" Gwen asked.

"I think that will be the least of our problems, little sister," Griffin replied.

Titus excused himself, so he could be alone. They all ascribed it to his advanced age and did not give it another thought. But the reality was that Titus was suddenly very unsure if he had done the correct thing and he felt very lonely, for there was no one in whom he could confide. Had he mixed truth and lies correctly? Or had he just doomed these eight broken beings and undermined the cause of the *Custodes*?

Chapter 32: The Sun and the Moon

"Griffin, why are you so morose all the time?" Gwendolyn asked. She was kneeling at the edge of the enchanted lake, feeding a rabbit some dandelions from her hand. Everyone else was busy securing supplies and making plans, having bid the Historian farewell. Yet there was his sister, feeding a snowy white rabbit as if it were her pet—pretending that a dark menace were not looming over everything.

"Am I morose all the time?" he asked as he came over and sank to a knee.

"Perhaps not *all the time*," she said with a smile, perfect dimples ready to charm anyone who dared glance.

"If I am morose, it is because I have always had to be," he said, adjusting the sword which the Historian had given to him. It still sat awkwardly on his belt and he hadn't found the right location, quite yet.

"Why?" she asked, looking at him with those dewy eyes.

"To balance you, Gwen," Griffin explained tenderly, "From the moment you burst into this world, you were an overflowing basket of sunshine. Mother never knew quite what to do with you, but from my earliest memories, you were always our father's favorite. I always failed to understand why—as his only son—I was not the favored child..." He chuckled a little. It was a bitter chuckle, but not entirely so.

"You are a good son," she said, patting him on the leg.

"Maybe, but as you were perpetually cheerful, I suppose I grew grim in response," he said, "I do not wish to be so, but we often become what people expect us to be." The rabbit hopped away, as if retreating from Griffin, even though it understood nothing of what he said.

"You make me out to be happier than I am, Griffin. I get sad. I weep. And there is truly only one skill in the world which I possess."

Griffin laughed and shook his head. "Your arrows always hit their mark, sister, but I have never thought that your work with the bow was made you really special."

"It is what labeled me an oddity amongst our people," she said, "My archery is the only thing which makes me exceptional. Although I suppose I am rather quick, as well." She shrugged.

"I disagree," he said severely, "You are a peerless archer and possess otherworldly quickness, but neither trait makes you Gwen. It's your love which makes you different. You love everyone and everything." He gestured to the rabbit which had stopped hopping away for a moment to turn and look at Gwendolyn with as much tenderness as a rabbit can display with a glance. "Gwen, once other children were old enough to know you were peculiar, they shunned you. Their parents told them girls didn't fire bows and they stopped going to your parties. I spent quite a bit of my youth convincing my friends to force their sisters to attend your garden parties, so you would not be alone." Again, he smiled.

"I never knew!" Gwen exclaimed.

"But you did," Griffin insisted, "You had to. You knew you were unloved by the other girls. And yet you loved them, anyway. That is what makes you special, Gwendolyn *y Bryniau*; you love without being loved. Who in the Four Realms does that? That is your gift, dear sister. That is why you have always been the sun and I have always been the moon—a pale imitation of a greater light."

"I do so love the moon," Gwen said, gazing up in the blue sky and imagining the cool pale disk which ruled the night.

"Of course you do," Griffin said, shaking his head, "Let's join the others. It may be hard to return to the land of the Elves, but I cannot help but be excited."

"That is not morose," she teased, "Perhaps there is sunshine in your heart." They embraced and she smiled long after the embrace had ended. This embrace was one Gwendolyn always remembered.

***

"Where should we go?" Quintus asked.

"The King's City seems to make the most sense," Hermes said, "Surely the king would have this artifact hidden and under guard."

"You presume he knows its significance," Octavia offered, "But it has been a thousand years. It could be buried in some library or discarded as rubbish."

"I will need some time to examine this book," Marcus said, "I am betting that the answer can be found in these pages."

"Do we have time for reading?" Alexia asked.

"I read quickly," Marcus snapped.

"What do you think?" Quintus asked Synthyya.

"I am positively delighted with this hat that Titus gifted to me," she said, "My old one was getting a bit tattered. And there is a second hat, too." She clapped. "For days when I want to wear ribbons."

"Those days do not appear near, Wizard Woman," Hermes said, arching his eyebrow. This Wizard was the only one whose name he had not caught; or if he'd caught it, he'd lost it, already. Wizard names were so odd and sat uncomfortably on the ear. It seemed too late to ask her without appearing rude, and—despite their reputation—even Morphs avoided such rudeness. He should have asked Titus when he had the opportunity. Now, he was going to have to call her "Wizard Woman" until someone called her by name.

"Hats bring her joy," Octavia said, stepping forward belligerently a few inches from Hermes's face, "Let her have her joy."

"I can see why you got kicked out of your realm," Hermes laughed, "You've known me less than a day and already that manly voice is issuing manly threats."

"I was exiled because I saved a Wizard child," she said, relaxing a little, "And I may sound like a man, but I promise I am a woman."

"I have no doubt, Flame Haired One," Hermes declared, "You saved a Wizard child? That surprises me."

"It surprised me, too," she admitted, "I never before cared if a Wizard child got killed. I wonder if the Wizards themselves even care. Such are their ways..." She chuckled, as did the two Morphs, but her laughter died when she saw Synthyya and Quintus exchange the gravest of looks.

"If you'll pardon me, I am going to read over there where the light is better," Marcus said, excusing himself.

"What did I do?" Octavia asked.

"Nothing, dear," Synthyya said in her motherly tone, "It's just…"

"We don't discuss such things," Quintus finished her thought, "It is simply not a good idea." He looked over at Marcus, sitting by himself under a tree and leafing through the book. His face was impassive, but there had been something in his voice.

"Should I apologize?" Octavia asked awkwardly.

Quintus and Synthyya exchanged another dark glance. "No, no, dear, best to let it be," Synthyya advised. Octavia had a hundred questions, but bit them all back.

"Anyway…" Alexia tried change the mood, "when do we get going?"

"We need direction," Quintus said, "We need to have some idea where the Elves put the unstrung bow."

"A thousand years ago," Hermes said, "The warrior woman speaks well. It could have changed places a hundred times or more since the breaking of the first fellowship."

"We need to start somewhere," Marcus said from the tree, clearly hearing every word of their conversation.

"Well, I want to start anywhere," Hermes insisted, "These wings need to fly." He held out his dark and muscled arms.

"I shall give you a starting place," Marcus said, getting up and motioning to the Elvin siblings to join the others. "From the first few chapters of this work, I think our best bet is not the King's City, but rather *Dinas o wirodyd.*" Huge sections of the book were in Elvish and Marcus was suddenly grateful he'd taken time to learn the language. He found it exceedingly bizarre that Elves had their own language which was only written and generally not spoken. To them, the language was sacred, but he always held it quite illogical to construct an entire language simply for reading and writing, but not speaking and hearing. Elves!

"*Dinas o wirodyd* , The City of the Spirits," Gwen observed, pursing her lips, "The holiest city in Elfland."

"And conveniently just east of here," Hermes said, pumping his fist. "Fate has smiled upon our fellowship."

"Let us be off while the sun spirit is still high," Griffin agreed.

"We need to figure out one important matter," Synthyya said.

"We know the way," Alexia said, "He just said we go east."

"No," Marcus said, reading Synthyya's intent, "We should figure out who will wield the bow in the event we ever assemble it." Synthyya nodded in agreement.

"You don't think it's premature?" Hermes chuckled, "There are four pieces, we possess none of them, and you want to name your archer, already?"

"The debate over who would fire the arrow is what split apart the first fellowship," Synthyya reminded him, "We must all agree before we even begin."

"We must learn from our shared history," Marcus agreed, "I think it should be Quintus. He is brave and unflinching and I have never seen a better archer."

"I disagree," Griffin said, "Gwendolyn is the finest archer in all the Four Realms."

"He's right, Marcus," Quintus said, "I have seen her. She is better than me."

Marcus studied him. "This is too important a situation for you to be thinking with your heart, Quintus Agrippa. I know you love her, but you are an unmatched archer and when we assemble this bow, I think you should draw the string."

"I respectfully disagree," Quintus said.

"You have to think with your head," Marcus whispered, "Your love clouds your judgment."

"I'll hit whatever target you want, Marcus, if you need to see to believe," Gwen said with a shrug, loading her bow.

"What do you want her to do?!" Griffin exclaimed, "Hit an acorn off a squirrel's tail? She's the best, just trust my judgment."

"I do not trust your judgment," Marcus said coolly, "You have seen very little of the world, Griffin *y Bryniau*." The Elf flinched at the Wizard's tone. "Alexia?"

"Yes, Marcus."

"Can you do squirrel?" She nodded. "Get an acorn, Quintus. Alexia will become a squirrel and balance it on her tail. Gwen can walk 100 steps, turn and fire at the acorn."

"That's absurd," Quintus said.

"An 'acorn off a squirrel's tail?' It's an Elvin *expression*, Wizard," pleaded Griffin, "I didn't mean it literally."

"I'll start walking," Gwen said with a shrug, "Do you have a needle point arrow I could borrow, Quintus?" He rummaged through his quiver and handed over his finest tipped arrow. He knew Marcus wouldn't trust Griffin, but Quintus himself had vouched for her. Shouldn't that be enough? Not for Marcus. Quintus sighed. Wizards!

Alexia balanced the acorn on her tail, pressed against the trunk of a nearby tree. The entire scene defied all logic. Quintus looked imploringly at Marcus, but the Wizard's face looked as if it had been sculpted out of marble. He was unmovable. He was going to make her shoot at an acorn on a squirrel's tail. And then what?

Thwump. The matter was settled.

"Let me be the first to remind you that Wizards are occasionally mistaken," Marcus conceded, clasping Gwen's hand. The arrow had been sunk into the tree. The two shards of acorn were still slightly rocking where they landed on either side of the squirrel.

"She *split* the acorn!" marveled Octavia. "Did you feel anything, Alexia?" Alexia morphed back and shook her head. She then just stared at Gwendolyn and picked up the split acorn to put with her things, while her heart throbbed in her chest.

"Now, I presume we're ready," Griffin said, swelling with pride at his sister.

"I hate to state the obvious," Octavia interrupted, "But we are planning on walking into an Elvin city—the holiest Elvin city of all—and we have two Humans and two Morphs. Not exactly the most popular races amongst Elves..."

"She's right. The Wizards will be fine," Hermes said, "The Elves will be fine."

"So long as no one recognizes us as exiles," Gwen offered.

"We will be fine, too," Alexia said, entwining her arm with Hermes's, "I am sure that eagles and robins fly into holy Elvin cities all the time."

"That leaves us," Quintus said, his face downcast as he looked at Octavia.

Synthyya picked up some soil and rubbed it between her palms, muttering the ancient Wizard words. She touched Quintus's ears and then Octavia's. Instantly, they became pointed. Synthyya was singing to herself while she touched each of their heads with her staff and their hair turned golden. She admired her work and said, "Their skin is already pale enough to carry it off, for Sunrise Elves come in many different shades of white. Many trees make up a forest." She winked.

"Look, Quintus is an Elf," Gwen squealed with delight.

"It will do," Synthyya nodded.

***

"Yes," Titus agreed as he stared into the bowl of water, "It will do." He sighed heavily with the burdens that only he bore. He would need to reveal all that he knew, eventually, but he understood the wisdom of letting them have their fantasy in the beginning. It seemed like the correct choice at that moment.

Chapter 33: The City of Spirits

The gleaming city stretched out in front of them, its buildings fashioned in snowy white marble with ample green from living plants interspersed. It seemed a compromise between a forest and a city. The City of Spirits was the holiest city for the Elves, where their sacred deities had inspired the sacred 12 writers of the Holy Book in an olive grove which still stood—miraculously—hundreds of generations later. Typical of Elf cities, the alabaster buildings were surrounded, even dwarfed, by the majesty of the natural world. Trees and bushes were ubiquitous and one could not walk 20 paces without disappearing into a grove of lemon trees or a tangle of grape vines or a small forest of maple trees. Music wafted up from stringed instruments and flutes, accompanied by the sonorous voices of random Elves. A cacophony of animal noises hummed in the background of the City of Spirits, as well. For Gwen and Griffin, it was home—even if Griffin had only visited the city once on a trip chaperoned by clerics and Gwen had never before laid eyes on the City of the Spirits. It was Elfish to the extreme and filled their hearts to the brim with all that was beautiful about their race.

Predictably, Octavia was less impressed. "Do they build in any color other than white?" she asked Marcus in a whisper as she sidled up to his left shoulder, his right being occupied by the owl. She was frightened she'd jeopardized their détente with her off-color joke about children which seemed to hurt him far worse than when she called him a "sorcerer"—the worst Wizard slur she knew.

"It's just *this* city," Marcus said, "White is holy and all that. Other Elf settlements are much more colorful, but no less absurd in their unfettered joy of being an Elf."

She nodded, as if she understood, then bit her lip. "Marcus?"

"Yes?" His face wasn't exactly joyous, but nor did it show the creases of grim determination which were so often there. The face almost seemed warm to her. Almost.

She bit her lip as she pondered how to proceed. "How do I look as a blonde with pointed ears?" she asked playfully. "Was I born in the wrong body? Do I make a beautiful Elf girl or what?"

He looked at her thoughtfully and pondered. What he pondered, no one knew, for such is the way with Wizards. But whatever the outcome of his pondering, it erupted into a slow grin. "I always prefer the original in these matters," he said. There was a dollop of cheer in his voice, for which Octavia was grateful.

She took his words as a compliment or at the very least as a statement in favor of her Human ear/red hair appearance, which was fortunate because Synthyya had warned them that the spell would fail after about a day and need to be constantly renewed. She wouldn't be blonde for long, so it was good that Marcus preferred the red. Or was it good? Did that complicate things? Or was *she* simply complicating them? Octavia hoped there would be a fight soon because she always thought clearer in battle than in other parts of life.

As they approached the city, the Morphs returned to mortal form to discuss strategy. "Where should we look in the city?" Alexia asked.

"A good question," Marcus said, stroking his chin. "I need more time with this volume."

"I would think the Sacred Space would make sense," offered Hermes.

"If this artifact is as important as you say, the holiest place in Elfland would be logical," Gwen agreed.

"But do the Elves even know the bow's importance?" asked Synthyya, "That is the question."

"That is *a* question," Griffin said, "But I do not think we should be parading all over the Sacred Space where the Spirits revealed their truths for…"

Quintus bit his tongue, but Marcus snapped, "For *what*? For the salvation of all Elves near and far, as well as every other creature which walks the black earth? For that?"

Gwen gently placed her hand on Marcus's arm as if to ask him in the sweetest wordless manner she had if he could please restrain himself. "What Marcus means is that the Spirits doubtless bless our efforts and are guiding us, brother," she said, "I am sure everyone will respect the traditions of our people." A chorus of affirmatives seconded her. "If I remember correctly, you told me the how large the Sacred Space is when you returned from your trip?"

"It is immense," he agreed.

"Perhaps it seemed so because you were young," Quintus offered.

"No no," Synthyya interjected, "I have been here before and the Elves have enclosed an entire olive grove and anything remotely nearby within the roofless walls of a temple."

"Temple is your word," Gwen said sweetly, anticipating her brother's fit of pique, "We do not worship our deities in a temple. We designate spaces as holy, but they are always open to the sun and rain. A temple is like a house. Elves do not wish to confine our sacred Spirits to a house." She smiled.

"Forgive me," Synthyya said graciously.

"Dear friend, you are always forgiven," Gwen replied, her cheeks pinking ever so slightly and her dimples standing out.

"How long will it take us to search the space?" Marcus asked.

"Thoroughly?" Synthyya asked, she looked at Griffin, "A week?"

"That sounds right," he agreed, "It is a bow, so it cannot be so easily hidden. The arrowhead will be a nightmare to locate..."

"I think we are getting ahead of ourselves," Alexia guffawed, "You may as well have Gwen start practicing her shots to the heart. Let's find the unstrung bow, first."

"Agreed," said Marcus, "But if the Sacred Space is that big and we don't even know the bow will be there, we will be in this city for some time. We need a place to stay. Surely, you know several innkeepers in this town?" Marcus turned to Synthyya.

"Not a one," she said, "I've only passed through briefly."

318

"Do you have any relatives in the City of Spirits?" Octavia asked the Elves.

"No, most of our family is either in the King's city or..." Griffin paused, "In the Hills which give us our family name." He seemed caught between wanting to clench his teeth or not. He chose not to. This was an absolute good. You must not judge Griffin too harshly, though it is tempting to do so. It is difficult for any creature to overcome lessons imbued during its upbringing and an Elf more so than most creatures. His love of Gwendolyn was unquestioned and beautiful in its own way, but love can sometimes bring out the worst in us as well as the best.

"No one thinks to ask Hermes if he and the Historian have anticipated this?" laughed the tall dark morph, "We have connections in many settlements close to the enchanted lake. We have friends in every city. They are our eyes." He pointed to his eyes which seemed whiter emerging from his ebony face than anyone else's could be.

"You have friends in the City of Spirits?" asked Quintus.

"Yes," Hermes said triumphantly, smiling so that his white teeth had much the same effect as his eyeballs, "I know a tavern owner named Owyn who has been very good to me and I to him. Perhaps we are not 'friends', but we have a mutual understanding."

"A tavern sounds good to me," Octavia cheered, "Elfish wine could quickly become my favorite if it's anything like what Thorbad was carrying."

"Here's an unwise question," Quintus said, with a puzzled look, "Does the tavern owner know you're a Morph?"

"He does not, Quintus, and I am sure he wouldn't like that about me," Hermes's smile wavered for an instant, "We have never met face to face. We use a mutual friend to communicate our needs."

"Is this friend readily available?" Marcus asked.

"No, I am afraid he is quite busy this time of year," Hermes said, "But in the back of Marcus's book is a token." Marcus turned to the back of the book where he found a ring pinned to the inside of the back cover. There was a large H on it with an eagle perched on the horizontal line in the letter.

"Your ring?" Marcus asked.

"I've never met a Morph who wore jewelry," Alexia said, "I am reconsidering my previous assessment of you, which was based entirely on your anatomy." She glanced down at Hermes's unclad form with a devilish grin.

"It is for sealing documents," he said, returning Alexia's grin with one of his own, as if to thank her for her appreciation of his bare body, "Owyn will recognize it. Tell him you are my friends and he will direct you where to stay. Alexia and I will fly ahead with the Wizard's owl and begin scouting the town. You six should go to the Crossed Spears Tavern and ask for Owyn. Show him the ring and doors will open for you." With that, Hermes morphed into an eagle and soared majestically towards the city. Alexia became a robin and followed him. Marcus's owl looked at him searchingly and the Wizard nodded, so it took flight with the other birds.

Octavia began to discuss the amount of wine she could drink and betting the others that she could drink more than them, especially if money were on the line. Griffin twitched. "Synthyya," Griffin said, "Wait." He looked at Octavia, as if struggling to put into words what he was thinking.

"Don't tell me you're in love with me because I'm blonde and Elfy, Griffin," cracked Octavia.

"No," Griffin said, "It's just that... Synthyya, I think it makes sense to darken Octavia's hair. Maybe Quintus's, too."

"Darken their hair?" Marcus asked, his eyebrows lowered suspiciously. "With light skin and dark hair, that would make them Low Elves, wouldn't it?"

Griffin nodded and swallowed. "Low Elves?" Octavia asked, "Why would I want to be a Low Elf? To be honest, I don't even want to be a...um...High Elf."

Griffin and Gwen giggled to each other. "We don't use the term 'High Elf,'" Gwen explained, "Why do you think it matters, brother?"

"Look at the muscles on Octavia," he said, "No normal Elf girl looks like that."

"Athletic pursuits are frowned upon for Elf-girls of the Sunrise or the Sunset," Gwen said wearily.

"But a Low Elf might carry heavy loads, so it is more explainable," Griffin said.

"I can hide the muscles under heavy clothes," Octavia said.

"And what about me?" Quintus asked, "Athletic pursuits are fine for your men. I am quite sure I can pass for a Sunrise Elf." Gwen nodded in vigorous agreement.

"Yes, Quintus, you probably can," Griffin allowed, reluctantly, "But not Octavia. It is more than Octavia's body. We will be in a tavern and she will be expected to act demure and quiet like a proper Sunrise Elf girl."

"Okay, not my usual tavern persona," Octavia agreed, "But I can try to be soft and demure." She couldn't even maintain a straight face.

"You can try," Griffin said, clearly unconvinced, "But if you were a Low Elf, no one would look twice if you were acting like...well...Octavia."

"Boisterous and charming?" she asked.

He nodded. "Boisterous, anyway."

"What if I don't want to be a slave Elf?"

"Low Elves aren't slaves," insisted Griffin, "They are just different sorts of Elves. With different rules of behavior which are more consistent with how you act."

"Aren't they prostitutes?" Marcus asked, clearly not sold on the idea.

"Yes, they often can be," Griffin said, "But if Octavia were with our group to help carry bags and to serve as a pleasure Elf, people would expect her to interact as she normally does. She could be loud and entertaining and...well...*Octavia* in a way she could not as a Sunrise Elf. If we keep her like this and she breaks character, we'll be found out."

"So I should be your donkey and whore? Gwen, surely this is too much," Octavia said, turning to the Elf she trusted. Gwen studied Octavia for a moment.

"I do not wish to admit it, but Griffin is probably right," Gwen sighed, "As a Low Elf, no one would find it suspicious if you were drinking and laughing with the men. No one would find your strength peculiar. You could act as a Human woman does, that is, yourself."

"And all because I had dark hair and light skin, it would be permissible?" Octavia asked, "Seems to me that the Low Elf girls are freer than the other Elf girls."

"In some ways, that might be true," Gwen said softly, "Synthyya, do you agree with Griffin's concern?"

"It is logical," Synthyya agreed. Marcus started to say something, but she touched him on the arm. "We cannot jeopardize the mission by getting detected. Octavia can try to act the part of a proper Sunrise Elf girl, but it would be easy for her to slip. Some words would fall off her tongue and we'd be discovered. Griffin gives us good counsel."

"Fine," Octavia said, "And I was just getting used to being a blonde. But let's be clear, I will only pretend to play the role of a prostitute. You all won't be getting any of me, even if the world is at stake." She gestured at her lower torso and winked. Only Gwen noticed her lip slightly quiver as she delivered the statement.

"That sort of speaking from a Sunrise Elf would reveal us, for sure," Griffin said, silently thanking her for proving his point.

With a wave of Synthyya's hand, Octavia's hair turned jet black. Griffin and Gwen handed over their bags to her, as did Quintus with great reluctance. "Come on, Marcus," Octavia said, "Load up the Low Elf donkey. I can handle it."

"Wizards carry their own bags," he said, then lowering his voice to a whisper, "And in case you were wondering, I still prefer the red."

***

The Crossed Spears Tavern was a warm respite from the chill. Even though they were deep in the south where summer was supposed to reign eternally, there was a bite in the air and a coldness which was not entirely natural. It was nearly winter, but Griffin and Gwen had told the fellowship that even in wintertime, the City of Spirits was very comfortable and never saw snow or ice. Yet the flowers seemed to be struggling with the drop of temperature and the animals appeared to shiver every once in a while. "Winter approaches, a dark winter," Synthyya said ominously to Marcus. He nodded solemnly.

Inside the tavern, a roaring fire kept things exceedingly toasty and the scattering of Elves nursing beer or wine paid little attention to the four Elves and two Wizards who entered. One Sunset Elf pointed at the Wizards and slurred "Two of them," but that was all. The tavern was dark, which suited Marcus fine. He kept checking Octavia and Quintus's ears, as if at any moment Synthyya's spell would wear off. He knew Synthyya was the best earth magic Wizard in the Gray Mountains and it was not rational to worry. But he worried. They had to find the bow and get out of this place before their enemies knew what was happening. All Marcus wanted to do was to sit at one of the tables with a dark Elvin beer and the book which he felt held the answers.

"Good day, my friend," Griffin said to the barkeeper, a fat Sunset Elf who was wiping the top of the bar.

"What will it be, friend?" he asked. Elves were curiously polite, noted Octavia.

"Six beers of your choosing," Griffin said, placing some coins on the dark wooden bar. Marcus was grateful the Historian had thought to give them Elvin coins with their silly trees and animals on them. He hated himself for not thinking of it first.

"A beer for the Low Elf, too?" the bartender asked as he counted the party.

"She is much more fun with several drinks in her," Griffin winked mischievously.

The bartender smiled lecherously, "I'll bet she is. Good day to you, fair maiden," he spoke to Gwendolyn.

She curtseyed as she was supposed to and smiled sweetly. "It is my pleasure to make your acquaintance, dear sir."

"And Lord and Lady Wizard, we have always welcomed your kind in this establishment," he said, doffing his knit cap for Marcus and Synthyya. They both nodded wordlessly because they knew that's what Wizards were supposed to do. The bartender did not speak at Octavia, although he was clearly undressing her with his eyes, while he poured the beverages. "Here is your change," he pushed some coins to Griffin.

Griffin pushed them all back, "For your trouble, friend," he said.

"Many thanks, my generous friend," the bartender said, his eyes growing wide.

Griffin pushed Hermes's ring across the bar. "We also seek Owyn, the one who owns this fine establishment." The bartender's eyes grew wider when he saw the ring.

"I had no idea," he stammered, "I shall fetch Owyn immediately."

The fellowship slipped into a table in the far corner and drank nervously. Octavia seemed perturbed that Griffin had to be the one carrying her battle axe and she eyed it constantly. Gwen sat demurely and refused to make eye contact with Quintus. Marcus simply brooded. As ever, Synthyya seemed unaware or simply unconcerned. The bartender had hurried through a small door, clutching the ring. Within moments, a very tall blond Elf who wore his hair long as many Elves did, emerged with the bartender. Griffin's eyes got very wide and Gwen choked a little on her beer.

"Maybe he won't recognize us," Griffin whispered to Gwen so faintly that even other sharp-eared Elves in the tavern could not hear.

Owyn strode confidently forward with the ring now in his possession and searched the tavern for the party described by his bartender. The bartender pointed and Owyn smiled. As he drew closer, the smile disappeared. He stopped short, screwing up his face, staring at Griffin and Gwendolyn. Putting his finger to his lips, he pondered for a long moment. Griffin and Gwen grimaced and Marcus discreetly placed his hand on the hilt of his sword, ensuring his cloak covered the action.

"Griffin? Gwendolyn? Is that you?" Owyn asked. Under the table, Octavia squeezed Marcus's leg, hoping he understood that she meant for him to ensure she got the axe from Griffin if it went bad. Marcus nodded almost imperceptibly and then exchanged a brief worried glance with Quintus, whose breathing had grown shallower while he sized up the situation.

Griffin swallowed hard and rose from his chair, yanking Gwen up next to him. "*You* are the Owyn who runs this tavern?" Griffin said with a huge insincere smile.

"I am," Owyn declared. Marcus could not read his tone. Did he know about Gwen and Griffin's legal difficulties? Had they been discovered? What was the next move? Marcus tried to make eye contact with Synthyya, but she simply smiled and adjusted her hat, never once taking her eyes off of Owyn.

"It has been too long," Gwen said in as disarming a tone as she possessed.

"It has," Owyn said, studying them both, "I had heard you two ran into some challenges in the King's City. Has that been resolved?"

"It has," Griffin said confidently, "When did you move here?"

Owyn studied them another moment. "I came into quite a bit of wealth a year ago and bought this tavern. I know business is not typical of our sort of Elf, but it has been a labor of love for me."

"Do you like the City of Spirits?" Gwen asked, still tense.

"I love it. This is why I chose this tavern and this life," Owyn said, "I feel as if the Spirits are closer in this place than in any other place in the Four Realms." He paused. "I am happy to hear that your troubles with the King have been resolved. That blessed news had not yet blown to our sacred city."

"We came to an understanding," Griffin lied, "And we have powerful friends." He gestured to Synthyya and Marcus.

"It is not rare to see a Wizard in this city," Owyn said, "But to see two together is quite a treat. Let me introduce myself properly, I am Owyn." He bowed.

"Owyn and I were educated together," Griffin explained, "From when we were little Elflings until we both took the belt of maturity."

"I remember that ceremony," Owyn laughed, "We had spent the evening before with great flagons of ale and the company of several talented Low Elves." He looked at Octavia with a combination of contempt and desire.

"I recall my head pounding when they buckled the belt on," Griffin offered.

"Those were happy days," Owyn said with a grin which looked sincere.

"This is Lord Cyrruzz and Lady Heqquba," Griffin introduced Marcus and Synthyya, "They are powerful Wizards and good friends." His lie was smooth and natural—clearly, he had pondered the problem of a Wizard with a Human name and decided to obscure both of their identities. Wise, Marcus thought to himself. There was more to Griffin than one might allow.

"Friends of yours are friends of mine," Owyn said, gesturing to get the attention of the fat Sunset Elf behind the bar, "The next round of drinks is on me."

"You are most generous," Synthyya said.

"Lady Heqquba, is it?" he asked. She nodded. He kissed her hand. "I am charmed to meet you. And Gwendolyn, how are you, these days?"

"I am well, Owyn," she said, "I have agreed to be married, finally. This is Arthur with whom I will be joined in the spring." Quintus recognized a beat slow that he was 'Arthur' in this lie and rose to clasp Owyn's forearm in a typical Elvin greeting.

"Congratulations to you, Arthur," Owyn said, "Spring is lovely for a joining ceremony. I am pleased that Gwendolyn has finally fallen in line. I presume she has abandoned the bow."

"I have learned my lesson," she lied sweetly.

"The bow was her first husband," Owyn laughed to Quintus, "You make a much better match. Is the Low Elf yours, Griffin?"

326

"She is," Griffin said, trying to avoid Octavia's piercing stare, "After a few drinks, she'll be dancing, telling stories, and entertaining your whole establishment."

"I cannot wait," Owyn said. Octavia noticed that he did not bother to ask her name because she was simply meant to carry bags and entertain. So strange, these Elves. They had so much respect for plants and animals, while they had so little respect for members of their own race.

Marcus stepped in, "We seek your advice, Owyn."

"Anything I can do, simply say the word, my Lord," Owyn said, "Not only are you friends with Griffin, who is one of my dearest companions from youth. But..." He lowered his voice to a tone of conspiracy, "You are with Hermes and that means you are with *us*."

"Of course," Griffin said, having no idea what Owyn meant, "But we will be in this town for a week or so and need lodging. Can you recommend a place where we can comfortably rest our heads? When we are not here, enjoying your fine beverages, of course." Griffin smiled broadly. He could be quite charming, Octavia allowed.

Owyn smiled back at him. "There are many fine places for lodging, but why not stay here? I have a dozen rooms upstairs where my own Low Elves ply their trade." He winked at Octavia. "I shall move two of them out and give you a room for the men and a room for the women. Gwen and the Wizard Woman can share a room and I will give the biggest room to you, this Wizard Man, and what was the name?"

"Arthur," Quintus said.

"Of course," Owyn smiled, "You may place your Low Elf wherever you please, Griffin, depending upon your needs." His grin became lewd. Octavia badly wanted to punch him, but resisted the urge. "And should you wish to rent her out to the Crossed Spears Tavern while you are here, I will split her earnings with you, my friend." Outwardly, Octavia simply looked ready to please should her master be willing to "rent her out." She presumed that was her proper expression. Inwardly, Octavia wondered how long it would take her to snatch up her axe from Griffin's hands and cleave this smug Elf in two.

327

"That won't do," Gwen spoke up, "Griffin does not like to share his possessions."

Owyn laughed and slapped the table. "So it was when we were Elflings, Gwen." Octavia's insides relaxed slightly. "I will not take your coin for the rooms, as Hermes is a trusted ally in our sacred cause—but you knew that. Now, let us get the drink flowing to celebrate the end of your troubles, Gwen and Griffin. Plus, I want to see your Low Elf laughing and dancing for my patrons. She looks a bit grim."

Octavia forced a smile and averted her eyes. "Three drinks is all I need, sir." She squeezed Marcus's knee so hard, he grimaced. There was no mistaking her meaning in that.

"Then, I shall see you in two more drinks," Owyn said, leaving the ring on the table and returning to the back room. "Griffin," he shouted, "when you have relaxed a little, come and speak with me. I would love to catch up on all I have missed since we parted."

"Of course," Griffin said, raising his cup.

"That was fortunate," Synthyya said.

"Let us hope you are right," Quintus said darkly.

Chapter 34: The Coming of Winter

"Something is wrong," Gwen said to Alexia. The robin merely nodded, for there were too many Elves around to morph into her mortal form. "These flowers are sad." Gwen caressed their slightly wilting petals. "The animals are frightened, aren't they?" Again the small head bobbed up and down and Alexia tweeted. The garden would seem gorgeous to you or me; it was quite late in the year for flowers to burst into bloom anywhere else in the world. Few would have sensed anything amiss with the plants or with the animals in the small, well-tended garden randomly placed in the Elvin city. Even a typical Elf might not look twice at the flowers' slight droop or the animals' excessive twitchiness. To most Elvin eyes, the garden and its inhabitants looked fairly ordinary. But Gwendolyn did not possess "most Elvin eyes." She keenly felt the stress of the animals and plants, and it troubled her greatly.

"Winter begins today," Synthyya observed, as she and Marcus strolled into the garden, their cloaks trailing behind them.

"It is never truly winter here," Gwen said, "We are so far south."

"This is unlike other winters," Synthyya explained in a faraway voice, looking knowingly at Marcus while she patted the robin gently on her head.

"What do you mean?" Gwen asked, as she tried to nudge a wilting rose.

"The seasons help amplify magic," Marcus explained, "Wizards believe that each of the children or grandchildren of Air and Earth have a season set aside for them and spells can be more powerful in the right season."

"There is a season for everything," Synthyya declared in that faraway voice.

"I agree with that sentiment," Gwen said as the robin hopped onto her delicate wrist, "I miss the seasons in Elfland. Each season is greeted with a festival and I can *feel* the changes stronger in Elfland than in other realms. I miss..." Her voice trailed off. "But please tell me about the Wizard sense of the 'right season'."

Marcus's owl hooted a greeting at Alexia who chirped back. Marcus continued, "In spring, it is light magic which is most powerful, in summer it is the Light goddess's father, the Fire god. Fall is best for water magic as the Water goddess pours forth from the sky her autumnal rains... Even those of us who struggle to believe in gods can see the changes in the magic, just as only an Elf can detect winter in this sun-splashed land."

"Is winter for the magic of darkness?" Gwen asked.

"Yes," Synthyya frowned, "Dark magic is always easier to cast in the winter. It was set aside for the god of Darkness. Few Wizards have used much dark magic in *decems* stacked upon *decems*, perhaps one hundred or more. But the Lord we fight must be the most powerful Wizard of such spells. His strength will be greater in this season."

"The season began today," Marcus sighed.

"The flowers feel it," Gwen lamented, "The animals, too. They do not understand why, but they feel a shift. I feel it, as well."

"Whether it is his season or not, we have no choice but to go forward," Synthyya declared grimly, as if she were not Synthyya for a moment, "We must find that bow no matter what the calendar shows. Have you had any fortune, Gwen and Alexia?"

The robin shook her head and Gwen giggled a little. "Alexia and I have been searching garden after garden and have found nothing," she said.

"Marcus, his owl, and I have done no better," Synthyya muttered. "Perhaps, Hermes's sky view has turned up something?"

"Or maybe Quintus, Griffin, and Octavia have had some success in the Sacred Space," Marcus said wistfully. "I am returning to the tavern to read. I feel strongly that there is an answer in this book, so long as I can find it."

***

"I cannot believe Griffin abandoned us to help prepare for the Elvin festival," Quintus moaned as quietly as he could, knowing that Elves hear keenly.

"I cannot believe these creatures *celebrate* the onset of winter," Octavia echoed his tone, "Who celebrates the changing seasons? In the North, it was winter for three seasons a year. A least that's how it felt. Why do they celebrate a slight cooling here in the south of the world? Foolish creatures..."

"Elves can appear frivolous," Quintus said in a low voice, "They seem to care about silly things. But not always..."

"I almost forgot you are in love with an Elf girl," Octavia said sarcastically. "I wish she were here. Or even Griffin. Or someone who understands Elvin society because I have no idea what I am supposed to do and I am terrified Synthyya's spell will weaken and we'll be discovered." She self-consciously touched her ears.

"The spell will last," Quintus said, "And I know Elvin society better than most Humans, so stick close to me. Just be yourself, Octavia. A Low Elf is not supposed to show the manners of a Sunrise Elf. I hate to admit Griffin was right, but you have just the personality for impersonating a Low Elf."

"You cannot imagine how horrible it is to 'be' a Low Elf, Quintus."

"What do you mean?" he asked.

"Every other Elf just looks through me as if I'm a ghost. It's not even like I don't matter to them—it's worse," she stumbled for a moment over her words, "It's like my continued existence is a gift they'll begrudgingly offer to me. As if I am lucky to be drawing breaths from air which is not my own. Does that make sense?"

"I have seen how the Elf boys look at you," he said, his voice rising slightly.

"Are you going to act like my elder brother, now?" she asked, "Truly? Does it bother you that they look at me like that?" She was secretly ecstatic that he had such brotherly feelings for her, as her own brothers were far far away. But she hid that ecstasy behind a shield of humor, the one shield she did not think was meant for sissies.

He shook his head. "You've managed quite well in your life without my help."

She sighed and pondered the untruth of his statement, but swallowed all of that bitterness down. "That's just it, I have been a soldier for four years...oops, 'sun cycles,'" she grinned, using the Elvin term, "I am accustomed to having men look at me with desire. That's just part of life when you're a Beaneater taking the coin of the Council. But these Elves look at me with more than just desire; it's desire mixed with contempt. Quintus, it is horrible and no one seems to recognize how unjust it is. Even Gwendolyn, the Elf who loves everyone and everything."

"It is hard to unlearn all that you have learned," Quintus said, "I have spent the last 20 'sun cycles' trying to do just that. Gwen was a slave once. She must understand better than most. It's hard for her..."

"I know," Octavia said, "But until you *are* a Low Elf, you can't imagine the rage they must feel. And I haven't even told you the looks that Elf girls give to me. I am less than a thing to them. I can't wait to get my ears and hair back to normal. Too much more of this existence and it will push me to a cartload of violence."

"The Low Elves would be an easy mark for the Dark one," Quintus observed softly.

"That might explain why our attackers in the desert were Low Elves," Octavia offered, "I might join him, too, if this were my real life." Quintus nodded.

"I suppose it is sort of like being a Morph and getting blamed for abandoning everyone."

"I don't entirely trust Morphs," Octavia said.

"Me neither," Quintus said. He smiled boyishly, "Just be grateful you're masquerading as an Elf. If we were in the Darkest Forest of Alexia's people, Griffin would probably insist you pretend you're a Morph and then you'd be stark naked. You'd get some looks in *that* disguise, especially from him— our allegedly righteous Elf..."

"Just so we're clear, a Low Elf would not punch a Sunrise Elf in the Sacred Space, would she?" Octavia asked with a lopsided smile.

"No," he said, "I am sure you'd be dismembered for that." He returned the smile.

"What if the spell wore off and we were recognized as Human?" she asked suddenly, "What would be the punishment for that?"

"I think we'd be lucky if all they did was dismember us," Quintus said gravely. "Now let's concentrate on finding that bow."

"One last question, Quintus," she said softly. Her face turned even more serious. He nodded. "The joke I made about Wizard children, how bad was that?"

"For Marcus?" he asked. She looked at him with a vulnerable expression which seemed as unnatural on Octavia as the evening gown had. "I won't lie to you, Octavia. It probably hurt him deeply. But he also knows you would not have understood why. Wizards are logical. I am sure he does not hold it against you."

"Can you tell me why it was such a horrible thing for me to say?" she asked.

He shook his head and shut his eyes. "Perhaps you can guess at part of it, but I promise, only he can tell you that story in its entirety." Then Quintus fell unusually silent and Octavia read the cue, a rare feat for her. They continued to look in vain for a curved piece of wood, which they thought was the first step in saving them all.

***

"I am so very pleased we reconnected," Owyn said, "And that we have some time together while your friends see the city."

"I have missed being in the company of a friend from my youth," Griffin agreed, lifting his glass as they downed the special 'liquid fire' Owyn had produced to quench their thirst.

"Are you right with the Spirits, Griffin?"

"You know I am," Griffin said.

"You always were," Owyn marveled, "Even when I was lost, you were always where you were supposed to be. I am not lost any more."

"I am glad to hear that."

"I believe that faith in the Spirits is very important to being a complete person," Owyn said, "And I believe that too many fail to make it a priority."

"In my travels, I have encountered all sorts of beings," Griffin lamented, the beverage loosening his tongue slightly, "Sun-worshipping Humans, godless Morphs, and Wizards who think they are gods."

"Really? You have met Humans? And Morphs?" Owyn was incredulous. Griffin nodded. He smirked slightly to think that Owyn did not know Hermes—whose name had inspired such loyalty—was a Morph. "Such disgusting creatures."

"Morphs?"

"Morphs and Humans, both," Owyn said, "Although I must confess that I have never met either. Did you actually speak with them or just slay them when you were a soldier?"

"I never spoke to them when I was a soldier, but I had to when I was a slave," Griffin said, pouring another drink.

"And were they horrible?" Owyn asked. Griffin nodded vigorously and refilled his glass. Owyn did the same. "And the Wizards who accompany you, are they good Wizards?"

"They are overconfident," Griffin answered, "They think they know more than the Spirits. I only feel truly at home with Elves."

"It is the same with me," Owyn said, downing more of the liquor. "There are a few Wizards who I respect, but they are Wizards who have accepted the truth."

"What do you mean?"

Owyn looked around suspiciously and bolted the door. "I will tell you because I trust you and I think we are of the same mind, especially because you have shown me Hermes's ring," Owyn said, "But you must swear you will speak of this to no one."

"Of course," Griffin said, putting down the cup.

"We are the Hands of the Spirits," he said, "The Ninth Holy Book tells us that the Spirits have no hands, so they must use ours to better the world. And there are times those hands must be clenched into fists, as the Book says. My brothers and I have joined a fellowship which will serve as the fists for the Spirits to better our world." He was very excited and his breathing had increased.

"Do the clerics run it?" Griffin asked.

"No, the clerics are part of the problem," Owyn said dismissively, "The King needs men who will live the truth. We pledge our lives to serving the Spirits, who work through us to achieve their goals. Too many of our kind have become infected by the ideas of Humans or Morphs."

"What do you mean?"

"Here is an example," Owyn said his lip curling into a sneer, "Several of the King's counselors have proposed the idea of Elf girls staying in schools after they reach 11 sun-cycles. For our whole history, females have left their studies at age 11 to learn from their mothers, while males remain to learn what is left to know. The authors of the 4th Holy Book tell us this is the way with Elf-boys and Elf-girls. But despite the war, the Humans and their One have influenced many good Elves who argue that men and women are the same and thus, Elf-girls should remain in school for the next ten sun cycles. As if there is no difference between us! The Spirits made us different. So it has always been, so it must remain."

"I hate Humans," Griffin said, thinking of Quintus.

"Tell me of your sister," Owyn said, "Has she accepted who she is, finally?"

"I am not always sure," Griffin exhaled, "She would probably squeal with delight at the idea of girls being educated until they had attained 21 sun cycles like boys."

"She remains lost," Owyn shook his head, "And be honest with me, does she still fire arrows like a boy?" The liquid fire had made Griffin more honest. Griffin nodded solemnly. Owyn winced as if in pain. "What about Arthur?"

"Who?"

"The Elf to whom she has pledged herself?" Owyn asked.

"Yes, they are to be married," Griffin said without expression, "Arthur."

"Is he like us?"

"He is most definitely not like us," Griffin scowled, "He is like the Humans."

"He will let her continue to act contrary to our beliefs?" Owyn asked.

"He certainly will," Griffin lamented, "He does not care for our ways."

"We must save your sister, Griffin," Owyn declared urgently. Whether it was his zeal for his religion or the impact of the liquid fire, it was difficult to disentangle.

"I have spent my life trying to do so, Owyn," Griffin said wearily, "But she loves this Arthur and she has never let me save her."

"It is worse than I had feared, my friend," Owyn said, "But do not worry. It is fortunate we ran into one another—clearly we live the will of the Spirits. The Hands are not numerous, but we are powerful, and there are several Wizards who have joined us and can work all kinds of wonders."

"Wizards? As Hands of the Spirits?"

"We show no mercy to Humans or Morphs," Owyn declared venomously, "We save the worst for Elves who do not live up to their race. But Wizards who consent to worship our Spirits are treated as Elves who know the truth. I have always cared for you Griffin, and I know you love Gwendolyn. We must save her from herself."

"If only I could separate her from...Qu...Arthur."

"It will be done," Owyn said, clapping his hands, "One of our greatest Wizard friends is in town. I shall speak with him about your problem. We will return Gwendolyn to the right path. And I will suggest you, my friend, for membership in our exclusive group. Would you like that?"

"To be accepted into such a fellowship would be a dream realized," Griffin said, finally feeling as he once did—before the King's sentence had fallen on him and Gwen.

336

"It will be done," Owyn said, "Now, tell your friends you were a great help in preparing for the Winter Festival. I have some important men to see."

***

"I have found something," Marcus said, as they sat around a small pond, obscured by trees. His owl was flying overhead as a sentry, and the thick foliage seemed to hide the fellowship, permitting them to speak in secret.

"You have located the bow?" Hermes grinned, pounding his chest.

"No," Marcus said, "I suppose it is too much to ask you to put some clothes on?"

"I am proud of my form," he said, "As is Alexia."

"I am proud of his form, too," she chuckled as she gestured lewdly at his unclad body. She had very much enjoyed her time with him last evening under the cover of darkness, when he had merged with her and she had remembered what it was like to join with another Morph. Still, her smile faded somewhat when her dark eyes fell upon Gwendolyn, sitting cross-legged in the tall grass and gracefully stringing flowers in a bracelet. Why did she have to think about this one sweet Elf-girl? Why couldn't she enjoy the dark-skinned Morph? Or the all-too-willing Elf boy? Or the previously ensnared Wizard? Why couldn't Alexia focus on finding other lovers? She still hadn't merged with the red-haired Human girl—that was a challenge worth pursuing. Why did her thoughts always return to the small pale Elf with eyes like the sky and hair like the sun itself? What was wrong with her? It was yet another example for Alexia of how she was not a normal Morph, and this gnawed at her.

Marcus simply looked back at the pages of his book, so as to avoid the Morphs' bodies with his eyes. Quintus spoke up, "Let Marcus speak. He's has been reading for half the day."

"And we cannot be together like this for long," Synthyya warned, her eyes darting about suspiciously.

337

"I have found out what happened just before the Dark Lord and his inner circle triggered the collapse of Classical Civilization," Marcus explained.

"Tell us, please," Gwen said, looking up from her flowers. She briefly met Alexia's eyes and then looked back down. Alexia could feel a warmth within her that only Gwen could bring on—simply by using her eyes. It was as if Gwen were the irresistible Morph and Alexia were some lesser being like an Elf, Human, or Wizard, a slave to the charms of Gwendolyn *y Bryniau.*

"The Classical Civilization elected an overking to rule them," Marcus said, referring to the book, "As Titus explained to you, there was a Council much like the Human Council with ten representatives from each of the five races…"

"*Five* races?" Griffin asked. Quizzical looks were exchanged.

"The Gnomes?" Octavia blurted out.

"Exactly," Marcus said, smiling proudly at her, "The Council of 50 elected one of their own as overking or overqueen, for women were equal in rights and dignity during the Ancient Times."

"Very enlightened times," Gwen sang sweetly. This time she did not look up or she'd have seen her brother grit his teeth.

"The ruler was elected for life but could never pass the throne to his or her children—the book says they detested the idea of traditional monarchy," Marcus explained, "And the only rule was that the next overking could not be from the same race as his or her predecessor. For at least 100 *decems*, that is a thousand years, this is said to have succeeded. Overkings and overqueens ruled with the advice of the council and rarely was there a wicked ruler."

"What if they chose in error?" asked Quintus, "And elected a tyrant for life?"

"They could invoke the sacred power of *vetamus*," Marcus said, fingering a page, "If six of the ten Councilors from each of the five races agreed—that is 30 of the 50—the overking could be removed and imprisoned for failing to 'love

338

the people of the realm.'" He thumbed through several pages. "It all seemed to work reasonably well…"

"Until?" Synthyya asked.

"There is a Wizard Councilor whose name is scratched out every time he is mentioned," Marcus said, "He conceived a desire to be overking and eagerly sought the title, but was passed over and the Council chose a Gnome. The Gnome overqueen then died under mysteriously circumstances—most appear to have blamed this Wizard."

"Was he elected in her place?" Quintus asked.

"No," Marcus read, "The Council chose another Wizard and voted to expel this nameless councilor from its ranks. They list the vote here as 29-11."

"Not such a popular guy," Octavia observed.

"Weren't there 50 councilors?" asked Quintus, counting quickly in his head.

"The Gnomes' representatives were all slain in their sleep on the night before the vote," Marcus read, "The expelled Wizard Councilor refused to recognize the vote and announced a rebellion because he claimed the Council failed to 'love the people of the realm.' Some rallied to his banner, although the Council did not take them seriously as a threat. Eight of its number, however, recognized the danger…"

"The fellowship which forged the bow?" Gwen marveled.

"Yes," said Marcus, "The book never uses the name, but this councilor must be the Dark Lord. The text goes on to describe the struggle and the appearance of the monsters we all call by different names—ogres, orcs, trolls, goblins. They seem to have not existed before this revolt. The names of his followers are not listed, although there are figures like 'the Golden Duke' or 'the Wild Wolf' who must represent actual collaborators. I presume their names were obscured by the time the author wrote this history. The account breaks off before *Dominus Maleficarum's* total victory. Those pages appear to be torn out."

"It sounds like a very valuable book," Gwen said, "Titus clearly trusts you."

"I've never read any history of this council," Marcus said, "It must be the only account in existence."

"Nice History lesson, Wizard," Hermes said insincerely, "But where does this leave us?"

"There is a passage after the bow has been split where the Elves hide it 'in plain sight at the City of Spirits for all who seek fairness.'"

"Is that supposed to be helpful?" Griffin asked, "Because we already suspected it is in the city. Your book has told us it is in plain sight, but we have been here for three days and none of us has seen anything."

"All who seek fairness?" Alexia asked, "Who does not seek fairness?"

"It is all I have right now," Marcus said, "I thought it might help."

"It is something," Synthyya said cheerfully, "We have confirmation that we are in the right city and we have some words to chew upon, as we ponder where in this city it may be located. Let's scatter before we are discovered. The Morphs will keep looking during the evening. Marcus and I will keep reading. I believe that all of our Elves and Elf imposters need to celebrate the Winter Festival or surely we will be unmasked."

***

He saw nothing in the bowl. This happened sometimes, especially if he was trying too hard to force the magic so it would show him what he wanted to see. Still, it was vexing for the Historian, who wanted to follow the exploits of his fellowship of outcasts. He breathed deep and resolved to try again on the next day, when he would be in a better frame of mind. Nevertheless, he was nervous. He had filled them up with grand thoughts, but he knew the truth to be far less epic than they might expect. The Historian emptied the bowl and tried to manage his breathing. All would be well, he consoled himself. His throat tightened. All would be well, so long as he knew what was occurring. He could not help them if the bowl remained blind.

***

The Crossed Spears Tavern was alight with dancing and singing Elves who downed huge cups of autumn-brewed beer to celebrate the coming of winter. Octavia, her hair magically darkened, danced around half-dressed like the fool she was supposed to be. At least a dozen Elves had pressed money into her hands for favors she would never grant, smitten by her ample breasts, which were so rare in Elf girls. Griffin seemed to be enjoying himself drinking in the company of Owyn and several other Elves. Marcus and Synthyya sat in the corner and pored over the book, discussing matters in their ancient tongue. Gwen complained that her head hurt and shuffled off to bed, but the other Elves would not let Quintus follow her—pressing more and more drinks into his hand to celebrate Winter, his impending fictional wedding, and the joy of being Elves. Synthyya went upstairs to check on Gwen, so Marcus took a break to watch his friends from across the room.

Quintus was drunkenly telling a story about fighting a pack of bear Morphs who had angered a beehive just prior to his arrival. The story told of how he fought them while angry bees swirled around. Suddenly, his blonde hair began to fade to a brownish hue and his ears slowly started to change. You might not have noticed it, were you there. But Wizards are uncannily observant. Marcus was frozen with fear. Synthyya's spell was wearing off and she was upstairs. What should he do? How would the Elves react? What was the logical move? Knowing this was earth magic, his worst magic, paralyzed him. Synthyya alone could make this right. Oh, how his father would have reveled in this failure, Marcus thought as his throat constricted. Earth magic. Always earth magic. His father. Always his father. Marcus found himself uncharacteristically rooted to his seat, incapable of figuring out how to save his friend—who was completely unaware that his disguise was disappearing. And if Quintus's disguise was evaporating, so was Octavia's.

Octavia coolly came over and plopped Quintus's helmet on his head, obscuring his hair and ears. "Just in case the bear

341

Morphs are nearby and want revenge," she joked. The entire tavern erupted in laughter. Her winged helmet was nearby for Griffin had been pretending it was his, along with her axe. She placed the beloved helmet on her own head, leaving it at a goofy angle for effect. She alertly tucked her hair inside. "I ought to keep myself safe, too." She mimed a fight against bear Morphs and pretended she had been stung in the rear end by a swarm of bees. The Elves fell off their chairs, laughing as they ogled her. "My friends, it has been fun," Octavia said, "But I think Lord Cyrruzz and I need to help Arthur upstairs before he tells any more stories and injures himself." She gestured to Marcus, who became unglued from his seat and hurried over to help Quintus. The howls of protests at her leaving were only quelled when she promised, "Perhaps, if you are good, then one of you may be able to help me soothe these beestings tomorrow." She shook her bottom theatrically. This set off a frenzy of activity amongst the Elves.

With that, Marcus and Octavia helped bring a groggy and Human-looking Quintus up the stairs, his ruined disguise obscured by the helmet. The revelry continued beneath them. After they had placed Quintus in bed, Marcus grabbed her shoulder. "Octavia?"

"Do you know a cure for fake beestings?" she asked with a wink. A few stray red hairs were peeking out from her winged helmet. Marcus tucked them back in for her.

"In truth," he said, "Quintus is the dearest man in the world to me. Your quick thinking saved his life and perhaps our whole quest. I owe you a life debt."

She paused for a moment. "We can call it even if you agree to forgive me the joke about the Wizard children." He closed his eyes and nodded gravely. "Will you tell me why it wounded you so, Marcus?" Her expression was unusually tender. He took her hand in his and looked directly into her emerald eyes.

"Someday," he said, "Someday…" She felt his breath on her ear, but his voice seemed so distant, she could barely hear it.

Chapter 35: A Horrible Misunderstanding

"Of course, you are right," Griffin said, as he and Owyn wandered through an orchard, "I was so ashamed that I did not reveal it to you."

"But we are bound to one another by the Spirits themselves," Owyn insisted, "You are part of our elite force for the truth. It all makes sense to me, now, Griffin. He is no Elf. I knew something was not right about him."

"It is a disguise. He is a Human," Griffin hissed through his teeth.

"Now, I know why you want so badly to part your sister from him," Owyn said, "Gwendolyn is further from the path than I had feared. I suppose the blessing is that it is a Human and not a Morph."

"She has merged with a Morph, as well," Griffin replied, his eyes moist with tears. Whether those tears indicated sorrow, wrath, or an even mixture of both, no observer could not tell.

"There is a Morph *here*? What form is he?" Owyn asked, looking around.

"She," Griffin said glumly. Owyn appeared perplexed for a moment, although realization swiftly washed over his features.

"Your sister and a...a...she-Morph!?" Owyn exclaimed, "Such an affront the the natural world. It is as if Gwendolyn has burned down a forest or poisoned a river. This beast-girl, is she a bear, a wolf, or an eagle?"

"She can take *any* form," Griffin said, "She could be with us, right now. Any bird or scurrying chipmunk could be the beast-girl who seduced my sister."

Owyn seemed genuinely frightened and then his expression relaxed as if he had thought of something. "Worry not, Griffin. It is no matter. We will save Gwendolyn."

"I hope we can," Griffin said, "She is my only sister. And as flawed as she may be, I love her, Owyn." He wondered whether he was correct to tell the fellowship's secrets to Owyn. You must understand that Griffin loved his sister more than every blade of grass which pushed through the earth. Temper your judgment of him, for he acted in service to that love. As you probably know, much that is wicked can be accomplished by those acting in service to love.

"Already, events are in motion," Owyn promised, his voice taking on a serene tone of one who knows more than his adversaries, "This very day, I have instructed one of our associates to bring Gwendolyn to our prayer-leader—a very powerful Wizard, who knows the truth of the Spirits. I have told him of the Human who appears to be an Elf. The prayer-leader will probably know about the she-Morph, in some way. Wizards see things that even we cannot see. They are useful in that way. He will save your sister, he promises me."

"How?"

"Wizards never tell you how," Owyn said, "They are not like us, but they do have power and this one has more than most. And if he cannot save her, he will turn to the supreme leader of our prayers. I am told that he is an even greater Wizard and it is said he can work unfathomable magic. They will not let Gwen fall down the path of evil. They will do all this for you."

"Why? They don't even know me." Griffin became suspicious and his eyes narrowed. He contemplated the choices he had made and wondered if they had been wrong. Owyn had already acted on his own and drawn another Wizard into this matter. Perhaps, a voice in Griffin's head whispered, he had been foolish to trust this old friend.

"I have spoken up for you, Griffin. I have told them of your woes. They will make it right," Owyn promised, "And when it is done, you will be able to return to the King's City. You and your sister will be able to hold your heads high in the King's presence and all will be forgiven for you, her, and your family."

Griffin's breathing relaxed. It was all he could have hoped for and more, so he permitted himself to believe in Owyn. "All this the Wizard has promised?" Griffin asked, incredulous.

344

"Now you know that you are on the right path, Griffin," Owyn said. Griffin smiled as he plucked a tart fruit from its branch and bit into it.

***

"Come closer," Marcus advised. Synthyya and Quintus leaned in further. The tavern was not so crowded, and he did not want the sharp ears of Elves to hear what he had to say.

"Is it about the bow?" Quintus whispered. Synthyya's spell had been renewed and he was looking Elvin once again.

"No, but it is just as interesting," Marcus said, "It is said here that Elves and Morphs loved one another as if they were cousins, long ago."

"Of course," Synthyya said, "In the Golden Age when all hatred was muted."

"No no," Marcus found the passage with his finger, "It's more than that the typical Classical Age lecture Quintus has grown to expect from you and me." He permitted himself a self-deprecating smile. "It is written here that once Elves and Morphs lived in the same lands, sang the same songs, and had a bond which surpassed that between any of the races. They considered one another kin and shared a love of the world and one another."

"It really says that?" Quintus asked, "Perhaps, you trust in books too much, old friend." Marcus looked at him sharply. "What does the text say happened?"

"All the text says is that there was a horrible misunderstanding," Marcus said, "The trust evaporated and the Elves shunned the Morphs. The Morphs were lost without the love of the Elves and…"

"They turned to the Dark Lord," Synthyya said, her eyes closed.

"They turned to the Dark Lord," Marcus repeated, nodding.

"All because of a misunderstanding?" Quintus winced.

"The author does not tell us what the misunderstanding was," Marcus said, frustrated, "Nor does he lay the blame at the feet of the Lord, but surely he was behind it. If only they knew…"

"Perhaps Gwen and Alexia's bond is reminiscent of these times," Synthyya said, "Like an echo which continues long after the speaker is silent." Marcus nodded. Quintus squirmed uncomfortably in his chair.

***

"If only they knew," he repeated Marcus's words as the shimmering waters of the enchanted bowl displayed the Wizards and the Ranger. "If only they knew…"

***

"You are sure we can trust him?" Alexia had asked her when Gwen told her about the invitation. Gwendolyn knew that this Elf standing outside her room was a friend of Owyn's and that Owyn was a friend of Griffin's. His name was Bruce and she had seen him in the company of her brother and the tavern's owner.

"He said that Owyn and Griffin wanted me to meet someone important," she said, "It cannot be dangerous if my brother is behind it."

"I want to go with you," Alexia insisted, "Place me in the pocket of your dress." She morphed into a mouse and crawled into Gwen's impossibly white hands. Gwen tucked her in the pocket of her green dress—worn only to avoid standing out in this pious city. She was grateful that her Morph friend wanted to accompany her. Gwen knew that if she'd have told Quintus, he would have insisted on coming and would have probably upset Griffin with his presence.

"Who are we going to see?" she asked Bruce, a very serious but not entirely unpleasant Sunrise Elf with long blond hair and piercing blue eyes.

"His Holiness, the Prayer Leader," he said, "Be not afraid. He is a Wizard and they can be frightening."

346

"I am not frightened of Wizards," Gwen smiled. The mouse squeaked.

"Why do you have a mouse in your pocket?"

"I love the animals and they love me," Gwen said, "She is my good luck charm."

Bruce let it go as odd. They had told him that Gwen was odd. "He is a Wizard with his heart in the right place," Bruce explained, "He supports our faith and is a lover of the truth."

"Truth is a tricky thing to love," Gwen observed but Bruce did not respond. He took them to the Hall of Righteousness, a gleaming white building where Gwen knew the King's governor sat in an oaken chair to dispense the King's justice to those in the city. She had learned during her too-brief schooling that the building was thousands of sun cycles old and some foolish scholars had thought it predated the Elves. Her teachers had scoffed at the idea of a time before Elves were in these lands. But what was the truth?

"Here is where I must leave you," Bruce said, "You must go in and see him alone. I will wait for you and escort you back to the Crossed Spears when you are through, for no unmarried woman may walk alone in our city. I have been asked to protect your reputation by my presence. May the Spirits walk with you as you enter the building."

Gwen looked around at the farms which surrounded the Hall. She knew many of the crops had sinister purposes and she briefly pondered the irony of that. Plants for neutralizing Wizards' powers, plants with horrifying poisonous qualities, plants that put one to sleep indefinitely were all cultivated in the shadow of this building. Elves had no qualms with putting their Hall of Righteousness in the midst of these farms. Gwendolyn decided she had qualms, but walked into the building nonetheless.

***

Octavia was getting angry. They had been over this ground at least four times and she'd seen no bow. The eagle's wings cast an enormous shadow on the ground while it circled overhead. She was supposed to look like she was gathering berries for the others, a menial task suited to a Low Elf. But in reality, she and Hermes were trying to find the bow—an increasingly frustrating endeavor. It was midday and the berry patch was deserted for the Elves had returned home to take their typical midday lunch and rest. Octavia fumed. These creatures only worked half the days in the year and they took a nap every day? Elves!

The Morph flew towards a small wooded area and seemed to signal that she should follow. She didn't want to follow. She didn't want to stay in this city any longer. She wanted her hair back, her ears back, her name back. Octavia wanted to be away from these superstitious Elves and their foolish notions of what females could do. Hermes flew down and then morphed into his mortal form, grabbing her arm and pulling her into the woods. "I would suggest keeping your talons off of me," Octavia said, pulling away. She did not like the way he had roughly handled her. It dredged up darkness within her.

"We still have no fortune with our task," he observed, avoiding her statement.

"This task seems utterly hopeless," she replied.

"The bow is important," Hermes said in his deep voice, "It is not meant to be easy for us to find. I cannot believe Titus knew of this weapon and never told me until you arrived at our home." He stood there and looked at her. She had averted her eyes at his nudity. Humans! "I smell desire on you, Octavia," he said with a grin, "Is it for me?"

"You flatter yourself," she shot back, "Why do you Morphs think we'll all be seduced by you?"

"You see me unclad. You know exactly why I think this," he said alluringly, "It would be good for you, I promise. Hike up your dress right here and I will ensure your fire hair burns with ecstasy right through the Wizard woman's spell." He began to stroke her magically darkened hair. A dull ache spread in Octavia's stomach. She pushed through it and caught his wrist in her grasp. He was strong but she was stronger. She needed to be.

"I reject your offer. I don't wish my hair to catch fire." Her words were laced with wrath beyond all measure. "I rejected Alexia. I reject you. Your Morph powers do not entice me. Are we clear?"

"Your desire is not for me? Who is it, then?" he asked, inhaling deeply, "For the desire is there." She exhaled gruffly. "Ah, I know. It is the male Wizard, isn't it? Marcus." He pronounced the name with a deep-seated joy, for he felt he had uncovered a secret. Hermes smiled broadly.

Octavia clenched her teeth and hissed, "The Historian said one or more of our fellowship would die before we were through, Hermes. Keep talking and it will be you." Her eyes narrowed and fixed a withering stare at him. He seemed unmoved by the stare which had made many men pass water and soil themselves.

"The temper you possess!" he exclaimed, laughing, "Your Wizard Marcus was seduced by a Morph. She told me. Alexia says this upset you. So wriggle out of those short pants and pull up that Elvin dress. If you join with me, you'll even the score with Marcus. I hear you both enjoy keeping score about any number of things. How about this?"

"A lovely offer, Hermes. I'll be sure to consider it," she said, her tone indicating that she did not intend to do so. She turned around and began walking away, praying to the One that the spreading discomfort in her stomach did not manifest itself as vomiting—at least not until the Morph had flown away. She concentrated on inhaling through her nose and exhaling through her mouth. It was advice she had once received in dealing with such feelings from one who had them, as well.

"You are lying to me," he stated simply.

"Can you smell that, too?" She stopped and wheeled around on him, wishing she had her axe and helmet instead of a basket of berries and a brown dress.

"What could stir your loins about that Wizard? You are young and tender. Marcus is old and weary," Hermes said, "He

349

was already older than you are now when you first burst from your mother's womb."

"Don't talk about my mother," she spat in clipped tones.

"I like you, Warrior Girl, even though you reject the promise I give freely to you," Hermes said, his lip curling, "Let me bring you joy. Let me help you."

"No, thank you."

He shrugged. "Then let me help you with words," he offered, "I'll give you some advice, which you cannot refuse. You have no future with the Wizard."

"If I listen to enough people, it appears I have no future at all," she said, "Surely you've heard about the Dark Lord destroying the world and all that?" Sarcasm dripped from her words.

"No," he said softly, almost empathetically, "Doom hangs over Marcus. Titus confided in me. You have said the fellowship will lose one or more members before our task is completed. It has been prophesied. Titus told me that the Wizard will be the first to die." She let out an audible gasp. "It is so. There is very little softness in you, Octavia Flavius," he said, putting his hand against her face and sliding it down to her breast, "Why waste what little tenderness you have on a hopeless creature like Marcus?"

***

Gwendolyn walked into the building, passing through the gathering room which was empty because it was midday. She knew that all such Halls in every Elvin city were set up the same—a gathering room, the governor's receiving room, and then a third private room where the governor might seek the counsel of his advisors. A door opened to the west for the Elves seeking justice to enter and a door opened to the east where the governor entered and exited. She entered the gathering room and saw the door to the central receiving room ajar, so she pushed through it. Carved into the wall facing her was the famous Elvin saying, "Many different kinds of tree make up a forest" and the name of King Diarmaid II who was credited with the words. As she entered the room, she saw the simple wooden chair on a small platform occupied by a large Wizard. He wasn't old, probably not much older than Marcus, although Wizard men never lost their hair like Elves or Humans, so it was sometimes hard to tell. He had large violet eyes, a pointed black beard speckled with white, and large jowls which quivered slightly even when he was sitting still.

"Gwendolyn of the Hills," he greeted her. He knew her name. All of it.

"Am I to address you as 'your Holiness?'" she asked, curtseying.

"Most Elves do not," he said kindly, "But I treasure those who do. I have been told of your situation and I can help make it right."

"You sit in the chair of Justice," she observed, ensuring she did not break character as the good little Elf girl.

"You want justice," he said, "for your parents and your brother."

She gasped, then caught herself, "Yes, sir." It was all Gwendolyn could do to avoid the appearance of being eager for his justice. She steadied her breathing.

"And you have desires for yourself," he said, "Which you will not speak to your friends, even to Quintus..." He let the name hang upon his thick lips.

"Who is Quintus?" she asked innocently.

"I promise that I am a far more powerful Wizard than those with whom you keep company," he said, but not malevolently, "And I answer to one greater than myself. I know about Quintus. I also know that you remain under the King's ban, even if you've convinced the Elves of this city that it has been resolved. I also suspect that is no mouse in your pocket. Alexia? Is that your name? You may join us without fear of harm."

Alexia morphed and stood between Gwen and the Wizard. "You cannot harm her," she said fiercely. "I will not permit it."

He looked amused. "I am here to help her, Alexia," he said, "And I can help you, too. Listen to me: Your brother,

351

Griffin worries about you. If I am correct, you share his worries. You want to return to Elfland, so long as your special skill is respected."

"I love this place," Gwen admitted, "But there is no place for me so long as the bow is forbidden and my blessing from the Spirits is despised by those around me."

"I can change that," he promised.

"You can change Elf Society?" Alexia asked suspiciously, "What a Wizard you must be!" Her tone was sarcastic, but he brushed it off.

"I cannot change the Elves, I can change you," he said, "At great personal expense, I have created a potion which will solve everything for you."

"There must be a cost for Gwen," Alexia said, narrowing her dark eyes.

"Everything has a cost, my good Morph," he said, "But you might like this one. Gwen must drink the potion of her own free will for it to work, but if she chooses to drink, she will be changed into an Elf-boy. A simple and logical solution to a thorny problem, wouldn't you agree? Her bow talent will be honored with this change. And so long as she returns to the King's city and pledges her bow to the King and his commands, then she will no longer be an outcast. Her parents will be freed, her brother will be pardoned, and you will finally fit in to your society, Gwendolyn."

"A boy?" Gwen asked.

"It would solve all of your woes. Because I know this will be a sacrifice, I will prepare a second potion for Alexia," he said, "which will transform her from a Morph-girl into an Elf-girl. No longer will she be burdened as the Morph who cannot be bear, wolf, or eagle. She could live with you as your wife and you could love one another in Elfland. All of your problems solved with my magic." He smiled in a satisfied fashion.

"What of Quintus?" Gwen asked.

"You cannot have everything," the Wizard said, "You must make choices. Quintus does not fit this solution. You must ask yourself if you truly love him or if perhaps you have let your emotions overtake you because of the circumstances of your meeting. What is most important to you, Gwendolyn?"

"What about my friends?" Gwen asked, "We are on a quest."

"A 'quest?' It sounds *very* important," he laughed, "You will need to leave your quest and your Human. But it seems as if it will all be worth it. You will fit, Gwendolyn. You will finally fit."

"Why would you do this for me?" she asked, wrinkling up her nose.

"I am moved by your brother's love of you," the Wizard said, "And I am very fond of Owyn, who spoke so powerfully on Griffin's behalf. And meeting you, I can tell that you are good. Very very good. Who would not want to assist such a lovely Elf? I can give you the potion, now. Or you may have until sunset tomorrow to ponder."

"I would like to ponder," she said.

"Of course, it is a big change for both of you," he agreed, "Seek me out tomorrow by dusk. I will be here. If I do not see you, I will leave and the potions will leave with me. If you come, you must come freely or the magic will not work. Be sure to break with Quintus and your friends before you depart. Do not come here with any ties. I look forward to solving your problem, Gwendolyn. It brings me great joy."

"Thank you, sir," beamed Alexia. Gwen said nothing as they strode out.

***

When the girls were long gone, a voice from the room behind the Wizard asked. "Why go through all of this trouble?"

"It is what he wants," the Wizard replied, annoyed by the question.

"Why not just kill them and be done with it?"

"Ask yourself." There was a pause.

"The bow? He believes they can find it for us?"

"Yes, that is part of it. We Wizards are known to be logical, unlike your kind," the prayer leader said disdainfully,

353

"But there is more to it. To just kill does not solve this problem. There is the hope which we will be able to strangle by following his plan. The hope is the key. This way will be better for that, even if it is more trouble."

Chapter 36: Not Good Enough

Griffin craned his head into the girls' bedroom. Synthyya, Gwen, and Octavia were in their beds and Alexia was sitting in the middle of the room. Griffin refused to look at the unclad Morph girl for fear of losing his way. He had finally started to get his life in order. He could not afford to slip because of her terrible charms. "Gwen?" he called. She slipped out of bed and walked to the door. "You asked for me?"

"Yes, brother," she said. She looked anxious and worried, an odd look for she was usually so carefree. "I saw the Wizard friend of Owyn's today."

"He told me," Griffin said, taking her hand. "Will he help you?" She nodded. "Will you let him?" He knew his sister better than anyone.

"I may," she whispered.

"Just this once," Griffin said, "Please allow me to be the elder brother and help you out of this. He is a great Wizard, according to Owyn, and he answers to an even greater one. These are beings who could help us undo all that has been done. Think of our mother and father."

"This could be a chance to start over," she admitted, "It's just…"

He put a finger to her pink lips. "Don't do what you always do," he said, "I have no idea what was offered, but I have known Owyn since we were children and I trust him. Let him solve this for us." Gwen nodded. She headed back to her room, although Griffin knew that it would not be for long. He knew the pattern of the last two evenings. He would go down to pray with Owyn and the Hands. Marcus would be ensconced in the table by the fire with Quintus. Once Griffin disappeared, Quintus would excuse himself and slip upstairs to make love to his sister. He knew it had been happening and he knew he was powerless to stop it, tonight. But he would not be powerless, tomorrow. That much had been promised. "Gwen," Griffin said. She turned back. "You know that I love you, right?"

"Of course, sweet brother," she said and for a moment her lighthearted tone reminded him of when they were young.

Griffin walked downstairs and saw Quintus eyeing him from the bar where he was procuring drinks for himself and the Wizard. Quintus would not be a problem if all promised were kept, Griffin consoled himself. How fortuitous to have found Owyn and finally have a solution to Gwendolyn—whatever it might be. Griffin smiled with confidence and strode right up to the Ranger, "If you truly love my sister, you would know that you cannot give her the life she wants," he said quietly, meeting Quintus's eyes.

"I will give her *everything*, Griffin," Quintus replied softly.

"It won't be enough."

"Because I am Human?" he asked in hushed tones.

"You are what you are," Griffin smiled, "She is what she is: an Elf. She has fought our society's rules from the moment she could pull back a bow, but the ways of our people are in her bones. You say you love her? Then leave her."

"Leave her?" Quintus asked, incredulous, "Because I was not born an Elf? I'm terribly sorry for that grievous error on my part!" he managed to exclaim in a whisper.

"You cannot begin to understand what she needs," Griffin said.

"I know that you have spent virtually your whole life in this land of fluttering butterflies and delightful songs and have seen little else of the world," Quintus said, "I know that you think you hate Humans because some fool with a crown told you to. But I am no typical Human." They had kept their tone low, but some patrons had sensed they were arguing.

"No, you are no typical Human," Griffin whispered bitterly, "You are Quintus Agrippa Aureus, son of a Duke."

"To the Realm of No Return with that rubbish," Quintus declared, "I traded that birthright for love of an Elf. I then forsook my race to live with those committed to loving your people. And how soon you've forgotten that I freed two Elves from slavery." His gray eyes flashed with wrath.

"You'll take all the credit?" laughed Griffin, "And leave none for the Wizard?" He gestured to Marcus, who was too far away to notice anything. His head was buried in the book, as expected.

"Do you think the Wizard got involved with your enslavement because of his thirst for justice?" Quintus asked, his whisper straining while his voice rose in pitch, "How little you know of Wizards. He got involved because we are brothers."

"I did not realize you shared a mother with Marcus," mocked Griffin.

"Brothers are bound by love, not blood," Quintus said, trying with effort to keep his voice from rising, "I left my blood brothers because not one stood with me when my time came. But Marcus has never let me down. He is truly my brother and I promise he only cared about you and Gwen's situation for love of me."

Griffin exhaled with the grace of one who has won the struggle, even if his opponent was unaware of the score. "You are not wicked, Quintus," he said, softening his tone, "Amongst Humans, you may be the best of men. But one simple fact remains: you are not good enough for my sister." With that, he turned away and headed for the backroom and the Hands of the Spirits.

It was long after Griffin had disappeared when Quintus did respond in a hoarse whisper. "Don't you think I know that?"

Quintus then looked up to see Gwen descending the stairs. This had not been their plan. What was she doing? She walked over to him, each step like the note of a musical scale. "You look so grim, Arthur," she said, "Go upstairs. I need to speak with Lord Cyrruzz for a moment." He looked perplexed. She whispered, "I'll be up shortly." He complied with the request.

Marcus's expression did not appear to change after she'd told her tale of Wizard's offer. He stared blankly at her for a long while. "Dear gods," Marcus finally said, "I have never heard of such magic, Gwendolyn. Never."

"Do you think he can do what he promises?" she asked.

"I do not claim to know about all the magic in the Realm, potions in particular," he admitted, "But I could not begin to understand how a Wizard could work such spells. Gender and race are fixed by powers greater than Wizards—at least in my experience. Such magic in a potion? It makes no sense. But I am the worst Wizard who walks the black earth, my powers fatally weakened with Human blood. Why not ask Synthyya?" She blushed.

"I am asking you because I have grown to trust your judgment above all others," she said sweetly. He studied her for several moments.

"Have you decided?"

"I think that I have."

"And you will drink it?"

"It is a chance like no other, Marcus," she said.

"It is, it is," he said, looking in her eyes, "But you have doubts?"

"Of course," she said, "But don't you think I should take the chance?"

"No," he said, "I do not."

"Because of Quintus?" she asked.

"Yes, in part, I readily admit," he said, "But whether the magic can be cast or not, I wonder why anyone would ask you to abandon our fellowship. It makes me suspicious. We cannot know if this Wizard is friend or foe."

"He does not know what quest we are on," she chided him.

"Perhaps. Perhaps not. But you will abandon us if you drink it, won't you?"

"It is part of his offer," she said, "But I will always love you and will pray for your success." He seemed mournful. More so than she had expected.

"The Historian said all eight would begin but not all eight would finish the quest," Marcus said despondently. His eyes had a helpless quality that Gwen had never seen, even in the desert which had nearly been the end of him. "What can I say, dear friend? Search your heart, Gwendolyn, and it will tell you the answer."

"You will not compel me to stay?"

"I would never do such a thing to you," he said, "Even if I could."

A thought entered her mind, "You will not tell the others, will you?" A pathetic worry flashed into her heavenly eyes.

"I will not," he agreed, "But you must tell Quintus yourself. I cannot do that."

"I will," she promised, "You promise that you will not stop me if I choose this?" He shook his head gravely. "I appreciate your friendship, Marcus." She stood.

"And I treasure yours, sweet Gwendolyn," he said, embracing her, "I wish you would reconsider because—and it is hard for a Wizard to admit this—I have come to believe that you are the most important member of our fellowship."

"That's not true," she whispered softly, "Quintus can shoot the arrow for you. I can be replaced."

"Gwendolyn," Marcus said, his face lined with gravity, "I truly believe that you will save us all, and not necessarily with your bow." He kissed her gently on the forehead as a father might kiss his child before bed. His eyes seemed deep and soulful. She tried to smile but it was too difficult.

***

An Elf, Alexia repeated to herself. Would she be as beautiful as an Elf? Would she be Alexia as an Elf? Would it be so bad to cease being Alexia? Would she submit herself to any magic in order to be with Gwendolyn? Could she trust a Wizard to solve her problems with his spells, as if it were a fairy tale? It all seemed so absurd when the Wizard had explained it, but she allowed herself to believe it would all be worthwhile. Quintus would be removed as an obstacle. Griffin would not oppose her. Gwen would be happy. Alexia could then love that sweet little Elf. And she could stop being Alexia, the Morph unlike the others. Perhaps, she mused, this was the sweetest part of the Wizard's offer.

***

"It is done," Owyn said, slapping Griffin on the back when the prayer had ended.

"What will happen?" Griffin asked. Owyn replayed what the prayer-leader had told Gwen and Alexia about the potions. "He can change her like that?" Griffin marveled, "And the Morph can become an Elf? Truly?" Wizards never ceased to amaze with what they could accomplish with some tired old words and a simple gesture.

"Griffin," Owyn shook him by the shoulders and laughed, "Not even our master, the founder of the Hands of the Spirits could work magic like that. A girl to a boy? A Morph to an Elf? That's like some silly tale for Elflings. Perhaps, they could find a magic ring under a stone for such a spell. We do not live in a fairy tale."

"I have found more truth in fairy tales than I had previously thought," Griffin offered, his eyes narrowed in confusion, "Then, if the potion will not do what he says, what will happen when she drinks it?" He was becoming agitated.

"It is brilliant," Owyn said, as he drew Bruce over. "Tell him."

Bruce smiled a dark smile. "It will erase her memory, as if you had drawn something on the shore and the waves made it vanish," Bruce explained, "She will fall asleep and then forget everything and everyone."

"Everything?" Griffin winced, "Everyone?"

"Yes," Owyn said, "She will forget Quintus the Human and all these foolish non-Elves. She will forget her love of the bow and arrow. She will be an empty vessel into which we can pour the truth."

"Will she forget me?" he asked.

"Yes," said Bruce, "But you will be able to explain to her who you are because you will be there for her when she awakes. You and your parents will get another chance to make her into a proper Elf girl. It is a fresh start, so the Wizard's promise was not a deceit. Not entirely so." He shrugged.

"With no memory of her archery, Gwen will be normal," Owyn said, "You can marry her to whichever Elf you choose and never have to worry about her chasing this wretched Human or bringing shame on your family with her archery."

"It will not do exactly what she thinks, but it is powerful magic, nonetheless," Griffin observed, "And the end will be what she desires, in a manner of speaking."

"The end is all that matters," Bruce agreed, "She wishes to be normal. She will have her wish. We are blessed with great friends, Griffin. But it is an unstable potion and will only work if she drinks it willingly. We cannot force it down her throat or drop it in her wine or it loses all potency. She must choose to drink it. A ruse is perfectly fine according to the Wizard, but she must take it and drink it with her own power, knowing that it is a Wizard's potion."

"What about the Morph's potion?" Griffin asked, "Will she forget, too."

"Griffin, you still have so much to learn," Owyn chuckled, "She is a Morph, the lowest form of life imaginable. Hated by the Spirits. Enemy of the Elves. There is no enchanted potion for her. There is poison. She will drink and die wretchedly."

***

Gwendolyn merged with him for the last time, trying to memorize his body and the feel of his touch. She noticed the shaggy hair of his chiseled chest had sprouted a few white hairs, for Quintus was in the middle of the lifespan for a Human. Gwen determined that she should love him as he was, for age should be no deterrent to love. Yet she could not love him into the Gray Hair portion of his life. She had to choose another path, the one offered to her. She kissed Quintus's face and his neck passionately, to leave him with a pleasant memory of their love. She wondered how odd she'd feel after the potion. Gwen had never regretted being a woman, nor had she really exhibited many "boyish" traits like Octavia. Gwen regretted Elf society, not how she was made. Still, she would be normal and Griffin and her parents would finally be proud of her. She would fit in. It would cost her Quintus, but Alexia was a worthy substitute, wasn't she? Alexia had begged Gwen to take the Wizard's offer. So not only would this one potion make Gwen whole, it would make her little robin whole, as well. Still, there was the cost. Marcus's suspicions about the Wizard's motivation were worth considering and she did consider them, or so she told herself. The outcome was just too hopeful to darken with the possibilities. She swallowed them down as best she could.

Gwendolyn looked deep into Quintus's eyes after they had finished. He was still flush from the ecstasy and always seemed even more loving in the aftermath. His breathing had not yet returned to normal and she knew his body was tingling. She had to tell him, now, so she did. Gwen explained everything to Quintus. He fought her for an hour, professed his love, and refused to accept that she had made up her mind. He echoed the cynicism of his Wizard best friend. He fought for her as if he would die if she parted from him. This was not a surprise. She knew he would fight her decision. In fact, it had gone just as she expected.

Until it did not.

"I love you," he said for the hundredth time. She opened her mouth and he held up his calloused hand. "I desire nothing in all the world more than your happiness, Gwendolyn *y Bryniau*. If you truly believe this Wizard's spell will make you happy, I will support your choice with all of my heart and wish you well, even if prevents me from feeling joy for the rest of my days. I love you above all else." His sad gray eyes focused on her and his lip quivered.

It was the last thing Gwendolyn expected and the only thing she'd ever wanted. He loved her. He truly and completely loved her. She felt as if a bubble in her chest were inflating while warmth coursed through her body to the tips of her fingers and toes.

"Oh Quintus," she said, falling into his arms. And with that mellifluous cry of his name, he knew that she had changed

362

her mind. He did not know why, but he did not dare to push the matter any further.

Chapter 37: The Unstrung Bow

"She has refused," Owyn said regretfully while he and Griffin fired their arrows at a lone fawn who foolishly believed she was camouflaged against their attack.

"Refused? How could she?" Griffin asked, "She told me she would accept. Your friend offered her everything she could want!"

"Almost everything," Owyn said as the deer fell over, twitching with death. "It is the Human," he snarled, "She truly believes that she loves him. As if an Elf could actually love a Human! Once more, it is far worse than we had thought, Griffin."

"I appreciate your aid, Owyn," Griffin said as he checked to make sure the beast was dead. Too much struggle after the arrow ruined the meat. "We came so close to saving her. But if she refused *this* offer…"

"You give up so easily? Dear Griffin, we will solve your problem," Owyn insisted confidently, "We will simply need to use other means."

"Other means?" Griffin asked as they both took out long knives and began to butcher the creature.

"Yes. Tell me, can you speak with the Morph girl?" Owyn asked.

"Alexia? Of course. Why?"

"Alexia," Owyn let the unfamiliar name hang on his tongue, "She has lost something due to Gwendolyn's choice, or at least she *believes* she has lost something. We can use that. And what's more, she thinks you were going to help her achieve her dream of being one of us. These are tools with which we can build."

"I am sure her dream is my sister and becoming one of us was a means to that end," Griffin said bitterly. Owyn looked ready to vomit. Whether it was the carcass or the image of a female Morph coupling with an Elf-girl, it was impossible to tell.

"Talk to the Morph. She will be a means to *our* end," Owyn said, "Alexia can help us with the Quintus obstacle because Gwen trusts her. Let me speak with the others and we will have a plan for you which cannot be denied by some willful girl's silly choices. We will make sure Quintus is never a problem again."

It took Griffin a moment to comprehend Owyn's meaning. "We will kill him?" Griffin asked. Owyn was up to his elbows in blood and so his smile looked horrifying in the context. Griffin understood the plan and nodded his consent. He saw no other path available and the tragedy was that he did not look closely enough.

***

"I am sorry she did not take the potion, Alexia," Griffin said as gently as he could.

"Not as sorry as I am," Alexia muttered.

"Would you have liked being an Elf?"

"I would have liked the chance to love your sister," Alexia said, "I would have done whatever it took to be with her. She is so…" Words failed her.

"You love her."

"I do," Alexia said, "It seems odd you would have tried to help me. I thought you did not approve of me and Gwen." It was true. Griffin had to think quickly. The lie fell easily from his mouth.

"You are different races and the same gender," he explained, "If that Wizard could have made you both Elves and you were a boy and a girl, it would have been natural. It would have been proper. That's what I want for Gwen."

She studied him a long time. "Why do you hate Quintus's love of Gwen more than mine when mine is so 'unnatural' according to your people?"

"Wizards aren't the only ones who are logical," Griffin said, "We have discussed this. Quintus can get her pregnant with a half-breed baby. That would be an unfathomable nightmare. Unless I am mistaken about Morphs, your acts with my sister—however distasteful—could not put a baby in her belly. So you are the lesser of two evils."

"You really make me feel cherished," she spat.

"I did try to help you," he insisted, "And if Gwen had made the right choice, then wouldn't your dreams have come true?" He sweat profusely, hoping Morphs could not smell deception as well as they could smell desire. Alexia would have died horribly if Gwen had made the choice and Griffin did feel faint guilt about that. But Gwen was the most important thing here and everything else was peripheral. Such was his love for her.

"You did help," Alexia admitted, "And I am grateful for what could have been. Are there any other Wizard potions available for us?"

"Not that I am aware of," he said, "She truly went down to the Hall of Righteousness and said no to that Wizard's face?"

"She did," Alexia said, "I followed them as a hummingbird."

"Them?"

"She went with Quintus," Alexia said bitterly, "They went in, and they came out. It was all over so quickly. I did not wish to reveal myself with Quintus there. I wish I had thought to fly into the building, just to see the Wizard's expression. I'll bet it was ridiculous. He didn't strike me as the type whose offers get refused very often."

"We must take other measures to rid ourselves of Quintus," Griffin stated, his dark tone indicating the gravity of the situation.

She pondered a brief moment. "I am in," Alexia said, "What is the plan?"

"I am still awaiting details from a friend," Griffin said, "But let me be clear: we will need to kill him or else Gwen will be lost to us both." Alexia gasped and Griffin was delighted to have surprised the Morph. After a minute, her eyes took on a feral quality and she agreed. One could always count on a beast-girl to have no respect for life, Griffin thought, especially when in pursuit of desire.

***

"Where is Marcus?!" demanded Quintus as he and Gwen burst into the portion of the Sacred Space where Synthyya and Octavia were searching.

"Shhh, keep your voice down," Synthyya said, "We are in the Sacred Space and saying a Human name will get us unwanted attention."

"Where is he?" Gwen echoed Quintus's demand.

"Marcus found a passage in the book and believes he might know the location of the bow," Octavia said. Both looked dumbstruck. "But it has been an hour and he has not returned with Hermes. I think it is likely another dead end."

"Where is my brother and where is Alexia?" Gwen asked.

"Your brother is with his little boyfriend Owyn, of course," Octavia laughed, "And I have not seen Alexia since last night. Why?"

"Marcus and Hermes *are* at a dead end. Quintus and I know where the bow is," Gwen said breathlessly. Synthyya looked at them both as if to discern whether they were joking. She detected no humor in either of them. This was it. Synthyya had thought it would feel different. It was mildly disappointing. She swiftly got a hold of herself, as you've come to expect from her.

"We must talk, but this place is not safe," Synthyya said with a tone of alarm, "There is a cave several minutes from here. Animals use it, but Elves avoid it. I shall owl Marcus, so that he and Hermes can join us there. We will speak of your belief." She did not fully permit herself to believe that the unstrung bow had been located. Too much depended upon this. Synthyya motioned with her hand and a snowy white owl left a nearby tree and landed on her arm.

"It is not a *belief*," Quintus declared, his gray eyes flashing, "It is so."

"Marcus will not be happy to learn he is on a fool's errand," observed Octavia.

"Let us speak no more until we are safely out of earshot," Synthyya cautioned, "Elves hear very well."

***

The cave was dark and made Gwen uncomfortable. Elves longed for the sun, even as they mocked Humans for worshiping it as the One, the unbreakable circle. She thought of her parents, rotting in a cave by order of the king. She regretted not saving them, but she could not doubt her decision. Not now. Not with all that had unfolded in the last few hours. Not with all that awaited in the next few hours. Gwendolyn was close enough to Quintus to feel his breath. He had done it. He had saved the world. Not just her world. *The* world. She beamed as she looked upon him.

"Where is the bow?" Synthyya asked when she was certain they were safe.

"If you enter the Hall of Righteousness, the words of the Elves are written over the chair of the governor," Quintus said.

"Many trees in the forest, whatever," Octavia said, "Where is the bow?"

"The author of the quote was the great king Diarmaid II," Gwen said, "and his name is inscribed under the words."

"I am not following," Synthyya said, loathe as the Wizard was to admit it.

"Quintus is so very clever," gushed Gwen.

"It is the 'D' of Diarmaid," Quintus explained, "As soon as I saw it, I knew it was true. The bow has been placed in the marble to form the rounded portion of the letter."

"You are sure?" Octavia asked, "Completely and totally sure?" They nodded vigorously. "A place where all seek fairness, in plain sight," she mused.

"Ingenious," marveled Synthyya. Her face then screwed up into a look of bafflement. "Why were you two at the Hall of Righteousness? You could have been recognized by an official of the King, Gwendolyn."

She took a deep breath and told the story of the offer and the potions and her refusal. "Wizards can do all that?" Octavia asked, "Turn a girl to a boy or a Morph to an Elf. Just like that? With a potion?"

"No," Synthyya said, gravely, "Even the dark magic has no spells for such things. You were lied to, Sweet Elf." Synthyya looked terribly concerned.

"It seemed very true," Gwen said, "I saw the potions myself when we went. He showed them to me."

"Eyes deceive," Synthyya muttered, "Even the earth magic which allows me to change your bodies is brief and fleeting. You cannot change one's gender or one's race except as an illusion for a day, as we have done with Quintus and Octavia. Who was the Wizard who made such promises? Describe him." Gwen described him and Synthyya seemed graver and graver to Octavia.

"Could you please explain what is going on?" Octavia asked.

"Yes, of course, it must be him," Synthyya muttered to herself, "It stands to reason he is in on it. So long he has done her bidding and so long she has done the bidding of her own master..."

"Hello, please forgive the dumb brute warrior!" Octavia exclaimed, snapping her fingers under Synthyya's dazed expression, "What in the Realm are you talking about?"

"The Dark Lord is in this city or else his minions are," Synthyya said, as she paused for a full minute, "They know too much. Titus warned us that these supporters would walk amongst us and I suspect that the Wizard doing the Dark One's bidding is one I already know. If I am correct, I know him all too well. It would make sense, but I must know for sure. Is he still there?"

"I think he left after I rejected his offer," Gwen said. Synthyya appeared disappointed for a moment and then a thought entered her mind. She tried to dismiss it, but the situation had become too dire for half-measures.

"There is another way," Synthyya said, swallowing audibly, "It is dark magic but there is no time for any other choice."

"You know dark magic?" Quintus asked, aghast.

"A little," Synthyya admitted, "If I cast the spell, I can see inside of Gwen's mind. It will hurt her, but I must see this

Wizard's face to confirm my fears. We need to know who lied to her. Will you consent to the spell, Gwen?"

Before she could answer, Quintus spoke up, "I saw him, too. I was with Gwen. I saw him as well as she did. Please, Synthyya, cast the spell on me," he insisted, "Let Gwendolyn be. Use my mind to see his face."

"Quintus..."

"Gwen, please," he said, "I want no darkness to touch her, Synthyya."

"Agreed," Synthyya said, "This will hurt you terribly. I am very sorry." She put her hands on Quintus's temples and muttered the words. He seemed to be in excruciating pain, but not a sound escaped his lips. Synthyya's eyes closed and then snapped open. All the blood drained from her face.

"Is it...him?" Octavia asked, "The Dark Lord?" Quintus flopped around for a moment before coming to some state of half-consciousness.

"No," Synthyya said, pausing for a minute, "It is the Archpriest Xanthu."

"Who?" Gwen asked. Quintus was still groggy but appeared to perk up slightly at the news, as if he recognized the title.

"Wizards mingle governing and religious belief in ways that are not always good for governing or religion," Synthyya explained, "The *Curia* of the Emperor or Empress contains the highest priests and the most masterful teachers because religion and education are paramount to my people. As a master of Earth magic, I sat on that council with this very man. The five Archpriests of the elements are powerful advisors like the five University masters. These are men and women who wield great influence in the Gray Mountains. Archpriest is an office which has been occupied by both the great and the wicked. It is my considered opinion that this Archpriest falls into the latter category."

"Why is an Archpriest of the Wizards here in Elfland?" asked Octavia, "And how do we know he is with the Dark Lord?"

"I do not know for sure why he is here," Synthyya admitted, "But I know him. Xanthu is infamous for his hatred of Humans and his support for the war. He was just a priest when he helped pave the way for the Empress to ascend the throne. She made him an Archpriest and he later married..." She paused.

"The Empress?" Gwen asked.

"No," Quintus said, looking at Synthyya, "Xanthu married Marcus's wife."

"Former wife," Synthyya corrected him.

"Marcus had a wife?" Octavia asked. Quintus and Synthyya nodded solemnly. "Did they have children?" Quintus looked at Synthyya, who spoke quickly.

"We cannot speak of such things now," Synthyya snapped, "Things have grown too dangerous. If a Wizard Archpriest is here as an agent of *Dominus Maleficarum* and knows us well enough to try and expose Gwen's weakness, then we are in unimaginable peril. How such things became known is unfathomable to me. But he knew exactly what he needed to offer to tempt Gwendolyn and thank the gods, she chose her love of Quintus or we would already be undone. When Marcus and Hermes come to this place, you must make a plan to secure the bow *immediately*. Tonight, if possible. Find Alexia and Griffin and let them know Gwen is safe."

"Safe? What do you mean, Synthyya?" Gwen asked.

"Can't *you* tell them when they get here?" Quintus asked, still a little befuddled from the spell. The pain in his head felt like Octavia's axe had split his skull in two. Quintus Agrippa Aureus endeavored to work through the pain, as he always did.

"No, I will not be able to tell them, nor help you formulate a plan," Synthyya said, "It is now far too dangerous for Gwendolyn to be in this city. I will use all the magic I possess to take her to the easternmost part of the southern shore—far from here."

"You expect me to *go to the beach*?" Gwen demanded, "While those I love risk their lives for the bow?"

"The sun rises over the ivory sands of Aurora Point," Synthyya said, "If the Darkness is weak anywhere, it will be there where the sun rises and the sand is pure. You are too important to this quest, my dear, sweet Elf. We will gather a few things and be off as fast as we can."

"I am a member of the fellowship," Gwendolyn protested.

"Listen to Synthyya," Quintus said.

"I will not leave you," Gwen insisted.

"They're right," Octavia said, "You are the archer, Gwen. What good is it if we collect the bow and the arrow and reassemble them, but have not you to fire the shot? Like it or not, you are the key to the quest, and if Synthyya says you need to go to safety, then you must listen to her. For all of our sakes. For the whole world, sister."

Gwen pouted and remembered Marcus's words to her. She fought a couple of minutes longer before submitting to the inevitable. Synthyya, Quintus, and Octavia had agreed and surely Marcus would support them. There was no conceivable way Griffin and Alexia would disagree with a plan which made Gwen's safety paramount. She was only wasting precious time by insisting on remaining. The lovely Elf swallowed her pride and nodded. "Fine," she conceded, "But please take care of Quintus, Octavia."

"I will," Octavia promised. Her husky voice was a comfort to Gwen when she uttered the words.

"And Alexia and Griffin?" Gwen pleaded. Octavia and Quintus nodded. "And Marcus, you both must take care of him, too."

"I have been doing that for many dark moons," Quintus said, kissing Gwen and embracing her so tightly that her breathing was labored. Synthyya magically scrawled something on a rock by tracing her finger on it.

"Give this to Marcus," she said to Quintus, "It is important he reads it." She then left the cave with Gwen and swiftly made for Aurora Point in the southeast through any means magical or non-magical.

"What does the rock say?" Octavia asked

372

"It's Wizard language," Quintus answered, "And in all my years with Marcus, I have not learned to read a word of it. The letters are the same as the Common tongue, but the words befuddle me. I have picked up very few words in that ancient language despite nine years with a Wizard as my best friend."

"Whatever the words say, this is our moment, isn't it, Quintus?" she asked.

"It is, Octavia," he said.

"It sounds like one of those epic tales of old, but it sure doesn't feel like one," Octavia said, "I suppose Titus warned us that this quest is no traditional epic."

"Perhaps, the epic heroes of old in all those tales felt much as we do," Quintus suggested, allowing himself a half-smirk, "Although they always get to slay the monster and then wealth, fame, and bliss follow swiftly. I don't imagine our heroism will be so neat or tidy."

"Heroism doesn't feel like heroism when you're doing it," she agreed, "I may be young, but I've learned that over the last few years. Even the word 'quest' suddenly seems so silly to me, as if dragons will darken the sky any moment."

"Marcus loves the old stories, which is why he insists on calling this a 'quest,'" Quintus said, permitting himself a nervous chuckle, "Use whatever word you want, we have a job to do and we need to do it, Octavia. We have both been soldiers. We know what it is like to do a job, which is incomprehensible to outsiders."

A haunted thought invaded her chest. "We'll succeed, won't we, Quintus?" she asked.

"We have no choice," he declared.

Chapter 38: Plans Unfold

Marcus's owl only narrowly beat Hermes to the cave. It hooted up a storm but without a Wizard to interpret it, the two Humans were left to presume it meant Marcus was coming. He arrived a few minutes after the Morph, and then Quintus and Octavia explained what had transpired in their absence.

"Too much has happened while we were away," Hermes growled, "Your book led us astray. This is why I hate books, Wizard!"

"Regardless," Marcus said calmly, "If Quintus is right, then we have our target."

"But it is fair to assume that the Dark Lord knows we are here," Octavia said.

"If this is true, we must act quickly," Hermes demanded, "We need a plan."

"We have a plan," Quintus said, "And a good one."

Marcus and Hermes looked surprised. "As we were the only ones here, we had to fill the void," Octavia explained.

"I cannot believe the Wizard woman left with the Elf-girl," Hermes said, shaking his head. "Did they say where they were going?"

"They did not," Quintus said abruptly. Octavia looked strangely at him, but he simply nodded and she nodded back.

"So my two favorite Humans have made a plan. Tell it to me. What is the *Human* plan?" Marcus asked, trying to hide his pique at not being part of the planning. He had clearly read the book incorrectly and wasted half the morning. He was furious at himself. And now, Humans were formulating strategy? Truly?

"We know the bow is in the center room of a three-room building," Quintus said.

"A very ancient building," Marcus offered.

"Great time for a history lesson," Octavia quipped, "World's in danger, so let's talk about old, dead stuff. Our goal is to slip in and slip out without being noticed by Elves or Archpriests or Dark Lords."

374

"Xanthu is here," Marcus growled, with hatred baked into each word.

"We also need to beware ambushes," Quintus said, steering his friend away from pondering the paying of old debts, "We do not know if the Dark Lord sees things as the Historian does, so we must be sure we are alone and the building is clear."

"How do you propose we do this?" Hermes asked.

"We split," Octavia explained, "Marcus, Quintus, and I will go in the western door. Quintus and I have until the end of today before our Elf disguises wear off without the earth magic and no one will look twice if a Wizard, his owl, a Sunrise Elf and a Low Elf enter the hall."

"When do you propose we enter?" Marcus asked, "Night is dangerous. He is more powerful then."

"Midday," Quintus said, "When the Elves are lounging around, stuffing themselves with food and napping. A few may linger at the Hall, but not many. Surely the governor and his advisors will be ensconced in some luxurious room at luncheon. The building will remain open, but should be briefly empty or close to it."

"Where will I be?" Hermes asked.

"Griffin, Alexia, and you will enter from the east," Quintus said, "That way we will be able to ensure that both the gathering room and the private room are clear before we meet in the center where the bow is located."

"You know a lot about Elf halls," Hermes remarked.

"I know a lot about Elves," Quintus insisted.

"It is a good plan," Marcus conceded, "The Humans have done well. I could have done no better." It was meant as a compliment, but Wizards often fumbled compliments they paid to other races. It was simply their way.

"It is a good plan, but I can make it better. You must make one change," Hermes said, after a moment of consideration, "You cannot put two Morphs with Griffin at the eastern entrance. It is too risky. Even in our animal form, it will look strange for an Elf and two beasts to be entering. Let me switch with Quintus. I will go in the west with Marcus and Octavia. You will go in the east with Alexia and Griffin."

"I suppose," Octavia said, "But you'll still need to be an eagle."

"This is the most important task of my entire life," Marcus declared, "This is a moment I would rather be with Quintus than you. No offense, Hermes."

"The Historian placed me with you to help," Hermes insisted, "I know Elves, too. The plan is good, but it will be better if the Morphs are split." Quintus looked at Marcus.

"As you say," Quintus shrugged, "It is an improvement, Marcus. I will go with Alexia and Griffin. It makes sense. Now, enough of our talking. Hermes, you must fly to Griffin and find Alexia to tell them the plan. Midday is in two hours. I will meet them at the east entrance to the building and our plan will unfold." Hermes nodded and flew away.

"I don't like the plan," Marcus said, "I trust *you* in these situations, Quintus Agrippa. I trust you above all the creatures in the Realm."

"It will be fine," Quintus said, "You trust Octavia, too. And Hermes…"

"You do not entirely trust Hermes," Octavia said, "Do you, Quintus?"

"I trust him," Quintus said, "He is in our fellowship and the Historian did place him with us, so that we'd fulfill the prophecy."

"Why did you not tell them where Gwen is?" asked Octavia.

"Perhaps, I remain in the grip of those old stories where the Morphs betray the other races, but the truth is that I fear that even now we are being watched," Quintus said, "And Gwendolyn is important to me for reasons even more compelling than our quest to save the world." He smiled and she nodded. "The fewer beings who know where she is, the better." Marcus studied the stone left by Synthyya and grimly nodded to no one in particular.

***

The bowl shimmered for only a few minutes before going dark again, but it was enough. It had all gone terribly wrong. He had been blind to the truth and he had endangered all of their lives, as well as the plans of the Custodes. All was in peril and it was his fault. Titus permitted himself to weep at his failure, but only briefly. He tried in vain to summon again the images which had floated on the enchanted bowl of water. It was likely too late to prevent disaster, but perhaps he could minimize some of the failure. To whom could he turn? He could not summon the Wizard girl. It would be too dangerous, given what was transpiring. She would be found out if she left at this moment. So who? A thought flitted into his old head. Yes. It would not undo what had been done, nor would it relieve him of the responsibility for his choices. But perhaps he could snatch a stick from the fire before all was consumed. If he acted swiftly...

***

"Hermes found you?" Griffin asked when Alexia crept into his room, slinking through the window as a cat.

"Yes, our fellowship is at the ready," she said, "They have found the bow. It was right in front of me, when I was in that hall. Griffin, I am shocked. This is truly the moment?" She could sense that Griffin believed he had a chance to bed her one last time before the quest reached its climax. She rejected that notion in her head.

"It is more than just the bow," Griffin said, "After Hermes visited me, I told Owyn of our plan."

"About the *quest*?" Her dark eyes grew as wide as dinner plates. "Griffin, what in the Four Realms were you thinking?"

"No, not exactly," he said, "I said nothing of a magic bow and a Dark Lord. He'd have thought me mad! But he knows we will be in the Hall to steal something and he knows when. Without knowing it, Quintus and Octavia's plan helps *our* cause."

"Our cause?"

"Quintus will enter with you and me, right? How fortunate! It is as if the Spirits had decreed it. When we enter from the east, Owyn and some others will be in the private room, waiting for us," Griffin said, "There will be a 'struggle' and Quintus will be slain. The others will praise us for our bravery, mourn poor Quintus, and focus on the bow. Gwendolyn will be sad, but we will console her. She will recover."

"Must we slay Quintus?" Alexia asked, "He is a good man. Surely, there is another way." Griffin was shocked. The Morph was suddenly worried about the value of a Human life, which stood between her and her desire. This was unexpected.

"*You* need not slay him, Alexia," Griffin explained, "The Hands of the Spirits will take care of that. You must simply repeat the tale that I tell about his unfortunate demise. It will not be difficult and you will get what you want out of it. It is important that you and I tell the same story, so that Gwen and the others do not suspect anything."

"Are we being selfish?" she asked.

"Do you love my sweet sister?"

"You know I do," Alexia said, on the verge of weeping, "She was the first being in all the Four Realms to love me. I adore her above everything else in creation."

"She appears to be the only desire you cannot move away from and replace with another," Griffin observed with some degree of sympathy. Alexia nodded.

"I hunger for her," she said sadly.

"Then Quintus must die," Griffin stated, "Violence in the service of the Spirits is permissible. The holy book is clear on that."

"Are we in the service of your Spirits, Griffin? Or are we serving ourselves?"

"Will you tell Quintus? Will you jeopardize this plan?" he demanded. Alexia thought about the advice the Historian had given her. Her chest ached as she grappled with unfamiliar feelings. She did not simply want to sleep with the Elf, she hungered for her. All of her. Not just her lithe little body, but her whole being. Alexia loved her. Yes, the Historian was a wise old man, who had warned her to let Gwendolyn go. But what did an old man know of young love? Alexia could tell Quintus and thwart Griffin's plan. She could change before Griffin blinked and be off to the hall with the warning. Alexia knew Gwen loved Quintus. She thought of Gwen's grief. It was an ugly feeling, even if Alexia was only playing a minor role in this dark deed. But then Alexia considered a future with Gwendolyn and how she could comfort the little Elf in her grief. That was a warm feeling. She looked at Griffin and shook her head to indicate that she would not betray him, she would play her part.

***

"You have a history with this Archpriest?" Octavia asked as they headed up the hill towards the gleaming Hall of Righteousness. Her axe and helmet were obscured in a blanket she was carrying.

"I do," Marcus said. Dariuxx's owl simply hooted from Marcus's shoulder.

"Would you like him dead?" she asked.

"Very much," he replied bitterly.

"If he is here, I will try to slay him for you."

"You are a wonderful friend," Marcus said, permitting himself a brief smile.

"I *am* a good friend, Marcus, aren't I?" she asked with uncharacteristic vulnerability.

"You are, Octavia," he said, "As good a friend as I could imagine." Before things got muddled, he added with some mirth, "Who would not want a savage warrior girl as a friend? A friend who would delight at cleaving his enemies? How lucky a Wizard I am!" She was grateful for his jest, as she knew why he made it.

Octavia smiled and brushed a strand of the magically darkened hair out of her face, "What were the words Synthyya inscribed on the stone for you?" Octavia asked, "She said they were important."

"*Quisque vita sacra est,*" he shrugged, "The words of Wizardkind. 'Every life is sacred.' It was an odd time to remind me of the saying, but I've always thought it an odd saying. I am not sure I know too many Wizards who live those words."

"Synthyya does," Octavia said, "And so do you."

"I try to, Octavia, I try to…." He had a good sense as to why she had inscribed the words, although he could not entirely grasp her intentions. So it was with women of all races, he conceded.

After a few minutes, they were there. As Quintus had predicted, the entrance to the gathering hall was very lightly populated when Midday began. There were a few Elves milling about chatting, but nothing like the throngs which one might see in the morning or late afternoon. Justice was closed for two hours and the King's banner had been lowered to indicate that the governor was enjoying a leisurely lunch and perhaps a brief rest along with most of the sacred city. It was a good time to strike, Marcus noted. Quintus certainly knew the Elves better than they knew themselves. The Wizard looked up at the eagle, soaring high, but slowly circling lower. He seemed a powerful ally, but Marcus wished Quintus had insisted on the original plan. Marcus simply felt better with Quintus at his side. It was no slight on the Morph, it was just that Quintus was Quintus and he had always come through in the past. Marcus put much stock in that. The eagle landed on the steps. Marcus and Octavia headed towards him. At this moment, Griffin, Quintus, and Alexia should be slipping through the eastern door. Soon, it would be over.

The door was bolted. A bit of a surprise. Marcus left Octavia and walked confidently towards the door (as a Wizard should), waving his hand across the lock, muttering the spell. The door unlatched and no Elf thought it odd that a Wizard might go where he so chose when in Elfland. Surely, they presumed, he had Wizardly business in the Hall. Marcus was about to step in when he heard his name. Not the disguised name of "Cyrruzz." His real name. "Marcus!" He turned to see Octavia, her red hair blowing in the breeze while a group of confused, but determined Elves moved to seize her. Her hair. The spell had been broken and she was herself again with rounded ears and fiery red hair. It was too soon. How had the spell been broken? A dozen or more Elves had identified her as a Human immediately and were beginning to beat her. Marcus could see her axe and helmet had tumbled onto the ground. The warrior girl was fighting savagely, but was vastly outnumbered. Everyone in the sparse crowd was fixed on this scene and no one spared Marcus a sideways glance. Marcus instinctively lurched towards her, when he felt a strong arm on his shoulder. He turned and saw Hermes in his mortal form.

"We must save her," Marcus said.

"She has given us a distraction," Hermes said, "Perhaps, that is her part to play in all of this. Do not miss the opportunity. Come now. We must get to the bow before the Dark Lord does."

"But Octavia..."

"Marcus," he said, "Our quest is too important. We have no time for her. She is brave and will die bravely. Come and let us get the bow. It is your quest. Nothing else matters."

"She matters."

"She is expendable," Hermes said, "We all are. Mind the words of Titus: not every member of our fellowship will survive, but no one in the Four Realms will survive if we do not get that bow!"

Marcus could not even see Octavia, for several more Elves had crowded around to get their blows in. Her cloak had been torn off and her winged helmet was rolling away from the crowd. Marcus squinted and saw the glint of her axe on the ground, out of reach. Octavia called his real name again, faintly. The two syllables of his name sounded like a desperate prayer. Marcus's owl was flapping its wings and hooting in alarm. Whether it wanted Marcus to save Octavia or to move towards the bow as Hermes had advised, he could not discern.

Hermes looked prepared to even strike the Wizard if he did not comply. He opened the door to the hall and pulled at Marcus's arm. "Marcus, this is our *world* we are talking about," Hermes insisted, "Will you weigh her life against all of the Four Realms? Marcus, she is just a girl."

Chapter 39: Every Life Is Sacred

Quintus stepped first after they'd forced the lock. Griffin had insisted on leading, but had suddenly relented—a rare moment of compromise from the brittle Elf. Quintus was still astonished that he had not yet won over Gwen's brother, for charm was an item the Ranger had always had in surplus. Surely, Griffin could see the love in his sister's eyes for Quintus. Why couldn't he move beyond the narrow world he had inherited? The room was dark, but Quintus saw well in the blackness. There was a movement. A shadow against the dark... He saw well, but there was much he did not see.

It gripped her so tightly that she could barely breathe. The shame. The guilt. The old stories. The wrongness of it all. She could live with it no longer. He was a good man. This was wicked. Desire was not all there was. Love was strange in so many ways. Gwen would never forgive her. She could not be defined by the old lie.

"Quintus, look out!" shouted Alexia, "It's a trap!"

A sharp pain entered his side. It was an arrow and he knew it. He fought blindly, swinging his sword, but the blows crashed down upon him and he crumbled to the ground. Torches were lit and he saw Owyn and two other Elves. He felt his arrow wound, leaking crimson blood. It took him several moments to piece together what had happened. Why hadn't Griffin unsheathed his sword? How had Alexia known? It was not until he heard Owyn call Alexia a "filthy beast-woman who nearly ruined us" that it became clear. Griffin had betrayed the fellowship. Alexia had known. She had tried to make amends, but she was too late. Quintus coughed and some blood came out. She was far too late. He wished he could save Alexia now, so that he might repay her kindness. But he was unable to save even himself. Quintus watched two of the Elves hold Alexia's arms while Owyn steadied his bow, aiming at her bare chest. Griffin just looked on, unblinking. This was the Elf's plan? Alexia would die, too? In one moment, Griffin would see two people who loved his sister snuffed out like candles? How could he be so hateful? He tried to catch Griffin's attention, but Griffin refused to look at Quintus.

Before the arrow could be released, Alexia got over her shock and morphed into a robin. The two Elves were left holding air. She evaded the shaft and flew towards an open window, listening to the raging Elves behind her cursing her and her kind. The quest was ruined, their cause undone. Griffin had killed Quintus and meant to kill her, too. All she could do now was fly to Gwendolyn and tell her the awful truth: her brother had betrayed them, her lover was dead, and the bow would fall into the hands of the Dark Lord and his wicked fellowship. She did not care anymore. She just wanted to hold Gwen in her arms and kiss her until the Darkness swallowed the world. It would not be much, but it would be enough. She beat her little wings and headed southeast where she knew her true love was waiting on the ivory beach revered by Elves as the land of the first sunrise. Alexia was grateful that Octavia had told her Gwen's location before the moment they parted to head for the Hall. It was an awkward attempt to assuage the Morph that her beloved was in no further danger. Octavia was soft under all of those hard muscles. A pity if she and Marcus and Hermes were doomed as well. How wrong it had all gone. How much of it was Alexia's fault? She concentrated on flapping her wings, knowing that if she paused to ponder her guilt, she'd fall from the sky.

"How surprising," jeered the third Elf who Quintus did not recognize with Owyn and Bruce. "A friend is wounded and the Morph has abandoned him. I suppose Humans should know better than to rely on Morphs. Surely, you know the old stories."

"You must realize it is over, now, Quintus," Owyn said, "You will not defile our kind." Quintus rubbed his ears and knew the spell had lapsed. They knew who he really was. And he knew who really Griffin was. And as these were Quintus's final moments, he consoled himself that this last truth was important to know.

***

"I worry about them," Gwen said, tracing her name in the white sand.

"You should," Synthyya said, "They are in peril, for certain."

Neither woman talked while they listened to the waves pound the shore. "But they will overcome, won't they?"

"Child, I cannot know that," Synthyya said.

"But Marcus is a great Wizard, isn't he? He will protect Quintus and Alexia and my brother, and the others?"

"He is a great Wizard," she smiled, "Greater than he believes. But what makes him great isn't always his Wizardness. There is much of his mother in him and my hope is in that."

"Hope is everything, isn't it?" Gwen asked.

"Yes dear, it is."

***

Hermes had opened the door and stepped through. His strong hand was pulling Marcus to join him. The words echoed in Marcus's skull. Octavia was a friend and a comrade for whom he had complicated feelings. But she was only one person. What about the many? What about his quest? What about the one thing in the entire world that made him useful and brought meaning to his tragic life? This solemn endeavor to find the pieces of the ancient bow and arrow was important in a way that nothing else he had ever done was. It would help him get past the pain and losses of his life. He inhaled and exhaled. And with that, the Wizard made his choice. It would not have been his father's choice. But he was not his father. "She's just a girl," the Morph repeated.

"No, she is not!" Marcus raged, his violet eyes aflame.

"Don't be so foolish, sorcerer," snarled the Morph.

"*Quisque vita sacra est,*" Marcus declared to Hermes as he turned from the doorway and pointed his staff at the crowd of Elves.

385

"You are a fool," Hermes fumed, "You'd trade our sacred mission for her, a nobody? Do not fail us, sorcerer!"

Marcus was not paying attention, he was casting an air spell to blow away the Elves and rescue Octavia. A fierce wind erupted from his staff and the Elves were momentarily scattered, exposing Octavia. She looked bruised and bloody. He ran towards her and he feared his moment's delay might have cost Octavia her life. With no regard to the angry Elves, Marcus stripped off his enchanted cloak and draped it on her barely moving body to protect her with its magic. The owl of his dead teacher was flying in front of his face hooting, but Marcus ignored it while he wrapped the girl in the enchanted cloak. Octavia looked up weakly and helped pull the cloak around herself. She was breathing, but it was shallow. The Elves reassembled and Marcus began to chant when he felt a sharp pain in his left shoulder and a force which drove him to the ground. As he tried to rise, he felt that it was a spear which had hit him from behind. He craned his head and saw Hermes. Marcus had no time to ponder why. He wrenched the spear from his left shoulder and drew his enchanted sword. The Morph became an eagle and swooped towards the Wizard. Marcus swung and singed some tail feathers, then prepared to swing again on the eagle's next approach. His owl had gone to Octavia and was hooting at the Elves who kept their distance from a Wizard's beast, even such a small one.

As Marcus focused on the traitorous eagle Morph, his sword leapt from his hand. He turned left to see his new assailant and caught the eagle's talons across his already wounded left shoulder. A blazing ball of fire was headed towards him from the left. He ducked and miraculously avoided it. He had no time to ponder, but cast lightning at the Wizard who was attacking him, who had conjured another fireball. Their spells met in midair and crackled. It was then that Marcus saw the caster.

"Xanthu," he said as he gripped the staff of his old teacher and tried to concentrate on the spell.

"Marcus," the Archpriest said, not appearing to exert much effort, "the last time I saw you, I left with a new wife. Today, I will have a new bow."

So that was it. He knew. It was all undone.

Marcus struggled fiercely, but he knew he was only half a Wizard and seriously injured on top of that. The eagle attacked Marcus again and his concentration lapsed when he turned to deal with it. The Archpriest had his opening. His fire singed the half-Wizard and Xanthu followed it immediately with a vicious gust of magical wind which knocked Marcus onto his belly, as his staff tumbled far away. Marcus lay exposed and cloakless, his violet eyes searching for movement where Octavia lay. The Morph then attacked his owl, which fell motionless beside the red haired warrior girl, still draped in the protective cloak. The history book about the last council leaked out of Marcus's leather sack. With a casual flick of the wrist and a few words, the Archpriest sent a fireball to consume it. He grinned. "Finish them, Hermes, so that I might kill their friends and secure the object," the Archpriest said with a satisfied grin. He entered the hall purposefully. Quintus, Alexia, and Griffin faced certain doom at the hands of Xanthu. Octavia was probably already dead. Marcus was sure to join her. The quest was over. It was not supposed to be like this, Marcus thought while he struggled to his knees. It was so far from the epic story he'd conjured up in his head. Marcus saw Hermes grab the enchanted sword, relishing its power as he cut the air with it. His white grin was impossible to miss and he slowly walked towards the wounded Wizard. At least Synthyya and Gwen are safe, Marcus consoled himself while he tried to summon the strength to cast something in his own defense. Only one spell occurred to him.

He muttered the words and the earth rose up and encased Hermes's feet. He strove to raise those mighty tree-trunk legs, but the ground would not release him. He morphed into an eagle and still the talons of the bird were stuck in the grasping earth. Marcus took a moment to delight that the earth spell had actually worked and lunged for his staff. He tried to make it come to him by an air spell, but he could not maintain both spells at the same time, for he was growing weary. His tragic challenge was clear: he could delay his death but he could not prevent it.

***

"Synthyya, I think I've figured it out," Gwen said, as she threaded her toes through the mud, feeling the salty water wash them clean. The cool ocean caressed her pale smooth legs and somehow, everything felt okay for a moment.

"What is that, dear Gwendolyn?"

"The words," she said with a smile, "I have memorized them since I was an Elfling, but only now do I understand them."

"The Elf words?" Synthyya asked, "It takes many kinds of tree to make a forest?"

"Yes," Gwen said, "The clerics and the teachers always told us it spoke of the three kinds of Elves and how we must do what comes naturally to our kind to keep the world in balance: Sunrise Elves sow and reap, Sunset Elves buy and sell, Low Elves serve."

"But you feel all those wise Elves have misread it?" Synthyya asked impishly.

"Oh yes," Gwen said, her blue eyes twinkling in the sunlight, "What if it refers to all the races? What if the forest is our world entire and all of us have a role to play, no matter the race?"

"Quite profound," marveled Synthyya.

"They say King Diarmaid was the wisest," Gwen shrugged.

"It was not the king I was complimenting," Synthyya said.

"Look Synthyya," Gwen said, pointing to the sky, "It's a robin flying towards us. I love robins. They always remind me of Alexia…" The bird bobbed down from the sky and landed on the soft powdery sand of Aurora Point.

***

"Forget the Morph, she will get what's coming to her," Owyn sneered, "It is this Human who we have agreed to eliminate for the Spirits."

"For the Spirits!" the others chanted.

"We are their Hands," Owyn declared.

"I warned you to leave my sister," Griffin said to Quintus. Quintus looked up at him with perfect calm. Suddenly, as life ebbed in his body, the words of those barren old monks and nuns made perfect sense. He would die and shine forth in the sky as a star in the night. He would be with all those comrades who had fallen in battle and with all those who had gone before him. Forever would he help light the night for the Golden One who shines in the day. Quintus would die on the earth, but he believed he would be reborn in the night sky, twinkling faintly and keeping watch over Gwendolyn. He would never take his eyes off of her, so long as she lived.

"Would you like the honor, Griffin?" Owyn asked, "You will derive great pleasure from the blow, I promise."

"Killing a Human is like drinking the liquid fire," Bruce declared.

"There are times those hands must be clenched in fists," quoted the third Elf whose name Griffin had never even asked. "Draw your sword, Griffin. Spill his Human blood. Save your sister from the shame!"

Griffin drew his sword. He was unnerved that Quintus seemed so unafraid, even though he had been totally disarmed and was bleeding like a river in flood. Quintus met the Elf with a steely gaze and simply said, "I will never stop loving her, even if you kill me, here." And that was it.

In a moment, Griffin saw it all. Quintus was not the enemy. He was the love his sister deserved. These Elves were not his friends. They had never even traveled outside of their own small world. They hated creatures they had never seen. They twisted their beliefs to justify a small little world where Elf girls like his sister could not learn and Low Elves existed to do the work they believed they were too good for. They were so sure of themselves, but had never seen anything to challenge their beliefs or complicate their world. They knew nothing of real life. Only too late did this all wash over Griffin, as if a veil had been raised. He could not save Quintus from a horrible death. But perhaps, he could undo a little of what he had done. He had betrayed his sister and only now was that clear. There was nothing left Griffin could do except end it the right way.

The look on Owyn's face was precious, for he was the unsuspecting first victim. The look of horror and surprise was frozen on his face after Griffin's sword pierced him and he sank to the floor. The nameless Elf was next, a clean blow and he was dead. Bruce realized what had happened and shot Griffin with two arrows, shredding his flesh and spilling his blood everywhere, for he caught Griffin in the throat. Griffin ran at Bruce and took a dagger blow to the side of his neck before he succeeded in driving his sword low and deep into Bruce's belly, just as he'd been taught. He reached into his pouch and thrust some potent healing herbs at Quintus, then stumbled and whispered hoarsely, "I am so sorry, Quintus. I approve," before falling dead. Darkness enfolded Griffin of the Hills and he was gone, perhaps to the Forest Above the Clouds, but who can be sure of such things?

Quintus tried to stanch his blood. The healing herbs might delay his death, so he used them, but his wounds were grievous and the gray-eyed Ranger knew the reality of the situation. He struggled to his feet and staggered to the next room. It was empty. He looked at the bow. Marcus should have been here by now, but at least Quintus knew that in his last moments, he could get the bow for the Wizard to help make the task easier. He would miss Marcus's friendship when the inevitable happened, but Quintus felt that he had at least one last act in his mangled body before he succumbed. He barely had time to savor Griffin's approval, which would all be for naught as the tragic story of Quintus Agrippa Aureus drew to a close. He reached for the "D" when a blast of air that felt like it was a stone wall drove him through the door and back into the governor's private room where the Elves lay dead. Quintus had thought he had been near death before, but it crept much closer after that horrible cold wind had struck his wounded body. Not even Elvin herbs can prevent the inevitable, he thought when he recovered from the shock.

"Owyn," he heard the Archpriest shout from the next room, "I know you still breathe. Finish the Ranger while I get the bow."

"I am grievously wounded, Prayer Leader..."

"You'll be dead if I must tell you again," shouted the Wizard, "I will see to our master's gift because magic surrounds it. You will see to the Ranger's death. I have done most of the work for you."

Quintus had no idea where the energy came from, but somehow, he scrambled to his feet and limped out the eastern door with the wounded Elf trailing him.

***

The Morph was monumentally frustrated by the spell, but Marcus could feel it weakening. Hermes was close to breaking free of the earthy embrace. Marcus could not fight it any more. He would die from a blow of his own sword, delivered by a treacherous Morph who had betrayed him to the Archpriest. How happy his former wife would be when she heard the story from her second husband.

Then, the story changed, as stories sometimes do.

It all took an instant and Marcus barely saw what happened, because he was focused on maintaining his earth spell. All he saw was the blow—Octavia was on her feet and had swung her axe and beheaded the immobilized Morph. His severed head still had a look of shock while it rolled away.

"I don't play damsel in distress. I don't like those tales," Octavia said through heavy breaths, "The score is even between us." She helped Marcus to his feet and secured his cloak on him. He went and scooped up the wounded owl.

"Octavia?" he demanded.

"He called you 'Sorcerer.' I heard him," she responded, "He had to die for that."

"The bow," Marcus croaked.

Suddenly, the crowd of Elves moved forward menacingly. "The Wizard helps the Human," one Elf declared, "He is no friend of the Elves."

"I killed a Morph," Marcus argued weakly.

The crowd grew hostile. "The Holy Wizard blessed the Morph you slew," one Elf called out. Another added, "A woman who kills is unnatural." The other ten Elves were grim-eyed as they nodded in agreement. They clutched weapons which ranged from well-crafted spears to crude pieces of wood. Some simply held large rocks as weapons.

Marcus and Octavia held one another tightly, for neither had the strength to fight the mob. On a typical day, twelve fairly ordinary Elves could have never challenged the Wizard and the warrior together, but the day had been far from typical. Marcus had little magic left and Octavia was bruised and bleeding. They could try to dash for the door to the Hall of Righteousness, but if they failed, they'd both be dead.

As they steeled themselves for the onslaught, a large Dark Elf emerged on the top of the hill, yelling and brandishing his spear. "Go away, don't you know they're trying to help you? Go! Go!" Surprised by the fierce new presence, the mob lost heart. As quickly as that, the Elves scattered like birds taking flight.

"Ardor? What are you doing here?" Marcus asked hoarsely.

"Let's say that a mutual friend told me some crazy story and that you might need some help."

"Do we have a mutual friend, Ardor? Octavia asked, "Why did you help us?" She'd remembered hitting his jaw in what seemed like a lifetime ago. She regretted it bitterly on this day.

The Sunset Elf grinned for he read her thoughts and rubbed his healed jaw to underscore that he did. "Let's say that it never hurts to have a Wizard in your debt. And if I score correctly, you now owe me, Marcus."

"You keep score with him, too?" Octavia whispered. Marcus grinned weakly.

"You are correct, Ardor," Marcus said, "Thank you."

"Oh, I am sure we will meet again and when we do, I will be happier knowing that you owe me," Ardor said, pausing as he looked at the two badly injured beings still clutching one another, "Plus, you two make the most ridiculous couple I have seen in all the Four Realms. But you're so charmingly awkward, I think you actually fit." He winked.

"Sorry about the jaw, Ardor," Octavia said.

"It's okay, Red. You owe me, too, understand?" Ardor smiled, "Now, go finish whatever you have planned. I'll guard the door and make sure no one follows you." He passed some Elvin healing herbs to them. "Take care of yourselves."

Marcus nodded, as if to endorse that plan.

Chapter 40: "He approved."

"Where are the others?" Marcus whispered as they peered through the doorway to the second room. All they saw was the Archpriest reaching for the bow. Quintus, Griffin, and Alexia were not in the room. Octavia had no words for Marcus, only a look of horror, as if the Archpriest had vaporized their friends. And he had married Marcus's ex-wife, she thought angrily. How sweet it would be to behead him, as she did the traitorous eagle Morph, who had called her friend a "sorcerer." Fortunately, the large Wizard gave no thought to Marcus and Octavia, who were peeking through the slightly open door. He assumed they were dead—a very reasonable assumption. His thoughts were entirely consumed with the hidden bow which— as he had predicted—they had unwittingly helped him find for his master. And yet the Archpriest Xanthu was vexed because each time he reached for the "D" in King Diarmaid II's name, he was repelled by some invisible force.

"What is happening?" Octavia asked, leaning so close to Marcus that he could smell her sweat and her blood.

Marcus narrowed his eyes. "Perhaps the ancient magic still protects the bow." He was not entirely correct, but nor was he completely mistaken.

Octavia wanted to sneak up and cleave the wicked Wizard's head off his shoulders, but knew she'd never be quick enough, though he was distracted. But the move for the bow had to be flawless and she was a better leaper than Marcus, even if she had been beaten quite nearly to death. "You take the Wizard, I'll get the bow," Octavia whispered hoarsely. He looked at her as if faintly amused by the audaciousness with which she spoke. He placed his unmoving owl gently on the floor. It seemed dead, but he was not ready to bury it without consulting Synthyya.

Marcus held Octavia's gaze, "Did you just ask me to 'take the Wizard?'" he asked, "You feel we ought to expose ourselves in our condition?"

"Why don't you be a Wizard and shoot some fire or lightning or something," she snickered darkly, her eyes sparkling because she knew they both should have been dead already and yet Ardor had prevented that outcome. It was like a night in the gambling dens where the games seemed rigged the wrong way. "Just get him out of the way, so I can make a jump for the bow. You must have some magic left?" He raised an eyebrow. "Marcus, we aren't dead yet and we should be. I am not the most pious girl in the Realm, but clearly, something good moves with us on this day. We have nothing left to lose?"

He nodded assent and took a deep breath. He could feel how little magic he had in his body and how exhausted he should be. Yet something was driving him forward, propelling him beyond his capabilities. Perhaps, it was the epic quest he thought he was on or the need to locate Quintus whose absence confounded him. Perhaps, it was this peculiar girl with the hair like flames. No matter the origin of his strength, Marcus poured all of his power into one perfect lightning bolt and sent it through Zarqqwell's old staff at the unsuspecting Archpriest. The Archpriest was driven into a pillar and it collapsed, sending a significant portion of the ceiling down on top of him. Marcus did not even hear him groan before the rubble buried him. Octavia—despite her injuries—took off as if this were a race and leapt with the grace of a deer. Sometimes, she moved so awkwardly and other times with such poise, he marveled. She easily plucked the bow from its slot and landed firmly. "Guess the ancient magic likes me," she said, "Should we make sure he's dead?" She gestured at the stones.

"We must find Quintus and the others," Marcus said, fear leaking into his voice.

Marcus scooped up Dariuxx's unconscious owl as tenderly as he could and placed it into his now-empty leather pouch. The book with the answers had been incinerated. Only now, did this dark thought enter his head. No time to dwell on that. Quintus was what mattered. They stumbled into the governor's secret room and found Griffin and two other Elves. "Is he...?" Octavia asked as Marcus knelt beside him. Marcus nodded solemnly. "Do you know these two?" She gestured at the other two Elves.

"They were at the Crossed Spear," Marcus muttered, "Friends of the owner, I think?"

"I don't see Quintus," she said between ragged breaths. She headed for the Eastern door and heard a sound. Octavia turned toward Marcus and saw him dragging Griffin's body. "What are you doing, Marcus?"

"If we can get back to Gwen, she deserves her brother's body. It is important."

"You and I are both half-dead and the journey to Gwen is probably days away on foot. This doesn't make sense. Leave it. It is no longer Griffin anymore," she said.

"Who is the logical Wizard, now?" he asked, "Gwen should be able to have the body. Elves have a way of mourning and she has the right to it."

Recognizing that it is usually best to let Wizards have their way, Octavia reluctantly helped him drag it out the door. They dragged Griffin's corpse several minutes before they almost tripped over something strewn carelessly in their path. "It's Owyn," Octavia said, rolling over the dead Elf. Quintus's body was a few paces further.

"Quintus!" Marcus threw himself on the ground next to the body of his friend. "Quintus, my brother, awake!" Octavia thought Marcus was going to explode. She had never seen him gripped by such madness.

"Mar…" groaned Quintus.

"He lives," Marcus said triumphantly. Octavia knelt on the other side. His wounds looked dire. Even Marcus had to notice that.

"We have the bow, Quintus," Octavia said, her hair brushing his ashen face.

Quintus attempted a smile, then it disappeared, "Griffin…betrayed."

"Griffin was betrayed?" Marcus asked.

"No…Griffin…betrayed…me," Quintus croaked.

Marcus and Octavia shared a look of pure terror. "What about Alexia?" Marcus asked. Quintus's lip quavered and his eyes shut for a moment before opening slowly.

"She flew away."

396

"Just like they say," Octavia spat, "never trust a Morph with your life or your love. How could she do that?"

"I had thought she was better than all the old stories," Marcus fumed.

"No..." wheezed Quintus, "tried to save me...Alexia."

"She tried to save you? But what about Griffin?" Octavia asked.

"In the end," Quintus whispered softly, "he approved, Marcus...He approved." He then closed his eyes and fell into darkness. How deep the darkness, no one could yet tell.

"Will he die?" Octavia asked. His chest still rose and fell, so he wasn't dead, yet.

"We had two friends with skills in healing. He was one," Marcus said flatly, "and the other is stone dead." He gestured at Griffin's corpse. "I see what looks like medicinal herbs in the wounds, but this is not a skill I possess. I am not even sure you and I used Ardor's herbs correctly. Quintus has tried to help himself, but to what end, I cannot tell. We must get him to Gwendolyn. She is an Elf. She must know their lore."

"Griffin betrayed Quintus. You heard him. That Elf broke the fellowship," Octavia raged, "He must have brought those other Elves there to kill Quintus. Do you still think Gwen deserves the body?" Angry sparks danced in her green eyes.

He thought briefly. "Yes," Marcus answered, "he is still her brother and he cannot hurt us, anymore. We must bring the body. There is a story...you wouldn't know it. It is important to me." He looked around for some way out of where they were; logic was failing him. "I should have seen it coming, Octavia. Of course, he hated Quintus because of his love for Gwen. I am sure our enemies used that to turn Griffin. Why didn't I see that?"

"You can't expect yourself to know everything," Octavia said, putting her hand heavily on Marcus's shoulder. It was not his wounded one, but he would not let her see him wince, anyway. "Even Wizards have limits. What about Hermes?"

397

"I probably should have seen that, too," Marcus muttered, "Working for the enemy all along. No wonder the Dark Lord knew us so well. He had a spy within the fellowship. We have much to ponder, but not at this moment. As the Morphs would advise, let's focus on right now, Octavia."

"We must make it to Gwen and Synthyya on the southeastern shore," Octavia said, "Where the sun rises."

"We'll never make it on foot."

"Not with two bodies."

"Not even with one," Marcus said, "We have managed to secure the bow and yet we are trapped in this city."

"And the Elves will be coming out of their little cottages soon and I doubt even Ardor can hold them off indefinitely," she lamented. Suddenly, she smiled. "But the Elves are still napping away the afternoon, right now. Is that correct?"

"Yes, as Elves do at midday. What is the point?"

"Isn't that a farm?" she asked, pointing, "Surely the farmer sleeps and we can wander about his property unnoticed. What farmer doesn't have a cart to bring his vegetables to the market and a horse or two?"

"No farmer I would want to know," he said with an involuntary smile. She returned the smile and they began to investigate the farm.

Within minutes, they'd discovered a large red cart with peeling paint and Octavia had hitched two strong horses to it. A lone Low Elf saw them and tried to stop the theft, but Octavia punched him in the jaw and he collapsed unconscious.

"Do you think every Elf you hit will turn out to be a friend like Ardor?" Marcus asked impishly.

"I am playing the odds," she shrugged. They hoisted Griffin's body into the cart and then checked on Quintus. "He still breathes," she said, "But it is growing shallower. Do you think Gwen can heal him?" She had not released the bow from her left hand for a moment, Marcus noticed.

"She is an Elf, she must have learned some of their healing arts," Marcus said, "Or else, perhaps Synthyya can help. He must be saved. We shall ride until these horses are ready to fall over. Once word leaks out, this city will be a beehive. We want to be well on our way before then." They gently put Quintus into the cart and covered both bodies with a large tarp. Marcus lowered the wounded owl into the cart, as well, and tried to cushion the poor bird with some straw.

"I will drive first," Octavia stated.

"I can drive."

"No," she insisted, "You need to sleep. We might have need for magic before we reach our friends and you seem all out."

"Agreed," he said, climbing into the cart and disappearing under the tarp. "Take this, Octavia." He passed her his cloak. "It is winter and it is a dire one, even for a brave woman of the North. This will help keep off the chill, amongst other things."

"Thank you," she said, pulling it around her shoulders and breathing easier knowing of its protective enchantment.

Chapter 41: The Cover of Darkness

They did not dare look back and reached the shore just as the horses were ready to drop from exhaustion. There were at least three near-misses along the way, but they had charmed their way out of two and resorted to magic to extricate themselves from the third. Marcus and Octavia arrived in the late afternoon the next day to find Gwendolyn hugging her knees and shuddering as if from a terrible chill. There was a dog next to her with sad eyes, which they recognized as Alexia. Synthyya was standing and looking out at the vast ocean. She did not notice them at first.

"Synthyya," Octavia called, "We are here."

She turned and looked at them, nonplussed. "Yes," was all she could say. It was vaguely interrogative but not excessively so.

"We have the bow," Octavia said, brandishing the magical item.

Synthyya looked relieved, but hardly euphoric. Octavia felt her reaction should have been bigger. But even if she attempted a smile with her mouth, Synthyya's eyes remained downcast.

"Is it true? Griffin betrayed us?" Synthyya asked with a thin crack in her voice.

Marcus nodded solemnly, "Griffin is dead."

"We know," Synthyya said, "Alexia told us that Griffin led Quintus to his death. He broke the fellowship. Alexia had thought the bow was lost."

"The bow is not lost," Octavia tried again, "And Quintus lives."

Immediately, Gwendolyn leapt up and ran to them at full sprint with the dog nipping at her heels. Those Elf ears, Octavia marveled. "Is it true that he lives?"

"He is gravely wounded," Marcus said mournfully, "We hoped that you might know some of the Elvin healing arts?"

"Hope? I fear I am almost out of hope," Gwen whispered sadly, "And I was never much good at healing. Let me see him, please. O, Quintus!" They threw off the tarp and she saw her brother's body next to Quintus's. Gwen keened at the top of her little lungs. "Why, Griffin? Why?" she implored the corpse. "You killed my one true love."

"Such dramatics! Your one true love is not dead, yet" Synthyya said, a stern edge to her words, "Do not focus on what was, but what *is*, Gwendolyn. Heal him of his wounds as best you can. Do not let Quintus slip away."

"But Griffin killed him," she bawled, "My own brother betrayed..."

"Quintus's last conscious words to us were that Griffin approved," Marcus said, gently stroking Gwen's golden hair.

"What does that mean?" she shrieked.

"Heal him and we can ask," Synthyya said.

Gwen nodded absently. Her eyes caught the injured owl in the cart and she wordlessly scooped it up and caressed its feathers. The bird opened its eyes for the first time since Hermes had attacked it. Gwen permitted herself as small smile while she tenderly stroked the bird. Gwen then began to work on Quintus, telling Alexia to fetch certain leaves and berries from their camp. The dog nodded and obeyed.

"What is wrong with Alexia?" Octavia asked Synthyya, "Why doesn't she morph?"

"She flew here and told us about Quintus and Griffin," Synthyya explained, "Gwendolyn's reaction was horrible to watch. It was as if she had been stabbed over and over again. It was even worse than all this. You must remember that for the last day, we knew Griffin was a traitor and we thought we knew Quintus was dead and the quest had failed. We presumed you were dead, too. Alexia was horrified by Gwendolyn's loss of hope and felt responsible as the teller of the tale. She morphed into a dog. She has not changed into anything else since." Synthyya pondered a moment. "I almost forgot to ask about Hermes," she said, "Is he dead? Did he fall in the struggle."

"Oh, he fell all right," Octavia snarled, "And he will not get up again."

"I don't understand."

"Synthyya," Marcus sighed heavily, "He was working for *Dominus Maleficarum* all along. Octavia and I were both on the precipice of death because of that wretched being."

Synthyya clapped her hand to her mouth in a rare display of Wizard emotion, "Someone must warn Titus. A traitor in his midst? We are beset with a swarm of bad news..."

"Marcus cast some earth magic during our struggle," Octavia piped up, "Quite well, if I noticed correctly."

Synthyya quite nearly beamed at that, "Earth magic? Well, that is something, isn't it? Let me see what I might do to fix the two of you up. You're not as close to death as Quintus, but neither of you looks particularly well."

"We didn't sit on the beach all day like you," quipped Octavia.

"How I missed that mouth of yours, warrior girl," Synthyya smiled, embracing Octavia like a daughter.

***

Quintus would live through the night, at least. Gwen threw all of her being into keeping his broken body from failing. Yet the Fellowship of Outcasts had been shaken. As the sun dipped into the horizon, suffering was ubiquitous. Griffin was dead. Alexia remained a dog, steadfastly refusing to return to her mortal form for reasons no one completely understood. The Historian's book had been destroyed in the City of the Spirits. Synthyya left that very night to see Titus— not knowing if he had been complicit in the Dark Lord's scheme or if he were dead because of Hermes's betrayal. When Synthyya would return, no one knew. The fellowship had secured the unstrung bow, but three pieces remained hidden in the world and the onset of winter would only make their enemy stronger. Gwen was tending to Quintus in a tent, while Alexia the dog slumbered outside. In the still of dusk, Marcus and Octavia sat on a rock and watched the churning white water together.

"There is something about impending doom which really gets the air crackling like a fire, isn't there?" she joked.

He marveled that only this Human could find the courage to joke in the teeth of all this tragedy. He admired that about Octavia.

"The real possibility of the world ending truly sets one's heart a flutter," he agreed in jest.

"Hearts are a flutter in that tent," she said, nodding towards Quintus and Gwen's tent before turning to Marcus and grinning, "I suppose there is something tragically beautiful about the end of the world for lovers,"

"Lovers? Is that an invitation?" he mocked, arching his eyebrow.

"I've never been all that romantic," she snickered.

"Do you want to hear about the beauty of a tragic romance?" he asked.

"I've got nothing better to do but wait for some Dark Lord to pull my little world into an abyss," she chuckled, "So will you finally tell your tale to me, Marcus? I daresay I've earned the right to hear it."

"I suppose you are right. It is as good a time as any for me to tell you the story of who I am..." Marcus began. He dared to put his arm around her because it was cold and Octavia leaned into him, resting her head on his chest. Marcus looked forward at the darkening sky while the waves pounded the sand rhythmically, yet mercilessly. For a moment, the Wizard thought of turning his face ever so slightly and kissing Octavia full on her pink lips. But the stars were not yet out, and Marcus could not risk anything so foolish until covered by darkness.

Made in the USA
Middletown, DE
05 December 2015